As a forensic anthropologist to the province of Quebec, Canada, Kathy Reichs has often said that she works *with* the dead, but *for* the living.

Forensics are an integral part of her world, with cases constantly coming in to her lab. And yet her chosen profession is, she says, like any other job. However, though you may get used to what's happening around you, and to the sounds and smells and sights of death, this doesn't mean you become immune to it.

Each of her books is based loosely on the cases she's worked on, or an experience she's had. She believes that her stories remain fresh because they originate from her being enmeshed and engaged in forensic work on a regular basis.

Kathy Reichs is one of only eighty-two forensic anthropologists ever certified by the American Board of Forensic Anthropology. She served on the Board of Directors and as Vice President of both the American Academy of Forensic Sciences and the American Board of Forensic Anthropology, and is currently a member of the National Police Services Advisory Council in Canada. She is a Professor in the Department at the University of North Carolina-Charlotte. She is a native of Chicago, where she received her PhD. at Northwestern. She now divides her time between Charlotte, NC and Montreal, Quebec.

www.kathyreichs.com
www.facebook.com/kathyreichsbooks
twitter.com/kathyreichs

Also available by Kathy Reichs

The Virals Series
with Brendan Reichs

Kathy
REICHS

BONES TO
ASHES

arrow books

Reissued by Arrow Books in 2012

5

Published by arrangement with the original publisher, Scribner,
an imprint of Simon & Schuster, Inc.

First published in Great Britain in 2007 by William Heinemann

First published in paperback in 2008 by
Arrow Books
The Random House Group Limited
20 Vauxhall Bridge Road, London, SW1V 2SA

www.randomhouse.co.uk

Addresses for companies within The Random House Group Limited
can be found at: www.randomhouse.co.uk/offices.htm

The Random House Group Limited Reg. No. 954009

A CIP catalogue record for this book is available from the British Library

Penguin Random House is committed to a sustainable future for
our business, our readers and our planet. This book is made from
Forest Stewardship Council® certified paper.

Printed and bound in Great Britain by Clays Ltd, Elcograf S.p.A.

Typeset by SX Composing DTP, Rayleigh, Essex

For those buoyant, bighearted, bodacious *Acadiens*.

On ouaira quosse que d'main nous amèneras . . .

This is the forest primeval; but where are the hearts that
    beneath it
Leaped like the roe, when he hears in the woodland the
    voice of the huntsman?
Where is the thatch-roofed village, the home of Acadian
    farmers.

– from "Evangeline" by Henry Wadsworth Longfellow

1

Babies die. People vanish. People die. Babies vanish.

I was hammered early by those truths. Sure, I had a kid's understanding that mortal life ends. At school, the nuns talked of heaven, purgatory, limbo, and hell. I knew my elders would "pass." That's how my family skirted the subject. People passed. Went to be with God. Rested in peace. So I accepted, in some ill-formed way, that earthly life was temporary. Nevertheless, the deaths of my father and baby brother slammed me hard.

And Évangéline Landry's disappearance simply had no explanation.

But I jump ahead.

It happened like this.

As a little girl, I lived on Chicago's South Side, in the less fashionable outer spiral of a neighborhood called Beverly. Developed as a country retreat for the city's elite following the Great Fire of 1871, the hood featured wide lawns and large elms, and

Irish Catholic clans whose family trees had more branches than the elms. A bit down-at-the-heels then, Beverly would later be gentrified by boomers seeking greenery within proximity of the Loop.

A farmhouse by birth, our home predated all its neighbors. Green-shuttered white frame, it had a wraparound porch, an old pump in back, and a garage that once housed horses and cows.

My memories of that time and place are happy. In cold weather, neighborhood kids skated on a rink created with garden hoses on an empty lot. Daddy would steady me on my double blades, clean slush from my snowsuit when I took a header. In summer, we played kick ball, tag, or Red Rover in the street. My sister, Harry, and I trapped fireflies in jars with hole-punched lids.

During the endless Midwestern winters, countless Brennan aunts and uncles gathered for cards in our eclectically shabby parlor. The routine never varied. After supper, Mama would take small tables from the hall closet, dust the tops, and unfold the legs. Harry would drape the white linen cloths, and I would center the decks, napkins, and peanut bowls.

With the arrival of spring, card tables were abandoned for front porch rockers, and conversation replaced canasta and bridge. I didn't understand much of it. Warren Commission. Gulf of Tonkin. Khrushchev. Kosygin. I didn't care. The banding together of those bearing my own double helices assured me of well-being, like the rattle of coins in the Beverly Hillbillies bank on my bedroom dresser. The world was predictable, peopled with relatives, teachers, kids like me from households similar to mine. Life was St. Margaret's school, Brownie Scouts, Mass on Sunday, day camp in summer.

Then Kevin died, and my six-year-old universe fragmented into shards of doubt and uncertainty. In my sense of world order, death took the old, great-aunts with gnarled blue veins and translucent skin. Not baby boys with fat red cheeks.

I recall little of Kevin's illness. Less of his funeral. Harry fidgeting in the pew beside me. A spot on my black patent leather shoe. From what? It seemed important to know. I stared at the small gray splotch. Stared away from the reality unfolding around me.

The family gathered, of course, voices hushed, faces wooden. Mama's side came from North Carolina. Neighbors. Parishioners. Men from Daddy's law firm. Strangers. They stroked my head. Mumbled of heaven and angels.

The house overflowed with casseroles and bakery wrapped in tinfoil and plastic. Normally, I loved sandwiches with the crusts cut off. Not for the tuna or egg salad between the bread. For the sheer decadence of that frivolous waste. Not that day. Never since. Funny the things that affect you.

Kevin's death changed more than my view of sandwiches. It altered the whole stage on which I'd lived my life. My mother's eyes, always kind and often mirthful, were perpetually wrong. Dark-circled

3

and deep in their sockets. My child's brain was unable to translate her look, other than to sense sadness. Years later I saw a photo of a Kosovo woman, her husband and son lying in makeshift coffins. I felt a spark of recollection. Could I know her? Impossible. Then realization. I was recognizing the same defeat and hopelessness I'd seen in Mama's gaze.

But it wasn't just Mama's appearance that changed. She and Daddy no longer shared a pre-supper cocktail, or lingered at the table talking over coffee. They no longer watched television when the dishes were cleared and Harry and I were in our PJs. They'd enjoyed the comedy shows, eyes meeting when Lucy or Gomer did something amusing. Daddy would take Mama's hand and they'd laugh.

All laughter fled when leukemia conquered Kevin.

My father also took flight. He didn't withdraw into quiet self-pity, as Mama eventually did. Michael Terrence Brennan, litigator, connoisseur, and irrepressible bon vivant, withdrew directly into a bottle of good Irish whiskey. Many bottles, actually.

I didn't notice Daddy's absences at first. Like a pain that builds so gradually you're unable to pinpoint its origin, I realized one day that Daddy just wasn't around that much. Dinners without him grew more frequent. His arrival home grew later, until he seemed little more than a phantom presence in my life. Some nights I'd hear unsteady footfalls on the steps, a door banged too hard against a wall. A toilet flushed. Then silence. Or muffled voices from my parents' bedroom, the cadence conveying accusations and resentment.

To this day, a phone ringing after midnight makes me shiver. Perhaps I am an alarmist. Or merely a realist. In my experience, late-night calls never bring good news. There's been an accident. An arrest. A fight.

Mama's call came a long eighteen months after Kevin's death. Phones gave honest rings back then. Not polyphonic clips of "Grillz" or "Sukie in the Graveyard." I awoke at the first resonating peal. Heard a second. A fragment of a third. Then a soft sound, half scream, half moan, then the clunk of a receiver striking wood. Frightened, I pulled the covers up to my eyes. No one came to my bed.

There was an accident, Mama said the next day. Daddy's car was forced off the road. She never spoke of the police report, the blood alcohol level of 0.27. I overheard those details on my own. Eavesdropping is instinctual at age seven.

I remember Daddy's funeral even less than I remember Kevin's. A bronze coffin topped with a spray of white flowers. Endless eulogies. Muffled crying. Mama supported by two of the aunts. Psychotically green cemetery grass.

Mama's relatives made the trek in even larger numbers this time. Daessees. Lees. Cousins whose names I didn't remember. More covert listening revealed threads of their plan. Mama must move back home with her children.

The summer after Daddy died was one of the hottest in Illinois history, with temperatures holding in the nineties for weeks. Though weather forecasters talked of Lake Michigan's cooling effect, we were far from the water, blocked by too many buildings and too much cement. No lacustrine breezes for us. In Beverly, we plugged in fans, opened windows, and sweated. Harry and I slept on cots on the screened porch.

Through June and into July, Grandma Lee maintained a "return to Dixie" phone campaign. Brennan relatives continued appearing at the house, but solo now, or in sets of two, men with sweat-looped armpits, women in cotton dresses limp on their bodies. Conversation was guarded, Mama nervous and always on the verge of tears. An aunt or uncle would pat her hand. Do what's best for you and the girls, Daisy.

In some child's way I sensed a new restlessness in these familial calls. A growing impatience that grieving end and life resume. The visits had become vigils, uncomfortable but obligatory because Michael Terrence had been one of their own, and the matter of the widow and the children needed to be settled in proper fashion.

Death also wrought change in my own social nexus. Kids I'd known all my life avoided me now. When chance brought us together they'd stare at their feet. Embarrassed? Confused? Fearful of contamination? Most found it easier to stay away.

Mama hadn't enrolled us in day camp, so Harry and I spent the long, steamy days by ourselves. I read her stories. We played board games, choreographed puppet shows, or walked to the Woolworth's on Ninety-fifth Street for comics and vanilla Cokes.

Throughout those weeks, a small pharmacy took shape on Mama's bedside table. When she was downstairs I'd examine the little vials with their ridged white caps and neatly typed labels. Shake them. Peer through the yellow and brown plastic. The tiny capsules caused something to flutter in my chest.

Mama made her decision in mid-July. Or perhaps Grandma Lee made it for her. I listened as she told Daddy's brothers and sisters. They patted her hand. Perhaps it's best, they said, sounding, what? Relieved? What does a seven-year-old know of nuance?

Gran arrived the same day a sign went up in our yard. In the kaleidoscope of my memory I see her exiting the taxi, an old woman, scarecrow thin, hands knobby and lizard dry. She was fifty-six that summer.

Within a week we were packed into the Chrysler Newport that Daddy had purchased before Kevin's diagnosis. Gran drove. Mama rode shotgun. Harry and I were in back, a midline barrier of crayons and games demarcating territorial boundaries.

Two days later we arrived at Gran's house in Charlotte. Harry and I were given the upstairs bedroom with the green-striped wallpaper. The

7

closet smelled of mothballs and lavender. Harry and I watched Mama hang our dresses on rods. Winter dresses for parties and church.

How long are we staying, Mama?

We'll see. The hangers clicked softly.

Will we go to school here?

We'll see.

At breakfast the next morning Gran asked if we'd like to spend the rest of the summer at the beach. Harry and I gazed at her over our Rice Krispies, shell-shocked by the thundering changes rolling over our lives.

'Course you would, she said.

How do you know what I would or wouldn't like? I thought. You're not me. She was right, of course. Gran usually was. But that wasn't the point. Another decision had been made and I was powerless to change it.

Two days after hitting Charlotte, our little party again settled itself in the Chrysler, Gran at the wheel. Mama slept, waking only when the whining of our tires announced we were crossing the causeway.

Mama's head rose from the seat back. She didn't turn to us. Didn't smile and sing out, "Pawleys Island, here we come!" as she had in happier times. She merely slumped back.

Gran patted Mama's hand, a carbon copy of the gesture employed by the Brennans. "We're going to be fine," she cooed, in a drawl identical to that of her daughter. "Trust me, Daisy darlin'. We're going to be fine."

And fine I was, once I met Évangéline Landry.
And for the next four years.
Until Évangéline vanished.

2

I was born in July. For a kid, that's good news and bad.

Since my summers were all spent at the Lee family beach house on Pawleys Island, my birthdays were celebrated with a picnic, then an excursion to Gay Dolphin Park on the Myrtle Beach boardwalk. I loved those amusement park outings, especially the Wild Mouse ride, white-knuckling up, down, and around narrow tracks, heart banging, cotton candy rising in my throat.

Good stuff. But I never got to bring cupcakes to school.

I turned eight that summer after Daddy died. Mama gave me a pink jewelry box with a music player and pop-up ballerina. Harry crayoned a family portrait, two big and two little stick figures, fingers spread and overlapping, no one smiling. Gran's gift was a copy of *Anne of Green Gables*.

Though Gran prepared the traditional picnic of

red velvet cake, fried chicken, boiled shrimp, potato salad, deviled eggs, and biscuits, there was no postprandial roller-coaster jaunt that year. Harry got sunburned and Mama got a migraine, so I stayed alone on the beach, reading about Anne's adventures with Marilla and Matthew.

I didn't notice her at first. She blended with the white noise of surf and seabirds. When I looked up she was less than two yards from me, skinny arms spiking from palmed hips.

Wordlessly, we assessed each other. From her height I guessed she had a year or two on me, though her waist was still child-thick, her faded swimsuit still flat on her chest.

She spoke first, jabbing a thumb at my book. "I've been there."

"Have not," I said.

"I've seen the Queen of England." Wind danced the dark tangle on her head, lifting and dropping strands like shoppers deciding on ribbons.

"Have not," I repeated, immediately felt stupid. "The queen lives in a palace in London."

The girl dragged wind-forced curls from her eyes. "I was three. My *grand-père* held me up so I could see."

Her English was accented, neither the flat, nasal twang of the Midwest, nor the vowel-bloating drawl of the Southeastern seaboard. I hesitated, uncertain.

"What did she look like?"

"She wore gloves and a lilac hat."

"Where was this?" Skeptical.

11

"Tracadie."

The guttural *r* sounded excitingly foreign to my eight-year-old ear.

"Where's that?"

"*En* Acadie."

"Never heard of it."

"'This is the forest primeval. The murmuring pines and the hemlocks.'"

I squinted up at her, unsure what to say.

"It's a poem."

"I've been to the Art Institute in Chicago," I said, feeling the need to match poetry with an equally high-brow response. "They have lots of famous pictures, like the people in the park painted with dots."

"I'm staying with my aunt and uncle," the girl said.

"I'm visiting my grandmother." I didn't mention Harry or Mama. Or Kevin. Or Daddy.

A Frisbee arced to earth between the girl and the ocean. I watched a boy scoop it and send it sailing with a backhanded toss.

"You can't really go to Green Gables," I said.

"Yes, you can."

"It's not real."

"It is." The girl worked one brown toe in the sand.

"Today is my birthday," I said, at a loss to come up with anything better.

"Bonne fête."

"That Italian?"

"French."

My school in Beverly had offered French, the pet

12

project of a Francophile nun named Sister Mary Patrick. Though my exposure had gone little beyond *bonjour*, I knew this girl sounded nothing like the language teacher who'd come to my first- and second-grade classes.

Lonely? Curious? Willing to listen to anything that transported me from the gloom in Gran's big house? Who knows why? I bit.

"Was the prince with her?"

The girl nodded.

"What's this Tracadie place like?" It came out "Track-a-day."

The girl shrugged. "*Un beau petit village.* A small town."

"I'm Temperance Brennan. You can call me Tempe."

"Évangéline Landry."

"I'm eight."

"I'm ten."

"Wanna see my presents?"

"I like your book."

I settled back in my chair. Évangéline sat cross-legged in the sand beside me. For an hour we talked of Anne and that famous farm on Prince Edward Island.

Thus the friendship began.

The forty-eight hours following my birthday were stormy, the daytime sky alternating between pewter and sickly gray-green. Rain came in wind-blown bursts, streaming salty wash across the windows of Gran's house.

13

Between downpours I begged to be allowed on the beach. Gran refused, fearing undertow in the swells breaking white on the sand. Frustrated, I watched from inside, but caught no sign of Évangéline Landry.

Finally, blue patches appeared and elbowed back the clouds. Shadows sharpened under the sea oats and the boardwalks traversing the dunes. Birds resumed discourse, temperatures rose, and the humidity announced that unlike the rain, it was not leaving.

Despite the sunshine, days passed with no sign of my friend.

I was biking when I spotted her walking along Myrtle Avenue, head tortoised forward, sucking a Popsicle. She wore flip-flops and a wash-faded Beach Boys T-shirt.

She stopped when I rolled up beside her.

"Hey," I said, one sneaker dropping from pedal to pavement.

"Hi," she said.

"Haven't seen you around."

"Had to work." Wiping sticky red fingers on her shorts.

"You have a job?" I was awed that a kid be permitted such a grown-up pursuit.

"My uncle fishes out of Murrell's Inlet. Sometimes I help out on the boat."

"Neat." Visions of Gilligan, Ginger, and the Skipper.

"Pfff." She puffed air through her lips. "I scrape fish guts."

14

We started walking, me pushing my bike.

"Sometimes I have to take care of my little sister," I said, seeking to establish parity. "She's five."

Évangéline turned to me. "Do you have a brother?"

"No." Face burning.

"Me neither. My sister, Obéline, is two."

"So you have to clean a few fish. It's still cool to spend the summer at the beach. Is it really different where you come from?"

Something glinted in Évangéline's eyes, was gone before I could read it.

"My mama's there. She got laid off at the hospital, so now she works two jobs. She wants Obéline and me to learn good English, so she brings us here. *C'est bon.* My aunt Euphémie and my uncle Fidèle are nice."

"Tell me about this forest primeval." I steered from the topic of family.

Évangéline's gaze drifted to a passing car, came back to me.

"L'Acadie is the most beautiful place on Earth."

And so it seemed.

All that summer Évangéline spun tales of her New Brunswick home. I'd heard of Canada, of course, but my childish imaginings went little beyond Mounties and igloos. Or dogsleds mushing past caribou and polar bears, or seals perched on ice floes. Évangéline spoke of dense forests, coastal cliffs, and places with names like Miramichi, Kouchibouguac, and Bouctouche.

She also spoke of Acadian history, and the expulsion of her ancestors from their homeland. Again and again I listened, asked questions. Astonished. Outraged at the North American tragedy her people call le Grand Dérangement. The French Acadians driven into exile by a British deportation order, stripped of their lands and rights.

It was Évangéline who introduced me to poetry. That summer we stumbled through Longfellow's epic work, the inspiration for her name. Her copy was in French, her native tongue. She translated as best she could.

Though I barely understood the verse, she turned the story to magic. Our childish minds imagined the Acadian milkmaid far from her Nova Scotia birthplace. We improvised costumes and acted out the tale of the diaspora and its ill-fated lovers.

Évangéline planned to be a poet one day. She'd memorized her favorites, most French, some English. Edward Blake. Elizabeth Barrett Browning. The New Brunswick–born bard Bliss Carman. I listened. Together, we wrote bad verse.

I preferred stories with plots. Though the English was difficult for her, Évangéline tried my favorite authors: Anna Sewell. Carolyn Keene. C. S. Lewis. And, endlessly, we discussed Anne Shirley and imagined life at Green Gables farm.

In those days I hoped to become a veterinarian. At my instigation we kept notebooks on egrets in the marsh and on pelicans gliding high on the wind. We constructed protective walls around turtle nests. We trapped frogs and snakes with long-handled nets.

Some days we staged elaborate tea parties for Harry and Obéline. Curled their hair. Dressed them like dolls.

Tante Euphémie cooked us *poutine râpée, fricot au poulet, tourtière*. I can see her in her ruffle-strapped apron, telling stories of the Acadian people in broken English. Stories she'd heard from her father, he from his. Seventeen fifty-five. Ten thousand forced from their homes.

Where did they go? Harry would ask. Europe. The Caribbean. America. Those in Louisiana became your Cajuns.

How could such things happen? I would ask. The British wanted our farms and dikes. They had guns.

But the Acadians returned? Some.

That first summer, Évangéline planted the seed for my lifelong addiction to news. Perhaps because hers was such an isolated corner of the planet. Perhaps because she wanted to practice English. Perhaps simply because of who she was. Évangéline's thirst for knowing everything was unquenchable.

Radio. Television. Newspapers. We absorbed and comprehended in our limited way. At night, on her porch or mine, June bugs banging the screens, transistor radio sputtering the Monkees, the Beatles, Wilson Pickett, the Isley Brothers, we spoke of a man with a rifle in a Texas tower. The deaths of astronauts. Stokely Carmichael and a strange group called SNCC.

At age eight, I thought Évangéline Landry the smartest and most exotic being I would ever know. She was beautiful in a dark gypsy way, spoke a foreign language, knew songs and poems I'd never heard. But, even then, despite the sharing of secrets, I sensed a reserve in my new friend, a mystery. And something else. Some hidden sadness of which she didn't speak and which I could not identify.

The hot, muggy days rolled by as we explored our little Lowcountry island. I shared places familiar from previous visits with Gran. Together, Évangéline and I discovered new ones.

Slowly, as it inevitably does, my pain receded. My thoughts dwelled on new things. Pleasant things.

Then it was August and time to go.

Mama never returned to live in Chicago. My life settled into a new comfortableness in Charlotte. I grew to love Gran's old house in Dilworth, the smell of honeysuckle crawling the backyard fence, the leafy dark tunnel formed by willow oaks arcing our street.

I made friends, of course, but none as exotic as my summer soul mate. None who wrote poetry, spoke French, and had seen Green Gables and the Queen of England.

While apart, Évangéline and I exchanged letters containing news of our winter lives, our poetry, our preteen impressions of current events. Biafra. Why didn't other countries feed these people? My Lai. Did Americans really kill innocent women and children? Chappaquiddick. Do celebrities have such troubles, too? We speculated on the guilt or innocence of Jeffrey MacDonald. Could any person be bad enough to kill his children? The evil of Charlie Manson. Was he the devil? We counted the days until summer with hash-marked calendars.

The school year ended earlier in Charlotte than in Tracadie, so I'd arrive first at Pawleys Island. A week later, *madame* Landry's rusted Ford Fairlane would roll across the causeway. Laurette would spend one week at her sister and brother-in-law's small house on the marsh, then return north to her jobs at a lobster cannery and a tourist motel. In August, she'd repeat the long trip.

In between, Évangéline, Obéline, Harry, and I lived our summer adventures. We read, we wrote, we talked, we explored. We collected shells. I learned about fishing for a living. I learned some bad French.

Our fifth summer unfolded like the previous four. Until July 26.

Psychologists say some dates remain permanently fixed in the mind. December 7, 1941. The Japanese attack on Pearl Harbor. November 22, 1963. President Kennedy assassinated. September 11, 2001. The World Trade Center in flames.

My list includes the day Évangéline disappeared.

It was a Thursday. The Landry children had been on the island six weeks, were scheduled to remain for another four. Évangéline and I planned to go crabbing early that morning. Other details remain as fragments.

Pedaling through a misty dawn, crab net angled across my handlebars. A car passing in the opposite lane, male silhouette at the wheel. Oncle Fidèle? One backward glance. One silhouette in back.

The *tic tic tic* of pebbles winged onto Évangéline's bedroom window screen. Euphémie's face through a barely cracked door, hair bobby-pinned, eyes red, lips dead white.

They are gone. You mustn't come here again.

Gone where, *ma tante*?

Go away. Forget.

But why?

They are dangerous now.

Pedaling hard, tears streaming my cheeks, watching a car swallowed by fog on the causeway. Gone? No warning? No good-bye? No "I'll write"? Don't come back? Forget?

My friend and her sister never summered on Pawleys again.

Though I returned over and over to the small house on the marsh, begging for information, I was always rebuffed. Tante Euphémie and Oncle Fidèle never spoke to me except to repeat "You must go. They are not here."

I wrote letter after letter. Some came back undelivered, others did not, but there was no response from Évangéline. I asked Gran what I could do. "Nothing," she said. "Events can alter lives. Remember, you left Chicago."

Distraught, I swore to find her. Nancy Drew could do it, I told myself. And I tried, as much as a twelve-year-old was able in the days before cell phones and the Internet. For the rest of that summer and into the next, Harry and I spied on Tante Euphémie and Oncle Fidèle. We learned nothing.

Back in Charlotte, we persisted. Though the libraries within our small orbit kept no phone directories for New Brunswick, Canada, we managed to obtain an area code for Tracadie-Sheila. There were more Landrys in the region than the operator could sort without a first name.

Laurette.

No listing. Thirty-two L. Landrys.

Neither Harry nor I could recall mention of Évangéline's father's name.

Realization. Through all those long days and nights, Évangéline and I had talked of boys, sex, Longfellow, Green Gables, Vietnam. By some unspoken agreement, we'd never ventured into the subject of fathers.

Using a pay phone and coins from our banks, Harry and I phoned every L. Landry in Tracadie. Later we tried the surrounding towns. No one knew of Évangéline or her family. Or so they said.

My sister lost interest in sleuthing long before I did. Évangéline had been my friend, five years Harry's senior. And Obéline had been too young, half a lifetime Harry's junior.

In the end, I, too, gave up searching. But I never stopped wondering. Where? Why? How could a fourteen-year-old girl be a threat? Eventually, I grew to doubt my recall of Tante Euphémie's words. Had she really said "dangerous"?

The emptiness left by Évangéline was a void in my life until high school crowded out reflection and regret.

Kevin. Daddy. Évangéline. The ache of that triple whammy has faded, dulled by the passage of time and displaced by the press of daily living.

But, now and then, a trigger. Then memory rears up in ambush.

3

I'd been in Montreal a full hour when LaManche phoned. Until then, my June rotation to the recently thawed tundra on the St. Lawrence had gone swimmingly.

The flight from Charlotte and the connection from Philadelphia had both operated on time. Birdie had given me minimal grief, protest-meowing only during takeoffs and landings. My luggage had touched down with me. Arriving home, I'd found my condo in reasonably good shape. My Mazda had started on the very first try. Life was good.

Then LaManche rang my mobile.

"Temperance?" He, alone, rejected the more user-friendly "Tempe" employed by the rest of the world. My name rolled off LaManche's tongue as a high Parisian "Tempéronce."

"*Oui.*" My brain kicked into French mode.

"Where are you?"

"Montreal."

"So I thought. Your trip was good?"

"As good as it gets."

"Air travel is not what it was."

"No."

"You will come early tomorrow?" I sensed tension in the old man's voice.

"Of course."

"A case has arrived that is . . ." Slight hitch. " . . . complicated."

"Complicated?"

"I think it best to explain personally."

"Eight o'clock?"

"C'est bon."

Disconnecting, I felt a vague sense of trepidation. LaManche rarely phoned me. When he did, it was never good news. Five bikers torched in a Blazer. A woman facedown in a senator's pool. Four bodies in a crawl space.

LaManche had been a forensic pathologist for over thirty years, directed our medico-legal division for twenty of that. He knew I was scheduled back today, and that I'd report to the lab first thing in the morning. What could be so complicated that he felt the need to double check my availability?

Or so gruesome.

As I unpacked, shopped, stocked the fridge, and ate a salade Niçoise, my mind conjured up scenarios, each worse than the last.

Climbing into bed, I decided to bump my arrival to 7:30 A.M.

One upside to air travel is that it wears you out.

Despite my apprehension, I drifted off during the eleven o'clock news.

The next day dawned as if auditioning for a travel brochure. Balmy. Breezy. Turquoise skies.

Having commuted to Quebec for more years than I care to admit, I was certain the climatic fluke would be short-lived. I wanted to bike in the country, picnic on the mountain, Rollerblade the path along the Lachine canal.

Anything but face LaManche's "complicated" issue.

By seven-forty I was parked at the Édifice Wilfrid-Derome, a T-shaped high-rise in a working-class neighborhood just east of centre-ville. Here's how the place works.

The Laboratoire de sciences judiciaires et de médecine légale, the LSJML, is the central crime and medico-legal lab for the entire province of Quebec. We've got the building's top two floors, twelve and thirteen. The Bureau du coroner is on ten and eleven. The morgue and autopsy suites are in the basement. The provincial police, La Sûreté du Québec, or SQ, occupies all other space.

Swiping my security card, I passed through metal gates, entered the restricted LSJML/Coroner elevator, swiped again, and ascended with a dozen others mumbling *"Bonjour"* and *"Comment ça va?"* At that hour, "Good morning" and "How's it going?" are equally perfunctory no matter the language.

Four of us exited on the twelfth floor. After crossing the lobby, I swiped a second security card, and passed into the lab's working area. Through observation windows and open doors I could see secretaries booting computers, techs flipping dials, scientists and analysts donning lab coats. Everyone mainlining coffee.

Past the Xerox machines, I swiped again. Glass doors swooshed, and I entered the medico-legal wing.

The board showed four of five pathologists present. The box beside Michel Morin's name said: *Témoignage: Saint-Jérôme*. Testimony in Saint-Jérôme.

LaManche was at his desk, assembling the case list for that morning's staff meeting. Though I paused at his door, he remained hunched over his paperwork.

Continuing along the corridor, I passed pathology, histology, and anthropology/odontology labs on my left, pathologists' offices on my right. Pelletier. Morin. Santangelo. Ayers. Mine was last in the row.

More security. Good old-fashioned lock and key.

I'd been away a month. The place looked like I'd been gone since we occupied the building.

Window washers had displaced the framed pictures of my daughter, Katy, and all other memorabilia from the windowsill to a filing cabinet top. Floor polishers had then placed the wastebasket and two plants on the conveniently emptied sill. New CSU coveralls and boots had been heaped on one chair, clean lab coats draped on another. My laminated Dubuffet poster had nosedived from the wall, taking out a pencil holder.

My desk was mounded with materials forwarded from my mail slot in the secretarial office. Letters. Fliers. Ads. In addition, I could identify the following: an updated list of personnel telephone extensions; four packets of prints from Section d'identité judiciaire photographers; two sets of antemortem X-rays and two medical dossiers; a copy of *Voir Dire*, the LSJML gossip sheet; and three demande d' expertise en anthropologie forms. Three requests for anthropological analysis.

After collecting the upended pens and pencils, I dropped into my chair, cleared a small section of desktop, and scanned the first form asking for my expertise.

Pathologist: M. Morin. Investigating officer: H. Perron, Service de police de la Ville de Montréal. SPVM. Formerly known as the Service de police de la Communauté urbaine de Montréal, or SPCUM, the SPVM are the city boys. Same force, new spin. *Nom: Inconnu*. Name: Unknown. Skipping over the LSJML, morgue, and police incident numbers, I went straight to the summary of known facts.

Skeletal parts had been bulldozed up at a construction site west of centre-ville. Could I determine if the bones were human? If human, the number of persons? Time since death? If recent, could I ascertain age, sex, race, and height, and describe individuating characteristics for each set of bones? Could I establish cause of death?

Typical forensic anthropology stuff.

The second form was also SPVM, city police. Emily Santangelo was the pathologist, and therefore coordinating all expertise concerning the cadaver. This case involved a house fire, an incinerated corpse, and a denture melted beyond recognition. I was being asked to establish congruence between the charred remains and the ninety-three-year-old man reported living at the address.

Third form. A bloated and badly decomposed body had been dredged from Lac des Deux Montagnes, near L'Île-Bizard. Beyond the fact that the victim was female, the pathologist, LaManche, could determine little. Teeth were present, but there'd been no hit when dental information was entered into CPIC, the Canadian counterpart of the American NCIS. Could I ascertain age and racial background? Could I check the bones for signs of trauma?

Unlike the first two, LaManche's case was SQ. The provincial cops.

One town, two police agencies? Sounds complicated. It's not.

Montreal is an island, part of an archipelago trailing from the confluence of the Ottawa and St. Lawrence rivers. Its southern tip is wrapped by the fleuve Saint-Laurent, its northern by the Rivière des Prairies.

The small island is only fifty kilometers long, and varies from five to thirteen kilometers in width, narrowing at its ends and thickening at its center. Its dominant feature is Mont Royal, an igneous intrusion rising a proud 231 meters above sea level. Les Montréalais call this tiny bump *la montagne*. The mountain.

For policing purposes, Montreal is parceled out according to those particulars of geology. On the island: SPVM. Off the island: SQ. Assuming there is no local PD. Though rivalries exist, in general *ça marche*. It works.

My eye fell on the name of the investigating SQ officer. Detective-Lieutenant Andrew Ryan.

My stomach did a wee flip.

But more of that later.

Pierre LaManche is a large man in a grandpa-was-a-lumberjack hunched-forward sort of way. Favoring crepe soles and empty pockets, the man moves so quietly he can appear in a room with no warning of approach.

"I apologize for disturbing you at home last evening." LaManche was standing in my doorway, clipboard in one hand, pen in the other.

"No problem." Rising, I circled my desk, gathered the lab coats, and hung them on a hook on the back of my door.

LaManche lowered himself into the chair. I waited for him to begin.

"You know *maître* Asselin, of course."

In Quebec, coroners are either physicians or attorneys. Odd system, but *ça marche*. It works. Michelle Asselin was a lawyer, thus the title *maître*.

I nodded.

"*Maître* Asselin has been a coroner for as long as I've been with this lab." LaManche stroked his jaw, as though verifying he'd shaved that morning. "She is close to retirement."

"The complicated case is hers?"

"Indirectly. *Maître* Asselin has a nephew who farms near Saint-Antoine-Abbé. Théodore Doucet. Théodore and his wife, Dorothée, have one child, a daughter. Geneviève is thirty-two, but has special needs and lives at home."

LaManche seemed to study the placement of my wastebasket. I waited for him to go on.

"Dorothée was a regular churchgoer, but stopped attending. No one is certain of the exact date. Though the family was known to be reclusive, neighbors grew worried. Yesterday two parishioners visited the Doucet farm. They found Dorothée and Geneviève dead in an upstairs bedroom. Théodore was downstairs playing *Silent Hunter* on his computer."

LaManche mistook my quizzical look. "It is a computer game. One does something with submarines."

I knew that. I was surprised LaManche did.

"You went to the scene?" I asked.

LaManche nodded. "The house was a nightmare, rooms crammed with useless trash. Oatmeal cartons. Newspapers. Tin cans. Used tissues. Feces in ziplock baggies."

"Théodore is being held for psychiatric evaluation?"

LaManche nodded. He looked tired. But, then, the old man usually looked tired.

"Both women were fully dressed, lying on their backs with bedding pulled to their chins. Their heads were tilted and touching, and their arms were entwined."

"Posed."

"Yes."

I was wondering what this had to do with me. Unless dismembered, mutilated, or stripped of identifiers such as fingerprints or teeth, fresh corpses were rarely my domain.

"My feeling is that Dorothée has been dead for at least two weeks," LaManche continued. "I will confirm that today. Geneviève is the problem. Her body was lying beside a heat vent."

"With the fan blowing on her," I guessed. I'd seen it before.

LaManche nodded. "PMI will be difficult."

Mummified corpse. Uncertain postmortem interval. Yep. That would be me.

"Signs of trauma?" I asked.

"I saw nothing during my external examination of Dorothée. Geneviève's body is far too dehydrated. I saw nothing on the X-rays of either mother or daughter."

"Top priority?"

LaManche nodded. Then the hound-dog eyes locked onto mine. "I'm confident this can be handled discreetly and compassionately."

Unlike the Doucet women, few who rolled through our doors had died in their beds. Ours were the murdered, the suicides, those whose lives were cut short by bad timing, bad judgment, or bad luck.

LaManche understood my commitment to the dead and to those left behind. He'd witnessed my interactions with families, and with journalists seeking footage for the five o'clock news.

LaManche knew the words he'd spoken did not need saying. The fact that he'd voiced them revealed an uncharacteristic level of emotion. The old man cared deeply for Michelle Asselin.

Administrative issues discussed, cases assigned, staff meeting wrapped up by nine. Returning to my office, I donned a lab coat and crossed to the anthropology lab. The bones found at the construction site covered two worktables.

One glance told me the case wouldn't need detailed analysis. After eyeballing each element, I wrote a one-line report.

Les ossements ne sont pas humains. The bones are not human. Twenty minutes. Done.

Next, I instructed my lab technician, Denis, concerning cleaning of Santangelo's incinerated cadaver. Burned bodies can be fragile, requiring careful disarticulation of the skeleton and removal of soft tissue by hand.

Then it was on to the morgue.

Clipboard. Calipers. Skeletal autopsy forms.

I had my hand on the doorknob when the phone rang. I almost ignored it. Should have, perhaps.

4

"Doc Brennan?" The voice was barbwire dragged across corrugated tin. *"C'est moé, Hippo."*

"Comment ça va?" As in the elevator, a formality. If queried sincerely, I knew the caller would respond in detail. Though I liked the guy, this wasn't the time.

"Ben. J'vas parker mon char. Chu—"

"Hippo?" I cut him off.

Sergent-enquêteur Hippolyte Gallant was with L'unité "Cold cases" du Service des enquêtes sur les crimes contre la personne de la Sûreté du Québec. Big title. Easy translation. Provincial police. Crimes against persons. Cold case squad.

Though Hippo and I had worked a case or two since the unit's creation in 2004, I'd never cracked his accent. It wasn't the *joual* of Quebec's Francophone working class. It was definitely not Parisian, Belgian, North African, or Swiss. Whatever its origin, Hippo's French was a mystery to my American ear.

Fortunately, Hippo was fluently bilingual.

"Sorry, doc." Hippo switched to English. Accented, and slang-heavy, but intelligible. "I'm downstairs parking my car. Got something to run by you."

"LaManche just handed me an urgent case. I was heading to the morgue."

"Ten minutes?"

Already my watch said 9:45.

"Come on up." Resigned. Hippo would find me, anyway.

He appeared twenty minutes later. Through the observation window, I watched him work the corridor, pausing to exchange greetings with those pathologists still in their offices. He entered my lab carrying a Dunkin' Donuts bag.

How to describe Hippo? With his extra poundage, plastic-framed glasses, and retro crew cut, he looked more like a code programmer than a cop.

Hippo crossed to my desk and parked the bag on it. I looked inside. Doughnuts.

To say Hippo wasn't into healthy living would be like saying the Amish weren't into Corvettes. A few members of his squad called him High Test Hippo. Ironic, since the man's stomach was perpetually upset.

Hippo helped himself to a maple syrup frosted. I went with chocolate.

"Figured you mighta skipped breakfast."

"Mm." I'd eaten a bagel with cream cheese and a half pint of raspberries.

"That your urgent case?" Hippo chin-cocked the construction site lamb chops and poultry.

"No." I didn't elaborate. It was already past ten. And my mouth was full of chocolate and dough.

"Want your take on something."

"I do have to get downstairs."

Hippo dragged a chair toward my desk. "Ten minutes, I'm outta here." Settling, he licked sugar from his fingers. I handed him a tissue. "It's not something you gotta do."

I hand-gestured "Give it to me."

"It's bones. I haven't seen the actual stuff. This comes from an SQ buddy. He's been with the provincial police for eighteen years, and was just transferred from Rimouski to Gatineau. We had a few beers when he was passing through Montreal."

I nodded, really thinking about the doughnuts. Had there been another maple syrup frosted in the bag?

"Me and Gaston, that's his name. We been buds since we was kids. Grew up in a spit little town in the Maritimes." Finally, an explanation of Hippo's accent. *Chiac*, a vernacular French similar to *joual* but specific to some of the Atlantic provinces.

"There's this skeleton's been bugging Gaston for a couple years. He's half Micmac, you know. First Nations?"

I nodded again.

"He's got a thing about the dead being buried proper. Thinks your spirit's screwed if you ain't planted six feet under. Anyway, some SQ dick at

35

Gaston's last posting keeps a skull in his desk. Has the rest of the skeleton in a box."

"How did this detective come to have these bones?" I lifted the bag and held it out. Hippo shook his head. I looked inside, barely interested. Yes! One maple syrup frosted. I set the bag down.

"Gaston doesn't know. But his conscience is kicking ass because he didn't do more to get the bones buried."

"No grave, no afterlife."

"Bingo."

"This is where I come in."

"Gaston asked me if I'd heard of some bone lady here in Montreal. I said, you kiddin'? Doc Brennan and me is *sympathique*." Hippo raised and joined two nicotine-stained fingers.

"He's certain these bones are human?"

Hippo nodded. "Yeah, and he thinks it's a kid."

"Why?"

"They're small."

"Gaston should call the local coroner." I reached in and took the maple syrup frosted, casual as hell.

"He did. The guy blew him off."

"Why?"

"These bones ain't exactly fresh."

"They're archaeological?" Maple syrup wasn't bad, but chocolate still ruled.

"As I understand it, they're dry, and there's cobwebs in the holes where the eyes used to be."

"Cobwebs would suggest time spent above-ground."

"Bingo." Hippo liked the word. Used it a lot.

"Coroner said the stuff had been kicking around too long."

I stopped chewing. That wasn't right. If the bones were human, technically they were unidentified remains and fell within the coroner's mandate. It was up to a forensic anthropologist to determine if death had occurred recently enough to be of forensic interest.

"Who is this coroner?" I reached for paper and pen.

Hippo patted his jacket, which is worth mentioning. The fabric had yellow and orange lines running vertically and horizontally through a russet background. With its gold polyester pocket hanky, the garment would have been haute couture in rural Romania.

Locating a spiral pad, Hippo flipped several pages.

"Dr. Yves Bradette. Want the number?"

I nodded, jotted.

"Look, Gaston doesn't want to jam anybody up."

My eyes rose to Hippo's.

"OK, OK." Hippo pointed two palms in my direction. "Just be discreet. The stuff's at SQ headquarters, Rimouski." Hippo looked at his notes. "That's the District of Bas-Saint-Laurent–Gaspésie–Îles-de-la-Madeleine." Typical Hippo. Too much information.

"I can't get to this right away."

"Yeah, yeah, yeah. *Pas d'urgence.*" Not urgent. "Whenever."

When a body clocks out it trips one of three pathways: putrefaction, mummification, or saponification. None is pretty.

In a warm, moist setting, with bacteria, insects, and/or vertebrate scavengers looking for lunch, you get putrefaction. Putrefaction features skin slippage, discoloration, bloating, eruption of the abdominal gases, caving of the belly, rotting of the flesh, and, way down the road, disintegration of the bones.

In a warm, dry setting, with bugs and critters excluded, you get mummification. Mummification features destruction of the internal organs by autolysis and enteric bacterial action, and muscle and skin dehydration and hardening due to evaporation.

No one's really sure, but saponification seems to require a cool setting and poorly oxygenated water, though the water can come from the corpse itself. Saponification features the conversion of fats and fatty acids into adipocere, a cheesy, stinky compound commonly called "grave wax." Initially white and soaplike, adipocere can harden with age. Once formed the stuff lasts a very long time.

But decomp's not as simple as door A, B, or C. Putrefaction, mummification, and saponification can occur separately or in any combination.

Geneviève Doucet's body had lain in a unique microenvironment. Air blowing from the heat vent had been trapped by blankets and clothing, creating a mini-convection oven around her corpse. Voilà! Door B!

Though head hair remained, Geneviève's features were gone, leaving only desiccated tissue in the orbits and overlying the facial bones. Her limbs and chest were encased in a thick, hard shell.

Gently raising Geneviève's shoulders, I checked her back. Leatherized muscle and ligament clung to her spine, pelvis, and shoulder blades. Bone was visible where she'd been in contact with the mattress.

I took a series of backup Polaroids, then crossed to the light boxes lining one wall. Geneviève's skeleton glowed white amid the gray of her tissues and the black of the film. Slowly, I moved through the X-rays.

LaManche was right. There were no obvious signs of violence. No bullets, bullet fragments, casings, or metallic trace. The bones showed no hairline, linear, depressed, or radiating fractures. No joint dislocations. No foreign objects. For a complete examination of the skeleton, the body would have to be cleaned.

Returning to the autopsy table, I started at Geneviève's head and worked toward her feet, seeking indicators of illness, injury, or insect activity. Anything that might clarify time and/or manner of death.

As with the X-rays, nada.

Next, I tried cutting into Geneviève's belly. It took some doing, since the overlying skin and muscle had become so hard. My scalpel finally broke through. As I enlarged the incision, a stench seeped out and permeated the room.

With some effort, I created an opening approximately eight inches square. Using a small flashlight, I held my breath, leaned close, and peered into Geneviève's abdomen.

The internal organs had been reduced to a dark, viscous paste. I spotted not a single maggot, egg, or puparial casing.

Straightening, I removed my goggles and considered.

Observations: Outer tissue dehydration. Skeletal exposure. Visceral breakdown. Absence of fly and beetle activity.

Deduction: Death had occurred the previous winter. Long enough back to account for tissue destruction, at a time when insects weren't out and about. Geneviève Doucet had died months before her mother.

Welcome to reality, TV crime show buffs. No date, hour, and minute of death. The condition of this body allowed no greater precision.

I didn't linger on the implications. Geneviève blow-drying in her bed. Dorothée joining her months later. All the while, Théodore commanding U-boats on his PC.

After giving instructions for the cleaning of Geneviève's remains, I changed from my scrubs, washed, and returned to the twelfth floor.

The old man was again in his office. He listened, face a taut replica of the one he usually wore. LaManche knew what the future held for Théodore Doucet. And, by association, for Michelle Asselin.

There was an awkward silence when I'd finished. I said I was sorry. Lame, I know. But I'm lousy at commiseration. You'd think in my business I'd have honed some skills. You'd be wrong.

LaManche raised, dropped both shoulders. Life is hard. What can you do?

Back in my lab, Hippo's bag was still on my desk. A lone pink doughnut remained. Pink? There's something wrong there.

I looked at the clock: 1:46 P.M.

The sheet with Hippo's coroner contact information caught my eye. Grabbing it, I crossed to my office.

The mound of papers hadn't diminished. The wastebasket and plants hadn't relocated themselves to the floor. The CSU supplies hadn't disappeared, neatly folded, into a locker.

Screw housekeeping. Sliding into my chair, I dialed Yves Bradette.

His answering service picked up. I left my name and number.

A stomach growl warned that doughnuts hadn't sufficed.

Quick lunch. Chicken salad in the first-floor cafeteria.

When I returned, my red message light was flashing. Yves Bradette had phoned.

Again, I dialed Rimouski. This time Bradette answered.

"What can I do for you, Dr. Brennan?" Nasal. A bit whiny.

"Thanks for returning my call so quickly."

41

"Of course."

I relayed Hippo's story, mentioning no names.

"May I ask how you came to know of this?" A cool and very formal *vous*.

"A police officer brought the situation to my attention."

Bradette said nothing. I wondered if he was trying to recall Gaston's report of the bones, or formulating a justification for his failure to seize them.

"I think it's worth a look," I added.

"I have investigated this matter." Even cooler.

"You examined the skeleton?"

"Cursorily."

"Meaning?"

"I went to SQ headquarters. I concluded these bones are old. Perhaps ancient."

"That's it?"

"In my judgment, the remains are those of a female adolescent."

Easy, Brennan.

A coroner or pathologist orders a textbook or takes a short course, and Sha-zam! He or she is a forensic anthropologist! Why not score a copy of *Operative Cardiac Surgery*, hang a shingle, and start opening chests? Though it's rare that an underqualified person attempts to practice my profession, when it happens on my turf, I am far from pleased.

"I see." I matched Bradette's cool with arctic.

"Under questioning, the officer admitted to having had these bones for many years. Furthermore, he stated that they originated in New

42

Brunswick. New Brunswick is outside the scope of my authority."

Months, perhaps years pass with no thought of Évangéline Landry. Then, unexpectedly, a synapse will flash. I never know what the trigger will be. A forgotten snapshot curling in the bottom of a box. Words spoken with a certain intonation. A song. A line from a poem.

Hippo's *chiac* accent. New Brunswick. The skeleton of a girl, dead many years.

Neurons fired.

Irrationally, my fingers tightened on the receiver.

5

"I want those bones confiscated and sent to my lab." My voice could have carved marble.

"In my professional opinion, this is a waste of—"

"Tomorrow." Granite.

"Pierre LaManche must submit an official request form."

"Give me your fax number, please."

He did.

I wrote it down.

"You will have the paperwork within the hour."

After completing the form I went in search of a signature.

LaManche was now at a side counter in the pathology lab, masked and wearing a plastic apron tied behind his neck and back. A sliced pancreas lay on a corkboard before him. Hearing footsteps, he turned.

I told him about Gaston's skeleton. I didn't mention Évangéline Landry or her disappearance from my life almost four decades earlier as something that was prodding me to look more closely at adolescent remains from New Brunswick. I didn't really believe there could be any connection, but somehow I felt I owed it to Évangéline to explore the identity of the New Brunswick skeleton.

Yet the tightness in my chest.

"Nouveau-Brunswick?" LaManche asked.

"The remains are currently in Quebec."

"Might they have come from an old cemetery?"

"Yes."

"You will be very busy this month."

Spring to early summer is high season in my business in Quebec. Rivers thaw. Snow melts. Hikers, campers, and picnickers sally forth. Ta-da! Rotting corpses are found. LaManche was gently reminding me of this fact.

"The construction site bones are nonhuman. I'll begin Dr. Santangelo's case now. Then do your Lac des Deux Montagnes vic."

LaManche gave a tight head shake. "Old bones kept as a souvenir."

"PMI is unclear."

LaManche said nothing.

"Dr. Bradette's attitude offends me. A skeleton is lying ignored within our jurisdiction. No human being should be treated with such cavalier disregard."

LaManche gazed at me over his mask. Then he shrugged. "If you think you will have time."

"I'll make time."

I lay the form on the counter. LaManche stripped off a glove and signed it.

Thanking him, I hurried to the fax machine.

I spent the rest of that afternoon with Santangelo's fire victim, a ninety-three-year-old man known to smoke in bed before removing his dentures and turning off his bedside lamp each night. The kids and grandkids had repeatedly warned, but the old geezer had ignored their advice.

Gramps wasn't smoking now. He lay on stainless steel in autopsy room four.

If it *was* Gramps.

The skull consisted of charred fragments collected in a brown paper bag. The torso was an amorphous black mass with upper arms and legs raised due to contraction of the flexor muscles. The lower limbs were shriveled stumps. The hands and feet were missing.

No fingers, no prints. No teeth, no dentals. And the false choppers looked like a blob of Bazooka.

But one thing simplified my task. In 1988, the presumed vic had treated himself to a brand-new hip. Antemortem X-rays now covered the light boxes previously occupied by Geneviève Doucet.

Gramps's prosthesis glowed white in his upper right femur. Postmortem X-rays showed a similar neon mushroom positioned identically within the burned right leg.

Making an incision along the outer pelvic edge, I peeled back charred muscle and tendon, manipulated the device from the hip socket, then buzzed through the proximal third of the bone with an autopsy saw.

Further cleaning revealed the serial number. Crossing to the counter, I checked the antemortem orthopedic records.

Bonjour, Gramps!

I photographed, bagged, and tagged the specimen, then returned to the body for a full skeletal exam. Although the implant made the ID a slam dunk, anthropological data would provide useful backup.

Cranial fragments showed large brow ridges and mastoid processes, and an occipital muscle attachment the size of my sneaker.

Male. I made notes and moved on to the pelvis.

Short, chunky pubic bone. V-shaped subpubic angle. Narrow sciatic notch.

Male. I was recording my observations when the outer door clicked open then shut.

I glanced up.

A tall, sandy-haired man stood in the anteroom. He wore a tweed jacket, tan slacks, and a shirt the exact startling blue of his eyes. Burberry. I knew. I'd given it to him.

Time to discuss *lieutenant-détective* Andrew Ryan, Section des crimes contre la personne, Sûreté du Québec.

Ryan works homicide for the provincial police. I work corpses for the provincial coroner. No-brainer how we met. For years I tried maintaining professional distance, but Ryan played by different rules. Libertine rules. Knowing his reputation, I didn't sign on.

Then my marriage imploded, and Ryan high-geared the legendary charm. What the hell? I gave dating a whirl. Things went well for a while. Very well.

Then fate played the family obligation card. A newfound daughter barreled into Ryan's life. My estranged husband, Pete, was shot by the village idiot in Isle of Palms, South Carolina. Duty didn't call. It pounded on the door in full battle gear.

To add further complication, Pete's brush with death resurrected feelings I'd thought long dead. They didn't look dead to Ryan. He withdrew.

Was the lieutenant-detective still leading-man material? Definitely. But the casting couch had grown a bit crowded. Ryan and I hadn't spoken since parting the previous month.

"Hey," I said. Southern for "hi" or *bonjour*.

"Car fire?" Ryan pointed at Gramps.

"Smoking in bed."

"A sign of our increasingly complacent society."

I gave Ryan a questioning look.

"No one bothers with labels."

The look held.

"Big bold font on every pack. 'Cigarette smoking is dangerous to your health.'"

My eyes rolled skyward.

"How are you?" Ryan's tone went softer. Or did I imagine it?

"I'm good. You?"

"All good."

"Good."

"Good."

The dialogue of middle-schoolers, not former lovers. Were we? I wondered. Former?

"When did you arrive?"

"Yesterday."

"Good flight?"

"Landed on time."

"Better than early and sudden."

"Yes."

"You're working late."

I looked at the clock. Isolated in room four with its special ventilation, I hadn't heard the autopsy techs depart. It was now six-fifteen.

"Indeed." God, this was strained. "How's Charlie?"

"Bawdy as ever."

Charlie is a cockatiel whose early years were spent in a brothel. A Christmas gift from Ryan, we share joint custody of the bird.

"Birdie's been asking about him." I wondered if Ryan was there to see me, or to talk about LaManche's Lac des Deux Montagnes case. I didn't wonder long.

"Had time to look at my floater?"

"Not yet." I kept the disappointment from my voice. "What's the story?"

"Fisherman was trolling off L'Île-Bizard yesterday. Thought he'd snagged the big one, reeled in a body instead. Guy probably has his bass boat on eBay right now."

49

"I haven't gotten to it yet."

"The vic is female. LaManche thought he spotted some unusual patterning around the neck, wasn't sure because of the severe bloating and discoloration. No signs of gunshot on the body or the X-rays. No hyoid fracture. LaManche has requested a tox screen."

"Has Bergeron charted the teeth?" Marc Bergeron is the lab's consulting odontologist.

Ryan nodded. "I entered her dental descriptors into CPIC, got zip. The odds may improve if you nail age and race."

"She's next on the docket."

Ryan hesitated a beat. "We're looking at some MPs and DOAs that may be connected."

"How many?"

"Three missing persons. Two bodies, both unknown."

"You're thinking serial?"

"We're considering the possibility."

"Time frame?"

"Ten years."

"Vic profile?"

"Female. Early to late teens."

I felt the usual anger and sadness. Fear? Could some predator be using Quebec as his killing field?

"You suspect the Lac des Deux Montagnes woman could be vic number six?"

"Maybe."

"First thing tomorrow?"

"Thanks."

Ryan started to leave, turned back at the door. "How's Pete?"

"Recovering nicely. Thanks for asking. Lily?"

"Good."

"Good." God. We were doing it again. "I'll pick Charlie up," I said.

"No need. I'll deliver him."

"You don't have to do that."

"Serve and protect." Ryan snapped a salute. "I'll give you a call."

"Thanks, Ryan."

After rewrapping the burned nonagenarian, and rolling his gurney into its bay, I cleaned up and headed home. Birdie met me at the door.

While changing to shorts I explained that Charlie would be joining us soon. Bird was thrilled. Or bored. With cats it's hard to be sure.

Following dinner, Birdie and I watched a *Sopranos* rerun, the one in which Adriana gets whacked. Throughout, I kept picking up the land phone. Checking for a dial tone. Tossing the thing back onto the couch.

Ryan didn't phone. Nor did he appear at my condo that night.

Though Birdie and I were in bed by eleven, sleep didn't come for a very long time. Thinking back on our exchange in autopsy room four, I realized what was bothering me. Ryan had scarcely smiled or joked. It wasn't like him.

Don't act like an insecure adolescent, I told myself. Ryan's busy. Concerned about his daughter. About a serial killer. About ear wax buildup. About the mustard spot on his tie.

I didn't buy it.

6

I use a home-rigged system for cleaning cadavers. Originally designed for institutional cooking, the apparatus consists of water intake and discharge pipes, grease filtration gear, a compartmentalized boiling tank, and submersion baskets, the kind used to deep-fry potatoes or fish.

In the square baskets I simmer small body parts—dissected jaws, hands, feet, maybe a skull. In the large, rectangular ones I reduce the big stuff—long bones, rib cages, pelves—once defleshing has been done by morgue technicians. Heat water to just below boiling, add enzyme detergent to minimize grease, stir. The recipe's a hit every time.

Unless the bones are too fragile, of course. Then it's hand laundry all the way.

That morning the "cooker" was full to capacity. The Lac des Deux Montagnes corpse. Parts of Santangelo's charred bed smoker. Geneviève Doucet.

Putrid, sodden flesh means quicker turn-around time. And Ryan's floater had gone in first. Denis was removing those bones when I arrived following the morning staff meeting.

First, I opened the brown envelopes containing the Lac des Deux Montagnes scene and autopsy photos. One by one I worked from recovery through autopsy completion.

It was obvious why LaManche needed help. When dragged from the river, the body looked like a marionette wrapped in moss-colored Spam. No hair. No features. Large areas of flesh devoured by crabs and fish. I noted that the woman wore only one red sock.

I began constructing the requested portions of the biological profile. It took all morning. Though I'd left word to call the minute anything arrived from Rimouski, no one phoned or popped into my lab.

That no one included Ryan.

At lunch, I told LaManche what I was finding out about the Lac des Deux Montagnes woman. He told me that Théodore Doucet had undergone the first in his series of psychiatric interviews.

According to the doctor, Doucet was oblivious to the deaths of his wife and daughter. Delusional, he believed Dorothée and Geneviève had gone to church and would be home shortly to prepare supper. Doucet was being held at the Institut Philippe-Pinel, Montreal's main legal psychiatric hospital.

Back in my lab, I found the fire victim's pelvis and upper arm and leg bones spread out on a counter. Gloving, I transferred the remains to a second worktable and began my exam.

Though severely damaged, sufficient structure remained to confirm the gender as male. The pubic symphysis, coupled with advanced arthritis, suggested a skeletal age consistent with ninety-three.

Age and sex consistent. Orthopedic implant serial number a match. Known resident at the address. Known bed smoker. Good enough for me. Now it was up to the coroner. By three I'd completed my report and delivered it to the secretarial office for typing.

It isn't protocol to notify me of a skeleton's arrival. Normally, a case goes to one of the lab's five pathologists, and via him or her, to me. But I'd asked for a heads-up on the bones Bradette was sending from Rimouski. On the chance they'd forgotten, I checked with morgue intake.

Nothing.

Geneviève Doucet's were the third set of remains that had simmered overnight. Using long-handled tongs, I fished out her skull, pelvis, and several long bones, then spent an hour teasing off flesh. The stuff was resilient as gator hide, so I accomplished very little.

I was lowering Geneviève's basket back into its compartment when my lab door opened. I turned.

Of course. Ryan has a knack for showing up when I'm looking bad. I waited for a crack about steam-lank hair and eau de poached flesh. He made none.

"Sorry I didn't bring Charlie last night."

"No problem." I settled the stainless steel cover over the well and checked the temperature gage.

"Lily," Ryan sort of explained.

"Nothing serious, I hope." Backhanding hair from my face with a lab coat sleeve.

"I'll come by tonight." Ryan jabbed a thumb at the skeleton laid out behind me. "That my floater?"

"Yes." I stepped to the table, holding wet, greasy gloves away from my body. "She's young. Fifteen to eighteen. Mixed racial background."

"Tell me about that."

"Except for the front teeth, I'd have said she was white. Nasal opening is narrow and spiked at the bottom, nasal bridge is high, cheekbones aren't especially flaring. But all eight incisors are shoveled."

"Meaning?"

"There's a high probability she's part Asian or Native American."

"First Nations?"

"Or Japanese, Chinese, Korean. You know, Asian?"

Ryan ignored the dig. "Show me."

I rotated the woman's skull so her upper dentition was visible. "Each of the four flat teeth in front has a raised border around its outer perimeter on the tongue surface." Picking up the jaw, I indicated a similar raised ridge. "Same with the lowers."

I set down the jaw.

"I took cranial measurements and ran them

through Fordisc 3.0. Metrically she falls in the overlap region for Caucasoid and Mongoloid."

"White and Indian."

"Or Asian." A teacher correcting a dull pupil. "Any interest in age indicators?"

"Hit me with the high points."

I indicated a roughened area on the base of the skull. "The basilar suture is fused."

"The wisdom teeth aren't fully out," Ryan observed.

"Correct. The third molars have emerged but aren't yet in alignment with the tooth row."

Moving farther down the table, I ran my finger over an irregular line curving below the upper edge of the right pelvic blade. "The iliac crests are partially fused." I picked up a collarbone and pointed to a similar irregularity on the throat end. "Same for the medial clavicular epiphyses." I waved my hand over the arm and leg bones. "Growth caps on the long bones are in various states of fusion."

"Anything else?"

"She stood about five foot three."

"That's it?"

I nodded. "No abnormalities or anomalies. No new or healed fractures."

"LaManche thought the hyoid was intact."

Ryan referred to a tiny U-shaped throat bone often damaged during manual strangulation.

I gathered a small ovoid disc and two slender spurs in the palm of one glove. "At her age the hyoid wings and body aren't yet ossified. That means there's elasticity, so the bone can undergo considerable compression without breaking."

"So she could still have been strangled."

"Strangled, smothered, poisoned, gut-stabbed. I can only tell you what the bones tell me." I replaced the hyoid.

"Which is?"

"She wasn't shot or bludgeoned. I found no bullet entrance or exit wounds, no fractures, no cuts or slash marks anywhere on the skeleton."

"And the autopsy revealed zip."

LaManche and I had discussed his findings at lunch. There hadn't been much to discuss.

"The lungs were too far gone to know if she was breathing when she went into the water. Marine scavengers took care of her eyes, so there's no way to check for petechiae."

Petechiae are red pinpoint hemorrhages caused by leaky capillaries under increased venous pressure. Since sustained compression of the neck causes the backup of blood returning to the heart, the presence of petechiae on the skin of the face, and particularly around the eyes, is strongly suggestive of strangulation.

"So she could have been dead when she went into the water."

"I could try playing around with diatoms."

"I know you're going to tell me what those are."

"Unicellular algae found in aquatic and damp terrestrial habitats. Some pathologists believe the inhalation of water causes penetration of diatoms into the alveolar system and bloodstream, with subsequent deposition in the brain, kidneys, and other organs, including the bone marrow. They see the presence of diatoms as indicative of drowning."

"You sound skeptical."

"I'm not convinced diatoms can't make their way into any submerged body, drowned or not. Neither is LaManche. But there is another application. Many diatom species are habitat specific, so assemblages found in or on bodies can be compared with assemblages found in control samples taken from different locations. Sometimes specific microhabitats can be identified."

"Use diatoms to narrow where the body's been. Salt water. River bottom. Swamp. Estuary."

"That's the general idea. But it's a long shot."

"Sounds good."

"Before boiling I removed bone samples for DNA testing. I could have a marine biologist check the marrow in those. Also the sock."

Ryan spread both hands, palms up. "Case practically solved."

I raised questioning brows.

"The girl died near the river or someplace else. She was alive or dead when she entered the water. If alive, she fell, jumped, or was pushed, so manner of death is suicide, homicide, or accidental."

"Unless she had a stroke or heart attack," I said, knowing the only categories left were "natural" and "undetermined."

"Unless that. But this is a teenager."

"It happens."

★　　　★　　　★

Ryan did show up that night. I'd showered and blow-dried my hair. And, yes, I confess, applied mascara and lip gloss and a spritz of Alfred Sung behind each ear.

The buzzer warbled around nine. I was reading about FTIR spectroscopy in the *Journal of Forensic Sciences*. Birdie was performing his evening toilette on the far end of the couch. Losing interest in intertoe spaces, he padded along to the foyer.

The security screen showed Ryan in the vestibule, birdcage at his feet. I buzzed them in, welcomed both warmly. After greeting and ear scratching the cat, Ryan accepted my offer of a beer.

While I poured Moosehead and Diet Coke, Ryan settled Charlie on the dining room table. Birdie assumed his sphinx pose on one of the chairs, head up, paws in-curled, every sense fixed on the cage and its occupant.

Charlie was in top form, perch hopping, seed spewing, head cocking right then left to eyeball the cat. Every now and then he'd fire off a line from his repertoire *noir*.

Ryan took Birdie's end of the couch. I took mine, feet tucked under my bum. Again, we established that our daughters were good. Lily was waiting tables at Café Cherrier on Rue Saint-Denis. Katy was doing a summer Spanish course in Santiago, Chile.

My Montreal condo is small. Kitchen, bedroom, den, two baths. Only the main living area is spacious. French doors open from opposite sides, the north set to a central courtyard, the south to a Lilliputian-sized patch of grass.

Stone fireplace. Glass dining table. Yellow and blue Provençal sofa and loveseat. Cherry-wood moldings, window trim, and mantel.

As we talked, Ryan's eyes roved from object to object. Pictures of Katy. My younger sister, Harry. My nephew, Kit. A ceramic plate gifted from an old woman in Guatemala. A giraffe carving purchased in Rwanda. Rarely did his gaze meet mine.

Inevitably, we drifted into shop talk. Safe, neutral ground.

Ryan had been working special assignments since the death of his partner several years earlier. He described his current investigation.

Three girls missing. Two others found in or near water. And now there was the Lac des Deux Montagnes floater. Six in all.

I told Ryan about the burn victim, the Doucets, and the Rimouski skeleton en route to my lab. He asked who was responsible for the latter. I described my meeting with Hippo Gallant.

Ryan said Hippo was inputting on his missing persons and DOAs. Thus, we drifted into the inevitable Hippo stories. The time he left his gun behind in a gas station men's room. The time he pulled a suspect from a culvert and ripped his pants up the ass. The time a collar took a dump in the back of his cruiser.

Conversation was genial and friendly. And brotherly as hell. No mention of the past or future.

No body contact. The only references to sex were those made by Charlie.

At ten-thirty Ryan rose. I walked him to the door, every cell in my brain screaming that what I was debating was a *lousy idea*. Men hate being asked what they're feeling. I hate it, too.

Not for the first time, I ignored the advice of my instincts.

"Talk to me, Ryan." I laid a hand on his arm.

"Right now Lily—"

"No," I blurted. "It's more than Lily."

The cornflower blues refused to meet mine. A beat passed. Then, "I don't think you're over your husband."

"Pete and I have been separated for years."

Ryan's eyes finally locked home. I felt something hot coil in my belly.

"Operative word," he said, "'separated.'"

"I hate lawyers and paperwork."

"You were a different person when you were with him."

"The man had been shot."

Ryan didn't reply.

"My marital status never mattered in the past."

"No. It didn't."

"Why now?"

"I hadn't seen you together."

"And now that you have?"

"I realize how much you care." Before I could speak Ryan added, "And how much I care."

That stunned me. For a moment I could think of nothing to say.

"Now what?"

"I'm trying to get by it."

"How's it going?"

"Not well."

With that he was gone.

As I lay in bed, emotions battled inside me. Resentment at the feeling that Ryan had suckered me in. All the asking. Then the striving to keep things light.

Annoyance at Ryan's cowboy-done-wrong act.

But Ryan had one valid point. Why didn't I divorce Pete?

I take offense slowly, store insult until the end of time. Ryan is the opposite, affronted quickly, but quickly forgiving. Each of us reads the other well.

Ryan was light-years beyond feeling slighted or piqued. His signals were unmistakable.

So, mostly, I felt sadness. Ryan was pulling away.

A tear slid from the corner of one eye.

"OK, wrangler." Spoken aloud in my party-of-one bed. "Adios."

7

Harry has lived in Texas since dropping out of high school her senior year. Long story. Short marriage. Her concept of phone etiquette goes something like this. I'm up. I want to talk. Dial.

The window shade was oozing toward gray when my cell phone sounded.

"You awake?"

I squinted at the clock. Six-fifteen. Like a pilot whale, Harry needs approximately five hours of sleep nightly.

"I am now."

My sister once had this motto printed on a T-shirt: *Never complain, never explain.* While she's lax on the front end, she's crackerjack on the back, following her whims and offering no apologies for the outcome.

She offered none now.

"I'm going to Canyon Ranch." Harry is blond, leggy, and trying hard to look thirty. Though that

64

checkpoint was cleared a decade ago, in kind light, in the right clothes, she succeeds.

"That makes how many spas this year?"

"Rump's dragging, tits are starting to look like thirty-eight longs. Gotta eat sprouts and pump iron. Come with me."

"I can't."

"I'm selling the house."

The abrupt shift left me off balance. "Oh?"

"Butt-pie was an egregious error."

I assumed Butt-pie was husband number five. Or was it six? I dug for a name. Donald? Harold? Gave up.

"I think I hinted the man wasn't a girl's dream come true."

"You hinted he was stupid, Tempe. Arnoldo isn't stupid. Problem is he's got just one string on his fiddle."

Harry loves sex. Harry is also easily bored. I didn't want to hear about Arnoldo's violin.

"Why sell the house?"

"It's too big."

"It was too big when you bought it."

Husband number something was an oil man. I never quite learned what that meant, but their brief nuptials left my sister well oiled, indeed.

"I need a change. Come help me look at real estate."

"I really can't."

"Working on a juicy one?"

I considered, decided against mentioning the Rimouski skeleton. Once ignited, Harry is nonextinguishable. Besides, there was no evidence of an Évangéline Landry connection.

"It's my busy season."

"Need sisterly support?"

Please, God. "You know I love your visits, but right now I'm so slammed we wouldn't be able to spend time together."

Silence hummed across the line. Then, "What I said about Arnoldo's not really true. Fact is, I caught the bastard coyoting around."

"I'm sorry, Harry." I was. Though I wasn't surprised.

"Yeah. Me, too."

After slipping into jeans and a polo, I fed Birdie and filled Charlie's seed and water dishes. The bird whistled and asked me to shake my booty. I moved his cage to the den and popped in a cockatiel-training CD.

At the lab, there was nothing in my mailbox. No flashing light on the phone. A mini-avalanche had taken place on my desk. No pink message slip lay among the wreckage.

I called down to the morgue. No bones had arrived from Rimouski.

OK, buster. You've got until noon.

At the morning meeting I was assigned one new case.

The purchasers of a funeral home had discovered an embalmed and fully clothed body in a coffin in a basement cooler. The previous operators had closed their doors nine months earlier. The pathologist, Jean Pelletier, wanted my input on X-rays. On the request form he'd written: *All dressed up and nowhere to go.*

Returning to my office, I phoned a biology professor at McGill University. She didn't do diatoms, but a colleague did. I could deliver the Lac des Deux Montagnes specimens late the next afternoon.

After packaging the sock and bone plug, and preparing the paperwork, I turned to Pelletier's lingering corpse case.

Antemortem-postmortem X-ray comparisons showed the deceased was a childless bachelor whose only living brother had moved to Greece. The man's funeral had been paid for by money order two years earlier. Our ID chucked the ball into the coroner's court.

Back at my lab, Geneviève Doucet's bones had finally come out of the cooker. I spent the rest of the morning and well into the afternoon examining each with my new Leica stereomicroscope with magnified digital display. After years of bending over a dinosaur that I'd had to herniate myself to position, I was now equipped with state of the art. I loved this scope.

Nevertheless, magnification revealed little. Lipping of the interphalangeal joint surfaces of the right middle toe. An asymmetrical raised patch on the anterior midshaft of the right tibia. Other than those healed minor injuries, Geneviève's skeleton was remarkably unremarkable.

I phoned LaManche.

"She jammed her toe and banged her shin," he summarized my findings.

"Yes," I agreed.

"That didn't kill her."

"No," I agreed.

"It is something."

"Sorry I don't have more to report."

"How do you like the new microscope?"

"The screen resolution is awesome."

"I am happy you are pleased."

I was disconnecting when Lisa entered my lab carrying a large cardboard box. Her hair was pulled into a curly ponytail, and she was wearing blue surgical scrubs. Wearing them well. Firm glutes, slim waist, breasts the size of the Grand Tetons, Lisa is very popular with cops. And the best autopsy tech at the lab.

"Say you're bringing me a skeleton from Rimouski."

"I'm bringing you a skeleton from Rimouski." Lisa often used me to practice her English. She did that now. "It just arrived."

I flipped through the paperwork. The case had been assigned morgue and lab numbers. I noted the latter. LSJML-57748. The remains had been confiscated from *agent* Luc Tiquet, Sûreté du Québec, Rimouski. In the case overview cell, Bradette had written: *adolescent female, archaeological*.

"We'll see about that, hotshot."

Lisa looked a question at me.

"Jerk thinks he can do my job. Are you busy downstairs?"

"All autopsies are finished."

"Want to take a look?" I knew Lisa liked bones.

68

"Sure."

As I collected a case report form, Lisa set the box on the table. Joining her, I removed the cover, and we both peered inside.

Bradette was right about one thing. This wasn't a grown-up.

"It looks very old," Lisa said.

OK. Maybe two things.

The skeleton was mottled yellow and brown and showed lots of breakage. The skull was misshapen, the face badly damaged. I could see spidery filaments deep in the orbits and in what remained of the nasal opening.

The bones felt feather-light as I lifted and arranged them in anatomical alignment. When I'd finished, a small partial-person lay on my table.

I took inventory. Six ribs, most of the finger and toe bones, one clavicle, one tibia, one ulna, and both kneecaps were missing. So were all eight incisors.

"Why no front teeth?" Lisa asked.

"Each has only one root. When the gums go, there's nothing to hold them in place."

"There's a lot of damage."

"Yes."

"Peri- or postmortem?" Lisa was asking if the injuries had occurred at the time of or following death.

"I suspect most is postmortem. But I'll have to study the fracture sites under magnification."

"It's young, yes?"

Flashbulb image. A girl in a swimsuit on a Carolina

69

beach. Carrying a small white book with pale green lettering. Reading poetry aloud with an odd French accent.

I pointed to a proximal right humerus, distal right ulna, proximal left fibula, and distal right femur. "See how some long bones look normal on their ends, while these look corrugated and incomplete?"

Lisa nodded.

"That means the epiphyses weren't yet fused to the shafts. Growth was still ongoing."

I lifted the skull and rotated the base upward.

Running between dunes. Dark curls dancing wild in the wind.

"The basilar suture is unfused. There are no wisdom teeth, and the second molars show minimal wear."

I exchanged the skull for an innominate.

"Each hemi-pelvis starts out as three separate bones: ilium, ischium, and pubis. Union takes place around the time of puberty." I indicated a faint Y trisecting the hip socket. "See that line? Fusion was just wrapping up when she died. Given the teeth, the long bones, and the pelvis, I'd estimate she was around thirteen or fourteen."

Évangéline Landry, eyes closed, hands clasped, blowing out candles. There were fourteen on the cake.

"And the pelvis shows female?"

"Yes."

"Was she white?"

"Race is going to be tough since the face is smashed and the palate is history, including the incisors."

I picked up the skull. And felt a flicker of relief.

70

"The nasal aperture is wide and rounded. Its bottom edge is broken, but it looks like the nasal spine was small. Those are non-European traits. I'll know better when I've cleaned out the dirt."

"Why does her head look so"—Lisa floated a palm, searching for the English—"odd?"

"In adolescence, the cranial sutures are still wide open." I referred to the squiggly gaps between the individual skull bones. "Following brain decomposition, with pressure, the bones can warp, separate, or overlap."

"Pressure, as in burial?"

"Yes. Although skull distortion can result from other factors, exposure to sunlight, for example, or to extremes of heat and cold. The phenomenon is very common with children."

"There's so much dirt. Do you think she was buried?"

I was about to answer when the desk phone shrilled.

"Can you check the box for anything we might have missed?"

"Sure."

"How's it hanging, doc?" Hippo Gallant.

I skipped pleasantries. "Your buddy Gaston's skeleton arrived from Rimouski."

"Yeah?"

"My preliminary exam suggests it's an adolescent female."

"Indian?"

"There's a good chance her racial background is mixed."

"So it ain't all that ancient?"

"The bones are dry and devoid of odor and flesh, so I doubt death occurred in the last ten years. Right now that's about all I can say. She needs a lot of cleaning and it will have to be done by hand."

"*Crétaque.* She got teeth?"

"Some. But there's no dental work."

"You going to do DNA?"

"I'll retain samples, but if no organic components remain, sequencing will be impossible. There's soil deep in crevices and in the medullary cavities, suggesting burial at some point. Frankly, I suspect the coroner up in Rimouski may be right. The remains may have washed out of an old cemetery or been looted from an archaeological site."

"How about carbon fourteen or some fancy gizmo?"

"Except for a few specialized applications, C14 dating isn't useful on materials less than hundreds of years old. Besides, if I report that this girl's been dead half a century, the powers that be won't pony up for DNA, radiocarbon, or any other type of test."

"Think you'll be able to sort it?"

"I'm going to try."

"How 'bout I talk with the mope that had her. Get his story."

"That would be good."

Replacing the receiver, I returned to Lisa.

"Why does that one look different?" She pointed to the second right metacarpal.

Lisa was right. Though dirt-encrusted, one finger bone seemed to be a misfit.

Brushing free what soil I could without causing damage, I placed the odd metacarpal under my fabulous new scope, increased magnification, and adjusted focus until the distal end filled the screen.

My brows rose in surprise.

8

The bone's outer surface was a moonscape of craters.

"What is that?" Lisa asked.

"I'm not sure." My mind was already rifling through possibilities. Contact with acid or some other caustic chemical? Microorganism? Localized infection? Systemic disease process?

"Was she sick?"

"Maybe. Or maybe it's postmortem. There's still too much impacted dirt to be sure." Taking the metacarpal from the scope, I moved toward the skeleton. "We'll have to clean and examine every bone."

Lisa looked at her watch. Politely.

"What a dope I am. Already I've kept you too late." It was five-twenty. Most lab workers left at four-thirty. "Go."

"Shall I lock up?"

"Thanks, but I'll stay a bit longer."

That "bit" turned into two and a half hours. I might have worked through the night had my mobile not sounded.

Setting aside a calcaneus, I lowered my mask, pulled the phone from my pocket, and checked the screen. Unknown number.

I clicked on. "Brennan."

"Where are you?"

"I'm great, thank you. And yourself?"

"I've been calling your condo since six." Was Ryan actually sounding annoyed?

"I'm not at home."

"There's a news flash."

"Guess I slipped out of my ankle monitor."

A moment of silence. Then, "You didn't mention you had plans."

"I do have a life, Ryan." Right. Teasing dirt from bones at 8 P.M.

I heard the sound of a match, then a deep inhalation of breath. After quitting for two years, Ryan was back on cigarettes. A sign of stress.

"You can be a pain in the ass, Brennan." No rancor.

"I work on it." My standard reply.

"You coming down with a cold?"

"My nose is irritated from breathing through a mask." I ran my dental pick through the cone of dry soil that had collected on the tabletop in front of me.

"You're in your lab?"

"Hippo Gallant's skeleton arrived from Rimouski. It's female, probably thirteen or fourteen years old. There's something odd about her bones."

Tobacco hit, then release.

"I'm downstairs."

"So who's the loser working after hours?"

"These MP and DOA cases are getting to me."

"Want to come up?"

"Be there in ten."

I was back at the scope when Ryan appeared, face tense, hair bunched into ragged clumps. My mind shot a stored image: Ryan hunched over a printout, restless fingers raking his scalp. So familiar.

I felt sick. I didn't want Ryan to be angry. Or hurt. Or whatever the hell he was.

I started to reach out and stroke his hair.

Nor did I want Ryan controlling my life. I had to take steps when I decided steps needed taking. I kept both hands on the scope.

"You shouldn't work alone here at night."

"That's ridiculous. It's a secure building and I'm on the twelfth floor."

"This neighborhood's not safe."

"I'm a big girl."

"Suit yourself." Ryan's voice wasn't cold or unfriendly. Just neutral.

When Katy was young, certain cases at the lab caused me to rein in her personal life. Transference of caution. It wasn't her fault. Or mine, really. Working a child homicide was like taking a step into my own worst nightmare. Maybe these missing and dead girls were making Ryan overly protective. I let the paternalism go.

"Take a look." I shifted sideways so Ryan could see the screen. When he stepped close I could smell Acqua di Parma cologne, male sweat, and a hint of the cigarettes he'd been smoking.

"New setup?"

I nodded. "She's a pip."

"What are we seeing?"

"Metatarsal."

"Uh-huh."

"Foot bone."

"Looks funny. Pointy."

"Good eye. The distal end should be knobby, not tapered."

"What's that hole in the middle of the shaft?"

"A foramen."

"Uh-huh."

"For the passage of an artery supplying nutrients to the bone's interior. Its presence is normal. What may be unusual is the size. It's huge."

"The vic took a shot to the foot?"

"Enlarged nutrient foramina can result from repetitive microtrauma. But I don't think that's it."

I exchanged the first metatarsal for another.

"That one looks scooped out on the end."

"Exactly."

"Any ideas?"

"Lots. But most of her foot bones are missing so it's hard to choose."

"Give me some 'for instances.'"

"Rodent scavenging, with subsequent erosion of the surrounding bone surfaces. Or maybe the feet lay in contact with something caustic. Or rapidly running water."

"Doesn't explain the big holes."

"Destruction of the toe bones accompanied by enlargement of the nutrient foramina could result from frostbite. Or rheumatoid arthritis. But that's unlikely, since the joints aren't affected."

"Maybe she just has really big holes."

"That's possible. But it's not just her feet."

I placed Lisa's oddball metacarpal under the scope. "This is a finger bone."

Ryan regarded the pockmarked surface in silence.

I switched the metacarpal for one of the two surviving hand phalanges. "So is this."

"That hole looks large enough to accommodate the Red Line metro."

"Foramina show a range of variation in size. As you say, it could be that huge was normal for her." Even to me, I didn't sound convinced.

"What about the rest of the skeleton?" Ryan asked.

"I haven't gotten past the hands and feet. And there isn't much left."

"Preliminary diagnosis?"

"Increased blood flow to the extremities. Maybe. Deformity of the toe bones. Maybe. Cortical destruction on a metacarpal." My hands floated up in frustration. "Localized infection? Systemic disease process? Postmortem destruction, either purposeful or natural? A combination of the above?" The hands dropped to my lap. "I don't have a diagnosis."

Though far from high-tech, my lab is adequate. In addition to the worktables, boiler, and sprightly new scope, it is equipped with the usual: overhead fluorescents, tile floor, sink, fume hood, emergency eye wash station, photo stand, light boxes, glass-fronted cabinets. The small window above the sink overlooks the corridor. The big one behind my desk provides a view of the city.

Ryan's eyes floated to the latter. Mine followed. Two ghost images played on the glass. A tall man and a slim woman, faces obscure, superimposed translucent over the St. Lawrence and the Jacques-Cartier Bridge.

A strained silence crammed the lab, a void begging to be filled. I acquiesced.

"But this skeleton looks pretty old."

"LaManche isn't going to pull out the stops."

"No." I switched off the scope light. "Would you like to talk about these cases you're working?"

Ryan hesitated so long I thought he wouldn't answer.

"Coffee?"

"Sure." It was the last thing I needed. My fourth cup sat cold on my desk.

Habitat 67 is a modern pueblo of stacked concrete boxes. Built as a housing experiment for Expo 67, the complex has always engendered strong feelings.

That's an understatement. Montrealers either love it or hate it. No one's neutral.

Habitat 67 is located across the St. Lawrence from the Vieux-Port. Since Ryan lives there and my condo is in centre-ville, we decided on a coffee shop halfway between.

Ryan and I both had cars, so we drove separately to Old Montreal. June is peak season, and, as expected, traffic was snarled, sidewalks were clogged, and curbs were bumper to bumper.

As instructed by Ryan, I nosed my Mazda into a driveway blocked by an orange rubber cone. A hand-painted sign said *Plein*. Full.

A man in sandals, shorts, and a Red Green T-shirt came forward. I gave him my name. The man lifted the cone and waved me in. Cop privilege.

Walking downhill through Place Jacques-Cartier, I passed old stone buildings now housing souvenir shops, restaurants, and bars. Tourists and locals filled the outdoor terraces and wandered the square. A stilt-walking busker juggled balls and told jokes. Another played spoons and sang.

Turning onto cobbled Rue Saint-Paul, I smelled fish and oil wafting off the river. Though I couldn't see it, I knew Ryan's home was on the far shore. My view? Habitat 67 resembles a huge cubist sculpture, like the cross on Mont Royal, better appreciated from afar than up close.

Ryan hadn't arrived when I entered the coffee shop. Choosing a rear table, I ordered a decaf cappuccino. Ryan joined me as the waitress delivered it. In moments she was back with his double espresso.

"You planning an all-nighter?" Nodding toward Ryan's high-test selection.

"I brought files home."

No invite there, cowgirl. I waited until Ryan was ready to begin.

"I'll take it chronologically. For the cold cases, there are three missing persons and two unidentified corpses. This week's Lac des Deux Montagnes floater raises the un-ID'd body count to three."

Ryan stirred sugar into his espresso.

"Nineteen ninety-seven. MP number one. Kelly Sicard, eighteen, lives with her parents in Rosemère. March twelfth, one-forty A.M., she leaves a group of drinking buddies to catch a bus home. She never makes it."

"The buddies checked out?"

"And the family and the boyfriend."

Ryan sipped. His hand looked jarringly male holding the tiny white cup.

"Nineteen ninety-nine. DOA number one. The body of an adolescent female is snagged by a boat propeller in the Rivière des Mille Îles. You worked the case with LaManche."

I remembered. "The corpse was putrefied. I estimated the girl was white, age fourteen or fifteen. We did a facial reconstruction, but she was never ID'd. The bones are in my storage room."

"That's the one."

Ryan knocked back the remainder of his espresso.

"Two thousand one. DOA number two. A teenaged girl is found in Dorval, on the shore below the Forest and Stream supper club. According to LaManche, the body's been in the river less than forty-eight hours. He does an autopsy, concludes the girl was dead when she hit the water, finds no evidence of shooting, stabbing, or bludgeoning. Pictures are circulated throughout the province. No takers."

I remembered that case, too. "The girl was eventually buried as a Jane Doe."

Ryan nodded, moved up in time.

"Two thousand two. MP number two. Claudine Cloquet pedals her Schwinn three-speed through a wooded area in Saint-Lazare-Sud. Claudine is twelve and mildly retarded. The bike is found two days later. Claudine is not."

"An unlikely runaway."

"Father's sketchy, but alibis out. So does the rest of the family. Father's since died, mother's been hospitalized twice for depression.

"Two thousand four. MP number three. September first. Anne Girardin disappears from her Blainville home in the middle of the night." Ryan's jaw muscles bulged, relaxed. "Kid's ten years old."

"Pretty young to take off on her own."

"But not unheard of. And this was a streetwise ten-year-old. Again, the old man's a loser, but nothing's found to tie him to the disappearance.

Ditto for the rest of the household. A canvass of the neighborhood turns up zip."

We both fell silent, recalling the massive search for Anne Girardin. Amber Alert. SQ. SPVM. Tracker dogs. Local volunteers. Personnel from NCECC, the National Child Exploitation Coordination Center. Nothing was found. Subsequent tips all proved bogus.

"And now I've got DOA number three, the Lac des Deux Montagnes floater."

"Six girls. Three recovered in or near water. Three missing and unlikely to be runaways," I summarized. "Any other links?"

Again, a tensing in Ryan's jaw. "We may have a fourth MP. Phoebe Jane Quincy, age thirteen. Lives in Westmount. Missing since leaving home for a dance lesson day before last."

Ryan took a photo from his pocket and placed it on the table. A girl mimicking Marilyn in *The Seven Year Itch*, dress ballooning around her. Back-lighting outlined the thin figure through the diaphanous white fabric.

Thirteen?

"Who took this picture?"

"Parents have no idea. Found it hidden in the bottom of a dresser drawer. We're looking into it."

I stared at the photo. Though not overtly sexual, the image was disturbing.

"Her friends say she wants to be a model," Ryan said.

She could be, I thought, studying the slender form, long hair, and luminous green eyes.

"A lot of little girls want to be models," I said.

"Did you?"

"No."

"Kelly Sicard also had runway dreams," Ryan said.

"Slim lead." I slid the photo back toward Ryan.

"Slim beats none," Ryan said.

We discussed the cases for a few more minutes. Mostly, I listened.

Ryan isn't rattled by violence or death. He sees both frequently, has learned to mask his emotions. But I know the man. Know that the abuse of those powerless to protect themselves affects him deeply. It affects me, too. I was keenly aware of my feelings at that moment, having spent the past hours with the bones of a child.

Though Ryan claimed only fatigue, I could see through to the sadness and frustration. Fair enough. Comes with the job. But did I sense something else? Was some further factor contributing to Ryan's agitation, robbing him of his usual lightheartedness, goading him to smoke? Was I being paranoid?

After a while, Ryan signaled for a check.

Returning to the lot, I started my Mazda and pointed the headlights for home. I needed to rest. To shower. To think.

Needed a drink I couldn't have.

Turning west onto René-Lévesque, I lowered a window. The air was warm and moist and unnaturally heavy, the sky a black screen on which occasional flickers of lightning danced.

The night smelled of rain.

A storm would soon break.

9

The next day passed without word from Hippo or Ryan. Harry was another story. Little sister had made appointments to view a downtown Houston penthouse, a horse ranch in Harris County, and beachfront property at South Padre Island. I suggested she take time to ponder what she truly wanted post-Arnoldo, instead of impulsively chasing around southeast Texas hoping for inspiration. She suggested I lighten up. I'm paraphrasing.

I slogged through the mess in my office, then resumed teasing dirt from the Rimouski remains. I often give nicknames to my unknowns. Somehow, it personalizes them for me. Though he'd been only marginally involved in the case, I'd come to think of the skeleton as Hippo's girl.

The more detail I revealed about Hippo's girl, the more puzzling the picture became.

Around eleven, a skull came in from Iqaluit, a

pinpoint on the Quebec map a zillion miles north on Frobisher Bay. I looked the place up. Though I wanted to stay with Hippo's girl, I stuck with my promise to LaManche, and started on the new arrival.

Leaving the lab around five, I delivered the Lac des Deux Montagnes bone plug and sock to the biologist at McGill, then stopped by Hurley's for my version of a pint: Diet Coke on the rocks with a twist. It wasn't for the soft drink, of course, but for the contact with friends the pub would provide.

As I passed through the game room, I glanced up at the wall-mounted TV. A classic school portrait showed as a backdrop to a grim-faced anchorman. The young girl's eyes were green and mischievous, her hair center-parted and pulled into shoulder-length braids. Phoebe Quincy.

A small group of regulars was gathered around the downstairs bar: Gil, Chantal, Black Jim, and Bill Hurley himself. They greeted me, faces somber, then recommenced airing their views on the Quincy disappearance.

"Sweet mother o' Jesus, thirteen years old." Chantal shook her head and signaled for another pint. A Newfoundlander, she could outdrink the best of the best. And often did.

"Hope to God she's just gone walkabout." Black Jim's accent changed with his story of the moment. No one knew where Jim really originated. Every time someone asked, he produced a different tale. Tonight he was speaking Aussie.

"How long's she been gone?" Bill signaled the bartender and a Diet Coke was set before me.

"Three days. Went to dance class. Sufferin' Jesus." Chantal.

"You involved?" Bill asked me.

"No."

"Ryan?"

"Yes."

"Where is Ryan? You finally manage to lose that slug?"

I sipped my Coke.

"It doesn't look good, does it?" Gil resembled an aging French version of the Fonz.

"She may turn up," I said.

"They think some bugger nipped her?" Black Jim.

"I don't know."

"Can you imagine what her poor parents are going through?" Gil.

"They catch the bastard, I'll volunteer to cut off his dick, bye." Chantal.

I stared into my mug, rethinking my decision to delay going home. I'd wanted to shed the mantle of sorrow and death, arrive home diverted and refreshed, but it seemed there would be no relief tonight.

What *had* happened to Phoebe? Was she out there on the streets, alone but stubbornly following her own play? Or was she being held in some dark place, helpless and terrified? Was she even alive? How were her parents surviving the endless hours of uncertainty?

And what about the corpse from Lac des Deux Montagnes? Who was she? Had she been murdered?

And the other girl in my lab. Hippo's girl. When had she died? An irrational leap of thought. Could the skeleton be Évangéline Landry? Where was Évangéline?

I realized Bill was talking to me. "Sorry. What?"

"I asked where Ryan is."

Obviously, word hadn't reached the pub that Ryan and I had split. Or whatever it was we'd done.

"I don't know."

"You OK? You look beat."

"It's been a tough couple of days."

"Fuckin' hell," said Chantal.

I listened to the conversation a few minutes longer. Then I downed my Coke and set out for home.

Friday morning brought no new anthropology cases. I was composing a report on the Iqaluit cranium when Ryan showed up in my lab.

"Nice do."

My left hand did an automatic hair-behind-the-ears tuck, then I realized Ryan's remark was directed at the skull. It was sun-baked white, its crown capped with dried green moss.

"It's been lying on the tundra a very long time."

Normally Ryan would have asked how long. He didn't. I waited for him to get to the point of his visit.

"Got a call from Hippo Gallant this morning. Guy named Joseph Beaumont is doing a nickel to dime at Bordeaux."

Bordeaux is the largest of Quebec's correctional facilities.

"Last night the CFCF six o'clock aired a story on Phoebe Quincy. Included footage on Kelly Sicard and Anne Girardin."

"Only those two?"

Ryan raised palms in a "who knows why?" gesture. "Beaumont caught the report, requested a sit-down with the warden. Claims he knows where Sicard is buried."

"Is he credible?"

"Beaumont could just be a con looking to better his life. But the guy can't be discounted."

"What's he saying?"

"Let's make a deal."

"And?"

"We're negotiating. Wanted to give you a heads-up. If the tip's legit, a team will go out immediately. We'll want to move before the press scents blood."

"I'll be ready."

I was checking my field kit when Ryan phoned.

"We're on."

"When?"

"CSU truck's already on the move."

"Meet you in the lobby in five."

Ryan took Autoroute 15 northwest out of the city, cut east, then north toward Saint-Louis-de-

Terrebonne. Midday traffic was light. He briefed me as he drove.

"Beaumont settled for getting his mail privileges reinstated. Three months back the dolt received a copy of *Catch-22* with LSD mixed into the binding glue."

"Creative pals. What's his story?"

"Six years ago, Beaumont shared a cell with a guy named Harky Grissom. Claims Grissom told him about a kid he'd waxed back in ninety-seven. Said he picked her up at a bus stop in the middle of the night, took her home, abused her, then smashed her skull with a socket wrench."

"Beaumont could have read about or listened to reports of Sicard's disappearance."

"Grissom told Beaumont the kid he killed was crazy for NASCAR. Claims he lured her with promises she'd meet Mario Gosselin."

I watched the yellow center line click up Ryan's shades.

"The bit about Sicard liking stock car racing was dead-on." Ryan glanced at me and the yellow dashes slid sideways. "And never made public."

"Where's Grissom now?"

"Paroled in ninety-nine. Killed in a car wreck the same year."

"He won't be of any help."

"Not without a séance, but he wouldn't have helped in any case. We have to rely on Beaumont's memory."

Ryan hung a right. To both sides lay woods. In moments, I saw what I'd been expecting. Pulled to the side of the asphalt were the LSJML crime scene truck, a black coroner's van, an SQ patrol unit, an unmarked Chevrolet Impala, and an SUV. Apparently the speed and stealth had worked. No cameras or microphones were present. Not a single poised pen. For now.

Hippo was talking to a pair of uniformed cops. Two morgue technicians smoked by their van. A guy in civvies was filling a bowl from a canteen for a border collie.

Ryan and I got out. The air hit me like caramel syrup. That morning's *Gazette* had called for rain and a high in the nineties. June in Quebec. Go figure.

Walking toward Hippo, Ryan explained the lay of the land.

"According to Beaumont, Grissom described an abandoned barn off Route 335, in woods backing up to a horse farm."

I followed the compass of Ryan's hand.

"The highway's behind us. The Parc équestre de Blainville is off through those trees. Saint-Lin-Jonction and Blainville lie to the south."

I felt a heaviness in my chest. "Anne Girardin disappeared in Blainville."

"Yeah." Ryan kept his eyes straight ahead.

We reached the group. Hands were shaken, greetings exchanged. Maybe it was the sticky heat. Maybe unease over what we might soon unearth. The usual humor and banter were absent.

"Barn's about ten yards in." Hippo's face was slick, his pits dark. "Good wind will bring her down."

"What's been done?" Ryan asked.

"Ran the dog through," Hippo said.

"Mia," the dog handler cut in.

The collie's ears shot up at the sound of its name. Hippo rolled his eyes.

"Her name is Mia." *Sylvain* was embroidered on the handler's shirt.

Hippo is famous for loathing what he dubs "hot-shit" technology. It was clear cadaver dogs got the same fish eye as computers, iris scanners, and touch-tone phones.

"*Mia* didn't seem overly impressed." Hippo took a tin from his pocket, thumbed open the lid, and palmed antacid tablets into his mouth.

"The place is full of horseshit." Sylvain's voice had an edge. "Throws her off scent."

"GPR?" I truncated the exchange with a question about ground-penetrating radar.

Hippo nodded, then turned. Ryan and I followed him into the trees. The air smelled of moss and loamy earth. The thick foliage hung undisturbed by even a whisper of movement. Within yards, I was perspiring and breathing deeply.

In thirty seconds we were at the barn. The structure rose from a clearing barely larger than itself, leaning like a ship in an angry sea. Its planks were gray and weathered, its roof partially collapsed. What I assumed had been its main double doors now lay in a heap of rotten lumber. Through the opening, I could see dimness pierced by shafts of dust-filtered sunlight.

Hippo, Ryan, and I stopped at the threshold.

Crooking two fingers, I pulled my shirt by the collar and flapped. Sweat now soaked my waistband and bra.

The barn's interior was ripe with the mustiness of moisture and age. Rotting vegetation. Dust. And something sweetly organic.

The CSU techs looked like astronauts in their masks and white coveralls. I recognized each by movement and body form. The daddy longlegs was Renaud Pasteur. The Demster Dumpster was David Chenevier.

Hippo called out. Pasteur and Chenevier waved, then resumed their tasks.

Chenevier was guiding a three-wheeled apparatus in parallel paths back and forth across the barn floor. A rectangular red box hung below the rig's main axle, its bottom inches from the ground surface. A small LCD screen rested on the handlebars.

Pasteur was alternating between shooting stills and video, and clearing debris in front of Chenevier. Rocks. Soda cans. A length of rusted metal stripping.

Drew the short straw, I thought, seeing Pasteur pick something up, examine it, then toss it aside.

Forty minutes later Chenevier was covering the last and farthest corner of the barn. Pausing, he made a comment. Pasteur joined him, and the two discussed something on the monitor.

A chill replaced my hotness. Beside me, I felt Ryan tense.

Chenevier turned. "We got something."

10

Ryan and I picked our way across the uneven ground. Hippo zigzagged behind. He was wearing a shirt that could only have been purchased at a discount store. A deep-discount store. Shiny penguins in mufflers and berets. The fabric looked flammable.

Chenevier and Pasteur opened a space to allow us a view of the monitor. A layer cake of colors squiggled across the screen. Reds. Greens. Blues. Centered in the cake was a pale gray hump.

GPR isn't as complicated as the name implies. Each system includes a radio transmitter and receiver connected to a pair of antennae coupled to the ground.

A signal is sent into the soil. Since a subsurface object or disturbance will have electrical properties different from those of the surrounding dirt, a signal reflecting off that object or disturbance will bounce back to the receiver slightly later in time. A different wave pattern will appear on the monitor.

Think of a fish finder. The thing tells you something's down there, but can't tell you what.

"Could be an animal burrow." Chenevier's face was soaked with sweat. "Or a trench for old piping."

"How far down?" I asked, studying the inverted gray crescent.

Chenevier shrugged. "Eighteen or twenty inches."

Deep enough for a hurried gravedigger.

Mia was summoned and led to the spot. She alerted by sitting and barking once, sharply.

By noon I'd marked off a ten-foot square with stakes and string. Ryan and I started in with long-handled spades. Pasteur shot pics. Chenevier sifted.

Hippo stood to one side, mopping sweat and shifting from foot to foot. Now and then one hand would go into a pocket. The jangle of keys would join the click of Pasteur's shutter and the hiss of soil trickling through mesh.

The barn floor was rich with organics, easy to dig, easy to sift.

By twelve-thirty we'd exposed an amoeba-like splotch visibly darker than the surrounding earth. Soil staining. A sign of decomposition.

Ryan and I switched to trowels and began scraping dirt, both anticipating and dreading what we'd find beneath the discoloration. Now and then our eyes would meet, drop back to the hollow we were creating.

The first bone turned up in the screen.

"Got something." Chenevier's voice cut the silence.

"Gaubine!" Hippo popped antacid.

Chenevier crossed to me and extended a hand.

Sitting back on my heels, I took what lay in his palm.

There are 206 bones in the adult human skeleton, all varying in size and shape. Singly, they yield few clues about a person's life story. But together, like interlocking puzzle pieces, they say a lot. Age. Sex. Ancestry. Health. Habit. The more bones, the more is revealed.

Chenevier's find, however, disclosed the jigsaw solo.

Slender and less than ten centimeters long, the bone looked like a pin that might be worn to keep a topknot in place. Thicker at one end, it tapered to a subtle knob on the other.

I looked up to eight curious eyes.

"It's a baculum."

Four blank stares.

"A bone found in the penis of most mammals. I'd guess this one comes from a large domestic dog."

Still no one spoke.

"The os baculum aids in copulation when mating must take place during brief encounters."

Pasteur cleared his throat.

"When animals have to perform quickly." I adjusted my mask.

"Pour l'amour du bon Dieu!" Hippo's expletive suggested the same emotions swirling in me. Relief. Bewilderment. Hope.

I handed the bone to Pasteur. As he photographed and bagged it, Ryan and I resumed digging.

* * *

By three, Grissom's "victim" lay fully exposed. The snout was broad, the cranium rugged. Caudal vertebrae snaked between hind legs seemingly too short for the torso.

"Long tail."

"Some kind of pit bull mix."

"Maybe shepherd."

The testosterone set seemed inordinately interested in the dog's heritage. I couldn't have cared less. I was sweaty, itchy, and desperate to shed my Tyvek coveralls. Designed to protect wearers from blood, chemicals, and toxic liquids, the things reduced air circulation and were hotter than hell.

"Whatever his breed, the guy was a player." Pasteur held up the ziplock containing the dog's penis bone. Chenevier raised a palm. Pasteur high-fived it.

Already the jokes had begun. I was glad I hadn't told them that the os baculum is sometimes called a hillbilly toothpick. Or that best in show goes to the walrus, whose males occasionally reach thirty inches. It was going to be bad enough as it was.

During graduate school a fellow student had studied the os baculum of rhesus monkeys. Her name was Jeannie. Now professors and respected researchers, my old classmates still tease her about "Jeannie's penies."

By two the dog's bones had been packaged and placed in the coroner van. Probably unnecessary, but better to err on the side of caution.

By six Ryan and I had taken the entire ten-foot

square down twenty-four inches. Nothing had turned up in the pit or the screen. Chenevier had resurveyed the barn and surrounding field, and found no indications of additional subsurface disturbance.

Hippo approached as I was peeling off my coveralls.

"Sorry to drag you out here for nothing."

"It's the job, Hippo." I was ecstatic to be out of the Tyvek. And relieved that we hadn't unearthed Kelly Sicard.

"How long since Old Yeller strutted his stuff?"

"The bones are fleshless, odorless, and uniformly soil-stained. The only insect inclusions I found were dried puparial casings. Buried at that depth, inside the barn, I'd estimate the dog's been dead at least two years. But my gut feeling says more."

"Ten years?"

"Possibly."

"Could have belonged to Grissom. Or Beaumont."

Or Céline Dion, I thought.

Hippo looked off into the distance. Grime coated his lenses, making it hard to read the expression behind them. I suspected he was scripting a chitchat with his erstwhile informant.

"You want to hang around a few, I'll give you a lift."

I looked over at Ryan. He was talking on a cell phone. Behind him, heat shimmered mirage-like above the blacktop and the vehicles parked along it.

Catching Ryan's eye, I gestured that I'd ride with Hippo. He flicked a wave, continued his conversation.

"Sure," I said.

"I'll fill you in on Luc Tiquet."

I stared at Hippo.

"Sûreté du Québec, Rimouski? My buddy Gaston's bones?"

"What's his story?"

"I'll tell you in the car."

Climbing into the Impala was like climbing into a pottery kiln.

As Hippo turned onto the highway, I maxed the AC and held a hand to the vent. Hot air blasted my fingers.

"L'air conditionné est brisé."

On Hippo's tongue the word for broken came out "breezy." Hardly.

Static erupted from the radio. I peeled damp hair from my neck as I waited it out.

"Have you checked the coolant?"

"Pain in the ass." Hippo waved dismissively. "Heat won't last. Never does."

I bit back a comment. Useless. Coolant was probably a mystery to Hippo's mind.

When I lowered my window, the smell of fertilizer and fresh-mown fields flooded the car.

I slumped back, shot forward as scorching vinyl contacted bare skin. Crossing my arms, I eased into the seat, closed my eyes, and let the wind whip my hair.

I knew from past experience that riding with Hippo was like riding "El Torro" at the Rodeo Bar. I gripped the armrest as we hurtled through the countryside at neck-snapping speed, Hippo's boot slamming gas pedal then brake.

"This Tiquet's not a bad guy."

I opened my eyes. We were looping onto the fifteen. "What did he tell you?"

"Says he got a call reporting a disturbance at a quarry maybe five, six years back. Busted a couple kids for trespass and destruction of property. Geeks claimed to be spray-paint artists creating timeless works of beauty."

I braced against the dash as Hippo swerved around a pickup. The driver gave him the finger. Hippo's expression suggested a rejoinder in the making.

"The skeleton?" I brought Hippo back on point.

"Turned up in the trunk when Tiquet tossed their car."

"Where was this quarry?"

"Somewhere near the Quebec–New Brunswick border. Tiquet's vague on that."

"Did he remember the kids' names?"

"No, but he pulled the file. I've got them written down."

"Fair enough. He got the skeleton in a bust. But why did he keep it?"

"Says he contacted the coroner."

"Bradette?"

"That's the guy. Bradette dropped in, took a

look, told him he should call an archaeologist. Tiquet didn't exactly have one in his Rolodex."

"And he never got around to looking one up."

"Bingo."

A pothole launched us both toward the ceiling.

"*Moses!* Sorry."

"What explanation did these kids give?"

"Claimed they bought the bones from a pawnshop operator. Planned to do some sort of spray-painted sculpture with them."

"Nice. Where did the pawnbroker get them?"

"Tiquet didn't know."

"Where was the pawn guy from?"

"Miramichi."

I turned and looked out the window. We were back in the city now, and exhaust fumes had replaced the smell of turned earth. An auto body shop flashed by. A seedy strip center. A Petro-Canada station.

"Where is Miramichi?"

"New Brunswick."

"It's a big province, Hippo."

Hippo's brow furrowed. "Good point, doc. Miramichi's a city of eighteen, maybe twenty thousand. But the name also refers to the river and the region in general."

"But where is it?"

"Northumberland County."

Fighting back an eye roll, I wiggled my fingers in a "give me more" gesture.

"Northeast coast of New Brunswick."

"Acadia?"

"Deep in the heart."

I listened to blacktop whump under our tires. Beyond the windshield, a layer of smog was buffing up the sunset, bathing the city in a soft, golden glow.

Miramichi. I'd heard of the place. In what context?

Suddenly, I remembered.

11

The summer I was ten and Évangéline was twelve, she described an event that had occurred the previous December. The incident had so troubled her, she'd been unable to write of it in her letters.

Entrusting Obéline to a neighbor, Évangéline's mother had driven to a nearby town for groceries. That was unusual, since Laurette habitually shopped in Tracadie. Leaving the market, she'd directed her daughter to return to their old Ford and wait for her.

Curious, Évangéline had watched her mother round the corner, then followed. Laurette entered a pawnshop. Through the window, Évangéline saw her in animated conversation with a man. Frightened, Évangéline had hurried back to the car.

Laurette owned a single piece of jewelry, a sapphire ring with tiny white diamonds. Though unaware of its history, Évangéline was certain the ring never left her mother's finger. When Laurette slid behind the wheel that day, the ring was gone. Évangéline never saw it again.

Our childish imaginations conjured stories of heartbreak and lost love. A handsome fiancé killed in the war. A Montague–Capulet feud, Acadian style. We wrote verse rhyming the name of the town. Peachy. Beachy. Lychee.

That's how I remembered.

Évangéline and her mother had gone to Miramichi.

Did Hippo's girl come from Miramichi?

"How far is Miramichi from Tracadie?" More crazy possibilities swept through my mind.

"'Bout fifty miles."

Impossible. There was no reason to think Évangéline was not alive.

"Straight down Highway 11."

Yet? Ask Hippo to run a missing persons check? Not realistic. She could have taken another name, now be living elsewhere.

Drawing a deep breath, I told Hippo the story of Évangéline Landry. When I finished, he was mute for so long I thought his attention had wandered. It hadn't.

"You really believe something happened to this kid?"

That question had tortured me over the years. Had Oncle Fidèle and Tante Euphémie, tired of nurturing their two young nieces, simply sent them home? Or had it been the other way around? Had

Évangéline grown bored with the Lowcountry? With my friendship? Had my summer soul mate merely outgrown me? I didn't believe it. She would have told me she was leaving. Why Tante Euphémie's remark about danger?

"Yes," I said. "I do."

We were crossing onto the island. I watched Hippo's gaze slide sideways to the turgid water of the Rivière des Prairies. I wondered if he was thinking of the girl snagged by the boat in the Rivière des Mille Îles in 1999, Ryan's DOA number one. Or the girl washed ashore in Dorval in 2001, Ryan's DOA number two. Or the one found last week in Lac des Deux Montagnes, perhaps DOA number three in the chain.

"You say the skeleton's of mixed race," Hippo said. "Was your friend?"

"That's my impression. But I haven't had time to fully clean the skull. I never thought of Évangéline that way. I just thought she was exotic in a mysterious sort of way."

Hippo took a moment to chew on that.

"You told me the stuff's pretty beat up. You good with a PMI pushing forty years?"

I'd given the question of postmortem interval considerable thought. "I'm certain this girl was buried, then the bones were held for some period aboveground. The problem is, I've got zip on context. Buried how? In sandy soil? Acid soil? Shallow grave? Deep? Coffin? Fifty-gallon Hefty? Time since death could be ten, forty, or a hundred and forty."

Hippo did some more mental chewing. Then, "How well did you know this kid's family?"

"I knew Évangéline's aunt and uncle, but only superficially. I didn't speak French and they were self-conscious about their English. Laurette was at Pawleys very little, and wasn't bilingual, so the few times I saw her it was mainly hello and good-bye."

"You said there was a sister?"

"Obéline, eight years younger than Évangéline."

Hippo turned onto Papineau. We were creeping now, with traffic bumper to bumper.

"*Ben.* You know the system, homicide cops gotta focus on fresh cases. They got time, they can look at old, unsolved ones. Problem is they never got time because people keep capping people. That's where Cold Case comes in. We take files no one's working."

Hippo signaled a left, waited while three teens slouched through the crosswalk. Each wore clothing large enough to house the other two.

"Nineteen sixty to 2005 we got five hundred seventy-three *dossiers non résolus* in this province. Cold Case squad was created in 2004. Since then we've cleared six of those unsolved cases."

Forty years. Six answers. Five hundred and sixty-seven victims' families still waiting. That depressed me.

"How can so many get away with murder?"

Hippo hiked one shoulder. "Maybe there's no evidence, no witnesses. Maybe someone screws up. Most investigations, you don't score a viable lead

107

the first couple days, the thing's going nowhere. Years pass. The jacket fills up with forms saying 'no new developments.' Eventually, the detective decides it's time to move on. Sad, but what's one more unsolved killing?"

We were just blocks from the Édifice Wilfrid-Derome. I wondered if Ryan was somewhere behind us, returning to SQ headquarters. Wondered if he would stop by my office or lab.

Making a right onto Parthenais, Hippo kept talking.

"Some of these murder squad cowboys think we cold-casers been put out to pasture. That ain't how I see it. My thinking, a killing's no less important because it happened ten years back. Or twenty. Or forty. Ask me, cold case vics should be getting priority. They been waiting longer."

Hippo swung into the Wilfrid-Derome lot, shot down a row of cars and braked beside my Mazda. Throwing the Impala into park, he turned to me.

"And you can double that for kids. The families of missing and murdered kids live in agony. Every year that anniversary rolls around, the day the kid disappeared or the body was found. Every Christmas. Every time the kid's birthday pops up on the calendar. A dead kid's just one big ugly wound that refuses to heal." Hippo's eyes met mine. "The guilt eats at 'em. What happened? Why? Why weren't we there to save her? That kinda hell don't ever go cold."

"No," I agreed, feeling a new appreciation for the man beside me.

Hippo reached through the space between us, snatched his jacket from the backseat, and dug out a small spiral pad. Taking a pen from the center console, he wet a thumb and flipped pages. After reading a moment, his eyes met mine.

"My main focus right now is this job with Ryan. And don't get me wrong, forty years is a long time. Witnesses leave town, die. Same for relatives, neighbors, friends. Reports go missing. Evidence gets lost. Forget the crime scene, if you ever had one. You do manage to unearth something, no one's gonna stop in their tracks to process it. No one's gonna fork over money for fancy tests."

Here comes the blow-off, I thought.

"But if nobody pushes, nothing gets done. That's what I do. I push."

I started to speak. Hippo wasn't finished.

"You think someone messed with this Évangéline, that's good enough for me. You think this skeleton might even be her, that's good enough, too. If not, it's still someone's kid."

Hippo's eyes dropped back to his spiral. He thumbed again, scribbled, then tore a page free and handed it to me.

"This thing is a long way from dead. We got leads."

I read what Hippo had written. The names Patrick and Archie Whalen, a Miramichi address, and a phone number with a 506 area code.

"Tiquet's spray-paint artists?" I asked.

"Apparently the genre ain't a rocket to upward

mobility. Mopes are in their late twenties now, still living at Mom and Dad's place. Give them a ring. I'm guessing they'll be more open with you."

Because I'm female? Anglophone? Civilian? Hippo's reasoning didn't matter. I couldn't wait to get to a phone.

"I'll call as soon as I get home."

"Meantime, I'll start working the kid and her family. Can't be that many Évangélines and Obélines walking the planet."

"Can't be," I agreed.

It was almost eight by the time I reached my condo. I could have devoured Vermont and still had room for dessert.

Birdie met me at the door. One sniff sent him under the couch. I took the hint.

As I stripped, Charlie sent wolf whistles down the hall.

"Nicest compliment I've had all day, Charlie."

"Strokin'!"

"The *only* compliment I've had all day."

Charlie whistled.

I started to answer.

It's a cockatiel, Brennan.

After a long, hot shower, I checked the answering machine.

Four messages. Harry. One hang-up. Harry. Harry.

My freezer offered two choices. Miguel's Mexican flag fiesta. Mrs. Farmer's country chicken pot pie. I went with the pie. It had been a barnyard sort of day.

As my frozen entrée baked, I dug out the number Hippo had provided.

No answer.

I phoned Harry. Thirty minutes later I'd learned the following.

Marital lawyers in Houston are plentiful. Divorce costs a bucket. Arnoldo's parts aren't zip-a-dee-doo-dah. A real ass-waxing lay in the man's future.

After disconnecting, I ate my pie, then tried the Whalen brothers again.

Still no answer.

Disappointed, I clicked on the news.

There'd been a pile-up on the Metropolitan, one dead, four injured. A judge had been indicted for money laundering. Health officials had grown concerned about bacteria plaguing the beach on Île Sainte-Hélène. Police had learned nothing about the disappearance of Phoebe Jane Quincy.

The only good news involved the weather. Rain was on the way and, with it, cooler temperatures.

Disheartened, I killed the set and checked the clock. Ten-twenty. What the hell. I dialed the Whalens one last time.

"Your dime." English.

"Mr. Whalen?"

"Might be."

"Am I speaking with Archie Whalen?"

"No."

"Patrick?"

"Who's this?"

"Dr. Temperance Brennan. I'm an anthropologist with the medico-legal lab in Montreal."

"Uh-huh." Wary or dull? I wasn't sure.

"Am I speaking with Patrick Whalen?"

"Depends on what you're peddling."

"About five or six years ago, you and your brother purchased bones from a Miramichi pawnshop. Is that correct?"

"Where'd you get this number?"

"From an SQ cold case detective."

"We bought that shit fair and square. Paid full asking."

"Am I speaking with Patrick?"

"The name's Trick."

Trick?

"Are you aware that trafficking in human remains is illegal?"

"I may pee my shorts." No question about IQ versus attitude there.

"We might be able to let the charges slide, Trick. Providing you cooperate with our investigation of the origins of that skeleton." I wasn't sure who "we" were, but it sounded more official.

"Already I'm breathing easier."

OK, asshole. Let's see how tricky you are.

"According to the police report, you claimed to have purchased the skeleton from a pawnbroker."

"Yes."

"Where did he get it?"

"I didn't background the guy. We saw it in his

112

shop, flashed on the idea of a death scene sculpture, something totally war zone, bones, bullets, lots of black and green paint."

"You made no inquiries as to the source of the skeleton?"

"Guy said it came from an old Indian cemetery. What did we care?"

"Uh-huh."

"Skulls, man. Rattlesnakes. Shrouds. Bleak mojo, know what I mean?"

A dead child. I tried to keep the distaste from my voice.

"You were arrested in Quebec. Why were you there?"

"Visiting a cousin. He told us about a quarry. We thought jazzing all that rock would be a real mind-fuck. Look, when that cop busted us we were as freaked as anyone. We'd totally zoned on those bones."

"How long had they been in your trunk?"

"A year. Maybe more."

"What do you do now, Mr. Whalen?"

There was a pause. I thought I could hear a television in the background.

"Work security." Defensive. "Nights at the high school."

"And your brother?"

"Archie's a fucking junkie." The macho tone now sounded whiny. "Do us both a favor. Arrest his ass and get him out of this shithole."

I had one last question.

"Do you remember the pawnbroker's name?"

"'Course I remember that dickhead. Jerry O'Driscoll."

I'd barely disconnected when my cell phone rang.

Hippo.

His news rocked my world.

12

"Laurette Philomène Saulnier Landry. DOB May 22, 1938. DOD June 17, 1972."

Death at age thirty-four? How sad.

I pictured Laurette in Euphémie's Pawleys Island kitchen. My child's mind had never slotted her age. She was simply adult, younger than Gran, more wrinkled than Mama.

"She died so young. From what?"

"Death certificate lists natural causes, but doesn't elaborate."

"You're sure it's the right Laurette Landry?"

"Laurette Philomène Saulnier married Philippe Grégoire Landry on November 20, 1955. Union produced two kids. Évangéline Anastasie, DOB August 12, 1956. Obéline Flavie, DOB February 16, 1964."

"Jesus. I can't believe you found this so fast." In addition to my early telephone probes, I'd periodically tried the New Brunswick Bureau of Vital Statistics. Never had a hit.

"Used my Acadian charm."

Hippo's charm and a token would get him on the subway. I waited.

"Back in the sixties, the church handled most of the vital stats record keeping. Some parts of New Brunswick, babies were still being birthed at home, especially in rural areas and smaller towns. Lot of Acadians had no time for government or its institutions. Still don't."

I heard a soft *whop*, pictured Hippo downing several Tums.

"Got a church-lady niece at St. John the Baptist in Tracadie. Knows the archives like I know the size of my dick."

I definitely did not want to hear about that.

"You found baptismal and marriage certificates through your niece?" I guessed.

"Bingo. Since I'm a homeboy, I started dialing for dollars. We Acadians identify ourselves by ancestral names. Take me, for example. I'm *Hippolyte à Hervé à Isaïe à Calixte*—"

"What did you learn?"

"Like I warned you, forty years is a long time. But the Acadian National Memory Bank's got a whopper of a vault. Found a few locals remembered Laurette and her kids. No one would talk much, respecting privacy and all. But I got the drift.

"When Laurette got too sick to work, hubby's kin took her in. The Landrys lived outside of town.

Kept mostly to themselves. One old-timer called them *morpions*. Trailer trash. Said they were mostly illiterate."

"Laurette had a driver's license."

"No. Laurette had a car."

"She must have been licensed. She drove across the border."

"OK. Maybe someone got paid off. Or maybe she was smart enough to read a little and to memorize road signs. Anyway, Philippe took off while Laurette was pregnant with Obéline, leaving her to support the two little girls. She managed for five or six years, then had to quit working. Eventually died of some sort of chronic condition. Sounded like TB to me. This guy thought she'd moved out toward Saint-Isidore sometime in the mid-sixties. Might have had family living that way."

"What about Philippe?"

"Nothing. May have left the country. Probably dead somewhere."

"And the girls?" My heart was thumping my rib cage.

"Obéline Landry married a guy named David Bastarache in eighty. I'm running him now. And following the Saint-Isidore lead."

"What about Évangéline?"

"I'll be straight. I ask about Laurette or Obéline, I get cooperation. Or at least what sounds like cooperation. I ask about the older sister, people go iceberg."

"What are you saying?"

"I'm saying I've been at this awhile. I got

117

antennae. I ask about this kid, the answers come too quick, too consistent."

I waited.

"No one knows shit."

"Hiding something?" My grip on the handset was raising the cords in my wrist.

"I'd bet money on it."

I told Hippo what I'd learned from Trick Whalen. The Miramichi pawnshop. The mojo sculpture. The Indian cemetery.

"You want I should call this guy O'Driscoll?"

"No. If you can get contact information, I'll follow the bone trail while you chase the leads in Tracadie."

"Don't go 'way."

Hippo put me on hold for a good ten minutes.

"Place is called Oh O! Pawn. Catchy name. Says we care." He supplied a phone number and an address on the King George Highway.

Cellophane crinkled. Then, "You said you found something wrong with the kid's skeleton."

"Yes."

"You figure that out?"

"Not yet."

"You willing to work on Saturday?"

The 82nd Airborne couldn't have kept me from those bones.

By eight-thirty I was at Wilfrid-Derome. Contrary to reports, there'd been no rain and the weather hadn't cooled. Already the mercury was pushing eighty.

I rode the elevator alone, passed no one in the LSJML lobby or corridors. I was pleased that I'd have no disruptions.

I was wrong. One of several misjudgments I'd make that day.

First off, I dialed O'Driscoll. The phone went unanswered.

Disappointed, I turned to the skeleton. Hippo's girl. Before being interrupted by the Iqaluit skull and the dog exhumation in Blainville, I'd cleaned what remained of her trunk and limb bones.

Going directly to her skull, I cleared the foramen magnum and emptied soil and small pebbles from the cranial base.

At nine-thirty, I tried O'Driscoll again. Still no luck.

Back to teasing dirt. Right auditory canal. Left. Posterior palate. The lab thundered with that stillness possible only on weekends in government facilities.

At ten, I lay down my probe and dialed Miramichi a third time. This time a man answered.

"Oh O! Pawn."

"Jerry O'Driscoll?"

"Speaking."

I gave my name and LSJML affiliation. Either O'Driscoll didn't hear or didn't care.

"You interested in antique watches, young lady?" English, with a whisper of brogue.

"I'm afraid not."

"Two beauties just come in. You like jewelry?"

"Sure."

"Got some Navajo turquoise that'll knock your socks off."

Navajo jewelry in a New Brunswick pawnshop? Must be a story there.

"Mr. O'Driscoll, I'm calling about human remains you sold to Trick and Archie Whalen several years back."

I expected caginess. Or lack of recollection. O'Driscoll was polite, expansive, even. And had recall like a credit card agency computer.

"Spring of 2000. Kids said they wanted it for a college art project. Said they were constructing some kind of homage-to-the-dead display. Sold it to them for sixty-five bucks."

"You have an excellent memory."

"Truth is, that was the first and last skeleton I ever traded. Thing was older than all the angels and saints. Lots of broken bones. Face smashed in and caked with dirt. Still, the idea of selling dead souls didn't sit well. Didn't matter if the poor devil was Christian or Indian or Bantu. That's why I remember."

"Where did you get the skeleton?"

"Fella used to come in every couple months. Claimed he was an archaeologist before the war. Didn't mention which war. Always had this mangy terrier trailing him. Called the thing Bisou. Kiss. No way I'd have put my lips anywhere near that hound. Guy spent his time searching for stuff to pawn. Poked through Dumpsters. Had a metal detector he'd run along the riverbank. That sort of thing. Brought in a brooch once was pretty nice. I sold it to a lady lives up in Neguac. Most of his finds were junk, though."

"The skeleton?"

"Guy said he found it when he went out to the woods to bury Bisou. I wasn't surprised. Dog acted a hundred years old. Old geezer looked like he could really use a lift that day. Figured I'd take a loss, but I gave him fifty bucks. Didn't see any harm in it."

"Did the man say where he'd buried his dog?"

"Some island. Said there was an old Indian cemetery there. Could have been hooey. I hear a lot of that. People think a good tale ups the value of what they're offering. It doesn't. An item's worth what it's worth."

"Do you know the man's name?"

O'Driscoll's chuckle sounded like popcorn popping. "Said he was Tom 'Jones.' I'd bet my aunt Rosey's bloomers he made that up."

"Why is that?"

"Guy was French. Pronounced the name *Jones*. Spelled it *Jouns*."

"Do you know what happened to him?"

"Stopped coming about three years back. Old duffer was frail and blind in one eye. Probably dead by now."

After the call, I returned to the bones. Was there truth to Tom Joun's Indian burial ground story? Could Hippo's girl be a pre-Columbian aboriginal?

Cranial shape was distorted by breakage and warping. No help there. I rotated the skull and looked at the remnants of the face. The nasal spine

121

was almost nonexistent. A nonwhite trait. Though dirt packed the opening, the orifice seemed wider than is typical of Europeans.

I went back to teasing dirt. Time passed, the only sounds in my lab the competing hums of the refrigerator and the overhead fluorescents.

The eyeballs are separated from the frontal lobe by the paper-thin bone forming the floor of the anterior cranial fossa. Clearing the right socket, I found jagged breaches in that floor. I moved on.

I'd emptied the left orbit when something caught my attention. Laying aside my pick, I dampened a cloth and swiped a fingertip over the orbital roof. Dirt came away, revealing pitted, porous bone in the upper, outer corner of the socket.

Cribra orbitalia.

Now we were getting somewhere. Or were we? While cribra orbitalia has a fancy scientific name, and the lesions are known to occur most commonly in kids, their cause has yet to be satisfactorily explained.

I did one of my mental rundowns. Iron deficiency anemia? Vitamin C inadequacy? Infection? Pathogenic stress?

All of the above? None of the above? A and B only?

I was as puzzled as ever.

Findings to this point included modification of toe bones, enlargement of nutrient foramina in the hands and feet, cortical destruction on at least one metacarpal, and now cribra orbitalia. Abnormally pitted orbits.

I had plenty of dots. I just had to connect them.

One thing was becoming clear. This girl had been sick. But with what? Had the ailment killed her? Then why the caved-in face? Postmortem damage?

Using warm water, I cleaned the entire left orbit. Then I picked up a magnifying lens.

And got my second surprise of the morning.

A black squiggle crawled the underside of the supraorbital ridge, just inside the thickened upper border of the socket.

A root impression? Writing?

I hurried to the scope and balanced the skull face-up on the cork ring. Eyes on the screen, I jacked the magnification.

Tiny hand-lettered characters leaped into focus.

It took several minutes, and several adjustments, but I finally managed to decipher the inscription.

L'Île-aux-Becs-Scies.

The quiet of the empty building enveloped me.

Had Jouns marked his skeleton with the name of the island on which he'd found it? Archaeologists did exactly that. He'd claimed to have been one in his youth.

I flew from my lab, down the corridor, and into the LSJML library. Locating an atlas, I flipped to a map of Miramichi.

Fox Island. Portage. Sheldrake. Though I pored over the map portions depicting the rivers and the bay, I found no Île-aux-Becs-Scies.

Hippo.

Back in my lab, I dialed his cell. He didn't pick up.

Fine. I'd ask him later. He'd know.

Returning the skull to my worktable, I began freeing dirt from the nasal orifice with a long, sharp probe.

And encountered my third surprise of the morning.

13

The aperture resembled an upside-down heart, narrow at the top, bulging at the bottom. Nothing spiked from the dimple on the heart's lower edge.

OK. I'd been right about the wide nasal opening and reduced nasal spine. But the nasal bridge was narrow with the two bones steepling toward the midline. And I could now see that the periphery of the orifice looked spongy, indicating resorption of the surrounding maxilla.

The girl's nasal pattern didn't mean she was Indian or African. The spike had been reduced, the shape modified by disease.

What disease?

Defects on the hands, feet, orbits, nose.

Had I missed something on the skull?

I examined every millimeter, inside and out.

The cranial vault was normal. Ditto for the base. What remained of the hard palate was intact. I was unable to observe the premaxillary, or most forward part of the roof of the mouth. That portion was missing, along with the incisors.

I rechecked the postcranial skeleton and found nothing beyond what I'd already spotted.

Hands. Feet. Orbits. Nose. What disease process would lead to that kind of dispersed bone damage?

Again, I considered possibilities.

Syphilis? Lupus vulgaris? Thalassemia? Gaucher's disease? Osteomyelitis? Septic or rheumatoid arthritis? Blood-borne parasite? Infection due to direct extension from the overlying skin?

Diagnosis would take research. And with so much bone missing or damaged, I wasn't optimistic.

I was pulling out Bullough's *Orthopaedic Pathology* when Hippo came through the door. He was wearing a shirt festooned with bananas and red palm trees, gray pants, and a hat that would have made a drug lord proud.

Despite the "don't worry, be happy" attire, Hippo did not appear to be having a good day. The bags under his eyes were heavier than usual, and he was frowning.

Hippo took a seat on the opposite side of the table. He smelled of bacon and stale deodorant.

"Saturday casual?" I asked, smiling.

Hippo didn't smile back.

"I found the kid sister."

"Where?" Suddenly Hippo had all my attention.

"I want you to hear me out."

I settled back, elated, yet anxious at the same time.

"I did some poking into the husband."

"David Bastarache."

"Bastard would be more fitting. Your pal's little sis married into a family of smugglers and bootleggers."

"You're kidding."

"David's granddaddy, Siméon, made a nice chunk of change running rum in the twenties, invested in real estate. Bars in Tracadie and Lamèque. A rooming house in Caraquet. David's daddy, Hilaire, put his inheritance to good use. Turned some of the old man's properties into 'hides,' safe havens for illegal booze and contraband."

"Wait. Rumrunners?"

"Remember that proud moment in American history brought to you by the Eighteenth Amendment and the Volstead Act?"

"Prohibition."

"Nineteen twenty to 1933. Republican and Prohibition parties jumped in bed with the Temperance Movement." Hippo gave a half grin. "That where you got your name?"

"No."

"But you're a Pepsi hugger, right?"

"Diet Coke. Back to Bastarache."

"As you will recall from your history lessons, some politicos and Bible thumpers may have taken the pledge, but a great many Americans did not. Familiar with Saint-Pierre et Miquelon?"

Lying south of Newfoundland, the little island cluster is the last remnant of the former colonial territory of New France. Essentially under French control since 1763, a 2003 constitutional reform changed its status from territorial collective to oversees region, like Guadeloupe and Martinique in the Caribbean, French Guiana in South America, and Réunion in the Indian Ocean. With its own postal stamps, flag, coat of arms, and sixty-three hundred fiercely Francophile souls, Saint-Pierre et Miquelon is the Frenchest of French outposts in North America.

I nodded.

"Americans still wanted their cocktails, and the French didn't give a rat's ass about Prohibition, so Saint-Pierre et Miquelon stepped up to the plate. In the twenties, the place was awash with booze. I ain't just talking Canadian whiskey. Champagne from France. West Indian rum. British gin. And all that hooch needed distribution. That meant good times for many small villages in Atlantic Canada."

Hippo misread my impatience for disapproval.

"A man could make more running one load of booze than he could freezing his ass all year in a fishing boat. What would you choose? Anyway, right or wrong, booze flowed down the eastern seaboard and into Rum Row."

Hippo gave me a questioning look. I nodded again. I'd also heard of Rum Row, the flotilla of ships anchored beyond the three-mile limit off the U.S. East Coast, waiting to offload liquor for entrepreneurs such as Al Capone and Bill McCoy.

"You know the outcome. Twenty-first Amendment pulled the plug on Prohibition, but

Uncle Sam taxed booze up the wazoo. So smuggling continued. Eventually, the States and Canada independently declared war on the Atlantic rumrunners. Ever hear the Lennie Gallant song about the *Nellie J. Banks*?"

"Maybe at Hurley's."

"The *Nellie J. Banks* was Prince Edward Island's most notorious rumrunner. Also her last. Boat was seized in thirty-eight. Ballad tells the story."

Hippo's eyes wandered to a spot over my shoulder. For one awful moment I thought he was going to sing. Mercifully, he continued talking.

"The RCMP and Canada Customs still got their hands full. But it's not like the old days. The slime-balls working the coast now mostly deal in drugs and illegal immigrants."

"Your knowledge is impressive."

Hippo shrugged. "Rumrunners are kind of a hobby. I've read up."

"This has something to do with Obéline's husband?"

"Yes. I'm getting to that. Hilaire Bastarache was second in line. Wanting to up the profits, after World War II, he added a new wrinkle."

"Not smuggling."

Hippo shook his head. "The skin trade. Titty bars. Whorehouses. Massage parlors. Proved very lucrative.

"David, the third in line, is a strange duck, kind of a cross between Howard Hughes and some sort of urban militiaman. Keeps to himself. Distrusts anything having to do with government or its institutions. Schools. Military. Health care. Guy's never registered for social security, Medicare, voting. Was hit by a truck once. Refused to be taken to the hospital. And, of course, cops. Bastarache especially hates cops."

"I can see why someone in vice would be wary of the police, but why the paranoia about authority in general?"

"Part of the blame goes to Daddy. Little David was homeschooled, kept on a very short leash for a very long time. Hilaire Bastarache wasn't what you'd call gregarious. But it goes deeper than that. When the kid was ten he saw his mother gunned down in a botched raid on one of the old man's warehouses."

"Was she armed?"

Hippo shook his head. "Wrong place wrong time. Ruby Ridge kind of thing."

Hippo referred to the 1992 siege of an Idaho cabin by U.S. Marshals. During the incident, an FBI sniper shot and killed a woman while she was holding her ten-month-old son.

"Despite his hang-ups, Bastarache manages to take care of business. Keeps himself insulated with layers of hired muscle. Granddaddy's establishment in Caraquet got busted several years back. The current Bastarache hadn't a clue the place was being used as a cathouse. Thought he was renting rooms to upstanding young women." Hippo snorted derisively. "The court bought it. Prossie named Estelle Faget took the fall.

"Bastarache owns a strip club in Moncton off Highway 106. Le Chat Rouge. Shifted his base there in 2001. But I understand he's spending a lot of time in Quebec City these days. Has a bar there called Le Passage Noir."

"Why the relocation?"

"Got caught nailing a stripper. Turned out the kid was sixteen. Bastarache decided it was in his interest to leave Tracadie."

"Christ." My voice dripped with disgust.

Hippo pulled a folded paper from his pocket. When I reached out, he pressed it to the tabletop.

"My sources say Bastarache doesn't payroll choirboys." Hippo's eyes locked onto mine. "Word on the street is his enforcers play very rough."

"Real stud," I snorted. "Cheating on his wife with a bubble-gummer."

"Let me share a story. Guy named Thibault sold Bastarache a car back in ninety-seven. Bastarache complained the crankshaft was bad. Guy blew him off. Three days later, a body turned up under the Little Tracadie River Bridge No. 15. Had a crank-shaft protruding from his rib cage."

"Was Bastarache charged?"

"There was nothing to link him and no one would roll."

"Could be coincidence."

"Could be I'll get drafted to play fullback for the Alouettes. Look, what I'm saying is, Bastarache is nuts, he's mean, and he runs a rough crew. That's a bad combination."

131

I couldn't disagree with that.

But why would Obéline have married such a loser? And why had *he* chosen *her*? What had happened to the little girl I'd known on Pawleys Island?

Hippo's eyes dropped. Scooping up the folded paper, he began rotating it from corner to corner, tapping the tabletop.

"I got another story."

I started to interrupt.

"Concerns your friend."

The change in Hippo's voice chilled me.

"Plot's not original. Fighting. Husband getting liberal with the fists. Anonymous calls to the cops. Wife refusing to press charges. Finally, him breaking her arm. She's in a cast, he's slipping it to a pole dancer."

"Obéline?"

Hippo nodded. "Unclear how she got him out of the house. May have threatened to prosecute this time if he didn't leave. Two weeks later there's a fire."

I swallowed.

"Third-degree burns over twenty percent of her body. Spent time in rehab. Came away pretty scarred."

I pictured a peach-skinned toddler with chestnut curls laughing and chasing gulls in the Carolina surf.

On the medial surface of the mammalian brain, right beneath the cortex, there's a nexus of neurons

132

called the limbic system. This little hunk of gray matter cranks our emotions in and out of gear: wrath, fright, passion, love, hate, joy, sadness.

A limbic switch flipped, and white hotness seared my endocranium. I didn't let my anger show. That's not how I am. When that circuit trips, and true fury blasts the inside of my skull, I don't scream or lash out. *Au contraire.* I go steely calm.

"Arson?" My voice was a monotone.

"Cops suspected the fire was deliberately set."

"Bastarache?"

"Everyone thought the turd did it, but there was nothing to nail him and no one would talk. Guy's goons have everyone scared shitless."

I held out a palm.

Hippo kept the paper clamped in his hand. "I know you like to do things your own way, doc. But I want you to steer clear of this guy."

I curled my fingers in a "give it to me" gesture.

Reluctantly, Hippo slid the folded sheet across the tabletop.

Flattening the page, I read the number and address.

The room receded. The humming fluorescents. The skeleton. Hippo's luau shirt. I was on a porch on a Lowcountry summer night. A transistor radio was playing "Ode to Billie Joe." Évangéline and I were lying with arms crooked behind our heads, knees up, singing along.

Was it really so simple? Dial these digits and

Obéline would answer? Perhaps solve the mystery that had troubled me all these years? Perhaps lead me to Évangéline?

"You OK?"

I nodded, barely aware of Hippo's question.

"Gotta boogie. Ryan's waiting downstairs."

I heard Hippo push to his feet, then the lab door open and close.

My eyes drifted to the bones.

Or would it go the other way? Would I provide answers to Obéline?

Seconds, perhaps epochs later, the door opened again. I looked up.

"Giving up Saturday morning cartoons?"

"Hey."

"Hippo told me you were up here."

Hippo must have shared more than the fact of my presence. Ryan's eyes were crimped with concern.

"A hale fellow." I managed a weak smile. "He tell you about Obéline Landry being married to this sleaze David Bastarache?"

Ryan nodded.

"He doesn't want me to contact her."

"But we both know you will."

"Do you think Bastarache would shoot me just for phoning his estranged wife?"

"I don't know. Just—"

Pointing a finger I finished Ryan's sentence. "Be careful out there." *Hill Street Blues*. The sergeant's daily send-off was an ongoing joke between us.

Ryan hesitated, as though collecting his thoughts. Or choosing an opening.

"Listen, Tempe. There's something I need to tell you."

I waited, curious.

"I've made—"

Ryan's cell warbled. Giving a "sorry" face, he turned a shoulder and clicked on.

"Ryan."

I heard a series of "*oui*."

"Lousy timing." Ryan waggled the phone. "But we may be catching a break on the Quincy kid."

"I understand." I kept very still. "Would you like to meet later?"

Ryan's answer was a long time coming. "Sure."

"Curry?"

"Ben's at seven?"

"Sounds like a plan."

Troubled blue eyes scanned my face. As though memorizing detail.

Something sucked at my heart.

"Come here." Ryan opened his arms. "Give me a hug."

Surprised, I rose and pressed my cheek to Ryan's chest. The embrace broke every rule I'd imposed about intimacy at work. I didn't care. It had been too long. It was Saturday. The place was deserted.

Ryan's arms enveloped me. His chin rested on my hair. I felt a flush climb my throat as warmth spread through me.

135

Breathing in the familiar scent of soap and Acqua di Parma, feeling the familiar muscles and hollows, I wondered if I'd misinterpreted Ryan's look.

Then I heard the words, whispered, more to himself than to me.

"You'll probably never do this again."

14

I refused to let myself think about Ryan.

I refused to let myself rush to the phone. Before punching those digits, I wanted to rehearse what to tell Obéline.

Instead, I focused on bone pathology.

Though the metatarsal was slender and unnaturally pointed on the distal end, its outer cortex appeared normal on X-ray. Similar changes occur in advanced cases of rheumatoid arthritis. But with rheumatoid arthritis, the joints are also affected. The girl's joints were fine.

Lupus can cause changes in the bones of the hands and feet. It can also affect the nasal spine and aperture and cause resorption of the premaxillary alveolar process. But lupus is an immune disease that attacks many internal organs and tissues. The damage to the girl's skeleton was not that widespread.

Venereal syphilis leads to atrophy of the nasal

spine and destruction of the anterior palate. But with syphilis, vault lesions are common. The girl's vault had none.

Congenital syphilis.

Yaws.

Tuberculosis.

On and on. Nothing fit.

At five, I gave up and headed home.

As I concentrated on traffic, my brain cells roamed free range.

Was Birdie due for a checkup?

You took him in March.

It was July.

Pull his shot record.

Haircut.

Go really short, like Halle Berry.

You'll look like Demi Moore in G.I. Jane.

Lousy movie.

Not the point.

No guts no glory.

Or Pee-wee Herman.

Ryan.

What the hell, I was tired.

As with the previous topics, cerebral opinions were split.

Breakup, a cadre of pessimist brain cells predicted.

No way, an optimist faction countered.

The pessimists floated an image. *Annie Hall.* Alvie and Annie separating belongings.

We'd never lived together, but I'd spent nights at Ryan's place, he at mine. Had possessions migrated? Did Ryan want to talk about reclaiming CDs?

I began a mental list of objects at my condo. The wine opener. A toothbrush. A bottle of Boucheron aftershave.

Charlie?

He's over the marital status thing.

He's outta here.

Why the hug?

He's horny.

"That's it." I hit the radio.

Garou was crooning "Seul." Alone.

I snapped it off.

Birdie greeted me by flopping onto one side, stretching all four limbs, and rotating to his back. Ryan called the maneuver his "drop and roll."

I scratched the cat's belly. He must have felt tension in my touch. Popping to his feet, he regarded me, eyes yellow and round.

Partly Ryan. Partly Obéline. And partly being afloat on coffee.

"Sorry, big guy. Got a lot on my mind."

Hearing my voice, Charlie weighed in. " . . . *love drunk off my hump.*"

Black Eyed Peas. Good job with the training disc, Ryan.

But why that line?

When its battery dies, my smoke alarm shrills until a replacement is inserted. This occurred once on a weekend when I'd left Charlie alone. The cockatiel shrilled for the next three months.

It's the rhythm, I told myself. Not the lyrics.

I popped in the cockatiel training CD, filled seed and water dishes, and fed the cat. Then I wandered from room to room, each time forgetting the point of my going.

I needed exercise.

Lacing on running shoes, I jogged up the hill, then turned west. On the opposite side of Sherbrooke sprawled the grounds of Le Grand Séminaire, recovery site of a dismembered body years ago. One of the first cases I'd worked with Ryan.

Still no rain, but the barometric pressure was at least a billion. Within blocks I was sweating and breathing hard. The physical exertion felt good. I pounded past the Shriner's Temple, Dawson College, Westmount Park.

A mile and a half out, I looped back.

This time, no greetings from Birdie. In my hurry to be off, I'd left the door to the study ajar.

The cat and bird were eyeball to eyeball. Though feathers and seed casings littered the floor, neither feline nor avian looked particularly excited. But there'd definitely been action while I was out.

Shooing Birdie from the room, I hurried to the shower.

While I was drying my hair, the brain cells piped in again.

Mascara and blush.

Tart yourself up for yesterday's news?

Smart looks, smart thoughts.

Puh-leeze!

I spritzed Issey Miyake.

Trollop.

Le Maison du Cari is located in a basement on Bishop, across from the Concordia University library. Ben, the owner, remembers the preferences of each of his regulars. No question about mine. Ben's korma is so rich it prompts a smile from the most jaded diner.

Descending the steps, I saw the top of Ryan's head through the small front window. Dimly. Curry, brilliant. Tandoori, phenomenal. Windex, forget it.

Ryan was drinking Newcastle ale and munching papadum. I'd barely taken my seat when a Diet Coke hit the table. Lots of ice. Slice of lime. Perfect.

After hearing news of Ben's daughter in Sweden, we ordered. Chicken vindaloo. Lamb korma. Channa masala. Cucumber raita. Naan.

Conversation launched from the neutral ground of Phoebe Jane Quincy.

"We may have a lead. Kid didn't have a mobile, but the best friend did. Finally 'fessed up to allowing Phoebe to make calls she couldn't make at home. Records showed one unfamiliar number. Dialed eight times in the past three months."

"Boyfriend?"

"Photography studio. Low end, over on the Plateau. Rented to a guy named Stanislas Cormier." Ryan's jaw muscles bunched, relaxed. "Cormier was promising to make the kid a supermodel."

"The friend told you?"

Ryan nodded. "Quincy pictured herself the next Tyra Banks."

"You picked Cormier up?"

"Spent a lovely afternoon interrogating the dolt. He's innocent as Bambi."

"His explanation for the calls?"

"Claims Quincy found him in the Yellow Pages. Wanted a photo shoot. Upstanding citizen asked her age, heard thirteen, told her no go without a parent."

"She called eight times."

"Cormier says she was persistent."

"You believe him?"

"What do you think?"

"Did he take the Marilyn shot?"

"Claims to know nothing about it."

"Can you hold him?"

"We'll find a charge."

"What now?"

"Waiting for a warrant. Once it's issued, we toss the studio."

"What about LaManche's Lac des Deux Montagnes floater? Anything pop with the new info I gave you on age and race?"

"She's not in CPIC or NCIC."

The food arrived. Ryan ordered another Newcastle. As we served ourselves, I remembered something from our earlier conversation.

"Didn't you say Kelly Sicard also wanted to be a model?"

"Yeah." Ryan forked curry into his mouth. "Fancy that."

We ate in silence. Beside us, two kids held hands, eyes locked, food cooling on their plates. Love? Lust? Either way, I envied them.

Finally, Ryan got to it.

Wiping his mouth, he carefully folded and laid his napkin on the table. Smoothed it with a palm.

"There's something I have to tell you. It's not easy, but you should know."

A fist grabbed my gut.

"Lily's problems are worse than I've let on."

The fist eased ever so slightly.

"Three weeks ago she was nailed boosting DVDs from a Blockbuster outlet. I got a courtesy call because I'm on the job. I managed to talk the owner down, made restitution. Lily didn't go into the system. This time."

Ryan's gaze floated up to the window, went through the glass to the darkness outside on Bishop.

"Lily's addicted to heroin. She steals to feed her habit."

I didn't blink, didn't look over toward the couple beside us.

"I own a big hunk of blame. I was never there."

Lutetia kept her existence from you. I didn't say it.

Ryan's eyes came back to mine. In them I saw pain and guilt. And something else. The sadness of ending.

The fist retightened.

"My daughter needs medical help. Counseling. She'll get that. But she also needs stability. A home base. The conviction that someone believes in her."

Ryan took both my hands in his.

"Lutetia has been in Montreal the past two weeks."

My chest turned to ice.

"We've spent hours wrestling with this." Ryan halted briefly. "We think we can give Lily the safety net she needs."

I waited.

"We've decided to try to make the relationship work."

"You're going back to Lutetia?" Calm, and wildly out of sync with the turmoil inside.

"This is the most painful decision I've ever had to make. I've barely slept. I've thought of nothing else." Ryan lowered his voice. "I kept remembering you with Pete in Charleston."

"He'd been shot." Barely audible.

"I mean earlier. He had his arms around you."

"I was overtired, overwrought from so much work. Pete was merely calming me down."

"I know. I admit when I first saw you two together I felt betrayed. Humiliated. 'How could she?' I kept asking myself. I wanted to see you burned alive. That first night, I bought a bottle of scotch, took it to my room and got drunk. I was so angry I threw my room phone through the TV screen."

My eyebrows floated up.

"The hotel charged me six hundred bucks." Strained smile. "Look, I'm not criticizing or casting blame. But I've come to understand you're never going to cut Pete loose." Ryan's thumbs caressed the backs of my hands. "That realization made me reassess. Maybe the poets and songwriters have gotten it wrong. Maybe we do get a second chance to get things right."

"Andrew and Lutetia. The way we were." It was small and mean. I couldn't help myself.

"This won't affect us on the job, of course." Another weak smile. "We'll still be Mulder and Scully."

X-Files. X-Lovers.

"I want your help with these MPs and DOAs."

I bit back a retort I would later have regretted.

"You're sure about this?" I asked.

"I've never been less sure about anything in my life. But I'm sure of one thing. I owe it to my daughter to try. I can't see her destroyed while I just stand by."

I needed fresh air.

I didn't offer reassurance. Or another Streisand line. Or a hug.

Molding my face into a smile, I rose and left the restaurant.

I felt leaden, oblivious to the Saturday night revelers with whom I shared the sidewalk. My feet rose, fell, moving me along without sensation. Then they stopped.

I looked up.

Hurley's.

It wasn't air that I craved. I'd run toward the old umbilicus. The ruby glow in the long-stemmed

145

glass, the friction on my throat, the heat in my belly. The bullet train to temporary gladness and well-being.

All I had to do was enter and ask.

But I know myself. I am an alkie. The fling wouldn't be brief. And, inevitably, the euphoria would give way to self-loathing. Hours, perhaps days would be gone from my life.

I reversed my course and went home.

Lying in bed, I felt totally alone in the universe.

My thoughts played like a *danse macabre*.

Dorothée and Geneviève Doucet, forgotten in an upstairs bedroom.

Kelly Sicard. Claudine Cloquet. Anne Girardin. Phoebe Jane Quincy. Vanished, perhaps molested and murdered.

Three young bodies, two bloated and grotesque.

Laurette, abandoned, dead at thirty-four.

My own mother, widowed, neurotic, dead at fifty-seven.

Baby Kevin, dead at age nine months.

A young girl's skeleton, wrenched from its grave.

Obéline, battered and disfigured.

Évangéline, gone.

Ryan, gone.

At that moment, I hated my job. I hated my life. The world was wretched.

There were no tears. Only an overwhelming numbness.

15

I awoke to the sound of the phone. I felt sluggish
and flat and didn't know why. Then I remembered.

Ryan.

Last night's numbness reasserted itself. That was
good. It got me through the call.

"Good morning, sugar britches."

Pete never phoned me in Montreal.

Katy! I shot upright.

"What's wrong?"

"Nothing's wrong."

"Katy's all right?"

"Of course she's all right."

"You spoke to her? When?"

"Yesterday."

"What did she say?"

"Buenos días. Chile's the bomb. Transfer money.
Adios."

Leaning back, I pulled the quilt to my chin.

"How are you?"

"Hunky-dory."

"Where are you?"

"Charlotte. There's something I want to tell you."

"You're engaged to Paris Hilton." I was so relieved Katy was safe, I laughed at my own joke. It felt good.

Pete didn't answer.

"Hello?"

"I'm here." Devoid of humor.

Apprehension rocketed through my war-torn nerves.

"Pete?"

"Not Paris. Summer."

Summer?

"You want to get married?" I couldn't keep the shock from my voice.

"You'll like her, sugar britches."

I'll hate her.

"Where did you meet?" I tried to sound bright.

"At the Selwyn Pub. She looked sad. I bought her a beer. Turned out a puppy had been euthanized that day. She's a veterinary assistant."

"How long have you and Summer been dating?"

"Since March."

"Jesus, Pete."

"She's very bright, Tempe. Wants to go to vet school."

Of course she does.

"How old is Summer?"

"Twenty-nine."

Pete would soon be waving hello to fifty.

148

"Three months is pretty quick."

"Summer wants to tie the knot." Pete laughed. "What the hell? I'm an old bachelor, kicking around on my own. Don't forget. You turned me out, babe."

I swallowed. "What do you want me to do?"

"Nothing. I'll handle the filing. Irreconcilable differences. All we need is an agreement on the spoils of empire. We can do the actual dividing later."

"Not many spoils."

"North Carolina is a no-fault state, no need for accusations of anything."

"How soon?" I gave up all pretense at brightness.

"You and I haven't cohabited for years, so there won't be any mandatory separation period. Assuming we agree on finances, the divorce should be granted quickly."

"What's your time line?" Lifeless.

"We're thinking about spring. Maybe next May. Summer wants a mountain wedding."

I pictured Summer. Barefoot, tan, head garlanded with daisies.

"Have you told Katy?"

"Not a topic for the phone. We'll have a heart-to-heart when she returns from Chile."

"Has Katy met Summer?"

A slight hitch. "Yes."

"Not good?"

"Katy finds fault with any woman I date."

That was untrue. On occasion my daughter talked of her father's exploits. For some, she felt

149

the attraction was boobs. For others, it was gar-
bonzas. Melons. Jugs. Hooters. A few of the ladies
she liked very much.

"It could be awkward," Pete said. "Summer
wants kids. Katy may find that difficult."

Merciful God.

"I'd like your blessing, sugar britches."

"Whatever." The numbness was dissolving like
fog in a hot morning sun. I had to hang up.

"You'll like Summer. Really."

"Yeah."

I sat motionless, the dial tone buzz in my ear.

My estranged husband loves women in the way
moths love a back-porch bulb. He likes to flirt and
hover, drawn, but never willing to settle. I'd learned
the hard way. And been burned. Marriage, any
marriage, seemed out of character for him. When
we'd been in Charleston, before the shooting, he'd
seemed to want to explore reconciliation. But now
Pete wanted to divorce me, marry Summer, and
have babies.

Sad Summer. Very bright Summer. Twenty-
something Summer.

Slowly, carefully, I placed the handset on the
base unit.

Slid down the pillow. Rolled to my side. Tucked
my knees to my chest.

And lost it.

I don't know how long the tears flowed or when I
drifted off.

Again, a phone jolted me awake. This time it

was my cell. I glanced at the clock. Nine forty-three.

I checked the screen.

Harry.

I couldn't handle melodrama at that moment. I let it keep ringing.

Seconds later, the land line shrilled.

Cursing, I grabbed the handset and clicked on.

"What?" I snapped.

"Well now, aren't we wearing our cranky pants."

"It's goddamn Sunday morning."

"Just found a great recipe for kitten. Thought you might like to rustle some up."

"You're a scream, Harry."

"Does our happy face need a little silicone injection?"

"This better not be round six on Arnoldo." Tossing the covers, I headed for the kitchen. I needed caffeine.

"Ancient history."

"Out with the old, in with the new, right?" Harsh, but I wasn't in the mood for tales of marriage gone bad.

"Pete called."

That threw me. "My Pete? When?"

"Just now. Doesn't sound like he's yours anymore."

"Why call you?" I pulled beans from the cupboard, filled the grinder.

"Thought you might need cheering up."

"Well, isn't that ever so considerate. I'm fine."

"You don't sound fine."

I said nothing.

"You want to talk, I want to listen."

I hit the button. Blades whirred. A warm, coffee smell filled the kitchen.

"Tempe?"

"Yeah."

"It's me. Baby sister."

I dumped grounds into the Mr. Coffee. Added water.

"Yo, Tempe?"

Did I want to talk?

"Let me call you back."

Ninety minutes later I'd unloaded everything.

Ryan. Lily. Lutetia. The cold case investigation of the dead and missing girls. Phoebe Jane Quincy. The Lac des Deux Montagnes floater. The Doucets.

My sister is flighty, volatile, and prone to hysterics. But she's also a world-class listener. She didn't interrupt.

Finally, I told Harry about Hippo and the skeleton I'd demanded from the coroner in Rimouski. Hippo's girl.

"I've got no words of wisdom on Pete or Ryan, so let's talk about this skeleton. Let me see if I have this straight. Hippo's the cold case guy. He learned about the skeleton from his pal, Gaston, who's also SQ. Gaston had spotted the thing in the company of a cop in the boondocks named Luc Tiquet. Tiquet had confiscated it from two spray-paint punks, Trick and Archie Whalen. They'd bought it from Jerry O'Driscoll's pawnshop. O'Driscoll had fenced it off an old coot named Tom Jouns. Jouns had unearthed it from an Indian burial ground. That track about right?"

"If everyone's telling the truth."

"Life's full of ifs."

"Indeed, it is."

"What kind of Indian burial ground?"

"I don't know. Maybe Micmac."

"So the girl was Indian."

"I think she's white."

"Why?"

"Facial architecture."

"You estimate she died at thirteen or fourteen."

"Yes."

"Of some kind of disease."

"She was sick, but I don't know that the illness killed her."

"What did?"

"I don't know."

"What kind of illness?"

"I don't know."

"Well, *there's* something we can put in the paper. How long's she been dead?"

"I don't know that either."

"A long time?"

"Yes."

Harry made a clicking sound.

I drew a deep breath.

"Do you remember Évangéline and Obéline Landry?"

"Think I'm ready for the Texas State Hospital?

'Course I remember. I was nine, you were twelve. They disappeared from Pawleys Island and clean off the face of planet Earth. We spent three years trying to get a bead on them. Burned a busload of coins calling Canada."

"This sounds a little far-fetched, but there's a remote possibility Hippo's girl could actually be Évangéline."

"Hippo's girl?"

"The Jouns-O'Driscoll-Whalen-Tiquet-Gaston-Hippo skeleton."

"How remote?"

"Very."

I told Harry about Laurette and Obéline. And David Bastarache.

"Miserable sonovabitch. Give me a clear shot at his pecker, and that asshole won't be setting any more fires."

Harry could mix metaphors like no one I knew. I didn't point out that this one redefined human anatomy.

Silence hummed across the continent. Then Harry said what I knew Harry would say.

"I'm coming up there."

"What about selling your house?"

"You think I'm going to stay here diddlin' with real estate? You're a smart woman, Tempe, but sometimes I wonder how you pull your undies up in the morning."

"What are you saying?"

"You've got Obéline's address and telephone number?"

"Yes."

"Do you need a giant finger pointing down at burning shrubbery?"

I let her go on.

"I'll get my heinie on a plane to *la Belle Province*. You book us tickets to New Brunswick."

"You're suggesting we visit Obéline?"

"Why not?"

"For one thing, Hippo will be pissed."

"Don't tell him."

"That would be unprofessional, and potentially dangerous. I'm not a cop, you know. I rely on them."

"We'll text him from the forest primeval."

155

16

Harry's plane was due in at ten. I'd booked a noon flight to Moncton. Our plan was to meet at the departure gate.

Montreal's main airport is situated in the west island suburb of Dorval. For years it was simply called Dorval. Made sense to me. Nope. Effective January 1, 2004, YUL was rechristened Pierre Elliott Trudeau International. Locals still call it Dorval.

By ten, I was parked, checked in, and through security. Harry wasn't yet at gate 12-C. I wasn't concerned. Dorval's "welcome to Canada" immigration line usually makes Disney World's snake-back-and-forth-through-the-ribbon-maze queue look short.

Ten forty-five. Still no Harry. I checked the board. Her flight had landed at 10:07.

At eleven I began to get antsy. I tried reading, but my eyes kept drifting to the tide of faces passing by.

At eleven-fifteen, I started running possibilities.

No passport. Maybe Harry didn't know that a government-issued photo ID was no longer sufficient to enter Canada by plane.

Missing luggage. Maybe Harry was filling out forms in triplicate and quintuplicate. From previous visits I knew she didn't travel light.

Smuggling. Maybe Harry was batting her lashes at some steely faced customs agent. Right. That works.

I went back to reading my Jasper Fforde novel.

The man to my right was beefy, wiry-haired, and overflowed a polyester sports jacket several sizes too small. He kept bouncing one knee up and down while tapping his boarding pass on the armrest between us.

Montreal is not Toronto. Unlike its stodgy Anglo neighbor to the west, the island city celebrates gender and sex. Nightly, bars and bistros host the pheromone ball into the wee, small hours. Billboards proclaim upcoming events with risqué double entendre. Along the highways, half-naked models hawk beer, face cream, watches, and jeans. The town pulses with hot blood and sweat.

But the Big Easy North is never prepared for my sister.

When wire-hair went motionless, I knew Harry had arrived.

She did so with her usual flamboyance, standing in the cart, arms spread like Kate Winslet on the *Titanic* bow. The driver was laughing, tugging her waistband to reconnect her rump with the seat.

The cart slowed, and Harry hopped out. In jeans tight enough to be mistaken for skin, rose and turquoise boots, and a pink Stetson. Spotting me, she whipped off and waved the hat. Blond hair cascaded to her waist.

I stood.

Behind me, wire-hair remained frozen. I knew others were sharing his sight line. Others with a Y in each of their cells.

Harry bore down. The driver followed, a Sherpa pack-muling Neiman Marcus and Louis Vuitton.

"Tem-pee-roo-nee!"

"I was starting to wonder if you'd gotten lost." Spoken from the confines of a spine-crushing hug.

Releasing me, Harry arm-draped the Sherpa. "We were parlay-vooing, weren't we, An-dray?"

André smiled, clearly at a loss.

As though choreographed, a microphone voice announced the boarding of our flight.

The Sherpa combined two of Harry's carry-ons and handed them to her, along with a saddlebag shoulder purse. The Neiman Marcus bag was offered to me. I took it.

Harry gave the Sherpa a twenty, a high-beam smile, and a big "mer-cee."

André zoomed off, a man with a story.

The rental car I'd booked at the Moncton airport was somehow unavailable. An upgrade was offered at the same price.

What type of vehicle?

Spacious. You'll like it.

Do I have a choice?

No.

While I signed the rental agreement, Harry learned the following.

The agent's name was George. He was forty-three, divorced, with a ten-year-old son who still wet the bed. Tracadie was a straight shot up Highway 11. Gas was cheap at the Irving station just past Kouchibouguac. Le Coin du pêcheur in Escuminac served a mean lobster roll. The trip would take about two hours.

The spacious upgrade turned out to be a shiny new Cadillac Escalade EXT. Black. Harry was pumped.

"Would you look at this bad buggy. Kickass engine, four-wheel drive, and a trailer hitch. We can boogie this iron pony uphill, downhill, and off the road."

"I'll stay on the pavement, thanks. Don't want to get lost."

"We won't." Harry patted her purse. "I've got GPS on my phone."

We climbed in. The iron pony had that new car smell and an odometer showing forty-five miles. I felt like I was driving a troop carrier.

Though dead on about the sandwich, George had been wildly optimistic on the drive time north.

When we pulled into Tracadie my watch said seven-twenty. Eight-twenty local. Why so long? You guessed it. Harry.

The upside? We'd made friends with an RCMP constable named Kevin Martel, and with most of the residents of Escuminac. We also had snaps of ourselves arm in arm before Le plus gros homard du monde. Shediac was a detour, but how often can one pose in front of the world's biggest lobster?

At check-in, the nice motel lady told Harry of a restaurant with traditional Acadian food and an outdoor deck. I waited while Harry blow-dried her bangs, then we headed to the waterfront.

Plastic tables. Plastic chairs. Plastic menus.

Nice atmosphere, though. We shared it with men in ball caps hauling on long-necked beers.

The air was cool and smelled of fish and salty mud. The water was dark and restless, flecked by white from a rising moon. Now and then an insomniac gull cried out, stopped, as though surprised by its own voice.

Harry ordered spaghetti. I went for the cod and potatoes. When the waitress left, Harry pointed to a newspaper abandoned on the adjacent table. *L'Acadie Nouvelle.*

"OK, chief. Background. Starting with where the hell we are."

"Tracadie-Sheila." I pronounced it Shy-la, like the locals.

"That much I know."

"In the belly of L'Acadie, homeland to the distinctive, four-century-old Acadian culture."

"You sound like one of those travel brochures in the motel lobby."

"I read four while you were doing touch-up on your bangs."

"They were greasy."

"Except for the little jog into Shediac, we traveled north today, paralleling the Northumberland Strait. We're now on the Acadian Peninsula. Remember driving past signs for Neguac?"

"Sort of."

"The Acadian Peninsula stretches approximately two hundred kilometers up from Neguac, along New Brunswick's northeastern coast, out to Miscou Island at the tip, then around Chaleurs Bay to Bathurst. There are about two hundred and forty-two thousand French speakers living in the province; about sixty thousand of those are right here on the peninsula."

Our food arrived. We spent a few moments adding Parmesan and shaking salt and pepper.

"People here trace their unique brand of French, their music, even their cooking style back to Poitou and Brittany."

"In France." Harry was a master of the obvious.

"Ancestors of today's Acadians started arriving in the New World as early as the late seventeenth century, bringing those traditions with them."

"Didn't they all move to New Orleans? Évangéline used to talk about that."

"Not exactly. In 1755, the English ordered the expulsion of some ten thousand French speakers from Nova Scotia. Acadians call the deportation le Grand Dérangement. Lands were confiscated and people were hunted down and shipped off, mainly to France and the United States. Today, maybe a million Americans claim Acadian ancestry, most of those in Louisiana. We call them Cajuns."

161

"I'll be damned." Harry pounded more cheese onto her pasta. "Why did the English want them out?"

"For refusing to pledge allegiance to the British Crown. Some managed to escape the sweeps, and took refuge up here, along the Restigouche and Miramichi rivers, and along the shores of the Bay of Chaleurs. In the late 1700s, they were joined by Acadians returning from exile."

"So the French were allowed to come back?"

"Yes, but the English were still dominant and hostile as hell, so an isolated finger of land jutting out into the Gulf of St. Lawrence seemed like a good bet for a place in which they'd be left alone. A lot of them hunkered in here."

Harry twirled spaghetti, thought working in her eyes.

"What was that poem you and Évangéline were always playacting?"

"'Evangeline,' by Henry Wadsworth Longfellow. It's about a pair of doomed Acadian lovers. Gabriel is carried south against his will by the English order of expulsion. Evangeline sets out across America looking for him."

"What happens?"

"Things don't go well."

"Bummer." Harry downed the pasta, retwirled another forkful. "Remember how I'd nag until you'd give me a part?"

"Oh, yeah." I pictured Harry, skinny arms crossed, suntanned face a mask of defiance. "You'd last about ten minutes, start whining about the heat, then wander off, leaving us with a gap in casting."

"I got lousy roles with no lines. A tree. Or a stupid prison guard."

"Stardom doesn't come overnight."

Rolling her eyes, Harry twirled more pasta.

"I always liked Évangéline. She was"—Harry searched for a word—"kind. I also thought she was exceedingly glamorous. Probably because she was five years older than me."

"I was three years older."

"Yeah, but you're my sister. I've seen you eating Cool Whip out of the carton with your fingers."

"No, you haven't."

"And Jell-O."

We smiled at each other, remembering a time of backseat car rides, roller-coaster birthdays, make-believe, and Nancy Drew searches for lost friends. A simpler time. A time when Harry and I were a team.

Eventually, conversation shifted to Obéline.

Should we call ahead, give warning of our upcoming visit? Obéline was barely six when we'd last been together. Her life since had been rough. Her mother was dead, perhaps her sister. Bastarache had abused her. She'd been disfigured by fire. We disagreed on the warmth of the welcome we'd face. Harry felt we'd be greeted like long-lost friends. I wasn't so sure.

When we settled the check it was well past ten. Too late to phone. Decision made. We'd arrive unannounced.

Our motel was across the inlet from the restaurant. Heading back down Highway 11, I guessed we were recrossing the Little Tracadie River Bridge No. 15. I remembered Hippo's story, pitied the hapless soul who'd stumbled onto the crankshafted corpse.

I had only one revelation that night.

When Harry wears jeans, she goes commando.

Harry insisted on pancakes in the morning.

Our waitress was squat, with maraschino lipstick and wispy hair somewhere between butter and cream. She provided copious coffee, advice on nail polish, and directions toward the address Hippo had given me.

Highway 11, then east on Rue Sureau Blanc. Right turn at the end of the green fence. Then another. What's the family name?

Bastarache. Do you know them?

The wrinkled lips crimped into a thin red line. No.

Obéline Landry?

That'll be all, then?

Even Harry couldn't cajole the woman into further conversation.

By nine we were back in the Escalade.

Tracadie isn't big. By nine-fifteen we were turning onto a residential street that might have fit into any suburb on the continent. Well-tended flower beds. Neatly edged lawns. Fresh-enough paint. Most of the houses looked like they'd been built in the eighties.

Hippo's address took us to a high stone wall at the far end of the block. A plaque gave notice of a residence beyond. An unclasped padlock hung from the rusted iron gate. Harry got out and swung it wide.

A mossy brick drive bisected lawn losing out to weeds. At the end loomed a brick, stone, and timber house with a weathered shingle roof. Not a mansion, but not a shack, either.

Harry and I sat a moment, staring at the dark windows. They stared back, offering nothing.

"Looks like Ye Olde Rod and Gun Club," Harry said.

She was right. The place had the air of a hunting lodge.

"Ready?"

Harry nodded. She'd been unnaturally quiet since rising. Other than a brief tête-à-tête concerning her aversion to underpants, I'd left her in peace. I figured she was sorting remembrances of Obéline. Bracing herself for the scarred woman we were about to encounter. I was.

Wordlessly, we got out and walked to the house.

Overnight, clouds had rolled in, thick and heavy with moisture. The morning promised rain.

Finding no bell, I knocked on the door. It was dark oak, with a leaded glass panel that yielded no hint of a presence beyond.

No answer.

I rapped again, this time on the glass. My knuckles fired off a sharp *rat-a-tat-tat*.

Still nothing.

A gull looped overhead, cawing news of the upcoming storm. Tide reports. Gossip known only to the *Larus* mind.

Harry put her face to the glass.

"No movement inside," she said.

"Maybe she's a late sleeper."

Harry straightened and turned. "With our luck, she's in Wichita Falls."

"Why would Obéline go to Wichita Falls?"

"Why would anyone go to Wichita Falls?"

I looked around. Not a neighboring structure nearby.

"I'll check in back."

"I'll cover the front, sir." Saluting, Harry slipped her saddlebag purse from her shoulder. It dropped by her feet with a *thup*.

Stepping from the porch, I circled to my right.

A stone deck ran almost the full length of the back of the house. A wing paralleled the deck's far side, tangential to and invisible from out front. It looked newer, its trim brighter than that on the rest of the structure. I wondered if I was looking at the site of the fire.

The deck held a patio set, a barbecue grill, and several lawn chairs, all empty. Climbing to it, I crossed and peered through a set of double glass doors.

Standard kitchen appliances. Pine table and captains chairs. Cat-cuckoo clock with a pendulum tail.

Center island. A paring knife, a paper towel, and a peeled apple skin.

I felt my nerves tingle.

She's here!

I turned.

Past an expanse of lawn stood a small gazebo-like structure. Past the gazebo, water, rough and gunmetal gray. An inlet of the Gulf of St. Lawrence, I presumed.

Strange columns flanked the gazebo's entrance, tall, with projections forward and to the sides. Atop each was an unidentifiable shape.

Through the gazebo's screening I could dimly make out a silhouette. My mind logged detail.

Small, probably female. Hunched. Still.

The maybe-Obéline woman had her back to me. I couldn't tell if she was reading, dozing, or merely gazing seaward.

I moved forward, senses still logging information. A wind chime tinkling notes. Wet grass. Explosions of froth against a seawall.

Drawing closer, I realized the columns had been carved into stacks of zoomorphic creatures. The projections were beaks and wings. The shapes on top were renderings of stylized birds.

Then, recognition, prompted by anthropology studies of years ago. The gazebo had once been a sweat house, later modified by replacing walls with screening.

The assemblage looked thousands of miles out of place. Totem poles and sweat houses were built by peoples of the Pacific Northwest, the Tlingit, Haida, or Kwakiutl, not by the Micmac or other tribes of the Maritimes.

Ten feet back, I stopped.

"Obéline?"

The woman's head snapped up.

"*Quisse qué là?*" Who's there? Acadian French.

"Temperance Brennan."

The woman didn't reply.

"Tempe. From Pawleys Island."

Nothing.

"Harry is here, too."

A hand rose, hovered, as though uncertain of its purpose.

"We were friends. You and Harry. Évangéline and I."

"*Pour l'amour du bon Dieu.*" Whispered.

"I knew Tante Euphémie and Oncle Fidèle."

The hand shot to the woman's forehead, dropped to her chest, then crossed from shoulder to shoulder.

"I've been looking for you for a very long time."

Pushing to her feet, the woman draped a shawl on her head, hesitated, then shuffled to the door.

A hand reached out.

Hinges squeaked.

The woman stepped into daylight.

17

Memory is capricious, sometimes playing straight, sometimes deceiving. It can shield, deny, tantalize, or just plain err.

There was no mistake or dissembling here.

Though I saw only half the woman's face, I felt I'd taken a body blow. Dark gypsy eye, petulant upper lip swooping down to a diminutive lower. Brown blemish on her cheek in the shape of a leaping frog.

Obéline giggling. Évangéline tickling, teasing. Frog-freckle face! Frog-freckle face!

The jawline was sagging, the skin deeply etched. No matter. The woman was an aged and weathered mutation of the child I'd known on Pawleys Island.

My eyes welled up.

I saw Obéline, little legs churning, crying to be included in our games. Évangéline and I had read her stories, costumed her in sequins and tutus, built her sand castles on the beach. But, mostly, we'd sent her away.

I forced a smile. "Harry and I missed you both terribly."

"What do you want?"

"To talk with you."

"Why?"

"We'd like to understand why you left so suddenly. Why Évangéline never answered my letters."

"How did you get this address?" Her voice was wire-thin, her breathing and swallowing measured, perhaps a product of speech therapy following the fire. "Do you work for the police?"

I told her I worked for the coroner in Montreal.

"This coroner sent you to find me?"

"It's a long story. I'd like to share it."

Obéline twisted the fabric bunched at her chin. The skin on her fingers was lumpy and waxy-white, like oatmeal congealed on the bottom of a pot.

"The horror comes real."

"I'm sorry?" Obéline's *chiac* accent was so strong I wasn't catching all her words.

"The nightmare made truth."

"Pardon?"

She ignored my question. "Harry is here?"

"At your front door."

Her gaze drifted past me, lingered, I suspected, on a moment long past.

Then, "Join her. I will let you in."

* * *

After sliding what sounded like a hundred dead-bolts, Obéline admitted us to a foyer giving onto a wide central hall. Light diffusing through leaded glass windows gave an ephemeral cast to the large, empty space.

Ahead, I noted an ornately carved staircase; suspended from the ceiling, a faux Louis-the-something chandelier. The hall was furnished with carved and painted high-backed benches, more artifacts from the Pacific Northwest.

In spots, the floral wallpaper was marked by brighter rose and green rectangles, evidence that paintings or portraits had been removed. The floor was covered by a massive antique Persian Sarouk Farahan carpet that must have cost more than my condo.

Obéline's shawl was now wrapped below her chin and tied at the back of her neck. Up close, the reason was obvious. Her right eyelid drooped and her right cheek looked like blistered marble.

Involuntarily, my eyes broke contact with hers. I wondered, How would I feel were I the scarred one and she the visitor from so long ago?

Harry said howdy. Obéline said *bonjour*. Both were restrained. Neither touched the other. I knew Harry was feeling the same pity and sadness as I.

Obéline indicated that we should accompany her. Harry fell into step, head swiveling from side to side. I followed.

Heavy pocket doors sealed off rooms to the right and left of the main hall. Beyond the staircase, regular doors gave onto other rooms and closets. A small crucifix hung above each.

Clearly, the architect hadn't been tasked with bringing Mother Nature into the back of the house. Even so, the small parlor to which we were led was much dimmer than mandated by the paucity of glass. Every window was shuttered, every panel closed. Two brass table lamps cast a minimum wattage of light.

"S'il vous plaît." Indicating a gold velveteen loveseat.

Harry and I sat. Obéline took a wing chair on the far side of the room, snugged her sleeves down her wrists, and cupped one hand into the other in her lap.

"Harry and Tempe." Our names sounded odd with the *chiac* inflection.

"Your home is lovely." I started out casual. "And the totem poles are quite striking. Am I correct in assuming the gazebo was once a sweat house?"

"My father-in-law had an employee whose passion was Native art. The man lived many years in this house."

"The structure is unusual."

"The man was . . ." She groped for an adjective. " . . . unusual."

"I noticed the carved benches in your foyer. Do you have many pieces from his collection?"

"A few. When my father-in-law died, my husband fired this man. The parting was not amicable."

"I'm sorry. Those things are always difficult."

"It had to be done."

Beside me, Harry cleared her throat.

"And I'm very sorry your marriage turned out badly," I said, softening my voice.

"So you've heard the story."

"Part of it, yes."

"I was sixteen, poor, with few choices." With her good hand, she flicked something from her skirt. "David found me beautiful. Marriage offered a way out. So many years ago."

Screw small talk. I went for what I wanted to know. "Where did you go, Obéline?"

She knew what I was asking. "Here, of course."

"You never returned to Pawleys Island."

"Mama got sick."

"So suddenly?"

"She needed care."

It wasn't really an answer.

I wondered what illness had killed Laurette. Let it go.

"You left without saying good-bye. Tante Euphémie and Oncle Fidèle refused to tell us anything. Your sister stopped writing. Many of my letters came back unopened."

"Évangéline went to live with Grand-père Landry."

"Wouldn't her mail have been sent there?"

"She was far out in the country. You know the postal service."

"Why did she move?"

"When Mama couldn't work, her husband's

people took control." Had her voice hardened, or was it a by-product of the painfully recrafted speech?

"Your parents reunited?"

"No."

Several moments passed, awkward, filled only by the ticking of a clock.

Obéline broke the silence.

"May I offer you sodas?"

"Sure."

Obéline disappeared through the same door by which we'd entered.

"You couldn't at least *try* English?" Harry sounded annoyed.

"I want her to feel comfortable."

"I heard you say Pawleys Island. What's the scoop?"

"They were brought back here because Laurette got sick."

"With what?"

"She didn't say."

"That's it?"

"Pretty much."

Harry rolled her eyes.

I took in the room. The walls were covered with amateur landscapes and still lifes marked by garish colors and distorted proportions. Cases of books and collections of bric-a-brac gave the small space a cluttered, claustrophobic feel. Glass birds. Snow globes. Dream catchers. White hobnail dishes and candlesticks. Music boxes. Statues of the Virgin Mary and her minions. Saint Andrew? Francis?

Peter? A painted plaster bust. That one I knew. Nefertiti.

Obéline returned, face fixed in its same unreadable expression. She handed out Sprites, making eye contact with neither Harry nor me. Resuming her seat, she focused on her soft drink. One thumb worked the can, clearing moisture with nervous up-and-down flicks.

Again, I honed in like a missile.

"What happened to Évangéline?"

The thumb stopped. Obéline's lopsided gaze rose to mine.

"But that's what *you* have come to tell *me*, no?"

"What do you mean?"

"You came to say they've found my sister's grave."

My heart somersaulted. "Évangéline is dead?"

Unable to follow the French, Harry had grown bored and begun scanning book titles. Her head whipped around at the sharpness of my tone.

Obéline wet her lips but didn't speak.

"When did she die?" I could barely form the words.

"Nineteen seventy-two."

Two years after leaving the island. Dear God.

I pictured the skeleton in my lab, its ruined face and damaged fingers and toes.

"Was Évangéline sick?"

"Of course she wasn't sick. That's crazy talk. She was only sixteen."

Too quick? Or was I being paranoid?

"Please, Obéline. Tell me what happened."

"Does it matter anymore?"

"It matters to me."

Carefully, Obéline set her drink on the gate-leg table at her side. Adjusted her shawl. Smoothed her skirt. Laid her hands in her lap. Looked at them.

"Mama was bedridden. Grand-père couldn't work. It fell to Évangéline to bring home a check."

"She was only a kid." I was doing a poor job of masking my feelings.

"Things were different then."

The statement hung in the air.

Tick. Tick. Tick.

I was too dejected to push.

No matter. Obéline continued without prodding.

"When we were separated, at first I wanted to die."

"Separated?"

"My mother and sister moved in with Grand-père. I was sent to live with a Landry cousin. But Évangéline and I talked. Not often. But I knew what was happening.

"In the mornings and evenings, Évangéline nursed Mama. The rest of the day she worked as a maid. A portion of her pay was sent for my support."

"What was wrong with your mother?"

"I don't know. I was much too young."

Again, too rapid?

"Where was your father?"

"If we ever meet, I'll make certain to ask. That will be in another life, of course."

"He's dead?"

She nodded. "It was hard on Évangéline. I wanted to help, but I was so little. What could I do?"

"Neither of you attended school?"

"I went for a few years. Évangéline already knew how to read and do math."

My friend, who loved books and stories, and wanted to be a poet. I didn't trust myself to comment.

"Mama died," Obéline continued. "Four months later it was Grand-père."

Obéline stopped. Composing herself? Organizing recollections? Triaging what to share and what to hold back?

"Two days after Grand-père's funeral, I was taken to his house. Someone had brought empty boxes. I was told to pack everything. I was in an upstairs bedroom when I heard yelling. I crept downstairs and listened outside the kitchen door.

"Évangéline was arguing with a man. I couldn't hear their words, but their voices frightened me. I ran back upstairs. Hours later, as we were leaving, I saw into the kitchen." She swallowed. "Blood. On the wall. More on the table. Bloody rags in the sink."

Sweet Jesus.

"What did you do?"

"Nothing. What could I do? I was terrified. I kept it to myself."

"Who was the man?"

"I don't know."

"What happened to Évangéline?"

"I never saw her again."

"What did they tell you?"

"She ran away. I didn't ask about the blood or whether she was hurt. She wasn't there and I had to go back to the Landrys."

Tick. Tick. Tick.

"I was eight years old." Obéline's voice was trembling now. "There were no safe zones or child abuse counselors back then. Kids had no one to talk to."

"I understand."

"Do you? Do you know what it's like to live with such a secret?" Tears broke from her eyes. Pulling a tissue from her pocket, she wiped them away, blew her nose, and tossed the wad onto the table. "Do you know how it feels to lose everyone you love at such a young age?"

Images competed for my attention. Évangéline reading by the light of my Girl Scout flashlight. Évangéline spreading peanut butter on graham crackers. Évangéline caped in a beach towel, off to rescue her lover. Kevin. Daddy. Hippo's girl, long dead, lying in my lab.

Crossing to Obéline, I squatted, and placed my hands on her knees. I felt trembling in her legs, caught the soft scent of *muguet*. Lily of the Valley.

"I do," I whispered. "Really, I do."

She wouldn't look at me. I dropped my eyes, unwilling to intrude on the ravaged face.

We sat a moment, heads bowed, a frozen tableau

of grief. Watching tears darken her skirt in small, perfect circles, I wondered how much to reveal.

Should I tell her about the young girl's bones? Could I have been off in my estimate of Hippo's girl's age? Could she have been as old as sixteen?

This woman had lost her mother, sister, and grandfather almost at once. Her father had abandoned her. Her husband had beaten, then left her, then tried to burn her to death. Mentioning the skeleton might raise hopes that would later be dashed.

No. I wouldn't compound her pain. I would wait until I was certain.

And now that was possible.

"I'm very tired." Obéline pulled another tissue, dabbed her lower lids.

"Let me help you to bed."

"No. Please. The gazebo."

"Of course."

Harry stood. "May I use the ladies'?"

I translated.

Obéline answered without raising her head. "Through the kitchen. Through the bedroom."

I translated again, then cocked my chin at Obéline's soft drink. Harry nodded, understanding my silent direction.

Arm-wrapping Obéline's waist, I eased her to her feet. She allowed herself to be supported through the kitchen, over the deck, and across the yard. At the gazebo, she stepped away and said good-bye.

I was turning to go, when a sudden thought stopped me.

"May I ask one more question?"

Obéline gave a half nod, wary.

"Évangéline worked as a maid. Do you know where?"

Her response stunned me.

18

"Droit ici." Right here.

"In Tracadie?"

"In this house."

"In this house?" I was too shocked to do other than ape her words.

Obéline nodded.

"I don't understand."

"Évangéline worked for my husband's father."

"Hilaire Bastarache."

Something flicked in her eyes. Surprise at the extent of my knowledge?

"The Landry and Bastarache families have been linked for generations. My father's father and his brothers helped my husband's grandfather, Siméon, build this house. When Mama got sick, my husband's father offered Évangéline a job. Hilaire was a widower and knew nothing about laundry or cleaning. She needed work."

"Ten years later you married his son."

"David was generous, paid my support after Évangéline was gone. Visited me. His father died in 1980. He proposed. I accepted."

"You were sixteen. He was thirty."

"It was my only option."

I found the answer peculiar but let it go.

"You've lived in this house ever since?"

"Yes."

"Are you all right here?"

Beat. "This is where I want to be."

I started to ask how she was supporting herself. Then didn't. I felt tight bands compressing my chest. I swallowed. Took her hand.

"I promise you, Obéline. I will do everything to discover what happened to Évangéline."

Her face remained impassive.

I gave her my card, hugged her.

"I'll speak with you again."

She didn't say good-bye as I walked away. Rounding the house, I glanced back. She was entering the gazebo, scarf tails dancing in the breeze.

Harry was waiting in the Escalade. When I got in, she smiled and patted her purse.

"You didn't touch the rim, right?"

"Any moron with a TV knows better than that." Harry grinned a grin that hoisted warning flags in my brain.

"What?"

"You'll be proud of your baby sister."

Oh no. "Tell me."

"I also bagged the tissues."

Pleased, and relieved, I held up a palm. Harry high-fived it. We both grinned, the Brennan sisters sleuthing again.

"What now?" she asked.

"Once back in Montreal, I'll ship the can and tissues and a skeletal sample to an independent lab. If they can extract DNA from the bone, and compare it to Obéline's DNA, we'll know if the skeleton is Évangéline."

"Why send it out?"

"Our lab doesn't do mitochondrial DNA."

"And I'm sure that's important."

"With old bone, you're much more likely to get mitochondrial than nuclear DNA. There are more copies in each cell."

"It's Évangéline," Harry said.

"The chance is one in a billion."

"Where do you get your odds?"

"OK. I made that up. But it's highly improbable that Évangéline's skeleton has just, out of the blue, landed in my lab."

"Think what you want. That little voice in my heart is telling me it's her."

When Harry makes one of her extraordinary leaps of imagination, it's pointless to argue. I started to do so anyway, stopped, remembering. Sometimes, illogically, my sister is right.

I looked at my watch. Eleven-ten. Our flight was leaving at six-something.

"Head toward Moncton?" I asked.

"How 'bout lunch?"

"We just ate five pounds of pancakes each."

"I'm hungry."

"I thought you were worried about your spreading derriere."

"A girl gumshoe's gotta keep up her strength."

"You lifted two tissues and a soda can."

"Mental exertion."

"Fine. Then straight to the airport."

Driving into town, my head reeled with images. Obéline's dead eyes and disfigured face. Laurette on her deathbed. A blood-smeared wall and table. Bloody rags. Appalling visions of Évangéline's last moments.

I was anxious to get to the lab to reassess the skeletal age of Hippo's girl. To package and FedEx the DNA samples. I began formulating arguments to get my case bumped to the head of the line. I could think of only one that might work. Money.

Harry chose a brasserie on the Rue Principale. She liked the awning. The menu was uninspired. We both ordered burgers.

The conversation wavered between past and present. Obéline now. The four of us decades earlier on Pawleys Island. As we talked I saw flashes of Harry and myself, pillow fighting, cookie baking, school bus waiting, backpacks filled with our young lives and dreams.

Despite my sadness over Obéline, Ryan, and the dead and missing girls, I couldn't help smiling. Harry's enthusiasm for finding Évangéline surpassed even mine. Sitting in that booth, listening to her ani-

184

mated planning, I realized how very much I love my little sister. I was glad she had come.

Emerging from the restaurant, we saw two men lounging on the Escalade.

"Well, if it isn't Cheech and Chong."

"Sshh."

"You gotta admit, those guys aren't auditioning for the cover of *GQ*."

Harry was right. The men were in total-body denim, boots, and black tees. Personal hygiene didn't appear to be a priority. Though the day was overcast, both wore shades.

"Pretty buff, though."

"Let me handle this." I didn't need Harry riling or seducing the indigenous folk.

"Bonjour." I smiled and waggled the car keys.

Cheech and Chong remained butt-leaning on the Escalade.

"Sorry, but we need to motor." Light, friendly.

"Nice wheels."

"Thanks." As I moved toward the driver's side, Chong extended an arm, catching me at chest level.

"No fly zone, buddy." Harry's tone was a million light-years from friendly.

Stepping back, I frowned at Chong, then repeated what I'd said, this time in French. Still, the men didn't budge.

"What the hell's wrong with you boys?" Harry was glaring from Cheech to Chong, hands on her hips.

Chong smiled from behind his dark lenses. *"Eh,*

mon chouchou. Big truck for little girls." *Chiac*-accented English.

Neither Harry or I answered.

"You pals with Obéline Landry?"

"I don't believe that's any of your business." Harry was in war mode.

"We were childhood friends," I said, trying to defuse the situation.

"Shame what happened to her." Chong's shades were now pointing at me.

I didn't reply.

"You two are going to hoist your bony arses from that vehicle right now so my sister and I can be on our way."

I crimped my eyes in a "cool it" warning. Shooting a hip, Harry pursed her lips and folded her arms.

"Mrs. Landry in good health?"

"Yes." Chilly.

"She claiming Bastarache is one sick bastard?"

I didn't reply.

Cheech pushed from the hood. Chong followed.

"You ladies have a good trip back to Montreal." Unlike his partner, Cheech was Anglophone.

Harry opened her mouth. I hushed her with a hand.

Stepping onto the curb, Cheech made a gun of his thumb and forefinger and aimed it in our direction. "And be careful with those fine wheels."

Driving off, I glanced into the rearview mirror. The men were still standing on the sidewalk, watching our departure.

On the plane, Harry and I again discussed Obéline, and speculated about our encounter with Cheech and Chong.

"Testosterone weenies trying to impress."

"I'm not so sure," I said.

"Probably amuse themselves making fart noises under their armpits."

I wasn't convinced that it was that casual.

The men knew we'd visited Obéline. Knew we'd come from Montreal. How? Had they been following us? Was Cheech's parting comment a threat or merely a macho adieu? Not wishing to alarm, I kept these concerns to myself.

Back at the condo, Birdie remained hidden, cheesed off at having been left alone. I was dumping my overnighter on my bed when Harry called out.

"Your bird's a Korn fan?"

"What did he say?"

"You don't want to know."

Though Charlie's quips weren't always approved for all audiences, I couldn't help but admire the breadth of his material. I was transporting him to the dining room when my cell phone chirped.

Depositing the cage, I checked the screen. No caller ID.

I clicked on.

"How's it going?" Ryan sounded tired.

"Good." Neutral.

"Got a minute?"

"Hang on."

"Do you have everything you need?" I asked Harry.

She mouthed "Ryan?"

I nodded.

She arm-pumped "Yes!"

Shaking my head, I walked to my bedroom and closed the door.

"Do you listen to Korn?" I asked.

"Who?"

"Black Eyed Peas?"

"No. Why?"

"Never mind."

"Someone there at your place?"

Ryan was good. Two queries in one casual question. Am I home? Am I alone?

"Harry's here."

"Unplanned trip?" Query three.

"She's split with her husband."

I heard a deep inhalation followed by a slow exhalation. Ryan was smoking. That meant he was anxious. Or angry. I braced for a rant about my trip to Tracadie. It didn't come.

"I need your help."

I waited.

"Warrant came through, so we tossed Cormier's studio. Took all friggin' day to get through maybe an eighth of the file cabinets. Guy's got crap going back decades."

"He doesn't store his images digitally?"

"Dickhead thinks he's Ansel Adams. Claims digital can't capture the same ethereal quality as

188

film. Uses a Hasselblad that went out of production sometime in the eighties. The guy's probably too thick to keep up with technology."

"There are other photographers who agree with him."

"Cormier does mostly portraits. Couples. Pets. Lots of women. Glamour shots. You know, heavy makeup, big hair."

"Uh-huh."

"You should try that. Maybe with a boa."

"Is that what you called to tell me?"

"Cormier also did kids. Hundreds of them."

"Phoebe Jane Quincy?"

"Nothing yet."

"Kelly Sicard?"

"No."

I didn't ask about Claudine Cloquet or Anne Girardin.

Ryan dragged smoke into his lungs, released it. I waited for him to get to the point.

"I want you to browse through the kiddie shots. See if you spot any of my MPs. Or the kid recovered from the Dorval riverbank."

"Her photo was circulated in 2001 when the body was found."

"It was an autopsy pic. People tune out."

Ryan was right. And I'd seen it go both ways. Next of kin giving a positive on a body that wasn't a relative, or failing to recognize one that was.

"You know bones." Ryan was still talking. "Facial architecture. You see someone resembling one of my MPs or DOAs, maybe at a younger age,

189

maybe all vamped up, you could do that thing you do with surveillance tapes."

Ryan was referring to a technique in which images are compared metrically, one of a known suspect, another of a perpetrator caught on camera. Measurements are taken between anatomical landmarks, ratios are calculated, and statistical probabilities are computed as to whether the suspect under arrest and the perp caught on tape are the same individual.

"Anthropometric comparison."

"Yeah."

"I suppose it's worth a shot. I could also dig out the facial approximation we did on the girl recovered from the Rivière des Mille Îles."

"I'll pick you up at eight."

"You really think Cormier is dirty?"

"The guy's a sleaze."

"What about his home?"

"Judge says get something from that studio linked to one of these kids. Then he'll cut paper."

I opened my bedroom door. Coincidentally, Harry just happened to be passing by.

"Your evidence." She held up her purse. Quickly.

"Lame."

"Are you suggesting I was eavesdropping?"

"I'll get some ziplocks."

When I returned from the kitchen, Harry was sitting cross-legged on my bed. Reversing each baggie over my hand, I removed the can, then the tissues from Harry's purse.

"You've done some doggie-poop scooping," Harry observed.

"I'm multitalented."

"I've got something else."

Reclaiming her purse, Harry pulled an object from the side pocket and laid it on the bed.

The significance didn't register at first. I picked the thing up.

And felt a buzz of excitement.

"Where did you get this?"

"Obéline's bedside table."

19

I was holding a small book with a delicate green ribbon curling from the binding. The cover was red. The lettering was black.

Bones to Ashes: An Exultation of Poems.

"Looks like one of those sixties things quoting Mao," Harry said.

"You stole this?"

"I liberated it." Sanctimonious. "Mao would approve."

I turned back the cover. The pages were grainy and yellow, the same cheap paper used in comic books. The print was faded and fuzzy.

No author. No date. No ISBN number. Besides the title, the volume's only identifier was the name of the publisher. O'Connor House.

I flipped to the last page. Sixty-eight. Blank.

I opened to the ribbon. It was marking a poem titled the same as the collection.

"It's poetry, Tempe." Harry's body language told me she was pumped.

"I've never heard of O'Connor House. Could be a vanity press."

"What's that?"

"A vanity press charges the author for printing and binding."

Harry looked confused.

"A commercial publisher's intended market is the general public. A vanity press's intended market is the author him- or herself."

The heavily mascaraed eyes widened.

"OK. That computes. Évangéline wanted to be a poet, right?"

"Right."

"What if she's the author?"

I looked at Harry's excited face.

"We have absolutely no reason to believe that's so," I said, knowing I was about to hear one of my sister's imaginative but virtually baseless hypotheses.

"Any guess why I snitched this particular little volume?"

I shook my head.

"Did you notice the books in that parlor?" She didn't wait for my answer. "'Course not. You were parlay-voo-ing. But I did. There were dozens. Scores. Every last one in French. Same in the bedroom. Which, don't get your gizzard twirling, I had to traverse to get to the loo. The one and only English book in that whole place was this one. And it was lying right by Obéline's bed."

"What's your point?"

"One lonely little English paperback? Right there at her bedside?"

"That hardly means—"

"Maybe Obéline rounded up Évangéline's poetry and had it printed. Like a memorial. You know? Her sister's dream made real?"

"I suppose it's a possibility. In that case it was very wrong of us to take it from her."

Harry leaned forward, eager. "We'll return it. It's a clue. We run this publisher to ground, maybe we learn something about Évangéline. Maybe we tank. So what? It won't hurt the book."

I couldn't argue with her reasoning.

"My thinking, it's worth a look-see."

"I have to help Ryan tomorrow. And I need to reexamine the skeleton."

Harry scrambled from the bed, tossed her hair over her shoulders.

"Leave it all to baby sister."

Ryan arrived at seven-forty. I buzzed him in, suspecting the early landing was geared toward a glimpse of Harry.

Sorry, buckaroo. The Starlet of Slumber won't rise for four hours.

I pointed Ryan to the coffee, then finished my morning toilette, wondering if he and Harriet Lee actually had "hooked up" during her previous visit. Katy lingo. My prurient curiosity.

When I emerged from the bathroom, Ryan was

deep in conversation with Charlie. Birdie was observing from the sofa back.

"Cheaper to keep her." Sidestepping back and forth on his perch.

"Buddy Guy." The cornflower eyes swiveled to me. "Charlie's a blues man."

"Charlie's a cockatiel with a bawdy beak." I forced my voice stern. "Are you using his training CDs?"

"Religiously." All innocence. "Aren't we, pal?"

As though complicit, Charlie whistled a line from "Pop Goes the Weasel."

"He's picked up Korn lyrics," I said.

"I told you. I'm not into Korn."

"Someone is."

Embarrassed realization. Pulling on his nose, Ryan looked away.

Something clicked in my mind.

New CDs. New musical taste. Lutetia had already moved in with Ryan. I wondered how long it had been.

"Let's go," I said, unhappiness settling in my stomach like lead.

Cormier's studio was in a redbrick three-flat near the intersection of Saint-Laurent and Rachel. The building's first floor was rented by a dentist named Brigault. The occupant of the third offered something that required a reading knowledge of Chinese.

Ryan noticed me studying the nameplate.

"Ho. Does acupuncture and Tui Na."

"What's Tui Na?"

"I was hoping you could tell me."

Hippo was unlocking Cormier's studio when Ryan and I clomped onto the second-floor landing. At his feet sat a cardboard tray holding a white paper bag and three plastic-lidded cups.

During my brief absence in New Brunswick, Montreal's heat spell had soldiered on undiminished. The cramped hall was cooking, the air reeking of dust and mildew.

Pushing open the door, Hippo pulled a hanky from his pocket and wiped sweat from his face. Then he looked at me.

"Jet-lagged?" he asked, not kindly.

Not waiting for an answer, he squatted, scooped the tray from the threadbare carpet, and disappeared into the flat.

"What was that all about?" Ryan asked.

I shook my head.

I'd telephoned Hippo from the Moncton airport, but as we were leaving, not when we'd arrived. His displeasure was apparent. He'd asked for detailed descriptions of Cheech and Chong, then rung off abruptly.

Cormier's apartment was what Montreal realtors call a four-and-a-half. He used the large living-dining room in front for his shoots. Arranged next to the walls were various types of photographic equipment. Lights. Backdrops. Meters. Sheets of colored plastic.

One bedroom functioned as an office, the other was strictly for storage. I estimated the rooms held maybe forty file cabinets between them.

The larger bathroom had been converted to a

darkroom. The source, I assumed, of the vaguely acrid odor permeating the flat. Curling irons, blow-dryers, and lighted mirrors suggested the smaller bathroom served as a makeup and changing area.

The tiny kitchen retained its original function. There, we had sticky buns and coffee, and discussed strategy.

"How are the cabinets organized?" I asked.

"They got drawers. Each drawer's stuffed with folders."

Ryan's brows lifted at Hippo's sarcasm, but he said nothing.

"Are the folders arranged alphabetically by client name? By date? By category?" I spoke patiently, a parent to a derisive teen.

"My best assessment, Cormier's system went something like this. Done. Paid. Shove it in the drawer." The rusty voice was cool.

"So he separated paid from unpaid accounts?"

"Convoluted, eh?" Hippo reached for his third sticky bun. "Probably take some air travel to crack this baby."

Ryan jumped in. "Cormier kept an in-basket on his desk for open accounts. Otherwise, his filing doesn't seem to follow any pattern."

"The cabinets should at least reflect a rough chronology, right?"

"They're not that old," Ryan said. "At some point, Cormier must have transferred materials from elsewhere. Looks like he just shoved crap into drawers."

The strategy we settled upon went something

like this. Take a cabinet. Work from top to bottom, front to back. Pull any file in which the subject was young and female.

Who says detective work isn't complex?

Though Ryan opened windows in the parlor and kitchen, little breeze penetrated to the windowless bedrooms in the back of the flat. Four hours into the task, my eyes itched and my shirt was saturated.

Cormier had stored many of his records in large brown or blue envelopes. The rest he'd placed in standard manila jackets, the kind you buy at Staples.

And Ryan was right. The guy was lazy. In some drawers he hadn't even bothered to set the files upright, choosing instead to dump them flat in piles.

Most envelopes were marked with the client's name in black felt-tip pen. Most file folders were labeled on their tabs. Both envelopes and folders contained contact sheets and negatives in shiny paper sleeves. Some contact sheets bore dates. Others did not. Some files held photocopies of checks. Others did not.

By early afternoon, I'd stared at hundreds of faces frozen in variations on "I'm so happy" or "I'm so sexy." Some had caused me to linger, pondering that moment when Cormier clicked the shutter.

Had this woman curled her hair and glossed her lips for a disinterested husband? Was her head filled with hopes of rekindled romance?

Was this child thinking of Harry Potter? Of her

puppy? Of the ice cream she'd been promised for cheerful compliance?

Though I'd set several folders aside, solicited the opinion of Hippo or Ryan, in the end, I'd added each to my stack of rejects. Some resemblance, but no match. The girls were not among the cold case MPs or DOAs of which I was aware.

Hippo was shuffling paper on the far side of the room. Now and then he'd stop to Dristan a nostril or swallow a Tums. Ryan was across the hall in Cormier's office. It had been almost an hour since either had sought my opinion.

My lower back ached from lifting armloads of folders, and from leaning at an ergonomically inappropriate angle. Rising from the small stool on which I was balanced, I stretched, then bent and touched my toes.

The shuffling stopped. "Want I should order pizza?"

Pizza sounded good. I started to say so.

"Maybe phone Tracadie?"

"Give it a rest, Hippo."

I heard the *thup* of paper hitting wood. Then Hippo's face rose above the far row of cabinets. It looked parched and cross.

"I told you this Bastarache is a real piece of work. It would have been useful to have some people keep an eye on you from a distance in case things got close."

He was right, of course. Hippo's informants were legion. He could have kept track of us, and perhaps learned who else was doing so.

"Who's the blonde?"

"My sister." So he *had* gotten feedback. Probably after my call. "We talked to Obéline. That's all. We didn't do any prowling around."

Hippo did the hanky thing on his brow and neck.

"Do you want to know what we learned?"

"Is the skeleton this kid you knew?"

"I'm holding out for the pizza."

Hippo circled his row of cabinets. His shirt was so damp it was almost transparent. It was not a good look.

"Anything you don't eat?"

"Knock yourself out."

When he'd gone, I remembered. Ryan hates goat cheese.

Little chance, however, that Hippo would think outside the traditional sausage and cheese box. If he did, tough.

I got through another shelf before Hippo returned. I was right. *Toute garnie.* All dressed. Sausage. Pepperoni. Green pepper. Mushroom. Onions.

As we ate, I described my visit to Tracadie, repeating the encounter with the two thugs outside the brasserie. Hippo asked if I'd caught any names. I shook my head in the negative.

"Bastarache's henchmen?" Ryan asked.

"Most of those guys are too stupid to hench." Hippo tossed his crust into the box and scooped another slice. "That don't mean Bastarache can't jam you up."

"All I did was visit his wife."

"The wife he beat up and set on fire."

I was determined to ignore Hippo's bad temper. "I'll send the DNA samples off tomorrow."

"Coroner likely to cough up the dough?"

"If not, I'll pay it myself."

"You put skeletal age at thirteen or fourteen," Ryan said.

"This kid was sick. If illness slowed her development, I could be low on my estimate."

"But Obéline said her sister was healthy."

"Yes," I said. "She did."

At five-fifteen, I heaved the last stack of files from the back of the bottom drawer of my eighth file cabinet.

The first was a glamour shot. Claire Welsh. Pouty lips. Pouffy hair. Pushy-up cleavage.

The second was a toddler. Christophe Routier. On a tricycle. In a rocker. Hugging a stuffed Eeyore.

The third was a couple. Alain Tourniquette and Pamela Rayner. Holding hands. Holding hands. Holding hands. The contact sheet was dated July 24, 1984.

Where was I the summer of '84? Chicago. Married to Pete. Mothering Katy. Finishing a doctorate at Northwestern. The next year Pete switched law firms and we moved to Charlotte. Home. I joined the faculty at UNCC.

My eyes drifted to the double row of gray metal cabinets. I felt overwhelmed. Not merely by the thought of plowing through that immense repository of human stories, but by everything. The

dead and missing girls. The skeleton I was calling
Hippo's girl. Évangéline and Obéline. Pete and
Summer. Ryan and Lutetia.

Mostly Ryan and Lutetia.

*Suck it up, Brennan. You were colleagues before you
were lovers. You are colleagues still. He needs your
expertise. If someone intentionally harmed these kids,
it's your job to help nail the bastard. Nobody cares
about your personal life.*

I opened the next file.

20

Scrawled on the tab was the name Kitty Stanley.

Kitty Stanley stared into the lens, blue eyes rimmed with impossibly long lashes, amber curls sprouting from a black cloche hat pulled low to her brows.

In some shots, she sat with her arms circling a chair back, head resting on them. In others, she lay on her stomach, chin propped on interlaced fingers, feet raised, ankles crossed. Several frames showed tight facial close-ups.

The intensity. The heavy, straight brows.

Adrenaline flowing, I opened an evidence packet, chose a print, and held it beside Cormier's contact sheet. The strips of images were so small it was hard to evaluate.

Dumping everything from my lap, I found a hand lens on a cabinet top and compared the faces under magnification.

Kelly Sicard. Ryan's MP number one. The girl

had lived with her parents in Rosemère, disappeared in '97 after a night drinking with friends.

Kitty Stanley.

Kelly Sicard.

Both had blue eyes, amber hair, and Brooke Shields brows.

Kelly Sicard was eighteen when she disappeared. Kitty Stanley looked maybe sixteen.

I flipped the contact sheet. No date.

Kelly Sicard.

Kitty Stanley.

Back and forth. Back and forth.

After studying the images for a very long time, I was convinced. Though lighting and focal distances varied, the girls shared the same high cheekbones, narrow interorbital distance, long upper lip, broad jawline, and tapered chin. I didn't need calipers and a computer program. Kitty Stanley and Kelly Sicard were one and the same.

Sicard looked so young. I wanted to launch my voice through the celluloid and speak to her. Ask why she'd come to this terrible place to pose for this man. Ask what had happened to her after that day. Had she gone to New York to pursue a dream? Had she been murdered?

And why the alias? Had Sicard hired Cormier without telling her parents? Lied about her name? Her age?

"I have Sicard." It came out dead calm.

Hippo shot to his feet and reached me in three strides. I handed him the lens, the photos, and the contact sheet.

Hippo squinted at the images. He really needed a shower.

"Crétaque!" Over his shoulder. "Ryan! Get your ass in here."

Ryan appeared instantly. Hippo passed him the lens and photos.

Ryan studied the images. He was also in need of soap and water.

"Sicard kid?" To me.

I nodded.

"You certain?"

"I am."

Ryan dialed his cell. I heard a faraway voice. Ryan asked for a woman I knew to be a crown prosecutor. There was a pause, then another voice came on the line.

Ryan identified himself, got straight to the point.

"Cormier photographed Kelly Sicard."

The voice said something.

"No date. Looks like a year, maybe two before she went missing."

The voice said something else.

Ryan's eyes rolled to me.

"Yes," he said. "I'm sure."

By seven, we'd searched half of Cormier's files. The three of us looked like Dorothy, the Cowardly Lion, and the Scarecrow, sweaty, dirty, and discouraged.

We were all cranky as hell.

Ryan drove me home. Except for a few exchanges concerning Cormier and my visit to Tracadie, we rode in silence. No mention of Charlie or Korn or Lutetia.

In the past, Ryan and I enjoyed challenging each other with obscure quotes in an ongoing game of "Who said that?" Goofy, I know. But we're both competitive.

A one-liner rapped at my forebrain. "Facts do not cease to exist because they are ignored."

Aldous Huxley.

Good one, Brennan.

I settled for congratulating myself.

We were pulling to the curb when Ryan got the call. A warrant had been issued for Cormier's home.

Did I want to be included?

Sure. But I had to go to the lab first. I would drive myself.

Ryan gave me the address.

Entering my front door, I was slammed by the odor of cooking. Cumin, onions, and chilies. Harry was whipping up her specialty. It was not what I needed after a day in a furnace.

I called out a greeting. Harry confirmed that dinner would be San Antonio chili.

Inwardly groaning, I beelined to the shower.

In a way, Harry's chili was therapeutic. What toxins I hadn't sweated out at Cormier's studio, I definitely offloaded at dinner.

Harry was jazzed about the poetry book. In all fairness, I had to admit I was impressed with her progress.

"You were right. O'Connor House was a press for frustrated writers wanting to self-publish. It was a family business, owned and operated by a husband-and-wife team named O'Connor."

"Flannery and spouse."

Harry's eyes went round. "You know them?"

Mine went rounder. "You're making that up. This woman wasn't really named after Flannery O'Connor?"

Harry shook her head. "She was once she got married. Flannery and Michael O'Connor. The operation was headquartered in Moncton. Printing and binding were done elsewhere."

Harry dropped a handful of shredded Cheddar onto her chili.

"Apparently self-publishing wasn't the fast track to prosperity the O'Connors envisioned. The press folded after churning out a whopping ninety-four books, manuals, and pamphlets. Salad?"

I held out my plate. Harry filled it.

"Chili needs sour cream."

While in the kitchen, Harry must have sallied on in her head. When she returned, she'd fast-forwarded a page or two.

"Of those, twenty-two fit the bill."

"Fit what bill?"

"Twenty-two were books of poetry."

"Get out! Did you obtain author names?"

Harry shook her head. "But I got contact information for Flannery O'Connor. She's living in Toronto, working for an ad agency. I called and left a message. I'll call again when we've finished supper."

"How did you learn all this?"

"Books, Tempe. We're talking about books. And who knows books?"

I assumed the question was rhetorical.

"Librarians, that's who. 'Course, libraries are called *bibliothèques* here. But I found one with a Web site in the good old King's lingo. Has a staff directory with names and e-mail addresses and phone numbers. You can't imagine what happened when I dialed the reference desk."

I couldn't.

"A human being spoke to me. In English. Nice lady named Bernice Weaver. Bernice told me I should hike right on in."

Harry swiped the dregs of her chili with a slice of baguette.

"Building looks like a big ole dollhouse." Harry pointed the baguette in a vaguely western direction. "It's just yonder."

"Are you talking about the Westmount Public Library?"

Harry nodded, mouth full of bread.

Founded in 1897 in commemoration of Queen Victoria's Diamond Jubilee, the Westmount Public Library does, indeed, reflect the era's architectural whimsy. Its collections are some of the oldest in the Montreal area, and its clientele is solidly Anglophone.

Good choice, Harry.

"So Bernice was able to identify O'Connor House, its owners, and its publication list?"

"Bernice is a pip."

Apparently.

"I'm impressed. Really."

"Not as impressed as you're going to be, big sister."

Harry took in my wet hair, tank, and drawstring PJ bottoms. Perhaps curious that I'd showered and jammied before dinner, she asked how I'd spent my day. Since Ryan's DOAs and MPs and the Phoebe Jane Quincy disappearance had been all over the media, I could think of no reason for secrecy.

I told Harry about the cold cases Ryan and Hippo were investigating. The MPs Kelly Sicard, Claudine Cloquet, Anne Girardin, and most recently, Phoebe Jane Quincy. The DOAs from the Rivière des Mille Îles, Dorval, and now, Lac des Deux Montagnes. I sketched out my stint in the studio, without mentioning Cormier's name, and described the photo of Kelly Sicard.

"Sonovabitch."

I agreed. Sonovabitch.

We finished dinner lost in our separate thoughts. Pushing away from the table, I broke the silence.

"Why don't you give Flannery O'Connor another shot while I clear this mess?"

Harry was back before I'd loaded the dishwasher. Still no answer in Toronto.

She looked at me, then checked the time. Five past ten.

"Sweetie, you look rode hard and put away wet." She took the plate from my hands. "Hit the hay."

I didn't argue.

Birdie trailed me to bed.

But sleep wouldn't come.

I thrashed, punched the pillow, kicked off the bedding, pulled it back. The same questions winged through my brain.

What had happened to Phoebe Jane Quincy? To Kelly Sicard, Claudine Cloquet, and Anne Girardin? Who were the girls found in Dorval, in the Rivière des Mille Îles, and in Lac des Deux Montagnes?

I kept seeing images of Kelly Sicard/Kitty Stanley. Why had Sicard used an alias? Why had Cormier photographed her? Was he involved in her disappearance? In the disappearances and/or deaths of the others?

And the skeleton from Rimouski. Hippo's girl. What was the meaning of the lesions on her digits and face? Where was Île-aux-Becs-Scies? Was the girl aboriginal? Or contemporary? Could the bones be those of Évangéline Landry? Had Évangéline been murdered as her sister believed? Or was Obéline's memory a childhood distortion of a frightening incident? Had Évangéline been sick? If so, why had Obéline insisted that she was well?

I tried to picture Évangéline, to visualize the woman she'd be today. A woman just two years my senior.

And, of course, Ryan.

Maybe it was fatigue. Or dullness from so many dispiriting developments. Or overload from the hundreds of faces I'd scrutinized that day. My mind floated dark curls, a blue swimsuit, a polka-dot sundress. Recall from snapshots, not real-time memories. Try as I might, I couldn't live-stream an image of Évangéline's face.

A great sadness overwhelmed me.

Flinging back the covers, I turned on the bedside light, and sat on the edge of my mattress. Bird nudged my elbow. I lifted an arm and hugged him to me.

Knuckles rapped lightly.

"What's wrong?"

"Nothing."

Harry opened the door. "You're thrashing like a fish in a bass boat."

"I can't remember what Évangéline looked like. Not really."

"That's what's keeping you up?"

"That's my fixation of the moment."

"Wait."

She was back in minute, a large green book pressed to her chest.

"I was saving this as a hostess gift, but you look like you could use it now."

Harry dropped onto the bed beside me.

"Are you aware that your sister is the all-time champ-een in the recorded history of scrapbooking?"

"Scrapbooking?"

Mock astonishment. "You've never heard of scrapbooking?"

I shook my head.

"Scrapbooking's bigger than Velveeta cheese.

'Least in Texas. And I am the monster-star of the genre."

"You paste stuff in scrapbooks?"

Harry's eyes rolled so high I thought they might stick.

"Not just stuff, Tempe. Memorabilia. And you don't just slap it in mishmash. Each page is an artfully crafted montage."

"I didn't know."

"Temperance Daessee Brennan." Harry's voice was Ralph Edwards dramatic. "This is your life." She opened the scrapbook. "But you can peruse the early years at a future time of your choosing."

Flipping several pages, Harry slid her opus onto my lap.

And there we were, tan and barefoot, squinting into the sun.

Harry had penned *Tenth Birthday* beside the grainy snapshot. Sharing the page with Évangéline and me were a photo of Gran's house, a napkin from a Pawleys Island fish camp, and a ticket from Gay Dolphin Park on the Myrtle Beach boardwalk. Sand dollar and dolphin stickers completed the artful montage.

"I love it, Harry." I threw my arms around her. "Really, I love it. Thank you."

"Don't go all slobbery." Harry stood. "Get some sleep. Even if he is a two-timing peckerwood, Ryan's still a biscuit. You need to look perky on the morrow."

My eye roll made Harry's look amateur.

Before turning out the light, I spent a long time studying Évangéline's features. Dark, curly hair. Strong, slightly humped nose. Delicate lips, tight around an impishly protruding tongue.

I had no idea how soon I'd see that face again.

21

I don't know what I expected. *Ah hah!* Head slap! Epiphany! If so, I disappointed myself.

Other than evidence of disease, I found nothing in Hippo's girl's bones to alter my original age estimate, and nothing to exclude the possibility that she was sixteen. The nature of the skeletal pathology still baffled me.

At nine, I phoned a private DNA lab in Virginia. Bad news: prices had skyrocketed since I'd last used their services. Good news: I was permitted to submit samples as a private citizen.

After downloading and completing the proper forms, I packaged the Sprite can, the tissues, a molar, and a plug from the girl's right femur. Then I went in search of LaManche.

The chief listened, fingers steepled below his chin. Évangéline. Obéline. Agent Tiquet. The Whalen brothers. Jerry O'Driscoll's pawnshop. Tom Jouns.

LaManche raised some points for clarification. I answered. Then he called the coroner.

Hippo was right. No way, José.

I leveled with LaManche about my personal agenda. Reluctantly, he granted my request to pay for the tests out of pocket.

LaManche informed me I had one new case. Nothing urgent. Long bones had been found near Jonquiére. Probably old cemetery remains.

He updated me on the Doucet situation. The psychiatrist had concluded that Théodore was mentally incompetent. Since no cause of death could be established for Dorothée or Geneviève, charges were not being laid.

I outlined the cold cases Hippo and Ryan were working, and described my involvement in them. The MPs, Kelly Sicard, Claudine Cloquet, and Anne Girardin. The DOAs from the Rivière des Mille Îles, Dorval, and Lac des Deux Montagnes. The phone rang as I was explaining the possible link to Phoebe Jane Quincy.

LaManche raised two palms in apology. What can one do?

Back in my lab, I directed Denis to send the DNA samples by Federal Express. Then I phoned the lab and begged for expedition. The man said he'd do what he could.

I was grabbing my purse when I remembered one of LaManche's questions.

"*Où se situe l'Île-aux-Becs-Scies?*"

Where was it, indeed? I'd been unable to find the island anywhere in the New Brunswick atlas.

And what did the name mean? Island of what? Perhaps the maps I'd consulted used an English translation.

I pulled out my Harrap's French–English dictionary.

I knew *scie* translated "saw." I'd encountered the word countless times on requests for analysis of dismembered corpses. I wasn't so sure about *bec*.

Lots of choices. Beak. Bill. Snout. Mouth. Nose (of tool). Nozzle (of tube). Lip (of jug). Spout (of coffeepot). Peak (of bicycle saddle). Mouthpiece (of clarinet).

Who can explain the French mind?

I checked for alternate meanings of *scie*.

Nope. Saw was pretty much it. Radial, wood, circular, hack, power, jig, turning, chain, scroll. Distinctions were handled with modifiers.

Island of Beaks Saws. Island of Snouts Saws. Island of Peaks of Bicycle Saddles Saws.

I gave up. Better to ask Hippo.

Cormier's apartment was located a block from his studio, in a white-brick box lacking a single redeeming architectural detail. Air conditioners jutted from all four floors, whirring and dripping. Gold script above the glass entrance provided the building's name: Château de Fougères.

Good concept, but nary a fern in sight.

Ryan's Jeep was parked at the curb. Up the block I spotted a dark blue Taurus. The plate told me the vehicle was SQ.

The Chateau's outer vestibule had collected the

usual unwanted fliers and brochures. Stepping around them, I pressed the button beside Cormier's name. Ryan buzzed me in.

The lobby was furnished with a brown plastic sofa and green plastic ferns. OK. I'd jumped to judgment on the flora.

I rode the elevator to the third floor. Doors stretched to my right and left along a gray-tiled corridor. I checked the number Ryan had given me: 307. The unit was unlocked.

The kitchen was to my right. Ahead was a parquet-floored living room. To my left a short hall gave onto a bedroom and bath. Mercifully, the place was small.

And clean. Every surface gleamed. The air smelled mildly of disinfectant.

Though heat and humidity fought for dominion outside, inside the temperature barely topped sixty-five. Cormier kept his AC cranked.

Terrific. After yesterday's sweatshop, I'd worn a sleeveless top and shorts. I could feel squadrons of goose bumps gathering for action.

Ryan was in the bedroom talking to the same CSU techs who'd GPR'ed the dog in the barn. Chenevier was dusting for prints. Pasteur was rifling drawers. Ryan was searching the closet. Their faces looked tense.

We exchanged *bonjour*s.

"No Hippo?" I asked.

"He's at the studio." Ryan was checking the pockets of a very dingy trench coat. "I'll roll that way when I finish here."

"Finding anything?"

Ryan shrugged. Not really.

"The guy has some sweet electronics." Chenevier chin-cocked the bedroom's west wall. "Check it out."

I returned to the living room.

The west end of the room was overfurnished with a discount-store chair-sofa-coffee-end-table grouping. The plasma TV was the size of a billboard.

A glass and steel workstation ran the length of the east wall and shot some distance up the north. On it sat a cable modem, a keyboard, a flatbed scanner, and a twenty-inch LCD monitor. A CPU tower occupied the corner on the floor.

I watched lights flicker on the modem, thinking. Something didn't track. Cormier had high-speed Internet at home, but ran his business out of envelopes and manila folders?

The wireless mouse glowed red. I jiggled it and the monitor flashed to life. Blue background. Black cursor blinking in a rectangular white box.

"Does the search warrant cover the computer?" I called out.

"Yeah." Ryan left the bedroom and joined me. "I spent a couple of hours trolling when I first arrived."

"Cormier doesn't use password protection?"

"Genius uses his last name."

I moved aside. Ryan sat and hit a few keys. Notes sounded, and the screen changed to the familiar Windows desktop. The wallpaper was a cityscape, taken at night from an overlook on Mont Royal. The picture was good. I wondered if Cormier had snapped the shot.

I recognized most of the icons. Word. HP Director. WinZip. Adobe Photoshop. Others were unfamiliar.

Ryan right-clicked the green *Start* button on the bottom tool bar, then clicked on *Explore,* followed by *My Documents.* A list of files and dates filled the screen. *Correspondence. Expenses. Mail Order. My Albums. My Archives. My eBooks. My Music. My Pictures. My Videos. Upcoming Events.*

"I checked every folder, every file. Tracked what Internet history I could. I'm no expert, but it looks like a whole lot of harmless crap."

"Maybe Cormier's clean."

"Maybe." Ryan didn't sound convinced.

"Maybe the guy's just what he appears to be."

"Which is?"

"A low-end photographer with a high-end PC."

"Uh-huh."

"Maybe Cormier's such a Luddite he got talked into buying way more than he needs."

Ryan ducked his chin.

"It does happen," I said.

"Cave canem."

"Beware of the dog? You mean *caveat emptor.* Let the buyer beware. Both are Latin proverbs, not quotes."

The way-too-goddamn-blue eyes held mine.

Something sparked in my chest. Ryan's lips tightened.

We both looked away.

"I called Division des crimes technologiques." Ryan changed the subject. "Guy should be here any time."

As though on cue, the techie walked in. Only it wasn't a guy.

"*Tabarnouche*. Traffic's the shits." The woman was tall and thin, with lank blond hair that cried out for a stylist. "Already preparation for the festival's gumming up the streets."

The Festival international de jazz de Montréal takes place in late June and early July. Every year it paralyzes a major chunk of centre-ville.

The woman extended a hand to Ryan. "Solange Lesieur."

Ryan and Lesieur shook.

The hand came to me. Lesieur's grip could have fractured billiard balls.

"This the system?"

Without waiting for an answer, Lesieur seated herself, gloved, and began clicking keys. Ryan and I moved behind her for a better view of the monitor.

"I'll be awhile." Lesieur spoke without looking up.

Fair enough. I, too, refused to work with breath on my neck.

Chenevier was still tossing the bedroom. Pasteur had shifted to the bath. Sounds of his search drifted up the hall. The ceramic clunk of a toilet tank cover. The squeak of a medicine cabinet door. The rattle of tablets in a plastic tube.

While gloving, Ryan and I decided to start in the kitchen.

I'd finished going through the refrigerator, when Lesieur spoke.

Abandoning his utensil drawer, Ryan went to her.

I carried on in the kitchen.

Four stainless steel canisters lined one counter. I opened the smallest. Coffee beans. I ran a spoon through them, found nothing of interest.

"This system can accommodate multiple hard drives, boosting capacity to one point five terabytes."

Ryan asked a question. Lesieur responded.

The second canister contained a brown sugar geodite. I poked at it. If anything was inside, we'd need a hydraulic drill to free it.

Lesieur and Ryan droned on in the next room. I took a moment to listen.

"A gigabyte equals one billion bytes. A terabyte equals one *trillion* bytes. That's a friggin' locomotive. But all this toad's doing is surfing the Net, storing a few files?"

I refocused on the canisters. The third held white sugar. My spoon churned up no booty.

"He's not an engineer. He's not storing videos. Why's he need all that capacity?" Lesieur.

"Guy's a gamer?" Ryan.

"Nope."

The largest canister was filled with flour. Too deep for the spoon.

"And what's up with the scanner?" Lesieur.

"He's not storing images?" Ryan.

"None that I've found."

Removing a stack of bowls from an upper cabinet, I extracted the largest and put the others back.

Ryan said something. Lesieur responded. The exchange was lost to the rattling of china.

I grasped the canister in both hands and poured, focusing on the flour cascading over its rim. A white cloud billowed up, dusting my face and hands.

A sneeze threatened.

I set down the canister. Waited. The sneeze made no move.

I resumed pouring. Half. Three-quarters.

The flour was nearly gone when an object dropped into the bowl. Setting the canister on the counter, I studied the thing.

Dark. Flat. About the size of my thumb.

I felt a fizz of excitement.

Though sealed in plastic, the item was familiar.

22

I hurried to the bedroom, flour-coated hands held away from my body.

"Find something?" Chenevier asked.

"In a canister. Better shoot it in situ then dust for latents."

Chenevier followed me back to the kitchen. Scribbling an evidence label, he photographed the bowl from several angles. When he'd finished, I extracted the object, tapped it on the rim, and laid it on the counter.

Chenevier snapped more photos, then checked for prints on the object's outer surface. There were none. Twirling a finger, he indicated that I should unroll the plastic. I did. He photographed every few inches.

Within minutes, a baggie, an eight-inch length of clear plastic wrap, and a thumb drive lay side by side on the Formica. None yielded prints.

"Got something," I called into the living room.

Ryan joined us. Floating one brow, he brushed flour from my nose.

I narrowed my eyes in a "don't say it" warning.

Ryan handed me a towel, then scanned the small assemblage beside the bowl.

"USB flash drive," I said. "Sixteen gigabytes."

"That's massive."

"You could store the national archives on this thing."

Ryan indicated that I should bring the thumb drive to the computer. Chenevier returned to the bedroom.

I passed the drive to Lesieur. She thumbed a button, and a USB connector slid from one end.

"We got paper for this?"

Ryan nodded.

Reaching under the workstation, Lesieur inserted the drive into the CPU tower.

The computer ding-donged, then a box appeared requesting a password.

"Try using Cormier," Ryan said.

Lesieur shot him a "you've got to be kidding" look.

"Try it."

Lesieur typed *C-O-R-M-I-E-R*.

The screen changed. A new box stated that a removable device had been detected, and that the disk contained more than one type of content.

"What a bonehead." Lesieur hit several keys.

Columns of text appeared. Folders. Files. Dates.

Lesieur opened a file. Another. Ryan and I leaned in for a better view of the screen.

"I'll be at this awhile." As before, her message was not subtle.

Ryan and I returned to the kitchen.

Several cabinets and a silo of cereal and cracker boxes later, Lesieur spoke. Ryan and I went to her.

"OK. Here's my take. Everything looks innocent enough on the surface. Tax returns. Business files. But I think your guy's got another whole layer buried in the unused space of his thumb drive."

Ryan and I must have looked blank.

"Some of the newer encryption programs provide plausible deniability by creating two layers. The user stores some innocuous files in the first layer. Tax returns, business contacts, information a reasonable person might want to encrypt. The second layer is a disk volume hidden in the 'unused' space of the drive."

"So Cormier uses a simple password for layer one because he doesn't really care about those files," I guessed. "It's a cover. He's really concerned about layer two."

"Exactly. With this type of setup, if someone starts poking around, they see some files, some open space, everything looks copasetic. When they view the open area of the disk byte by byte, all they find is gibberish."

"That's not suspicious?" Ryan asked.

Lesieur shook her head. "Operating systems don't normally delete deleted files. They just change a marker that says, 'This file has been deleted and can be written over.' Everything that was in the file is still on the drive until its space is needed, so if you look at the unused areas on a normal disk drive, you'll see bits and pieces of old files. Remember Ollie North?"

Ryan and I both said yes.

"That's how Irangate investigators recovered information Ollie had deleted. Without those chunks of old files, whether plain text or recognizably patterned computer data, pure gibberish stands out for what it lacks."

Lesieur cocked her chin at the monitor. "The giveaway with your guy is that I'm finding megabyte after megabyte of gibberish."

"So you suspect there are encrypted files, but you can't read them."

"*C'est ça.* Your guy's running Windows XP. When used with a sufficiently long and completely random password, even the tool that comes with XP Pro creates encryption that can be a bitch to crack."

"You tried typing in 'Cormier'?" Ryan asked.

"Oh yeah."

Lesieur checked her watch, then stood.

"A mondo thumb drive stashed in a flour bin. Double-layered encryption. This guy's hiding something he sincerely doesn't want found."

"Now what?" Ryan asked.

"If your warrant allows, confiscate the hardware. We'll get whatever it is he's snaked away."

At one, Ryan and I left Chenevier and Pasteur to finish and lock up. I drove straight to Cormier's studio. It was like moving from the cool of the arctic to the heat and grime of the tropics.

Hippo was wearing another aloha shirt. Red turtles and blue parrots, all damp and wilted. He'd finished two more cabinets.

I told him about the thumb drive. His response was immediate.

"The guy's into porn."

"Maybe."

"What? You think he's storing church music?"

Since images and videos require a lot of disk space, I, too, suspected porn. But I bristle at knee-jerk reactions.

"We shouldn't jump to judgment," I said.

Hippo blew air through his lips.

To avoid an argument, I changed the subject.

"Ever hear of an island called Île-aux-Becs-Scies?"

"Where?"

"Near Miramichi."

Hippo thought a moment, then shook his head.

"What does the name mean?"

"I think a *bec scie* is some kind of duck."

Something rolled over in my hindbrain.

Duck Island? What?

I chose a cabinet and began pulling file after file. Kids. Pets. Couples.

I found it hard to concentrate. Was I really championing judicious thinking? Or was I in denial? Cormier a pornographer. Cormier a photographer of women and children. Were the implications simply too awful?

And why the heads-up from my subconscious? Duck Island?

Partly heat. Partly hunger. A headache began organizing on the right side of my skull.

Ryan was to have bought lunch and come directly from Cormier's apartment to his studio. Where the hell was he? Cranky, I continued plowing through folders.

It was two-thirty before Ryan made his appearance. In lieu of the salad and Diet Coke I'd requested, he'd gotten hot dogs and fries from Lafleur's.

As we ate, Ryan and Hippo discussed the thumb drive. Ryan agreed that Cormier was probably hiding smut. Hot, irritable, and stuffed with greasy wieners, I played devil's advocate.

"Maybe Cormier got sick of dealing with this disorganized mess." I waved an arm at the cabinets. "Maybe he was scanning all his old images and files."

"To a thumb drive stashed in his flour bin."

Ryan had a point. It irked me.

"OK, so it's porn. Maybe Cormier's just a perv trying to hide his dirty little secret."

Both men looked at me as though I'd suggested anthrax was harmless.

"Think what you want." I bunched my wrappers and shoved them into the greasy brown bag. "I'll wait for proof."

Cabinet twelve. I was looking at a photo of an exceedingly unattractive baby when my cell phone chirped.

Two-eight-one area code. Harry.

I clicked on.

"You certainly were up early this morning."

"I'm up early most mornings."

"How's that French buckaroo?"

"If you mean Ryan, he's a jerk."

"I just spoke to Flannery O'Connor." Harry's voice was jittery with excitement.

"I'm listening."

There was a pause.

"Are we having another cranky pants day?"

"It's hot." I placed the ugly baby on the stack of finished files, and opened another.

"This isn't even close to hot."

"What did you learn?"

"You want hot, you try Houston in August."

"O'Connor House?"

"The business folded when Flan and her husband went splitsville. She goes by Flan. I didn't ask if she'd changed it official or not. Anyway, Flan cut bait after catching hubby *au flagrant* with a guy named Maurice."

"Uh-huh." The new file was labeled *Krenshaw*. The subject was a cocker spaniel. I closed it, and selected another.

"She's a hoot, Tempe. We talked for over an hour."

I could only imagine that conversation.

"What did you learn about Obéline's book?" I opened another file. *Tremblay*. A very fat lady posed with a very fat child. The Tremblays went onto the stack.

"Following the divorce, Flan kept all the O'Connor House records. Client names, book

229

titles, number of pages, number of copies, what type of binding. 'Course we're not talking Simon and Schuster here."

"Obéline's book?" Keeping Harry on track was like herding sheep on uppers.

"During its existence, O'Connor House printed twenty-two poetry collections. Six of the orders were placed by women." I heard paper rustle. "*La Pénitence,* by Félice Beaufils."

What Harry did to the French language was truly remarkable.

"*Lie Down Among the Lilies,* by Geraldine Haege. *Peppermint Springtime,* by Sandra Lacanu. *Un besoin de chaleur humaine,* by Charlene Pierpont. That title means something about needing human warmth."

I opened another folder. *Briggs.* Blushing bride. Done.

"The other four had no authors. You know, the poet preferred to remain anonymous. *Ghostly Mornings.* Flan thought that was a literary club project. A woman named Caroline Beecher handled the transaction."

The headache was banging at the back of my eyeball. Using a thumb, I rubbed circles on my temple.

"*Parfum* was paid for by Marie-Joséphine Devereaux. *Fringe* was paid for by Mary Anne Coffey. Each of those books was about fifty pages in length. Each print run was a hundred. Beecher and Devereaux had Moncton addresses. Coffey lived in St. John—"

"Obéline?" It came out sharper than I intended.

Harry allowed me several moments of dead air.

"I'm sorry. I know you're working hard on this. It's just a little too much information for now."

"Mm-hm."

"What did you learn about *Bones to Ashes*?"

I opened a new file. *Zucker*. Three kids wearing plaid.

"Virginie LeBlanc." Curt.

"LeBlanc placed the order?"

"Yes."

"Did O'Connor have LeBlanc's address?"

"Post office box."

"Where?"

"Bathurst."

"Any other contact information?"

"No."

"Did you try tracing LeBlanc?"

"Yes."

"And?"

Sulky silence.

I rolled my eyes. It hurt.

"Look, Harry. I'm sorry. I do appreciate what you're doing."

From across the room, I heard a phone, then Hippo's voice.

"Gallant."

"Can I buy you dinner tonight?" I asked Harry.

"Quand? Où?" Staccato questions in the background. Where? When?

"I'll be here," Harry said.

"Bon Dieu!"

"You pick the restaurant," I said.

I heard a soft grunt, then footsteps clumping my way.

"You can give me a full report on everything you've learned."

Harry agreed. Coolly.

I clicked off.

Hippo was standing over me.

I looked up.

Something was dreadfully wrong.

23

Hippo's jaw was clamped like a screw press.

"What?" I closed the Zucker file.

Hippo glowered silently.

"Tell me."

"Just got a courtesy call from the RCMP in Tracadie. Obéline Bastarache is missing and presumed dead."

I shot to my feet. The Zucker file flew across the floor. "Dead? How?"

Flicking a shirttail, Hippo pocket-jammed the phone and turned away.

"How?" I repeated, too shrill.

"Neighbor downriver from the Bastarache place found a shawl wrapping one of the pilings under his pier. Recognized it. Checked. Got suspicious that Obéline wasn't home. Says the lady never goes out."

"That hardly means Obéline drowned."

"RCMP searched the property. Found blood on the breakwater."

"That could—"

Hippo continued as though I hadn't spoken. "Clothes on the end of the breakwater. Folded. Shoes on top. *Note d'adieu* shoved into one toe."

I felt the blood drain from my head. "A suicide note?"

Hippo didn't square to face me.

Didn't speak the words I knew were goading his tongue.

There was no need. Already, I felt the deadening weight of self-blame.

I swallowed. "When?"

"Yesterday."

I'd visited Obéline on Tuesday. Wednesday she was dead.

"What did the note say?"

"*Adieu.* Life sucks."

Shame boiled inside me.

And anger.

And something else.

Though far from happy, Obéline had seemed content. Had told me she was at the one place she wanted to be.

"I detected nothing to suggest she was suicidal."

"Where was it you earned that psychology degree?"

My face flamed. Hippo was right. What did I know of this woman? Until two days ago, our last interactions had been as kids.

"No one is questioning that she's dead? I mean, there's no body. Are they dragging the river?"

"The river's a freight train right there." Hippo

was squinting down the hall, into sunlight oozing through one of the living room's dirt-caked windows. "Body's probably in the Gulf of St. Lawrence by now."

"Where was Bastarache?" Hearing agitated voices, Ryan had left Cormier's office.

"Quebec City."

"He alibi out?"

"That bastard always alibis out."

With that, Hippo stomped from the room. In seconds, the studio door opened, slammed.

"I'm sorry." Ryan's eyes said he meant it.

"Thanks." Weak.

There was a moment of strained silence.

"What's up with Hippo and you?"

"He's pissed that I went to Tracadie."

"I doubt it's you. You're just handy."

"He asked me not to make contact."

"Bastarache is a flesh bandit. Hippo thinks it reflects badly on all Acadians."

I didn't trust myself to answer.

"Don't let him get to you. Hippo'll never say it, but your finding Cormier's thumb drive impressed the hell out of him. Once Lesieur cracks it, we'll be able to reel this dirtball in."

"If I hadn't found it, CSU would have."

Ryan knew that was true. Was trying to be nice.

"If you want to knock off, I understand," he said.

I shook my head. But I'd already lost Ryan's attention.

"I have court tomorrow. If we don't finish today, we'll wrap up on Monday."

With that, Ryan disappeared down the hall. And proceeded to ignore me for the rest of the day.

Fine. I could concentrate on Cormier's bloody files.

Only I couldn't. All afternoon, I kept seeing Obéline. The gazebo. The breakwater. The shawl.

Leaden, I forced myself through file after file.

Pets. Brides. Kids. None of them Phoebe. None of them a cold case MP or DOA.

At six I gave up.

Inching home through rush hour traffic, I worried about telling Harry that Obéline was dead. My sister feels things intensely, emotes unabashedly. Joy. Anger. Fear. Whatever Harry's reaction, it's always over the top. I was dreading the conversation.

At the condo, I parked underground. A light indicated the elevator was holding on three. I trudged up the stairs.

Both the outer and inner front doors were open. Runners crisscrossed the lobby floor. Winston, our caretaker, stood on one of them.

"Someone moving?" Not really interested. Thinking about Harry.

"Three-oh-four," Winston answered. "Transferred to Calgary."

I rounded the banister, started toward my corridor.

"You thinking about selling?"

"No."

"Funny."

I turned. "What's funny?"

"Couple guys wandered in here this morning. Asked about your place."

I stopped. "Asked what?"

"How many rooms. If the backyard was yours." Winston shrugged, thumbs hooking his jeans. "The usual."

I felt a tickle of apprehension. "Did they leave contact information?"

Winston shook his head.

"Did they use my name specifically?"

Winston gave the question some thought. "Not sure. It's been a zoo here today. They're probably gawkers. We get a lot of those."

"Release absolutely no information on my condo."

Winston's smile crumpled. His arms came up and crossed on his chest.

"I'm sorry. I know you'd never do that."

Winston ran a finger and thumb along the corners of his mouth.

I smiled. "Thanks for telling me."

"That sister of yours is a hoot."

"Isn't she." I made the turn toward my hallway. "I better feed her or she'll start gnawing the woodwork."

Still wounded, Harry had declined participation in restaurant selection. I took her to one of my favorites. Milos is pricey, but this wasn't the night for counting coins.

Conversation upon departure went something like this.

"Is the fish fresh?"

"Still swimming."

Upon arrival.

"Where are we?"

"Saint-Laurent near Saint-Viateur."

"Holy mackerel."

We shared a Greek salad and an order of deep-fried zucchini. Harry had crab legs and I had snapper.

After much prompting, she agreed to discuss *Bones to Ashes*.

"When I called the Bathurst post office, I was directed to a Miss Schtumpheiss." Harry pronounced the name with a hokey Colonel Klink accent. "Frau Schtumpheiss would neither confirm nor deny that Virginie LeBlanc had rented a postal box in her facility. I swear, Tempe, you'd think the woman was running a gulag."

"Stalag. What did she say?"

"That the information was confidential. I think Frau Schtumpheiss just didn't want to move her *frauenhintern*."

I bit. *"Frauenhintern?"*

"Buttocks. Female."

"How do you know that?"

"Conrad spoke German."

Conrad was hubby number two. Or three.

"I could ask Hippo to give her a call," I said. "He hails from that neck of the woods."

"Might work." Aloof, but not hostile. Harry's mood was improving.

For the rest of the meal, I kept it light. When

coffee arrived, I reached across the table and took my sister's hand.

"Hippo gave me some very bad news today."

Harry fixed me with two worried eyes.

I swallowed. "Obéline may be dead."

The eyes clouded. "Ohmygod!" Whispered, "How? When?"

I relayed what I knew. Braced.

Harry picked up a spoon and stirred her coffee. Tapped the rim. Set the spoon on the table. Leaned back. Bit her lip thoughtfully.

No tears. No outburst.

"Are you OK?"

Harry didn't respond.

"Apparently the current is very strong."

Harry nodded.

My sister's composure was unsettling. I started to speak. She flapped a hand for quiet.

I signaled for the check.

"There is something we can do," she said. "In homage to Évangéline and Obéline."

Harry waited as the waiter refilled my mug.

"Remember the guy who mailed bombs to universities and airlines?"

"The Unabomber?"

"Yeah. How'd that go?"

"From the late seventies to the early nineties, Theodore Kaczynski killed three and wounded twenty-nine people. The Unabomber was the target of one of the most expensive manhunts in FBI history. What does Kaczynski have to do with Obéline?"

239

A manicured nail jabbed the air. "How did they finally catch him?"

"His manifesto: *Industrial Society and Its Future*. Kaczynski argued that the bombs were necessary to attract attention to his work. He wanted to inspire others to fight against subjugation facilitated by technological progress."

"Yeah. Yeah. Yeah. But how did they nail the skank?"

"In the mid-nineties, Kaczynski mailed letters, some to his former victims, demanding that his manifesto be printed by a major newspaper. All thirty-five thousand words. Verbatim. If not, he threatened to kill more people. After a lot of debate, the Justice Department recommended publication. Both the *New York Times* and the *Washington Post* ran the thing, hoping something would break."

"And?" Harry turned her palm up.

"Kaczynski's brother recognized the writing style and notified authorities. Forensic linguists compared text samples provided by Kaczynski's brother and mother with the Unabomber's manifesto, and determined they'd been authored by the same person."

"There you go." Harry added a second upturned palm.

"What?" I was lost.

"That's what we do. In Obéline's memory. And Évangéline's, of course. We get a linguist to compare the poems in *Bones to Ashes* to poems Évangéline wrote as a kid. Then we make Évangéline an official poet."

"I don't know, Harry. A lot of her early stuff was just adolescent angst."

"You think young Kaczynski was William Friggin' Shakespeare?"

I tried not to look dubious.

"You talked to Obéline about Évangéline's murder. I don't speak French, but I listened. I know what I heard in her voice. Guilt. Terrible, horrible, gut-wrenching guilt. The woman's whole life was one giant guilt trip because she hid the fact that she knew about her sister's killing. Wouldn't she want this?"

"Yes, but—"

"Do you know a forensic linguist?"

"Yes, but—"

"Well enough to ask him to do a comparison?"

"I suppose."

Dropping both hands to the table, Harry leaned forward onto her forearms. "Évangéline and Obéline are both gone. That book is all we have left. Don't you want to know if Évangéline wrote it?"

"Of course I do, but—"

"And get Évangéline's name on record? Make her the published poet she always wanted to be?"

"But wait. This makes no sense. You're suggesting Évangéline wrote the poems and that Obéline had them printed by O'Connor House. But why would Obéline use the name Virginie LeBlanc? And why wouldn't she cite Évangéline as the author of the collection?"

"Maybe she had to hide the project from her creepozoic husband."

"Why?"

"Hell, Tempe, I don't know. Maybe he didn't want old dirt stirred up."

"Évangéline's murder?"

Harry nodded. "We know Bastarache used to beat the crap out of Obéline. He probably scared her." Harry's voice went hushed. "Tempe, do you think he's now killed her?"

"I don't know."

"Do you think she's even dead? I mean, where's the body?"

Indeed, I thought. Where is the body?

The check arrived. I did the math and signed.

"There's a problem, Harry. If I still have any of Évangéline's poems, and that's a big 'if,' they'd be in Charlotte. I have nothing here in Montreal."

A smile crawled Harry's lips.

24

When Harry plays coy, there's no cracking her. Though I asked repeatedly, she'd tell me nothing. My sister loves being on the giving end of surprises. I knew I was in for one.

Twenty minutes later we were in my bedroom, the odd samplings of my past staring up at us. The arm-in-arm friends. The ticket. The napkin.

But Harry didn't linger on that page of the scrapbook. On the next she'd pasted three items: a tiny Acadian flag, that being the French tricolor with one yellow star; a quill pen sticker; a cream-colored envelope with metallic lining and *Évangéline* stenciled on the outside.

Raising the flap, Harry extracted several pastel sheets and handed them to me.

The room fell away. I was twelve. Or eleven. Or nine. Standing by the mailbox. Oblivious to everything but the letter in my hand.

By reflex, I sniffed the stationery. Friendship Garden. Sweet Jesus, how could I remember the name of a childhood cologne?

"Where did you find these?"

"When I decided to put my house on the market, I started gophering through boxes. First thing I hit was our old Nancy Drew collection. Found them stuck in *The Password to Larkspur Lane*. That's what sparked the scrapbook idea. I like the pink one. Read it."

I did.

And stared into the unfinished country of Évangéline's dream.

The poem was untitled.

Late in the morning I'm walking in sunshine,
awake and aware like
I have not been before. A warm glow envelops me
and tells all around,
"Now I am love!" I can laugh at the univers for
he is all mine.

"Now listen to this."

Opening the purloined copy of *Bones to Ashes*, Harry read,

"Laughing, three maidens walk carelessly,
making their way to the river.
Hiding behind a great hemlock, one smiles as
others pass unknowing
Then with a jump and a cry and a laugh and a
hug the girls put their

Surprise behind them. The party moves on
through the forest primeval
In a bright summer they think lasts forever. But
not the one ailing.
She travels alone and glides through the shadows;
others can not see her.
Her hair the amber of late autumn oak leaves, eyes
the pale purple of dayclean.
Mouth a red cherry. Cheeks ruby roses. Young
bones going to ashes."

Harry and I sat in silence, lost in memories of four little girls, smiling toward life and what it would bring.

Harry swallowed. "The two poems kinda ring the same, don't you think?"

I felt an ache so deep I couldn't imagine it ever ending. I couldn't answer.

Harry hugged me. I felt her chest heave, heard a tiny, hiccupping intake of air. Releasing me, she slipped from the room. I knew my sister was as devastated by Obéline's death as I.

I couldn't bear to read the other poems right then. I tried to sleep. Tried to put everything from my mind. I failed. The day kept replaying in flash-point fragments. Cormier's thumb drive. Hippo's anger. Obéline's suicide. Évangéline's poetry. The skeleton. Île-aux-Becs-Scies.

Bec scie. Duck. Far away, in my head, a whisper. Faint, unintelligible.

Most distressing, try as I would, I could summon only a watercolor impression of

Évangéline's face. A blurry countenance at the bottom of a lake.

Had my memory run out, used up by countless visits over the years? Or was it the opposite? In medicine we talk of atrophy, the shriveling of bone or tissue due to disuse. Had Évangéline's face evaporated because of neglect?

I sat up, intending to study the scrapbook snapshot. While I reached for the lamp, a disturbing thought struck me.

Had recall of my friend grown dependent upon photographic feeding? Were my recollections of Évangéline being shaped by the vagaries of light and shadow at frozen moments in time?

Settling back, I cleared my mind, and dug deep.

Unruly dark curls. A tilt to the chin. A careless tossing of the head.

Again, the nagging *pssst!* from my unconscious . . .

Honey skin. Ginger freckles sprinkling a sunburned nose.

A comment . . .

Luminous green eyes.

A link I was missing . . .

A slightly too-square jaw.

An idea. Bothering me . . .

Willowy limbs. A tender suggestion of breasts.

Something about a duck . . .

And then I fell asleep.

Eight A.M. found me in my office at Wilfrid-Derome. It was to be a day of interruptions.

My phone was blinking like a railroad crossing signal. I reviewed the messages, but returned only one call. Frances Suskind, the marine biologist at McGill.

I'd completely forgotten about the diatom samples I'd taken from the teenaged girl found in Lac des Deux Montagnes. Ryan's DOA number three.

Suskind answered on the first ring.

"Dr. Brennan. I was about to phone you again. My students and I are very excited about our findings."

"You shared information with students?"

"Graduate level, of course. We found your challenge extraordinarily invigorating."

Challenge? Invigorating?

"Are you acquainted with the field of limnology?"

"Diatoms have their own ology?" Intended as a joke. Suskind didn't laugh.

"Diatoms are part of the class Bacillariophyceae of the Chrysophyta phylum of microscopic unicellular plants. Did you know that the members of this group are so numerous they represent the single most abundant oxygen source in our atmosphere?"

"I didn't."

I began doodling.

"Let me explain our procedure. First, we collected twelve samples from each of seven sites along the river and around Lac des Deux Montagnes, which is actually part of the river, of course, including L'Île-Bizard, near the point where the body was recovered. Those samples acted as our controls in examining diatom assemblages recovered from the victim. The ones we obtained from the specimens you provided. The bone plug and sock."

"Uh-huh." I drew a shell.

"At each site we collected from a variety of habitats. Riverbed. Riverbank. Lakeshore."

I added spirals to the shell.

"Our control samples yielded ninety-eight different diatom species. The various assemblages are similar and share many species."

I started a bird.

"The dominant ones include *Navicula radiosa, Achnan*—"

There are over ten thousand diatom species. Suspecting Suskind was launching into a full roll call, I interrupted. "Perhaps we could let that go until I have your written report."

"Of course. Well, let me see. There are variations in the presence or absence of minor species, and changes in the proportions of the dominant species. That's to be expected given the complexity of the microhabitats."

I added tail feathers.

"Basically, the samples divide into three cluster zones. A midchannel habitat with a depth of over two meters, which experiences moderate water flow. A shallow water habitat of less than two meters, which experiences slow water flow. And a riverbank or lakeshore habitat, above water level."

An eye. More plumage.

"Perhaps I should explain our statistical treatment. We do cluster analysis, to determine the clusters I just described." Suskind made a honking sound, which I assumed to be laughter. "Of course. That's why it's called cluster analysis."

I sketched a bill.

"To compare the control samples to the victim samples, we use a transfer function called modern analog technique. We calculate the dissimilarity between a victim sample and the most similar control sample, using the squared chord distance as the dissimilarity coefficient—"

"May we also leave quantitative analysis for the report?"

"Of course. The bottom line. We found that the diatom assemblages recovered from the sock show strong similarity to samples taken from the midlake channel and from the lakeshore."

Webbed feet.

"Our analog matching technique suggests that the closest lakeshore analogy is with a control sample collected at the bottom of a boat ramp situated in the Bois-de-L'Île-Bizard nature preserve, not far from the body recovery site."

My pen froze.

"You can pinpoint with that much precision?"

"Of course. What we do—"

"Where is this park?"

She told me. I wrote it down.

"What about the bone plug?"

"I'm afraid that's a bit more complex."

Suskind now had my full attention. "Go on."

"The diatom flora from the bone's outer surface is similar to that recovered from the sock. We recovered no diatoms from the marrow cavity."

"Meaning?"

"Interpretation of negative evidence is always risky."

"Suggest some scenarios."

"Diatoms find their way into the body via inhalation, via ingestion, and via the aspiration of water. Whatever the initial pathway, assuming they are sufficiently tiny, the diatoms then circulate into the body's organs and marrow. Diatoms are recovered from the bone marrow of approximately thirty percent of all drowning victims. They occur at significantly lower rates, perhaps as low as ten percent, in cases of bathtub or other city water drownings."

"Because diatoms and other impurities are filtered out of domestic water," I guessed.

"Of course. If present in domestic water, they've most likely come from household cleaners. But those are unique and recognizable species."

"You found none."

"We found nothing in the marrow cavity."

"So it's possible the victim may have drowned in treated or filtered water, not in the river?"

"It's possible. But let me continue. The diatom concentration in bone marrow is usually proportionate to the diatom concentration in the drowning medium. That concentration varies due to the natural cycle of blooms and die-offs. In the northern hemisphere, diatom blooms occur in the spring and fall, creating persistently high levels in rivers and lakes throughout the summer. In winter, levels are typically at their lowest."

"So the victim could have drowned in the river, but before this season's bloom."

"It's another possibility."

"When did this season's bloom occur?"

"April."

I was scribbling notes next to my doodles.

"Aspiration of water is required to transport the diatoms," Suskind continued. "The transportation process works because diatoms are resistant to the mucus of the respiratory system and are able to embolize from the circulatory system into the internal organs."

I knew where she was going. "Blood has to be pumping to get diatoms into the marrow."

"Of course."

"So the victim may not have been breathing when she hit the water."

"It's another possibility. But remember. Diatoms are found in only one third of all drowning cases."

"Why such a low percentage?"

"Many reasons. I'll give you the primary three. First, it may have to do with method of collection. If very few diatoms are present in the marrow cavity, they may simply be missed in sampling. Second, victims who hyperventilate and pass out under water or who experience laryngeal spasm may die more quickly, leading to a reduced quantity of inhaled water. Third, as I am sure you

251

know, a relatively low volume of blood flows to and through the bone and bone marrow. And, for this individual, one bone plug was all I had. No samples from lungs, brain, kidney, liver, spleen."

"When may I expect your report?"

"I'm completing it now."

Thanking Suskind, I disconnected.

Great. The girl drowned or didn't. In the river or elsewhere.

But the boat ramp. That was useful.

I called, but Ryan didn't answer his cell. Of course. He was in court. I left a message.

The receiver had barely hit the cradle when the phone rang again.

"Having a nice day, kitten?" Male. Unaccented English.

"Who is this?"

"No matter."

My mind looked for matches.

Cheech, the thug from Tracadie? I couldn't be sure. He'd only spoken a sentence or two.

"Where did you get this number?"

"You're easy to find."

"What do you want?"

"Working hard fighting crime?"

I refused to be goaded.

"Noble endeavor, that. Protecting the good citizens of this province."

Down the hall, a phone rang.

"But hazardous."

"Are you threatening me?"

"That's one fine-looking sister you've got."

A cold tentacle curled in my gut.

"What's little sis do while big sis plays cop?"

I didn't react.

"She's pretty easy to find, too."

"Screw you," I said, and slammed the receiver.

I sat a moment twisting and untwisting the phone cord. Cheech? If so, was he a threat, or merely a yokel with a bad approach and an overblown opinion of his own appeal? No. He was delivering a threat from someone.

Why? Did he work for Bastarache? What did he mean by "this province"? Where was he?

Who was he?

Phone Hippo?

No way.

Fernand Colbert.

Good one, Brennan. Colbert was a techie cop who owed me for bringing him barbecue sauce from North Carolina.

I phoned.

When Colbert answered, I explained the anonymous call. He promised to try a trace.

I was hanging up when my gaze fell on my doodles.

Duck . . .

Shell . . .

Forget it. Focus on current cases. Ryan's MPs: Kelly Sicard. Anne Girardin. Claudine Cloquet. Phoebe Quincy. Ryan's DOAs: Rivière des Mille Îles. Dorval. Lac des Deux Montagnes.

Duck . . .

Shell . . .

The whisper broke through, and jumped all thoughts of MPs, DOAs, or Cheech and the threat.

25

Hurrying to the library, I pulled out the same New Brunswick atlas I'd consulted on Saturday, and flipped to the same map. Sheldrake Island lay in the mouth of the Miramichi River.

I checked an English dictionary.

Sheldrake. Any of several varieties of Old World ducks of the genus Tadorna . . .

Duck. Shell. Sheldrake.

Duck Island. Sheldrake Island.

A *bec scie* was a duck.

Could Sheldrake Island be the English equivalent of Île-aux-Becs-Scies? Was that the short-circuiting message to my cerebrum? Could Jerry O'Driscoll's drifter, Tom Jouns, a one-time archaeologist, have taken the girl's skeleton from Sheldrake Island?

Returning to my office, I logged onto the Internet. Before Google opened, my phone rang again. This time it was Harry.

"Did you call the forensic linguist?"

"Not yet."

Harry used silence to express her disapproval.

"I will."

"When?"

"This morning."

More censuring nothing hummed across the line.

"I'll do it now."

"Good."

"What are you up to?"

"Not much. Reading through these poems. They're really quite beautiful."

I could tell she was down.

"Harry, do you remember how we used to cook when Mama was having one of her bad spells?"

"Yes."

"Let's do that tonight. You and me."

"You were pretty bossy."

"Pick a recipe. I'll be sous chef."

"You'll call the linguist?"

"As soon as we hang up."

"How about that thing we used to do with chicken and smashed potatoes."

"Perfect."

"Will they understand me at that little grocery store on Sainte-Catherine?"

"Speak English. Not Texan."

"Hee haw!"

"And, Harry." I hesitated. Yes. "Keep your head up."

"For what?"

"Just be careful."

Rob Potter was finishing his doctorate in anthropology when I began my grad studies at Northwestern. Older, wiser, he'd been an ear to listen and a shoulder to cry on. Not to mention everyone's secret crush. Improbably, before turning to academia, Rob had been a bona fide seventies rock star. Sang at Woodstock. Wore leather jackets and butt-molding gold lamé pants. Knew Hendrix, Lennon, and Dylan. In Rob's words, he quit the limelight because for him, rock lost its luster after Jimi and Janis died, and he preferred looking ahead to being an aging professor than an aging—or dead—rock star.

While I'd poked bones Rob had parsed language, focusing on its context in other semiotic systems, modalities, and channels. He once explained what that meant. And I understood. Sort of.

Rob was now on the faculty at Columbia. Like me, he'd been pulled into forensics by cops and lawyers in need of expertise. Though we'd worked no cases jointly, we frequently joked about the possibility.

I checked my American Academy of Forensic Sciences membership directory. Rob was listed.

I dialed. He answered. I identified myself.

"I've been thinking about you."

"I didn't do it," I said.

"What if you were supposed to have?"

"Then I did it."

"Glad that's cleared up. Since you're so conscientious, would you consider being program chair for next year's AAFS meeting?"

"Can I think about it?"

"Only you can answer that."

"I'll think about it."

"Fair enough. What's on your mind?"

"I have a favor to ask."

"Not until I know how much money it will cost."

"Could you analyze two samples of poetry?"

"I could."

"Would you?"

"Of course. For you, anything. Is this to extract author demographic information, or to test for common authorship?"

"To determine common authorship."

"Go on."

"One poem was written by an adolescent girl. The author of the others is unknown."

"You suspect the poems were penned by the same hand."

"It's a possibility."

"Realize that these analyses can take a long time."

"Whenever you can. But there's a catch."

"As am I."

"This isn't an official request."

"Meaning no money. Or am I to forget the analysis after I give it to you?"

"Well, both."

"So. A favor. And an unofficial one. And secret. And no pay."

"I'll—"

"Oh, you'll pay, all right. Maybe your next trip through New York?"

"Lunch. We're on."

"Tell me about this gig."

"Some of the poems appear in a self-published volume. Others are handwritten."

"Give me some background."

I did. Pawleys Island. Évangéline's sudden disappearance. The recent trip to Tracadie. Harry's liberation of *Bones to Ashes*. O'Connor House. I left out only that Obéline had killed herself.

"I'll send the materials today," I said.

"You start with a theme."

"What?"

"A conference theme. A conceptual framework."

"Organizing an AAFS program is massive, Rob."

"It's a piece of cake."

"Like landscaping the Mojave is a piece of cake."

"I'll provide fertilizer."

"You always do."

I called Harry, gave her Rob's address, and suggested a shop on de Maisonneuve for FedEx shipping. She was thrilled to have another mission.

I turned back to my computer. As though on cue, Hippo appeared. His frown did not say forgive and forget. I braced for more disapproval.

"Might be we got us one less MP."

That caught me off guard. "What do you mean?"

Hippo was chewing gum, carefully not looking at me. "Girardin's old man took himself out last night."

"Anne Girardin? The little girl from Blainville?"

Tight nod. *Sans* orbital contact.

"What happened?"

"Girardin was a boozer. Wednesday he got wasted, told a drinking buddy he offed his kid and buried her in the woods. Wanted sympathy because her ghost's now haunting his sleep. Upstanding citizen thought it over, moral dilemma, you know, loyalty versus civic duty. This morning he went to see Girardin. Found him in the bathtub, pump-action Remington between his toes, brains on the ceiling."

"Sweet mother of God."

Hippo spit his gum into his palm, popped two antacids, reengaged the wad. "Dog insists there's something out behind the trailer."

"Were you able to reach Ryan?"

Hippo nodded. "He's rolling."

I stood.

"Let's go."

"Girardin hated crowds, distrusted strangers. Lived in a single-wide miles from anywhere."

"Lonely life for a ten-year-old girl."

"Yeah." Hippo's eyes stayed on the road.

Again, I was on my way toward Blainville. Again, I was being briefed on a child whose corpse I might soon dig up.

"Kid disappeared in '04. Adelaide, that's Mommy, split six months later. Girardin stayed put."

"What'd he do for a living?"

"Construction. Pickup jobs, mostly."

"Where is Adelaide now?"

"In the wind."

"Is she a local?"

"Thunder Bay, Ontario." Hippo made a turn. "Don't worry. We'll find her."

As we approached our destination, signs of habitation faded away. The few shacks and mobile homes we did pass were straight out of *Deliverance*.

Girardin's trailer was a rectangular box with dull yellow siding and pumpkin trim. A makeshift porch had been nailed around the entrance. On it sat an avocado refrigerator and an orange Barcalounger with herniated stuffing.

The yard was cluttered with the usual trash. Old tires, rusted barrels, plastic furniture, the skeleton of a lawn mower. Larger items included a boat trailer and an ancient Mustang.

The CSU truck was there. The coroner's van. Chenevier and Pasteur. Sylvain and the cadaver collie, Mia. Ryan.

The air was hot, the humidity a notch below rain.

It was the Kelly Sicard search all over again.

With a sadly different outcome.

The sun was low when we finally lifted the small bundle. Threads of light cut the foliage, casting odd patterns on the shallow pit, the plywood, the fifty-gallon Hefty.

The grave was not unexpected. We'd found a half-empty bag of quicklime under the trailer. A long-handled spade.

And Mia had been emphatic.

The others watched as my blade slit the plastic. Odor drifted out, rotten-sweet, like spoiled vegetation. A sole cawing crow broke the hush.

The child had been buried in pink flowered jeans, a pink hoodie, pink Keds. Carrot pigtails still clung to the skull, dirt-crusted, death-dulled. The teeth were in that stage between kid and adult.

As one, we recalled the snapshot. The police report filed by Anne Girardin's mother.

No one spoke. No one had to.

We all knew that Anne had been found.

I asked Ryan to drive me to the lab. He said that was crazy, that my analysis could wait until Monday. Daddy was dead. Finding Mommy might take time.

No good. Next-of-kin notification couldn't occur without an official ID. As a mother, I knew the anguish filling Adelaide Girardin's days. I wanted to be ready.

Hippo stayed to help Chenevier and Pasteur process the trailer. Ryan drove me to Wilfrid-Derome. On the way, I called Lisa, the autopsy technician. She agreed to work overtime. I asked her to determine if Anne Girardin's dental records were on file. And to call Marc Bergeron, the LSJML odontologist.

I also phoned Harry, filled her in on the day's events, and told her our culinary caper would have to wait. She asked when I'd be home. Late. I hated leaving her alone so much. What if the pair asking about my condo had had more than real estate in mind? What if the anonymous call really had been a threat?

Harry offered to get take-out whenever I was ready. I thanked her, reminded her to always set the security system. In my mind I could see her rolling her eyes.

The child was at the morgue when I arrived. She'd been assigned case number LSJML #57836–07. Dental X-rays had been taken.

People think quicklime hurries decomposition. They're wrong. Calcium oxide only masks the odor of decay. And its presence deters scavengers.

But time will have its way with flesh. Though the remains had suffered no animal damage, skeletonization was complete. Some hair remained, but there was no soft tissue at all.

Lisa photographed as I removed the rotting garments and spread them on the counter. Hoodie. Jeans. Training bra with expandable AAA "cups." Cotton briefs, Barbie doll pattern.

I'd been doing well. Despite the sadness and fatigue. But the underwear hit me hard. Barbies and bras. Monkey bars and lipstick. A child-woman on the brink. The sight was heartbreaking.

"Good thing the bastard is dead, yes?" Lisa gave me a look as heavy as a tombstone. I could tell she felt as wretched as I did.

"Yes," I said.

Focus, I thought, arranging bones on the autopsy table.

Lisa shot stills as I worked through my analysis.

The child's cranial and facial features indicated Caucasoid ancestry.

Fusion of the ischial and pubic pelvic rami suggested an age over eight. Absence of a tiny round bone at the base of the thumb, a sesamoid, suggested prepubescence. Long-bone development suggested a range of nine to ten years.

Sex assessment is imprecise with children. Though the clothing and pigtails pointed to female gender, I left that part of the biological profile blank.

Bergeron phoned as I was making final notes. He was upstairs and had Anne Girardin's antemortem records. The dentals were a match.

No surprise.

It was almost ten when I finally got home. After I showered, Harry and I ate Thai from the corner restaurant, then I excused myself. She understood and did not press.

Again, my brain resisted sleep. When I finally drifted off, it was into a landscape of disjointed dreams. Anne Girardin. Évangéline. The skeleton from Sheldrake Island. Hippo's girl. Pawleys Island. Ryan.

Then I was awake. I checked the clock. Two-forty. I closed my eyes. Checked again. Three-ten. Three-fifty.

At four, I gave up. Throwing back the covers, I went to the kitchen and brewed a cup of jasmine tea. Then I booted my laptop and began researching Sheldrake Island.

Dawn lit the shade when I finally sat back. Stunned. Appalled.

Certain of two things.

Sheldrake Island was, indeed, Île-aux-Becs-Scies.

Hippo's girl had suffered a hideous death.

26

I suspect lack of sleep muddled my thinking.

Or maybe it was Pete's early morning call about grounds. And filing papers. And young Summer's inability to find a caterer.

Or maybe Hippo's shocker.

In looking back, there's always the mental cringe. The suspicion that I could have done better.

After speaking with Pete, I woke Harry and explained what I'd learned on the Net. Then I apologized for abandoning her again.

I need to be certain, I said.

We could be back to square one, she said.

Yes, I agreed.

Harry went shopping. I went to the lab.

It took only an hour with the skeleton. The diagnosis seemed so obvious now. How could I have been so dense about the lesions?

It's the horror of other places, other times, I told myself. Not twentieth-century North America.

True. Nevertheless, a sorry defense.

When I'd finished with the bones, I logged onto my computer, wanting to arm myself fully for the upcoming conversation with Hippo. I was closing the Web browser when a *ping* told me a new e-mail had landed.

Contacting a government office on a weekend is like phoning the Pope on Easter morning. Curious who'd e-mailed on a Saturday, I clicked over to my in-box.

I didn't recognize the sender: watching@hotmail.com.

When I opened the message, icy-hot barbs shot through my chest.

Temperance:
Staring your severed head in the face . . .
Death. Fate. Mutilation.

A photo had been inserted below the text.

Thursday night. Harry and I, backlit by the bulbs at Milos's entrance.

I stared at the photo, breath stuck in my throat. It wasn't only the shock of seeing myself. Or the idea that I'd been watched by a stranger. Something was off. Wrong.

Then it registered.

Harry's head was on my body, mine on hers.

My gaze drifted to the italicized line in the message. Poetry? Lyrics?

I did another browser search using the words

"death," "fate," and "mutilation." Every link pointed me the same way.

Death was a heavy metal band formed in 1983, disbanded in 1999. Its founder, Chuck Schuldiner, was considered the father of the death metal genre. The group's *Fate* album was released in '92. One cut was titled "Mutilation."

When I brought up the lyrics, my pulse jackhammered. The line from the e-mail was there. And the refrain. Over and over.

You must die in pain.

Mutilation.

Jesus Christ! Where was Harry?

I tried her cell. She didn't answer. I left a message. Call me.

Who was this creep, watching@hotmail.com?

Same gut reaction I'd had to the phone call.

Cheech?

Same line of questions.

Alpha male courtship? Threat? Why?

And then I was angry.

Pulling air into my lungs, I punched Fernand Colbert's number. He answered.

"Working on Saturday?" I asked.

"Got a wiretap in place."

I knew not to ask details. "Hope my request isn't jamming you up."

"*Mais non.* And I need the barbecue sauce."

"Any luck with the trace?"

"Yes and no."

"Well, then."

"Let me explain. Phone companies track

everything going in or out of a landline, with the possible exception of local calls that are handled within the same switcher. This is also true of cell phones."

"This is the yes part."

"Yes. Here's how a cell call to a landline works. You dial a number on your mobile. It calls the closest tower. Using the same technology as your caller ID, it says, 'I'm Tempe's phone and I want to call 1-2-3-4-5.' The tower sends your call to the MTSO, the central Mobile Telephone Switching Office, which connects to the land-based phone system. You with me?"

"So far. I have a feeling you're getting to the no part."

"The MTSO connects with the landline's main exchange, which sends the call to the main exchange serving your destination. From there your call goes to the destination's local exchange and then to the destination phone.

"At every stop your phone's identification is logged because everybody who touches the call wants to get paid. Your number is not only associated with you but also with your carrier. The kicker is, all your information isn't kept in one place, and companies won't release it without a subpoena and reimbursement of the cost of looking it all up.

"The other kicker is that with some wireless services, you don't need to provide any ID, much less valid ID, to start the service."

"And any mope can buy a convenience store throwaway mobile."

"Exactly. Having the phone number doesn't help if you don't know who owns the phone."

"My mope called from a cell phone bought at a Wal-Mart," I guessed.

"Or Costco or Kmart or Pop's Dollarama. If it's really important, we could find out where the phone was purchased, then check the store's surveillance cameras, maybe nail the guy that way."

"No. That's a bit extreme at this point. But I have another request."

"It'll cost you a case."

"You've got it, barbecue boy."

I described the e-mail, but not the contents.

"Same jerk?"

"I'm not sure. Probably."

"He threatening you?"

"Not overtly."

"If the guy's that canny with the phone, it's probably pointless to try to track him through e-mail."

"I thought you might say that."

"Scenario. Guy drives around with a laptop equipped with a wireless card, lets it detect networks. When he finds one that's unsecured, he sets up a Hotmail account using false information. Sends e-mail. Shuts down his laptop and drives away."

"You can just sit in a car using another person's network?"

"*Oui*. The originating IP address belongs to someone who probably doesn't even have logging to show there was another user on his network. Some geeks do it for sport. Call it wardriving, even if they're on foot. They wander around looking for vulnerable wifi networks, sometimes make directional antennas out of Pringles cans. You can buy pens that flash green when you're within thirty feet of a signal."

Great. Something else to worry about.

"Here's another trick," Colbert said. "Many hotels have wireless networks they leave open so they don't have to train the guests how to log in with a Service Set Identifier, or SSID, which can be up to thirty-two characters long. With a closed system the user has to key in, but with an open system the SSID is broadcast to all wireless devices within range. So if you pull into a parking lot between a couple of airport hotels, you can probably log into their wireless network completely anonymously."

"Discouraging."

"Yeah. But I'm game to give it a shot."

Thanking Colbert, I disconnected.

OK. Time to bring Ryan into the loop.

Instead, I phoned Hippo.

He answered immediately. So much for weekend leisure in the glam world of law enforcement.

"I have news on the skeleton from Rimouski," I said.

"Yeah? I've been buried in these freakin' cabinets so long, Gaston's problem's gone out of my head."

"Agent Tiquet got the bones from the Whalen

brothers, who bought them at Jerry O'Driscoll's pawnshop in Miramichi. O'Driscoll purchased them from Tom Jouns, who claimed to have dug them from a Native burial ground."

"Sounds like one of those road rallies where you follow clues." Hippo slurped like he was chewing a caramel.

"O'Driscoll said the cemetery was on an island. I found the name Île-aux-Becs-Scies written on the girl's skull."

"Yeah, I remember you asking about *becs scies*."

"Île-aux-Becs-Scies is now called Sheldrake Island."

Hippo said something indecipherable.

"Are you eating caramels?"

"Taffy."

"Sheldrake is a thirty-two-acre island located in the Miramichi River, about eight miles east of Chatham. In the early nineteenth century the place served as a quarantine station for newly arriving immigrants. In 1844, the New Brunswick government turned Sheldrake into a leper colony."

All mastication stopped. "Say what?"

"There was an outbreak of leprosy in the province."

"Like in the Bible? People with fingers and toes falling off?"

"In some cases. Leprosy is caused by the *Mycobacterium leprae* bacillus. It's now called Hansen's disease."

"There were lepers in New Brunswick?"

"Yes, Hippo. New Brunswick."

"How come I never heard of that?"

"There's a lot of stigma attached to leprosy. More so in those days. Many said lepers brought the disease on themselves through sin or lack of cleanliness. Entire families were shunned. People were reluctant to talk about it. When they did, they called it *la maladie*."

"When did this happen?"

"The first cases appeared around 1820. During the next two decades more and more people began showing symptoms, at first within families, later among neighbors. Seven died. Public health officials began to panic."

"No shit."

"Keep in mind, leprosy is one of the most feared of all diseases. It's been around for thousands of years, causes disfigurement, and, until the 1940s, had no known cure. Back then, no one even knew if leprosy was contagious."

"Is it?"

"Yes, but the mechanism is unclear. For many years, transmission was attributed to long-term contact between affected and healthy persons. Today, most researchers think the bacterium is spread through respiratory droplets. Like tuberculosis."

"So it *is* dangerous to be around lepers?"

"Leprosy is neither fatal nor highly infectious. It's a chronic condition communicable only to persons with a genetic predisposition, probably about five percent of the population. But that wasn't known in the nineteenth century."

"So they banished people?"

"In 1844, the New Brunswick government passed legislation mandating the isolation of anyone showing symptoms of leprosy. A board of health was named and authorized to visit, examine, and remove from their homes people suspected of being infected. Sheldrake was chosen because there were a few ramshackle buildings on the island."

"Like that place in Hawaii."

"Molokai. Yes. Only Sheldrake was worse. The sick were abandoned with little food, only crude shelter, and virtually no medical care. The colony existed for five years. Of the thirty-seven patients admitted, fifteen died and were buried on the island."

"What happened to the rest?"

"A handful escaped. One was a ten-year-old kid."

Barnabé Savoie. His story had almost made me cry. Terrified, the child had fled Sheldrake for the only haven he knew. Home. Barnabé was taken from his father at gunpoint, bound with ropes, and hauled back to the island.

"They put kids out there?"

"Many. Babies were born on Sheldrake."

"*Crétaque!* These escapees, they get caught?"

"Most were rounded up and returned to the island. After that, even worse restrictions were imposed. All the sick were confined to one building, boundaries were set around it, and time was limited for fresh air and exercise. An armed guard was hired to enforce the new regulations."

An image flashed in my head. Children with twisted features and rag-wrapped fingers. Coughing. Weeping for their mothers. I willed it away.

"What about the others, the ones that survived?"

"I'm not sure what happened to them. I'm going to do more research."

"What's this got to do with Gaston's skeleton?"

"The girl had leprosy."

I heard rattling. Pictured Hippo switching ears, considering the implications of my statement.

"You're saying the kid died a hundred and sixty years ago?"

"It looks that way."

"So that's the end of it."

"I know an archaeologist on faculty at UNB in Fredericton. Once the remains have been officially cleared for release, I can give her a call."

Something banged, then a voice called out in the background.

"Hold on."

The connection muffled as Hippo must have pressed the phone to his chest. When he reengaged, his voice was jazzed.

"You still there?"

"Yes."

"You won't believe this."

27

"Someone popped our favorite photographer."

"Cormier?"

"Body was spotted early this morning behind a warehouse near the Marché Atwater. Two slugs to the back of the head. Ryan just left the scene. Says Cormier was capped elsewhere, then dumped. Time line points to sometime after midnight."

"Jesus. Is he there?"

"Yeah. Hold on."

I heard rattling, then Ryan came on the line.

"Whole new twist," I said.

"Yeah."

"In all the uproar over the Anne Girardin exhumation, I forgot to tell you that I heard from Dr. Suskind."

"Uh-huh." I could tell Ryan was hardly listening.

"Suskind is the marine biologist at McGill. Her findings on the Lac des Deux Montagnes case are complicated."

"Summarize."

"She recovered diatoms from the outer bone surface, but not from the marrow cavity."

"Meaning?"

"Either the girl was dead when she hit the river, she drowned elsewhere in treated water, she drowned before April, she hyperventilated and died quickly, or Suskind's recovery technique was flawed."

"Terrific."

"Suskind did learn something useful. The diatom assemblages found on the sock best match a control sample collected at the bottom of a boat ramp in a park not far from where the body was snagged off L'Île-Bizard."

"Say that again."

I did.

"Could be where the vic went into the water," Ryan said.

"Or a spot the body hung up for a while. Anything further on the ID?"

"I floated an interagency query about female white-Indian or white-Asian teenaged MPs. Nothing yet."

"Any success locating Adelaide Girardin?"

"I'm running some leads. But right now Cormier's taking center stage. Hit fell to me because he's a player in the Phoebe Quincy disappearance."

"Have you told Phoebe's parents?"

"No. I'm really looking forward to that conversation. Cormier was all we had. But the good news is his murder gives us the thumb drive. All that subpoena crap is now history."

I started to speak, halted. Ryan picked up on my hesitation.

"What?"

"Your plate's already full."

"Tell me."

"It may be nothing."

"Let me decide."

"I mentioned it to Hippo, but thought maybe you'd want a heads-up, too."

"You plan to get to it sometime today?" Friendly enough.

I described the anonymous phone call at the lab, and the e-mail containing the photo and Death lyrics.

"Fernand Colbert hit a dead end tracing the call. He's not optimistic about the e-mail."

"You're thinking one of the two slugs who hassled you in Tracadie?"

"Who else could it be?"

"You have a way of irking people."

"I work on it."

"You're good."

"Thanks."

"Leave this to me."

"My hero."

Humor intended. Neither of us laughed. New topic.

"I've resolved the issue of Hippo's girl," I said, unconsciously using my nickname for the case.

"Hippo's girl?"

"The skeleton I ordered confiscated by the

coroner in Rimouski. The one that had upset Hippo's friend Gaston."

"Yeah?"

"The bones are probably old."

"Not your lost chum."

"No. When you have time, I'll fill you in. Or Hippo can."

"You two kiss and make up?"

"Hippo's not one to bear grudges."

"Unload, move on. Healthy."

"Yes."

Again, awkwardness hummed across the line.

"Tell Hippo I'll help with Cormier's files tomorrow."

"I'll let you know what I dig up on these Tracadie thugs."

He did. Sooner than I would have imagined possible.

Sunday morning, the long-promised rain finally arrived. I awoke to water streaking my bedroom windows, warping the courtyard and the city beyond. Wind tossed the branches of the tree outside, now and then mashed a leaf into the screening with a soft ticking sound.

While Harry slept, I set off for Cormier's studio.

As I drove across town, my wipers slapped a rubbery beat on the windshield. My thoughts kept time to the rhythm of the blades. *Cormier's dead. Cormier's dead. Cormier's dead.*

I didn't yet know the reason for the photographer's murder. Knew it wasn't good news.

Sliding to the curb on Rachel, I raised the hood on my sweatshirt and sprinted. The building's outer door was unlocked. The inner door was propped open with a rolled copy of *Le Journal de Montréal*. I assumed Hippo was already at work.

Brushing water from my hair, I crossed the dingy lobby. A sign hung on the door of Dr. Brigault's dental office. *Fermé*. Closed.

I started climbing toward the second floor. The storm made the stairwell seem darker, more menacing than on my previous visit. The erratic wind filled it with a hollow, ululating whine.

As I continued upward, the narrow passage grew dimmer and dimmer. I stopped, allowed my brain to take this in. What little light was penetrating was doing so from below.

I looked up. One bare bulb jutted from high in the wall. It was dark. Making the turn, I leaned over the railing and checked the bulb on the second floor. It, too, was dark.

Had the storm knocked out the power?

At that moment, I sensed movement above.

"Hippo?"

Nothing.

"That you, Hippo?"

Again, no response.

Senses on high alert, I climbed to the second-floor landing. The door to Cormier's flat was ajar. Relief. Of course. Hippo was in the rear, out of earshot of my voice.

Opening the door wide, I stepped into the flat. Shadows of wind-jostled things played on the walls. Branches. Phone lines. Against the backdrop of the storm, the air in the studio seemed eerie in its stillness. I started down the hallway.

At the kitchen, I felt the tiny hairs rise on my neck. The digits on the microwave were glowing green. The power was on. I wiped damp palms on my jeans. Why the dark corridor? Had someone unscrewed the bulbs?

Breathing carefully, I listened. Wind. Rain pounding the top of a window AC one floor up. My own pulse. Then another sound separated itself out. Rummaging. Impatient.

Moving as quietly as possible, I crept down the hall until I had a view through the open bathroom door. What I saw made me drop to a crouch, trembling fingers bracing on the wall.

A man stood with his back to me, feet spread. He was looking down, as though examining something in his hands. The man was not Hippo.

Every hair on my body joined those already upright on my neck.

Outside, the wind made a fierce lap of the building, rattling windows and sending a metal object winging the length of Rachel.

Inside, at my feet, a floorboard shrieked.

Cold adrenaline flooded my neurons. Without thinking, I half rose and scuttled backward. Too fast. My heel caught a torn edge of carpet. I went down with a thud.

From the bathroom I heard soles hitting linoleum. Footsteps.

My mind raced through options. Try to outrun

him? Lock myself in a bedroom and phone for help?

Did those doors have locks?

Bypassing the higher centers, my legs decided. Get out!

I bolted down the hall. Across the studio. Out the door. For a brief moment I heard nothing. Then feet pounded behind me.

I was at the first riser of the staircase when a truck barreled into my back. I felt my hair twisted. My head jerked backward.

The dead lightbulb whipped past my eyes. I smelled wet nylon. Oily skin.

Muscular arms pinned my elbows to my body. I struggled. The grip crushed me tighter.

I kicked back, made contact with a shin. Flexed my knee to kick again.

One side of the vise loosened. A blow clipped me hard to the temple.

My vision splintered into shards of white light.

Grunting, my assailant lifted. My feet left the carpet. He spun me and shoved.

Arms windmilling, I tumbled backward, head bouncing, vertebrae scraping the edge of step after step. I came to rest on the first-floor landing, cheek flat to the carpet.

I lay there, head pounding, lungs burning. Then, through the din in my ears, I heard a muffled bang. In the lobby below? Inside my head?

Seconds or hours later, I felt more than heard another bang. Footsteps climbed toward me, hitched, accelerated.

Through a fog, a tinny voice spoke.

I pushed myself upright. Leaned my shoulders to the wall. Fought to inhale.

I felt pressure on the back of my neck. Lowered my head. Compliant. A rag doll. My whole being focused on one desperate thought.

Breathe!

The mosquito voice whined again, words lost to the roaring in my ears.

Breathe!

A shape crouched beside me. A hand patted my shoulder.

Breathe!

Slowly, the spasm eased its grip on my lungs. I drew air. The droning in my eardrums began to fade.

"—Doc, you sick?" Hippo. Anxious.

I wagged my head.

"You want I should—"

"I'm OK," I choked out.

"You fall, or what?"

"Pushed."

"Someone shoved you?"

I nodded. Felt a tremor under my tongue. Swallowed.

"Where were you?"

"Cormier's studio."

"He still in there?"

"I don't think so. I don't know."

"Did you get a look at him?"

I probed my addled brain. The man's back had been to me. Then the attack had happened too quickly.

"No."

"I didn't see no one." Hippo's tone was hesitant. I knew he was torn between attending to me and dealing with my attacker.

Why had I been attacked? Was I recognized, targeted specifically? Or had I been incidental, an impediment blocking a getaway? Whose getaway?

I lifted both arms, indicating I wanted to get to my feet.

"Hold on."

Hippo dialed his cell, described what had happened, answered questions with a few crisp *oui*. When he clicked off our eyes met. We both knew. A patrol unit would come and cruise the street, canvass neighbors. With no witnesses, the odds of catching the guy were a notch north of zero.

I flapped my hands.

"Moses." Hippo arm-wrapped my waist and hoisted.

I rose, legs trembling.

"Gotta check upstairs," I said.

"Maybe you should let a doctor—"

Grasping the rail, I climbed to Cormier's studio. Hippo followed. Murky light oozed from a gap between the door and the jamb. Motioning me behind him, Hippo drew his weapon.

"Police!"

No response.

"Police!" Tension curdled Hippo's speech. *"On défonce."* We're coming in.

More silence.

Raising a "stay here" palm, Hippo kicked out. The door slammed inward and ricocheted. Elbowing it back, he moved forward, weapon gripped two-handed at the side of his nose.

I heard footsteps as Hippo moved through the flat. A minute later, he called out.

"Clear."

I entered.

"Here." Hippo's voice came from the bathroom in which I'd spotted the intruder.

I hurried down the hall and peered in. This time I took in details that had escaped my earlier quick glance.

The overhead pipes were concealed by a drop-ceiling arrangement of twelve-inch panels framed in thin metal strips. Several panels had been ripped free and tossed into the sink.

Hippo was standing on the commode, shining his flashlight into the newly created breach.

Anger overpowered the pain in my head. "How could someone just waltz in here?"

Hippo raised up onto his toes.

"The bastard knew exactly what he wanted. And exactly where to look," I ranted on, despite the fact that Hippo wasn't listening.

"Sonova—?"

Hippo handed me his light without looking down.

"What? Do you see something?"

Hippo reached forward into the gap. Sensitized to issues of balance and gravity, I positioned myself below him in case of a slip.

Hippo rolled back onto his heels. His hand dropped to me. I relieved it of one crumpled sheet.

A photo. I glanced at the subject.

My heart jacked into high.

28

I'd been expecting porn. Silicone-bloated women twisting in fake erotic joy. Or kneeling like cats with their bums in the air. I was ready for that.

Not for this.

The picture was a contact sheet. Sepia. Either old or made to look old. The paper was so creased and faded I couldn't be sure.

The sheet contained twelve frames lined up in four sets of three. Each frame showed a girl. Young. Thin. Naked. Perhaps owing to misuse of the flash, perhaps to an intentional trick of exposure, the girl's flesh glowed ghostly pale in the darkness around her.

In the first series of shots, the girl was seated, back rounded, shoulders turned slightly from the camera. Ropes bound her ankles and wrists.

In the next series, an additional rope had been added, coiling the girl's neck, then looping to a hook on the wall above her head. Cracks spiderwebbed the plaster where the hook had been nailed.

The final two series showed the girl on the floor, first supine, then prone. Ropes came and went in varying patterns of torture. Hands bound behind her back. Wrists bound to her ankles. Wrists bound and hoisted to the overhead hook.

In shot after shot the girl averted her gaze. Embarrassed? Frightened? Following orders?

Suddenly, I was rocked by a blow harsher than the one on the staircase. The room receded. I heard the dull pounding of blood in my ears.

The cheeks were more hollowed, the eyes more recessed. But I knew that face. That wild jumble of curls.

I closed my eyes, wanting to disconnect from the girl avoiding the lens. To pretend that the horror I was seeing had not taken place.

"That's it." Hippo's shoes hit the floor behind me. "Musta got missed when this mooncalf made his grab."

Had she agreed to be exploited in this way? Had she been forced?

"You gotta sit down, doc." Hippo was at my shoulder. "Bring some color to your cheeks."

"I know her." Barely audible.

I felt Hippo slip the sheet from my fingers.

"It's my friend," I whispered. "It's Évangéline."

"Yeah?" Dubious.

"She was fourteen when I last saw her on Pawleys Island. She's older in these photos, but not by much."

I felt a ripple of air as Hippo flipped the sheet. "No date. You're certain it's her?"

I nodded.

"Ciel des boss." Again, the air stirred.

I raised my lids, but didn't trust myself to speak.

Dragging his eyes from the girl, Hippo voiced my thought. "This maybe ties Cormier to Bastarache."

"You'll arrest him?"

"You bet your ass I'll arrest him. But not until I can nail—"

"Then do it!" Angry.

"Look, I want to take this sleaze down so bad it hurts." Hippo waved the contact sheet. "But this isn't enough."

"She's just a kid!"

"A low-rent photographer has dirty pictures of a kid that cleaned Bastarache's daddy's house thirty years ago? Hardly a smoking gun. Some pinstripe would have Bastarache walking before he needed to pee."

Between my headache, my anguish over Évangéline, my fury at Cormier, and my frustration that Hippo wouldn't collar Bastarache, I'm not sure how I got through the rest of that day. Adrenaline, I guess. And cold packs.

When I refused to go home, Hippo bought a bag of ice and a pair of socks. Every hour or so he'd mash a revamped compress to my cheek.

By five, we'd finished the last of Cormier's cabinets. Between us we'd uncovered only one file of interest.

Opale St-Hilaire's proofs showed a smiling adolescent with almond-shaped eyes and gleaming black hair. The envelope was dated April 2005.

Hippo and I agreed Opale looked Asian or First Nations, making her a candidate for the Lac des Deux Montagnes floater. Ryan's DOA number three. Hippo promised to check her out on Monday.

Though Hippo's ice therapy had minimized the swelling on my cheek, Harry spotted the bruise as I came through the doorway.

"I fell."

"Fell." Harry's eyes narrowed.

"Down some stairs."

"You just lost it and went ass over teakettle." When suspicious, Harry makes the inquisition priests look amateur.

"Some jerk clipped me on his way by."

Harry's eyes became slits. "Who?"

"The gentleman didn't stop to give me his card."

"Uh-huh."

"The incident is hardly worth mentioning."

"Some Hun sends you sailing into tomorrow and it's not worth mentioning?" Harry folded her arms. For a second I really thought she was going to tap one foot.

"The worst part was Hippo. He kept mashing ice-filled argyles into my face."

I smiled. Harry didn't.

"Any other *incidents* that are not worth mentioning?"

"All right. All right. I've had one odd phone call and one strange e-mail."

"Strange? As in threatening?"

I waggled a hand. Maybe yes. Maybe no.

"Tell me."

I did.

"You think it's this same goober that knocked you off your pins?"

"Doubtful."

A red manicured finger pointed at my chest. "I'll bet it's those weenies in Tracadie."

"Cheech and Chong? That's a stretch. Let's eat."

After leaving Cormier's studio, I'd gotten smoked meat sandwiches from Schwartz's deli on Saint-Laurent. Chez Schwartz Charcuterie hébraïque de Montréal. Cultural syncretism. A city specialty.

As we ate, I told Harry about the false ceiling and the contact sheet. Her reaction was an exaggerated replay of mine. How could Évangéline have done something so demeaning? I had no answer to that. Why would Cormier have the proofs? Nor to that. Why would someone break in to steal them? Or that.

To lighten the mood, I asked Harry what she'd done for the past two days. She described her visit to the Oratoire Saint-Joseph, and showed me the spoils of Saturday's shopping trip. Two silk blouses, a bustier, and a truly extraordinary pair of red leather pants.

After I cleared the table, Harry, Birdie, and I watched an old movie. An evil scientist was creating female robots genetically programmed to kill men over forty. Normally, the film would have

291

given rise to much laughter. That night there was little.

As we headed to our rooms, Harry surprised me by saying she'd made plans for the following day. No amount of cajoling could pry them from her.

"Well, stay out of deserted alleys and pay attention to what's around you," I told her. "Both the e-mail and the phone call made reference to you."

Harry gave a dismissive wave of her hand.

Ryan was flirting with Marcelle, the LSJML receptionist, when I stepped off the lab elevator Monday morning. On spotting me, Marcelle's brows shot to her hairline. I wasn't surprised. My bruise was now the size of Morocco.

Ryan trailed me from the lobby. In my office, he grasped my chin and swiveled my face from side to side. I batted down his hand.

"Hippo told you?"

"In Technicolor detail. Can you ID this peckerwood?"

"No."

"Anything strike you about him?"

"He'd make one badass linebacker."

Taking my shoulders, Ryan maneuvered me into my chair, unpocketed several mug shots, and tossed them on the blotter.

Goon. Goon. Cheech. Subgoon. Chong.

"Bachelors number three and five." My skin burned where Ryan's fingers had touched my face. I kept my eyes lowered.

Ryan tapped the goons I'd chosen. "Michael Mulally. Louis-François Babin."

"And the rest of the dream team?" I swept a hand over Ryan's lineup.

"Bastarache muscle."

"Have you seen the contact sheet from Cormier's hidey-hole?"

"Yes." Pause. "I'm sorry."

I studied Mulally's face. Scraggly hair framing dark-stubbled cheeks. Gangsta glare. Babin was shorter and more muscular, but otherwise a clone.

"The e-mail. The phone call. The staircase." Ryan leaned a haunch on my desk. "Give me your take."

"It would be pure speculation."

"Speculate."

"I've been poking around in Tracadie and talking to Bastarache's wife." A vision surfaced in my consciousness. Obéline's face outside the gazebo. I felt a cold heaviness in my chest. Kept talking. "I'm looking at Cormier. Cormier is hooked to Bastarache, but he doesn't think I know that. Bastarache dislikes my snooping, so he whistles up the dogs to chase me away."

"Why?"

"I'm chaseable."

Ryan's look said he wasn't amused.

"OK. Say Bastarache can't understand why I'd make a sudden visit to Tracadie, and make straight for Obéline. This concerns him. He tells Cheech and Chong to find out what I'm up to. Or to scare me off."

"Cheech and Chong?"

"Mulally and Babin. You've talked to them?"

"Not yet. But I'm familiar with their rap sheets. Impressive."

"Hippo says it's too early to arrest Bastarache."

"Hippo's right. We don't want to move until our case is airtight."

"You know his whereabouts?"

"We're on him."

Ryan studied his shoe. Cleared his throat.

"Call me Ishmael."

Surprised by his sudden swerve to game playing, and the pansy lob, I identified Ryan's quote. *"Moby-Dick."*

"The book's about?"

"A guy chasing a whale in a wooden boat." I smiled.

"The book's about obsession."

"Your point?"

"You're being a pit bull with this Évangéline thing. Maybe you should ease back."

The smile faded. "Ease back?"

"You're acting obsessively. If the sister was on the level, the kid died over thirty years ago."

"Or was murdered," I snapped. "Isn't that the point of cold case investigations?"

"Did you listen to what you said a few moments ago? Has it entered your thinking that Hippo may be justified in his concern for your safety?"

"Meaning?" I hate it when Ryan plays protector. I sensed him assuming the role, and it made me churlish.

"Obéline Bastarache is missing and presumed drowned. Cormier is definitely dead."

"I know that."

"Some asshole tried to take you out on a staircase yesterday. There's a good possibility it was Mulally or Babin."

"You suspect they sent the Death lyrics e-mail?"

"Everything I'm hearing says these clowns need instructions to use Velcro. The Internet may be beyond their learning curves."

"Then who?"

"I'm not sure." Ryan stood. "But I intend to find out. It's very likely that more people are involved. People you wouldn't recognize. So you ought not be setting yourself up as a target. Free for lunch?"

"What?"

"Lunch? Peanut butter and jelly? Tuna on rye?"

"Why?" Petulant.

"You gotta eat. After that, I know a good place to start asking questions."

Over the weekend, a thirty-eight-foot Catalina had been discovered at the bottom of the Ottawa River, near Wakefield, Quebec. Bones littered the sloop's V berth. The remains were believed to be those of Marie-Ève and Cyprien Dunning, a couple missing since setting sail in rough weather in 1984.

Following Ryan's departure, I spent the day with the boat bones.

At ten, Hippo phoned to say that Opale St-Hilaire was alive and well and living with her parents in Baie-D'Urfé. The St-Hilaires had scheduled a sitting with Cormier on the occasion of Opale's sixteenth birthday. They'd been satisfied with the experience.

At eleven, Ryan phoned to cancel lunch. No reason given.

At noon, Harry phoned while I was in the cafeteria. No message. I returned her call but got voice mail.

By four, I was outlining a preliminary report on the boat bones. One male. One female. All skeletal indicators pointed to Mr. and Mrs. Dunning.

Ryan phoned again at four thirty-five.

"Heading home?"

"Shortly."

"I'll meet you there."

"Why?"

"Thought I'd float Mulally and Babin past your caretaker."

"The pair that inquired about my condo. I'd totally forgotten."

I heard the flare of a match, then deep inhalation. When Ryan spoke again, his voice had changed subtly.

"I came down on you pretty hard this morning."

"Forget it. You're frustrated with your cold cases. With the Lac des Deux Montagnes and Phoebe Quincy investigations. I'm frustrated over Évangéline." I swallowed. "And you're concerned about Lily."

"She's doing her part. Sticking with the program."

"I'm really glad, Ryan."

"How's Katy?"

"Still in Chile."

"Pete?"

"Engaged."

"Seriously?"

"Seriously."

I heard Ryan draw smoke into his lungs. Exhale.

"It's hard to go back."

Lily to sobriety? Ryan to Lutetia? I didn't ask.

"Tempe—"

I waited out another long inhalation, unsure where this conversation was heading.

"I'd like to hear about Hippo's buddy's skeleton." Ryan's tone was all business again.

"Any time."

"Tonight?"

"Sure."

"Dinner?"

"I'll have to check with Harry."

"She's welcome to join us."

"Somehow, that invitation sounded deeply insincere."

"It was."

Whoa, something whispered from deep in my brain.

29

Ryan was sitting cross-legged on his Jeep when I turned onto my street. Sliding from the hood, he flicked a wave. I returned it. His image flashed in my rearview as I plunged into my underground garage. Faded jeans. Black polo. Shades.

A decade down the road and the man still gave me that jolt. For once, Harry's appraisal was perfect. Ryan was hot-damn good-looking.

All the way home I'd replayed our phone conversation. What was it Ryan had started to say? *Tempe, I'm the happiest man on the planet. Tempe, I miss you. Tempe, I have heartburn from the sausage at lunch.*

My neural factions squared off for their usual debate.

You were attacked. Ryan's looking for excuses to keep you in his sights.

You've been threatened before. Your safety is no longer Ryan's personal concern.

He wants to question Winston.
He could do that on his own.
He wants to know about Hippo's girl.
The Rimouski skeleton is not his case.
He's curious.
It's an excuse.
Those were his words.
His voice said otherwise.

After parking, I checked Winston's basement workshop. He was there. I explained what Ryan wanted. He agreed. I could tell he was curious about my bruised cheek. He could tell from my demeanor it was a bad idea to ask.

Ryan was in the outer vestibule when Winston and I arrived on the first floor. I buzzed him into the lobby.

"Nice shoes," I said of Ryan's red high-top sneakers.

"Thanks." Ryan looked at Winston. "Undercover."

Winston nodded knowingly.

I rolled my eyes.

"Dr. Brennan explained why I'm here?" Ryan.

"Yes." Winston, solemn as a mortician.

Ryan produced the mug shots of Mulally and Babin.

Winston stared at the faces, brows furrowed, upper teeth clamping his lower lip. After a few moments, his head wagged slowly.

"I don't know. I just don't know."

"Take your time," Ryan said.

Winston refocused, then shrugged both shoulders.

"Sorry, man. It was so hectic that day. These dudes bothering Dr. Brennan?"

Ryan pocketed the pictures. "If you see them again, do let me know." Grave.

"Absolutely." Graver.

Ryan dug a card from his wallet and handed it to Winston. "I feel better knowing you're here."

The men locked gazes, acknowledging responsibility for the womenfolk.

I'd have done another eye roll, but it would have bothered my head.

Ryan held out a hand. Winston shook it then left, a soldier with a mission.

"Undercover?" I snorted. "With whom? The Disney police?"

"I like these shoes."

"Let's see what Harry's doing." I headed toward my corridor.

Whatever my sister was doing, it required her presence elsewhere. A fridge note explained that she'd left and would return later in the week.

"Maybe she got bored," Ryan suggested.

"Then why come back?"

"Maybe something came up that needed her attention at home."

"She'd need a passport to go to Texas."

Ryan followed me to the guest room.

Clothes were everywhere. Scrambled in suitcases, heaped on the bed, draped on the chair back and over the open closet door. Relying on memory, I lifted sweaters from the desk and opened the top drawer.

Harry's passport lay among my old bills and receipts.

"She's gone somewhere in Canada," I said. "Oh God. She's probably cooking up another of her surprises."

"Or maybe she figured the little side trip wasn't worth mentioning."

Worth mentioning. The phrase triggered a worrisome thought.

"Yesterday, I told Harry about the phone call, the e-mail, and the guy on the stairs. She was incensed. Immediately fingered the pair in Tracadie."

"Mulally and Babin."

"Harry didn't know their names. You don't suppose she's gone to Tracadie?"

"That would be nuts."

We looked at each other. We both knew Harry.

"Harry's not convinced Obéline killed herself." My brain was starting to spin possibilities. "Actually, though I've never said so, neither am I. Obéline seemed content when we visited her. Maybe Harry's suspicions drove her to do some snooping on her own."

"While there, ferret out Mulally and Babin. Ream them. Kill two birds with one stone."

Even Harry wouldn't do something that stupid. Or would she? I searched my mind for alternative explanations.

"Last night we also discussed *Bones to Ashes*."

Ryan gave me a questioning look.

I told him about the book Harry had filched

301

from Obéline Bastarache's bedside table. And about Flan and Michael O'Connor's vanity press, O'Connor House.

"Harry thinks Évangéline wrote the poems. Maybe she's gone to Toronto to talk to Flan O'Connor."

Another thought.

"Harry found out that the print order for *Bones to Ashes* was placed by a woman named Virginie LeBlanc. LeBlanc used a post office box in Bathurst. Maybe Harry's gone to Bathurst."

"Not the easiest place to get to."

"Jesus, Ryan. What if she *has* gone to Tracadie?" Even to myself I was starting to sound a bit loony.

"Call her."

"What if—"

Ryan placed a hand on my arm. "Call your sister's cell phone."

"Of course. I'm an idiot."

I picked up the portable, punched Harry's number, and listened to clicks as the call was routed. In my right ear, a phone rang. In my left, Buddy Holly and the Crickets chirped "That'll Be the Day."

Ryan and I both looked at the chair.

Grabbing Harry's new red leather jeans, I dug through the pockets. And almost flinched when my fingers touched metal.

"She changed pants and forgot," I said, extracting Harry's sparkly pink cell.

"She's fine, Tempe."

"The last time Harry did this she wasn't so fine."
My voice cracked. "The last time she almost got
herself killed."

"Harry's a big girl. She'll be OK." Ryan opened
his arms. "Come here."

I didn't move.

Taking my hands, Ryan reeled me in. As though
by reflex, my arms went around him.

Frightening images played in my head,
memories of my sister's long-ago brush with
crazies. An ice-pelted windshield. The crack of
bullets.

Ryan made comforting noises. Patted my back.
My cheek nestled into his chest.

Harry drugged and helpless.

Ryan stroked my hair.

A puppet dance of bodies in a darkened house.

I closed my eyes. Tried to calm my overwrought
nerves.

I don't know how long we stood there. How long
it took for the pats to elongate into strokes. Grow
more languid. Morph into caresses.

Other memories slowly took over. Ryan in a tiny
Guatemalan *posada*. Ryan in my Charlotte bedroom. Ryan in the bedroom just beyond the wall.

I felt Ryan bury his nose in my hair. Inhale.
Mumble words.

Slowly, imperceptibly, the moment redefined
itself. Ryan's arms tightened. Mine responded.
Unconsciously, our bodies molded to each other.

I felt Ryan's heat. The familiar curve of his chest.
His hips.

I started to speak. To protest? Doubtful.

Ryan's hands slid to my throat. My face. He lifted my chin.

I realized I was still clutching Harry's mobile. I turned to place it on the desk.

Ryan twisted my hair in his fist, kissed me hard on the mouth. I kissed back.

Tossed the phone.

Our fingers groped for buttons and zippers.

The digits on my clock glowed 8:34. At some point I, or we, had migrated to my bed. Rolling to my back, I extended an arm.

Cold needles prickled my chest. I was alone.

The refrigerator door whooshed, then a drawer rattled.

Relieved, I grabbed a robe and hurried to the kitchen.

Ryan was fully dressed, holding a beer, staring off into space. Suddenly it struck me. He looked exhausted.

"Hey," I said.

Ryan started at my voice. "Hey."

Our eyes met. Ryan grinned a grin I couldn't interpret. Sadness? Nostalgia? Postcoitus languor?

"You good?" Ryan asked, extending an arm.

"I'm good."

"You look tense."

"I'm worried about Harry."

"If you want I can put out a few feelers, check airlines, trains, car rental agencies."

"No. Not yet. I—" I what? Overreacting? Being

cavalier? The anonymous call and e-mail had implied a threat to my sister as well as to me. "Harry's just so impulsive. I never know what she'll do."

"Come here."

I moved to Ryan. He hugged me.

"So," Ryan said.

"So," I repeated.

Awkward tension filled the kitchen. Birdie wandered in and broke it.

"Birdster!" Ryan squatted to deliver an ear scratch.

"Do you have to rush off?" I asked. To Lutetia? I meant.

"Is that a hint?"

"Not at all. If you're hungry I can throw something together. But I understand if you have to get back . . ."

Ryan's knee popped as he rose. "I'm starving."

I made my standard bare-cupboard meal. Linguine with clam sauce and a tossed salad. As we prepared the food and ate, I told Ryan what I'd found out about Hippo's girl. He listened, asked good questions.

"Leprosy. Like, clapper and bell, unclean, go away?"

"The bells were as much to attract charity as to warn people they were approaching the sick. By the way, it's now called Hansen's disease."

"Why?"

"*Mycobacterium leprae* was discovered by Hansen in 1873. It was the first bacterium identified as causing disease in man."

"Whatever the label, it's a bad trip."

"Leprosy actually exists in two forms, tuberculoid and lepromatous. The former is much milder, sometimes resulting in little more than depigmentation spots. Lepromatous leprosy is far more serious. Skin lesions, nodules, plaques, thickened dermis. In some cases the nasal mucosa becomes involved, resulting in chronic congestion and nosebleeds."

"Not to mention the little buggers cause your flesh to rot."

"That's actually a misconception. It's the body's attempt to rid itself of the bacterium that causes tissue destruction, excessive regeneration, and eventually mutilation, not the bacterium itself. More salad?"

"Bring it on."

I handed Ryan the bowl.

"I keep seeing that scene from *Ben Hur*."

I raised both brows.

"Ben Hur's mother and sister got leprosy so they had to live in a cave in a deserted quarry. The colony was fed by lowering food over the quarry rim."

"OK."

Ryan twirled and downed the last of his pasta. "Now that I think about it, I vaguely recall rumors of leprosy in the Maritimes. But it was always hush-hush. I think there was a leprosarium somewhere out there."

"Yes. Sheldrake Island."

"Nah." Ryan's forehead wrinkled in thought.

"This was a hospital. I'm thinking New Brunswick. Campbellton? Caraquet?" Ryan swallowed, then air-jabbed his fork in sudden realization. "I'll be damned. It was Tracadie. There was a lazaretto in Tracadie."

"The town of Tracadie? As in Évangéline? Obéline? Bastarache?" I was so shocked I sounded like a moron. Or a teacher calling roll.

"Trendy burg."

"No one ever heard of Tracadie. Now the place is in my face every time I turn around." I pushed back my chair. "Let's see what we can dig up online."

Ryan's eyes dropped to his plate. Sighing, he laid down his fork. I knew what was coming.

"Time to go?" I tried for cheery. Failed.

"I'm sorry, Tempe."

I shrugged, a false smile slapped on my face.

"I'd rather stay." Ryan's voice was very quiet.

"Then stay," I said.

"I wish it was that simple."

Ryan stood, touched my cheek, and was gone.

Hearing the door, Birdie lifted his head.

"What happened tonight, Bird?"

The cat yawned.

"Probably a bad move." I rose and gathered our plates. "But the nookie was great."

After showering, I logged onto the Internet and Googled the terms "leprosy" and "Tracadie."

Ryan's memory had been dead on.

30

I surfed long into that night, chasing loops into loops into loops. I explored the history of the Tracadie leprosarium, or lazaretto in local parlance. I read personal stories. Educated myself on the cause, classification, diagnosis, and treatment of leprosy. Worked through shifts in public policy concerning the disease.

With regard to Tracadie, I learned the following.

In 1849, after five years of staggering mortality, the New Brunswick board of health recognized the inhumanity of forced quarantine on Sheldrake Island. A site was chosen in a backwater called Tracadie, and meager funds were appropriated for the construction of a lazaretto.

The building was a two-story frame, upstairs for sleeping, downstairs for sitting and dining. Privies were out back. Small and basic, the new digs must have seemed lavish to the seventeen individuals who survived the island.

Though still imprisoned, the sick now had some lifelines to the outside world. Families were closer and could manage visits. Over the decades, doctors showed varying degrees of commitment. Charles-Marie LaBillois. James Nicholson. A. C. Smith. E. P. LaChapelle. Aldoria Robichaud. Priests came and went. Ferdinand-Edmond Gauvreau. Joseph-Auguste Babineau.

Despite better conditions, the number of deaths remained high in the early years. Moved by compassion, a Montreal-based nursing order, les Hospitalières de Saint-Joseph, volunteered to care for the sick. Arriving in 1868, the nuns never left.

I stared at grainy images of these brave sisters, somber in their stiff white wimples and long black veils. Alone, in the dark, I pronounced their musical names. Marie Julie Marguerite Crére. Eulalia Quesnel. Delphine Brault. Amanda Viger. Clémence Bonin. Philomène Fournier. I asked myself, Could I ever have been so selfless? Would I have had the fortitude to sacrifice and to such degree?

I pored over patient photos, scanned from the archives of the Musée historique de Tracadie. Two young girls, heads shaved, hands hidden under their armpits. A bushy-bearded man with a concave nose. A babushkaed granny with bandaged feet. Circa 1886, 1900, 1924. Fashions changed. Faces. The expressions of despair remained ever constant.

Eyewitness accounts were even more heartbreaking. In 1861, a lazaretto priest described a sufferer's appearance in the end stage of the disease: " . . . features are not but deep furrows, the lips are big running ulcers, the upper one greatly puffed and turned up towards the seat of the nose which has disappeared, the lower one hanging over the glossy chin."

The lives of these people were too painful to imagine. Despised by strangers. Feared by family and friends. Exiled to a living tomb. Dead among the living.

Now and then I had to leave the computer. Walk the rooms of my home. Brew tea. Take a break before I could continue.

And, always, my thoughts were plagued by the question of Harry. Where had she gone? Why didn't she phone? My inability to contact my sister made me feel restive and helpless.

The lazaretto was rebuilt three times. Repositioned slightly. Expanded. Improved.

Various treatments were attempted. A patent medicine called Fowle's Humor Cure. Chaulmoogra oil. Chaulmoogra oil with quinine or syrup of wild cherry. By injection. By capsule. Nothing worked.

Then, in 1943, Dr. Aldoria Robichaud visited Carville, Louisiana, site of a four-hundred-bed leprosarium. The Carville doctors were experimenting with sulfas.

On Robichaud's return, diasone treatment was introduced at Tracadie. I could envision the joy, the hope. For the first time a cure was possible. The postwar years saw more pharmaceutical breakthroughs. Dapsone. Rifampicin. Clofazimine. Multidrug therapies.

The final tally shows 327 souls treated for leprosy in New Brunswick. In addition to Canadians, the sick included patients from Scandinavia, China, Russia, Jamaica, and elsewhere.

Besides the fifteen corpses left on Sheldrake Island, 195 were buried in Tracadie, 94 in the founders' cemetery, 42 in the church cemetery, and 59 in the lepers' cemetery beside the final lazaretto.

Hippo's girl had come from Sheldrake Island. Thinking of her, I scanned the names of the dead. Some were pitifully young. Mary Savoy, seventeen. Marie Comeau, nineteen. Olivier Shearson, eighteen. Christopher Drysdale, fourteen. Romain Dorion, fifteen. I wondered, Did I have another young victim in my lab? A girl of sixteen who died an outcast?

My eyes drifted from my laptop to my cell. I willed it to ring. Call, Harry. Pick up a phone and dial. You must know that I'm worried. Even you can't be that inconsiderate.

The thing remained obstinately mute.

Why?

I left my desk, stretched. The clock said two-twelve. I knew I should sleep. Instead, I returned to the computer, horrified yet fascinated by what I was learning.

The lazaretto's last patients included two elderly women, Archange and Madame Perehudoff, and an ancient Chinese gentleman referred to as Hum.

All three had grown old in the facility. All three had lost touch with their families.

Though cured with diasone, neither Madame Perehudoff nor Hum ever chose to leave. Both died in 1964. Ironically, Archange never contracted leprosy, though her parents and seven siblings had had the disease. Admitted as a teen, Archange endured to become the lazaretto's final resident.

Down to one patient, the good sisters decided it was time to close shop. But Archange posed a problem. Having lived her whole life among lepers, she was unacceptable to any senior citizens' residence in town.

I didn't cry when I read that. But it was close.

After much searching, a place was found for Archange away from Tracadie. One hundred and sixteen years after opening, the lazaretto finally closed its doors.

The year was 1965.

I stared at the date, hearing yet another subliminal whisper.

As before, I struggled to bring the message to clarity. My exhausted brain refused to process fresh data.

A weight hit my lap. I jumped.

Birdie *brrrp-ed* and rubbed his head on my chin.

"Where's Harry, Bird?"

The cat *brrrp-ed* again.

"You're right."

Gathering the feline, I crawled into bed.

★ ★ ★

Harry was sitting on a carved wooden bench outside Obéline's gazebo, the totem pole casting zoomorphic shadows across her face. She was holding a scrapbook, insisting I look.

The page was black. I could see nothing.

Harry spoke words I couldn't make out. I went to turn the page, but my arm jerked wildly. I tried over and over, with the same spastic result.

Frustrated, I stared at my hand. I was wearing gloves with the fingers cut off. Nothing protruded from the holes.

I tried to wiggle my missing fingers. My arm jerked again.

The sky darkened and a piercing cry split the air. I looked up at the totem pole. The eagle's beak opened and the carved bird screeched again.

My lids dragged apart. Birdie was nudging my elbow. The phone was ringing.

Fumbling the handset to my ear, I clicked on.

"—lo."

Ryan made none of his usual sleeping-princess jokes. "They've cracked the code."

"What?" Still sluggish.

"Cormier's thumb drive. We're in. You available to scan faces?"

"Sure, but—"

"Need a ride?"

"I can drive." I checked the clock: 8:13.

"Time to make yourself useful, princess." The old Ryan.

"I've been up for hours." I looked at Bird. The cat looked back. Disapproving?

"Right."

"I was online until three-thirty."

"Learn much?"

"Yes."

"Surprised you could stay awake after such rigorous physical activity."

"Cooking pasta?"

Pause.

"You OK with last night?" Ryan's voice had gone serious.

"What happened last night?"

"Headquarters. ASAP."

Dial tone.

Fifty minutes later I entered a conference room on the fourth floor of Wilfrid-Derome. The small space contained one battered government-issue table and six battered government-issue chairs. A wall-mounted chalkboard. Vertical-slat blinds on one dingy window.

The table held a cardboard box, a phone, a rubber snake, a laptop, and a seventeen-inch monitor. Solange Lesieur was connecting the latter two pieces of equipment.

Ryan arrived as Lesieur and I were speculating on the provenance of the serpent. Hippo was two steps behind. Bearing coffee.

Seeing me, Hippo frowned.

"Brennan's good with faces," Ryan explained.

"Better than she is with advice?"

Lesieur spoke before I could think of a clever rejoinder. "No coffee for me."

"I brought extra," Hippo said.

Lesieur shook her head. "I'm already stoked."

"What's Harpo doing here?" Sideswiping the reptile, Hippo placed his tray on the table.

Lesieur and I exchanged glances. The snake's name was Harpo?

Everyone sat. While Lesieur booted the laptop, the rest of us stirred powdered cream and/or sugar into the opaque brown sludge in our Styrofoam cups. Hippo went with two packets of each.

"All set?"

Nods around.

Lesieur inserted Cormier's thumb drive. The PC *bong-bonged.*

"Cormier was security-conscious but amateur." Lesieur's fingers worked the keyboard. "Want to know his system?"

"Talk quick, this stuff is lethal." Ryan pounded a fist to his chest.

"Next time get your own freakin' coffee." Hippo flipped Ryan the bird.

Ryan fist-pounded his chest.

I recognized the jesting for what it was. Morgue humor. Everyone was on edge, jittery about the images we might soon see.

"The best passwords are alphanumeric," Lesieur began.

"Sheez." Hippo doing derisive. "It's the jargon not the coffee that's gonna take us out."

"An alphanumeric password is composed of both numbers and letters. The more random the combination, and the more characters included, the safer you are."

"Don't rely on your puppy's name backward," I said.

Lesieur continued as though no one had spoken.

"Cormier used an old trick. Pick a song or poem. Take the first letter of each word of the opening line. Bracket that string of letters with numbers, using the date of the password's creation, day at the front, month at the back."

The Windows screen opened and Lesieur entered a few more keystrokes.

"Generates a pretty good encryption chain, but a lot of us geeks are wise to the trick."

"A double-digit, multiletter, double-digit pattern," I guessed.

"Exactly."

Ryan was right. The coffee was undrinkable. Sleep-deprived as I was, I gave up trying.

"Working on the assumption that the password was created this year, I checked music charts, created letter sequences from the opening lines of the top fifteen songs for each of the fifty-two weeks, then ran combinations of all month-day number pairs with all-letter strings. Hit with the program's four hundred and seventy-fourth alphanumeric chain."

"Only four seventy-four?" Hippo's distaste for technology was evident in his sarcasm.

"I had to try both French and English."

"Lemme guess. Cormier was hot for Walter Ostanek."

Three blank looks.

"The polka king?"

The looks held.

"The Canadian Frank Yankovic?"

"You're into polka?" Ryan.

"Ostanek's good." Defensive.

No one disputed that.

"You should know him. He's your homeboy. Duparquet, Québec."

"Cormier used Richard Séguin," Lesieur said.

Hippo shrugged. "Séguin's good, too."

"The week of October twenty-ninth, Séguin's "Lettres ouvertes" charted at number thirteen in Montreal. He used the opening line of a song from that album."

"I'm impressed," I said. I was.

"A fourteen-character alphanumeric code will keep the average hacker out." Lesieur hit *Enter*. "But I'm not your average hacker."

The screen changed to black. On the upper right was a graphic showing old-fashioned spool film, below it a playlist offering a dozen untitled selections. Digits indicated the duration of each. Most ran between five and ten minutes.

"The thumb drive contains video files, some brief, some with running times of up to an hour. I've opened nothing, figuring you'd want the first look. I also figured you'd want to start with the shorter clips."

"Go." Ryan's tone was devoid of humor now.

"This is virgin territory, people." Lesieur double-clicked the first listing.

The quality was poor, the duration six minutes.
The scene showed things I never imagined possible.

31

The video had been shot with a single handheld camera. There was no sound.

The setting is a room done in roach-motel cheap. The side table is wood-grain plastic. The double bed is plaid-quilted. A shadow hairlines from a nail on the wall above the headboard.

Normally my mind would have played with that. What had been removed? Terrible mass-market art? A print of beer-drinking dogs playing cards? Something fingering the motel's name or location?

No speculation this time. All my senses were focused on the horror center stage.

A girl lies on the bed. She is pale and has cornsilk hair. Bows double-loop from the ends of her pigtails.

My breath stopped in my throat.

The girl is naked. She can be no more than eight years old.

Rising onto her elbows, the girl turns her face toward

something off camera. Her eyes sweep past the lens. The pupils are caverns, the gaze unfocused.

The girl lifts her chin, tracking someone's approach. A shadow crawls onto her body.

The girl shakes her head no and lowers her lids. A hand comes into frame and presses her chest. The girl drops back and closes her eyes. The shadow moves down her torso.

Opposing reflexes shot through my nerves.

Turn away!

Stay! Help the little girl!

I kept my eyes glued to the monitor.

A man moves into frame. His naked back is to the camera. His hair is black, bound at the nape of his neck. Ugly red zits speckle his buttocks. Around them, the skin is the color of pus.

My fingers sought each other, clenched hard. I felt dizzy, anticipating the nightmare that was about to play out.

The man takes the child's wrists and raises her frail little arms. Her nipples are dots on the curvy shadows defining her rib cage.

I looked down. My nails had carved crescents into the backs of my hands. Drawing two steadying breaths, I refocused on the monitor.

The girl has been turned. She lies prone, helpless and mute. The man has climbed onto the bed. He is on his knees. He moves to straddle her.

Shooting to my feet, I bolted from the room. No conscious thought. Limbic impulse straight to motor neurons.

Footsteps echoed mine. I didn't glance back.

In the lobby, I stood by a window, arms wrapping my chest. Needing reality to ground me. Skyline. Sunlight. Concrete. Traffic.

A hand touched my shoulder.

"You OK?" Ryan spoke softly.

I answered without turning to face him. "These bastards. These evil fucking perverted bastards."

Ryan didn't reply.

"For what? For their own depraved gratification? To so injure an innocent child to get their jollies? Or is it really for the gratification of the viewing audience? Are there so many sickos out there that there's a market for videos of such injurious depravity?"

"We'll get them."

"These degenerates pollute the world. They don't deserve to suck air from the planet."

"We'll get them." Ryan's tone reflected the loathing I was feeling.

A tear broke from my lid. I backhanded it from my cheek.

"Get who, Ryan? The scum who make this garbage? The pedophiles who pay to watch, collect, and swap it? The parents who pimp their children to pocket a few bucks? The predators who cruise Internet chat rooms hoping to make a contact?"

I whirled to face him.

"How many kids will we see on that drive? Alone. Frightened. Powerless. How many childhoods were destroyed?"

"Yes. These guys are moral mutants. But my job

321

is Phoebe Quincy, Kelly Sicard, Claudine Cloquet, and three girls found dead on my patch."

"It's Bastarache." Through clamped teeth. "I can feel it in my gut."

"Being a flesh peddler doesn't make him a kiddie porn dealer."

"This is Cormier's dirty little collection. Cormier had photos of Évangéline. Évangéline worked for Bastarache."

"Thirty years ago."

"Cormier—"

Ryan placed a finger on my lips.

"Bastarache may turn out to be dirty. Cormier may turn out to be a link. Or he may turn out to be just another twisted perv. Either way, everything on that drive goes to NCECC."

Ryan referred to Canada's National Child Exploitation Coordination Center.

"Right." Wanting to lash out. "What will they do?"

"They investigate this type of thing full-time. NCECC maintains a database of images of exploited children and has sophisticated programs for digital enhancement. They're developing ways to ID the pricks who download this trash from the Net."

"Annually, there are more investigations into auto theft than into child exploitation." Scornful.

"You know that's unfair. There are a whole lot more auto thefts to investigate. The guys at NCECC bust their butts to rescue these kids." Ryan flicked a hand at the conference room.

I said nothing, knowing he was right.

"My focus is here." Ryan's fingers curled. "Quincy. Sicard. Cloquet. The DOAs." His fist pumped the air for emphasis. "I won't quit until I close the file on every last one of them."

"Watching is pure agony." My words were almost inaudible. "I can't do a goddamn thing to help her."

"It's gut-wrenching. I know. I can hardly bear to stay with it. But I keep telling myself one thing. Spot something. A street name. A sign on a delivery truck. A logo on a bath towel. Spot something and you're one step closer to finding one kid. And wherever that one kid is, there will be others. Perhaps some of mine."

Ryan's eyes burned with an intensity I'd never seen before.

"OK," I said, drying my cheeks with my palms. "OK." I started back toward the conference room. "Let's spot one."

And that's exactly what happened.

The next three hours were some of the worst of my life.

Before leaving, Lesieur explained that Cormier had stored his collection in a series of digital folders. Some were titled. "Teen Dancers." "Kinders." "Aux privés d'amour." "Japonaise." Others were numbered or coded with letters. Every file bore the same date, probably the day of transfer to the thumb drive.

Hippo, Ryan, and I slogged our way through, folder by folder, video by video.

Not every clip was as horrific as the opener. Some showed overly made-up kids in sex-kitten lingerie. Others featured girls or adolescents awkwardly vamping, or mimicking strippers or pole dancers. A large number portrayed torture and full penetration.

Artistic skill and technical quality varied. Some videos looked old. Others appeared to have been shot recently. Some showed aptitude. Some were amateur.

The collection was formed around one common element. Every video featured one or more young females. A ghastly few involved toddlers.

Periodically, we took breaks. Drank coffee. Battled back revulsion. Refocused on the goal.

Each time, I checked my phone messages. No calls from Harry.

By noon nerves were frayed and the mood was tense.

I was opening a new folder when Hippo spoke.

"What the hell good's this doing? I say we slide this garbage to NCECC and get our asses back on the street."

The new folder was untitled. It contained eight files. I double-clicked the first and the video began loading.

"One familiar face." Ryan's fingers drummed the table. I could tell he wanted a cigarette. "One background detail."

"Yeah?" The rusty voice dripped irritation. "What's that give us?"

Ryan tipped his chair and thrust his feet onto the tabletop. "Right now, it's our best shot at a lead."

"Cormier was a perv. He's dead." Hippo took his zillionth antacid hit.

"He took photos of Quincy and Sicard." Ryan wasn't being goaded by Hippo's ill temper.

"Hell-o. The guy was a photographer."

Was Hippo being serious? Or playing devil's advocate?

"Cormier may lead us to Bastarache," I said. "Isn't it your life's dream to nail that bastard?"

The monitor went black, then a scene opened.

The camera is focused on a door.

"We've got nothing." Hippo shifted and vinyl popped.

"We've got the contact sheet."

"It's older than Astroturf."

"The *child* on that contact sheet was my friend. She worked in Bastarache's house."

"At the gray dawn of history."

"When she was murdered!"

"Let's concentrate." Ryan. Sharp.

A girl appears in the doorway, young, maybe fifteen or sixteen. She is in a low-cut halter-top evening gown. Black. Her hair is up. She is wearing too much lipstick.

The camera zooms in. The girl looks straight into the lens.

Beside me, I heard a sharp intake of breath.

The girl's eyes stare directly at us. She tilts her head, subtly raises one brow. Hints a smile.

"Mary mother of the sweet baby Jesus," Hippo exhaled.

Ryan yanked his feet from the table. His chair legs smacked the floor.

Reaching behind her neck, the girl unties the halter. The dress falls, but she catches it to her breast.

The room was absolutely still.

Bending at the waist, the girl opens her mouth. Her tongue circles her lips. The camera zooms in and her features fill the screen.

Ryan jabbed a finger. "Stop it there!"

I moved to the keyboard. Hit *Pause*. The frame froze.

We all stared at the face.

Ryan spoke the name.

"Kelly Sicard."

"Sicard posed for Cormier as Kitty Stanley," I said.

"Crétaque."

"The sonovabitch used his photography business to make contact with young girls." Ryan was thinking out loud. "Then piped them into the skin trade."

"Probably got a head fee every time he delivered a warm body." Hippo.

"Maybe. But pedophiles aren't like your regular criminals for profit. They don't play just for money. They play for product. It's an obsession."

"You think the little perv hooked up girls to grow his collection?"

I jumped in. "Cormier's motive doesn't matter. If we're going to find out what happened to Sicard, or Quincy, or any of his other victims, it's the buyer we need. The creep who's producing this filth."

Ryan and Hippo exchanged glances.

"Bastarache," I said. "It's got to be him."

Hippo ran a hand across his chin.

"Could be she's right. Bastarache makes his living in the skin trade. Massage parlors, strip joints, prostitution."

"It's a short hop into porn," I said. "Then kiddie porn."

"Bastarache is a flesh bandit," Ryan said. "But we've got nothing to tie him to this."

"The contact sheet," I said.

"He'll deny knowing anything about it," Ryan said.

"Even if he does, it's still kiddie porn."

Ryan shook his head. "It's too old."

"Évangéline worked for him."

"You're like an old record."

"What will it take?"

"A direct link."

Frustrated, I slumped into my chair and hit *Play*.

The camera zooms out. Sicard straightens, turns her back, playfully crooks one finger. Follow me.

The camera trails Sicard's languid stroll across the room.

Still holding the halter straps, Sicard lowers herself onto the mattress. Curls, catlike.

Watching, I wondered what dreams filled her head. Lighted runways? Glossy magazines and red carpet openings?

Sicard smiles conspiratorially. Allows one strap of the halter to fall. A man enters and moves to the bed. Sucking one finger, Sicard looks up and smiles. Rises to her knees, allowing the dress to slip to her waist.

It took until midafternoon. The folder was titled *Vintage*. The footage was old. Hairstyles and clothing in some scenes suggested the fifties and sixties.

Video file seven. The script was hardly original.

The girl is in her midteens, tall, with center-parted dark hair. She is wearing a black bustier, garter belt, and fish-net hose. She appears ill at ease.

The girl glances to her left. The camera follows as she crosses a room and sits on a bench below and to the right of a window. Again she looks to her left, as though seeking direction. Sunlight falls on her hair.

My eyes drifted to the window framing the girl. Scanned the drapes. The woodwork. The misty landscape beyond the glass.

It took a few moments to register.

Hitting *Pause,* I studied the screen. Studied the shape. The hazy contour below it.

Somewhere, a million miles away, voices were talking.

I hit *Play. Stop. Play.*

Rewound. Did it again. And again.

"I've got him." Calm, though my heart was in my throat.

The voices stopped.

"I've got the wife-beating sonovabitch."

32

Hippo and Ryan joined me.

"This video was shot at Bastarache's house in Tracadie." I pointed at the image frozen on the monitor. "You can see totem poles through the window."

Hippo leaned so close the toothpick jutting from his lips nearly grazed my cheek.

"Beside that funny-looking shed?"

"It's a gazebo."

"Why the tom-tom kitsch?"

"That's not the point."

Scowling, Hippo rolled the toothpick to the front of his mouth.

"You saw the poles and gazebo on Bastarache's property?" Ryan asked.

"In the backyard."

"You're sure?"

"Yes. I may have also seen the carved bench the girl's sitting on."

Straightening, Hippo pointed the toothpick at Ryan and spoke around it.

"Video's old."

"Kid's not."

"And she's getting her ta-tas immortalized in Bastarache's crib."

"She is."

"Enough to net him?"

"Enough for me."

"Probable cause?"

"I think a judge will buy it."

"I call Quebec City while you chase a warrant?"

Ryan nodded.

When Hippo left, Ryan turned to me.

"Good job, hawk eye."

"Thanks."

"You think you can stick with this a little while longer?" Ryan chin-cocked the monitor.

"Indubitably."

"Good word, that."

By four, Bastarache was in custody, and Ryan had warrants allowing searches of his apartment and bar in Quebec City. No go on Tracadie, since Bastarache wasn't living in that house.

Ryan found me in the conference room still plodding through smut. Other than the times I'd stopped to check my home, office, and cell phones for input from Harry, I'd taken no breaks.

"Bastarache's lawyer was at the jail before the door clanged shut. Outraged. Can you imagine?"

"Is he aware that his client is a child porn-ographer?"

"She. Isabelle Francoeur. According to Francoeur, Bastarache is about to be short-listed for the Order of Canada."

"Did he walk?"

"Francoeur's working on it. QC cops say they can hold him for twenty-four. Then it's charge him or kick him."

"What happens now?"

"Hippo paws through Bastarache's shorts while I engage him in verbal discourse."

"You're going to Quebec City?"

"Hippo's pulling the car around now."

"I want to go with you."

Ryan looked at me for a very long time, undoubt-edly sensing my hidden agenda.

"If your friends are mentioned it's because *I* bring them up."

I started to protest, thought better of it. "It's your bust."

"What are their names?"

"Évangéline and Obéline."

"You are strictly an observer."

"I'll observe my ass off."

Ten minutes later we were motoring northeast on Highway 40, paralleling the shore of the St. Lawrence River. Hippo was at the wheel. Ryan was riding shotgun. I was in back, lurching and bouncing and trying not to barf.

On the way, Ryan explained the plan. I could barely hear him over the sputtering static from the radio. At my request, Hippo turned it off.

The strategy. Ryan and I would go to la prison d'Orsainville, where Bastarache was being held. Hippo would continue on into the city to oversee the tossing of Bastarache's bar.

The drive from Montreal normally takes three hours. Hippo made it in a little over two. Throughout, I checked my phone. No Harry. I told myself she was always going AWOL. Nevertheless, my apprehension was growing. Why didn't she phone?

Ryan called ahead as we approached the city's outskirts. Hippo dropped us at the prison then gunned off. By the time we cleared security, Bastarache was already in an interrogation room. A guard stood by the door, looking like his feet hurt.

Perhaps I'd seen too many *Sopranos* episodes. I was expecting mode de mobster. Oiled hair. Gold chains. Steroid-swollen muscles. I got a beluga in polyester with small piggy eyes.

The room held the usual four chairs and a table. Ryan and I took seats on one side. Bastarache filled the other. I was surprised not to see Francoeur.

Ryan introduced himself, explained that he was SQ and that he'd come from Montreal.

The piggy eyes slid my way.

"Would you prefer to wait for your attorney?" Ryan asked, refusing to assuage Bastarache's curiosity. Good. Let him wonder about me.

"*Frippe-moi l'chu.*" Roughly translated from *chiac*, "kiss my ass." "I own lounges. I run 'em clean. When will you assholes figure that out?"

"You own strip bars."

"Last I checked, exotic dancing's still legal in this country. Every one of my girls is over eighteen." Bastarache spoke with a cadence similar to Hippo's.

"You sure of that?"

"I check IDs."

"One or two manage to slip under your radar?"

Bastarache crimped his lips tightly and breathed through his nose. It made a wheezing sound.

"Way under. Sweet sixteen. I wonder. She have the braces off yet?"

A flush crept north from Bastarache's collar. "The kid lied."

Ryan clucked and gave a short wag of his head. "Kids today."

"She wasn't complaining."

"You like the young stuff, Dave?"

"The kid swore she was twenty-three."

"Age-appropriate for a guy like you."

"Look, there's two kinds of women in this world. Those you slip it to and those you take home to Sunday dinner. This chick wasn't going to Grandmère's for pot roast, know what I'm saying?"

"You nailed the third type."

Bastarache tipped his head.

"Jail bait."

The flush spread upward to Bastarache's face. "Same old recycled bullshit. She said she was legal. What you want me to do, check her teeth?"

"How about hooking? That legal?"

"A girl leaves the bar, we got no control over her personal life."

Ryan responded with silence, knowing most

interviewees feel compelled to fill it. Bastarache wasn't one of them.

"We've got some girls missing down our way," Ryan continued. "Some dead ones. You know anything about that?"

"Got no ties to Montreal."

Ryan used another interrogation trick I'd seen him employ. Sudden switch of topic.

"You like movies, Dave?"

"What?"

"Lights! Camera! Action!"

"What the hell are you talking about?"

"Let me guess. You decided to branch out. Go Hollywood."

Bastarache's hands were resting on the table, fingers interlaced like short, fat sausages. At Ryan's question, the sausages tightened.

"Bare tit on a pole. That's pretty low-rent action."

Bastarache glowered mutely.

"Motion pictures. That's the big time."

"You're goddamn crazy."

"Let's just say, for argument's sake, you got a kid eager to earn a few bucks. You propose a little poontang on camera. She goes along."

"What?"

"Am I going too fast for you, Dave?"

"What are we talking about here?"

"You know what I'm talking about."

"Porn flicks?"

"Of a very special genre."

"You lost me, pal."

Ryan's voice turned glacial. "I'm talking kiddie porn, Dave. Children."

Bastarache disengaged his hands and slapped them down on the table. "I. Don't. Mess. With. Kids."

The guard poked his head into the room. "We good here?"

"Jim dandy," Ryan said.

While Bastarache locked glares with Ryan, I observed him covertly. The rolls in his neck and stomach looked hard and his arms were corded with muscle. The guy wasn't the lardo I'd first taken him for.

Never breaking eye contact with Bastarache, Ryan reached into a pocket and withdrew one of several stills I'd printed from the video in Cormier's *Vintage* folder. Wordlessly, he slid the print across the table.

Bastarache looked down at the girl on the bench. I watched his body language. Saw no tensing.

"You check this little girl's ID?" Ryan asked.

"I never laid eyes on her."

"What's her name?"

"I told you." The piggy eyes rolled up. "I never met the young lady."

"You know a photographer named Stanislas Cormier?"

"Sorry." Bastarache started running a thumbnail through a scratch on the tabletop.

Ryan pointed at the print. "Got this from Cormier's computer. Part of a nasty little video. Drive holds quite a collection."

"The world's full of degenerates."

"That your house?"

The thumbnail froze. "What the fuck are you talking about?"

"Nice landscaping."

Bastarache squinted at the print, then flicked it toward Ryan with one meaty finger.

"What if it is? I was barely out of high school when this kid was playing Indian princess."

A tiny bell pinged in my head. What was wrong there? I set it aside until later.

One by one, Ryan laid out the photos of Phoebe Quincy, Kelly Sicard, Claudine Cloquet, and the facial reconstruction of the girl from the Rivière des Mille Îles. Bastarache barely glanced at the faces.

"Sorry, pal. Wish I could help you."

Ryan added autopsy shots of the Lac des Deux Montagnes floater and the girl from the Dorval shoreline.

"Jesus friggin' Christ." Bastarache blinked, but didn't look away.

Ryan tapped the photos of Quincy and Sicard. "These girls also appear in Cormier's collection." Not exactly true for Quincy, but close enough. "They have now vanished. I want to know why."

"I'll say it one more time. I don't know shit about porn flicks or missing kids."

Bastarache glanced up at the ceiling. Seeking composure? Clever answers? When his face came down it was devoid of expression.

"You employ a pair of cretins named Babin and Mulally?" Ryan pulled another topical switch.

"I am now going to await the arrival of counsel. Much as I'm enjoying this, it's time I roll outta here. Got a business to run."

Ryan leaned back and folded his arms.

"You surprise me, Dave. Sensitive guy like you. I figured you'd still be in mourning for your wife."

Was it my imagination, or did Bastarache tense at Ryan's reference to Obéline?

"But then, hell, it's been almost a week."

Two beefy palms came up. "Don't get me wrong. I'm not the coldhearted bastard you think I am. I feel it. But my wife's passing was no shocker. The woman's been suicidal for years."

"That why you had to tune her up now and then? To reinvigorate her zest for life?"

Bastarache drilled Ryan with a porcine stare. Relaced his fingers. "My lawyer will have me out of here before you hit the on-ramp to the forty."

I looked at Ryan, willing him to confront Bastarache with the contact sheet of Évangéline. He didn't.

"Your lawyer has plenty of time." Ryan held Bastarache's stare. "CSU's at your place right now. When I leave here, I'll be helping them take your life apart, nail by nail."

"Fuck you."

"No, Dave." Ryan spoke with a voice of pure steel. "We find one name, one phone number, one snapshot of a kid in a two-piece swimsuit, you'll be so fucked you'll wish your parents had decided on celibacy."

337

Shoving back his chair, Ryan rose. I followed. We were at the door when Bastarache barked, "You haven't a clue what's going on."

We both stopped and turned.

"How 'bout you tell me, then," Ryan said.

"These girls call themselves performance artists. Every single one's got dreams of being the next Madonna." Bastarache shook his head. "Artists, my ass. They're vipers. You block 'em, they'll take you off at the dick."

Though I'd promised to remain mute, the man was so repugnant I couldn't hold myself back.

"How about Évangéline Landry? She ask to appear in one of your dirty little films?"

The sausage fingers went so tight the knuckles bulged yellow-white. Again, the lips crimped. After several wheezy nasal intakes, Bastarache replied to Ryan, "You're way off base."

"Really?" Loathing glazed my response.

Still Bastarache ignored me. "You're so far off base you might as well be in Botswana."

"Where *should* we be looking, Mr. Bastarache?" I asked.

Finally, the response was directed at me.

"Not in my backyard, baby." A serpentine vein pumped the midline of Bastarache's forehead.

Ryan and I both turned our backs.

"Look in your own motherfucking backyard."

33

Quebec City is simply Québec to Quebeckers. It is the provincial capital. And oh-so-very-thoroughly *très* French.

The Vieux-Québec, the old quarter, is the only fortified town in North America up latitude from Mexico. The same zip code boasts the Château Frontenac, the Assemblée nationale, and the Musée national des beaux-arts. Hotel, parliament, and fine arts museum to us Anglophones. Quaint and cobbled, the Vieux-Québec is a world heritage site.

Bastarache's small corner of the *ville* definitely was not.

Located on a seedy street off Chemin Sainte-Foy, Le Passage Noir was a dive in a row of dives featuring women taking off their clothes. Short on charm, the neighborhood filled a niche in Quebec City's urban ecosystem. In addition to strippers flaunting T and A on runways, dealers hawked drugs on street corners, and hookers sold sex out of flophouses and taxis.

An SQ cop drove us to the address on Ryan's warrant. Hippo's car was at the curb along with a CSU van and a cruiser with Service de police de la Ville de Québec on its side panel.

When Ryan and I pushed through Le Passage's heavy wooden door, the air was thick with the smell of stale beer and dried sweat. The place was as small as a bar can be without becoming a kiosk. It was clear Bastarache didn't spend a lot on lighting.

A bar shot the center of the room. A crude platform spanned its rear wall. At stage right glowed a Rock-Ola jukebox straight out of the forties. At stage left was a pool table helter-skelter with balls and cues abandoned by hastily departing patrons.

A uniformed cop stood by the entrance, feet spread, thumbs hooking his belt. His badge said *C. Deschênes, SPVQ.*

A man slouched on one of the eight stools at the bar, heels catching one rung. He wore a white shirt, razor-creased black pants, and shined black loafers. Gold cuff links. Gold watch. Gold neck chain. No name tag. I assumed Mr. Sharp was the abruptly idled bartender.

A pair of women smoked and talked at one of a dozen tables facing the stage. Both wore shocking pink polyester kimonos.

A third woman sat apart from the others, smoking alone. Unlike her colleagues, she was dressed in street clothes. Shorts. Sequined tank. Roman sandals laced to her knees.

Otherwise, the place was empty.

While Ryan spoke to Deschênes, I scoped out the ladies.

The youngest was tall, maybe eighteen, with dull brown hair and tired blue eyes. Her companion was a thirty-something redhead who'd definitely put part of her salary into a boob job.

The lone smoker had fried platinum hair that wisped down past her ears. I put her age at somewhere around forty.

Hearing voices, or perhaps sensing my interest, the blonde flicked her eyes sideways in my direction. I smiled. She glanced away. The other women continued their conversation, uncurious.

"Bastarache has an office in back. Hippo's there." Ryan was speaking in hushed tones at my shoulder. "His digs are on the second floor. CSU's working that."

"Has the staff been questioned?" My gesture took in the women and the bartender.

"Bastarache is the boss. They're employees and know nothing. Oh. And the bartender says kiss his hairy French ass."

Again, the blonde's gaze slid to us, darted off.

"Mind if I speak to the talent?" I asked.

"Looking for new dance moves?"

"Can we lose the bartender and the kimono sisters?"

Ryan gave me a questioning look.

"I've got a feeling the blonde might be a talker if company's not present."

"I'll ask Deschênes to bring the others to me."

"OK. Now play along."

Before Ryan could respond, I stepped back and snapped, "Stop telling me what to do. I'm not stupid, you know."

Ryan got it. "Hard to tell most of the time," he said, loud and very condescending.

"May I *at least* have my pictures?" I held out a haughty palm.

"Suit yourself." Disgusted.

Ryan produced the envelope containing the prints, facial repros, and autopsy photos. Snatching it, I stomped across the room, yanked a chair, and threw myself down at a table.

The blonde had watched our "spat" with interest. Now her eyes were on the jar lid she was using as an ashtray.

After a brief exchange with Deschênes, Ryan disappeared through a rear door marked with a red electric *sortie* sign.

Deschênes collected the bartender, then crossed to the kimono twins. "Let's go, girls."

"Where?"

"I hear the joint's got a lovely green room."

"What about her?"

"Her turn's coming."

"Can we at least get dressed?" the redhead whined. "I'm freezing my ass."

"Occupational hazard," Deschênes said. "Let's go."

Reluctantly, the women followed Deschênes and the bartender through the same exit Ryan had used.

While appearing to act in a huff, I'd chosen a table near enough to allow conversation with the blonde, but far enough away that my move wouldn't look like an approach.

"Ass wipe," I muttered under my breath.

"The male sex is one long parade of ass wipes," the woman said, jamming her cigarette into the jar lid.

"That one is the grand marshall."

The woman made a chuckling noise in her throat.

I turned to face her. Up close I could see that her hair was dark down close to her scalp. Dried makeup caked the corners of her eyes and mouth.

"That's funny." The woman picked a speck of tobacco from her tongue and flicked it. "You a cop?"

"Now *that's* funny."

"Mr. Macho over there?"

I nodded. "Tough guy. Got a *big* badge."

"Officer Ass Wipe."

Now I chuckled. "Officer Ass Wipe. I like that."

"But not him."

"Jerk's supposed to be helping me."

The blonde didn't take the bait. I didn't push it.

Seemingly still fuming, I crossed my legs and began agitating one ankle.

The blonde lit another cigarette and inhaled deeply. Her fingers were nicotine yellow below fake pink nails.

We sat without talking for several minutes. She smoked. I tried to remember what I'd learned from Ryan about the art of interrogation.

I was about to take a chance when the blonde broke the silence.

"I been rousted so often I know the first name of every vice cop in town. Never encountered your Officer Ass Wipe."

"He's SQ, from Montreal."

"A bit off his patch."

"He's searching for some missing kids. One of them is my niece."

"These kids missing from here?"

"Maybe."

"If you're not on the job, why the tag-along privileges?"

"We've known each other a very long time."

"You doing him?"

"Not anymore," I said disdainfully.

"He give you that bruise?"

I shrugged.

The woman inhaled then blew smoke toward the ceiling in an inverted cone. I watched it drift and dissolve, backlit by neon over the bar.

"Your niece work here?" the blonde asked.

"She may have hooked up with the owner. Do you know him?"

"Hell, yeah, I know him. Worked for Mr. Bastarache off and on for twenty years. Mostly in Moncton."

"What's your take?"

"He pays OK. Doesn't let customers rough up his girls." Her lips pooched forward as she shook her head. "But I rarely see him."

That seemed odd with Bastarache living upstairs.

I filed the comment for future consideration.

"My niece may have gotten herself involved in something," I said.

"Everyone's involved in something, sunshine."

"Something more than dancing."

The blonde didn't respond.

I lowered my voice. "I think she was doing porn flicks."

"Gal's gotta earn a living."

"She was barely eighteen."

"What's this niece's name?"

"Kelly Sicard."

"What's yours?"

"Tempe."

"Céline." Again, the chuckling noise. "Not Dion, but not without flair of my own."

"Nice to meet you, Céline Not Dion."

"Ain't we a pair."

Céline sniffed, then backhanded her nose with a wrist. Reaching into my purse, I moved to her table and handed her a tissue.

"How long you been searching for this Kelly Sicard?"

"Almost ten years."

Céline looked at me as though I'd said Kelly had marched off to Gallipoli.

"The other kid's only been missing two weeks." I didn't mention Évangéline, who'd been missing over thirty years. "Her name is Phoebe Jane Quincy."

Céline took a very long drag, then the current butt joined the others in the lid.

345

"Phoebe is only thirteen. She disappeared while walking to dance class."

Céline's hand paused, then resumed mashing the butt. "You got a kid?"

"No," I said.

"Me neither." Céline stared at the jar lid, but I don't think she saw it. She was looking at a place and time far removed from the little table in Le Passage Noir. "Thirteen years old. I wanted to be a ballerina."

"This is Phoebe." I slipped a picture from Ryan's envelope and placed it on the table. "It's her seventh-grade class photo."

Céline considered the image. I watched for a reaction, but saw none.

"Cute kid." Céline cleared her throat and looked away.

"Ever see her here?" I asked.

"No." Céline continued gazing off into space.

I replaced Phoebe's photo with that of Kelly Sicard.

"How about her?"

This time there was a twitch in her lips and movement in her eyes. Nervously, she rubbed her nose with the back of a wrist.

"Céline?"

"I've seen her. But like you said, it was a long time ago."

I felt a ripple of excitement. "Here?"

Céline looked over her shoulder and around the bar.

"Mr. Bastarache has a place in Moncton. Le

Chat Rouge. This kid danced there. But not for long."

"Her name was Kelly Sicard?"

"Doesn't click."

"Kitty Stanley?"

A fake pink nail came up. "Yeah. That was it. She danced as Kitty Chaton. Cute, eh? Kitty Kitten."

"When was this?"

She gave a bitter smile. "Too long ago, sunshine."

"Do you know what happened to her?"

Céline tapped another cigarette from her pack. "Kitty hit the lottery. Married a regular and got out of the business."

"Do you recall the man's name?"

"It's not that kind of business."

"Can you remember anything about him?"

"He was short and had a skinny ass."

Céline lit up, idly waved the smoke from her face with one hand. "Wait. There is one thing. Everyone called him Bouquet Beaupré."

"Because?"

"He owned a flower shop in Sainte-Anne-de-Beaupré."

Céline's gaze was steady now, her mouth skewed with the hint of a grin. "Yeah. Kitty Kitten got out."

Looking at the woman, I felt an unexpected sadness. She'd been pretty once, might still be save for the overdone makeup and bleach.

"Thank you," I said.

"Kitty was a good kid." She flicked her ash to the floor.

"Céline," I said. "You could get out, too."

She shook her head slowly, eyes suggesting the abandonment of all illusion.

At that moment, Ryan appeared.

"Found something curious."

34

Céline and I followed Ryan through the illuminated *sortie* into a dim back hall. Deschênes watched our approach, heavy-lidded and bored. To his right was a small dressing room, door ajar. Through a smoky haze I could see the bartender and the kimono girls amid mirrors and makeup and sequined things that must have been costumes.

A faux-wood-paneled room was on the left. Hippo was in it sorting through papers at a desk.

Céline joined her coworkers. Ryan and I joined Hippo.

"Anything?" Ryan asked.

"Doesn't look like he's used this office for a while. Bills and receipts are all at least two years old."

"I got something."

Both men looked at me.

"The blond dancer, Céline, said Kelly Sicard worked at Bastarache's place in Moncton under the name Kitty Stanley. Billed herself as Kitty Chaton. Married a florist from Sainte-Anne-de-Beaupré."

"When?"

"Céline is a bit hazy on dates."

"Shouldn't be tough to track the guy down," Ryan said.

Hippo was already digging out his phone. "I'm on it."

A side door in the office gave onto stairs. Ryan and I climbed them into a loft-style flat.

The place was one big square with sleeping, eating, and living spaces demarcated by furniture groupings. The kitchen was separated by an island and bar stools. The parlor was a sofa-chair-lounger affair of chrome and black leather. The combo faced a flat-panel TV on a glass and steel stand. The boudoir consisted of a queen bed, a very large wooden desk, a side table, and a wardrobe. The area was bounded by an L of black metal filing cabinets. A corner bath was sectioned off with walls and a door.

Two CSU techs were doing what CSU techs do. Dusting for prints. Rifling closets. Looking for anything suspicious or illegal. It appeared they hadn't found much.

"I want you to listen to this."

Ryan led me to the desk and hit a button on the phone. A mechanical voice reported no new messages, thirty-three old ones, and admonished that the mailbox was full. Ryan hit "1" as instructed for old voice mail.

Twenty-nine callers had answered an ad about a Lexus. A woman had phoned twice to reschedule a housecleaning service. A man named Léon wanted Bastarache to go fishing.

The last voice was female, the French clearly *chiac*.

"It is not a good day. I need the prescription. Ob—"

The tape cut off.

"Was she saying Obéline?" Ryan asked.

"I think so." I felt totally jazzed. "Play it back."

Ryan did. Twice.

"It sounds like Obéline, but I can't be sure. Why didn't the jerk empty his mailbox?"

"Check this out," Ryan said. "The phone has caller ID. Unless blocked by the dialer, names or numbers are displayed, along with the time and date the connection was made. If blocked, the call comes up 'private number.'" Ryan began scrolling through the list, pausing on private-number records. "Notice the times and dates."

"A 'private number' phones at roughly seven each evening," I said.

"The truncated message was the last one to enter the mailbox. It came up 'private,' and was left at seven-oh-eight last night."

"Obéline may be alive," I said, realizing the implication. "And checking in every evening."

"Exactly. But why?"

"If it is Obéline, why the staged suicide?" I asked. "And where is she?"

"Shrewd questions, Dr. Brennan. We'll get a trace."

I noticed the CSU tech working the kitchen. "Are they finding anything to tie Bastarache to Quincy or Sicard? Or to Cormier?"

"Doesn't look like Bastarache spent much time living in this place."

"That jives. Céline said she hardly ever saw him. So where's he living?"

"The shrewdness never ends." Ryan smiled.

It slayed me. Ryan's smile always does.

I began to wander, opening closets, cupboards, and drawers already dusted for prints. Ryan was right. In addition to frozen shrimp and a carton of badly crystallized Ben & Jerry's, the refrigerator contained olives, clamato juice, a half-eaten jar of pickled herring, a dried-out lemon, and some fuzzy green chunks that were probably cheese. Save for aspirin, Gillette Foamy, and a Bic, the medicine cabinet was bare.

We'd been in the flat twenty minutes when Hippo bounded up the stairs.

"Got Sicard. Married name's Karine Pitre. Hubby's still hawking lilies and tulips in Sainte-Anne-de-Beaupré."

"Sonovabitch," Ryan said.

"She'll be at a café on Route 138 at eleven."

Ryan and I must have looked surprised.

"Lady's got kids. Prefers to discuss her good times in show biz away from the fam."

Le Café Sainte-Anne was a typical Quebec truck stop. Counter. Vinyl booths. Sun-faded curtains. Tired waitress. At that time of night the place was pretty much empty.

Though she was older, and the amber hair was short, Kelly was recognizable from her pictures. Same blue eyes and Brooke Shields brows. She was in a back booth, a half cup of hot chocolate on the table before her. She wasn't smiling.

Ryan flashed his badge. Kelly nodded without bothering to look.

Ryan and I sat. He began in French.

"A lot of people have been looking for you, Kelly."

"It's Karine now. Karine Pitre." She answered in English, barely above a whisper.

"We're not interested in jamming you up."

"Yeah? My past makes the papers, it won't be real easy setting up play dates."

"You know what they say about reaping and sowing."

"I was young and stupid. I've been out of that life for almost eight years. My daughters know nothing about it." As she spoke her eyes scanned the café. I could tell she was jumpy and on edge.

A waitress appeared at our table. Her name was Johanne. Ryan and I asked for coffee. Karine ordered another hot chocolate.

"I'll do my best to keep this discreet," Ryan said when Johanne had gone. "Our interest isn't in you."

Karine relaxed a little. "Then what?"

"David Bastarache."

"What about him?"

Ryan drilled her with the butane blues. "You tell us."

"Bastarache owns bars." Again, Karine's eyes ran the room. "I danced in one of them. Le Chat Rouge in Moncton. That's where I met my husband."

"When's the last time you saw Bastarache?"

"Sometime before I quit. It was cool. Mr. Bastarache didn't have any beef with me."

"That it, Karine? Just dirty dancing?"

Johanne returned and distributed mugs and spoons. Karine waited her out.

"I know what you're getting at. But turning tricks wasn't my thing. All I did was strip."

"Never flashed a little tit on film?"

Karine lifted her mug, set it down without drinking. I noticed a tremor in her hand.

"Tell us about Stanislas Cormier," Ryan said.

Karine's eyes crawled to me. "Who's she?"

"My partner. Stanislas Cormier?"

"You guys are thorough."

"Not as thorough as we could be."

"I was fifteen. I wanted to be a Spice Girl." She swirled her hot chocolate. "Wanted to live in Hollywood and appear in *People* magazine."

"Go on."

"I went to Cormier to have a composite made. You know, glamour-shot stuff. I'd read an article saying that was the way to break into acting and modeling. What did I know? During the shoot we got to talking. Cormier offered to hook me up with an agent."

"If you agreed to some questionable poses."

"It seemed harmless."

"Was it?"

She shook her head.

"Go on."

"It's hard to talk about."

"Try."

Karine's eyes stayed on her mug. "A man called about a week after my sitting, said he had a small part for me in a film called *Wamp Um*. I was so excited I nearly wet my drawers. Thought I'd found a ticket to freedom from my Nazi mother and father."

Karine shook her head sadly. Mourning what? I wondered. Her lost parents? Lost youth? Lost dreams of stardom?

"The man took me to a rat bag motel. I wore moccasins while a guy in a loincloth fucked me. I got fifty bucks."

"Bastarache."

Karine looked up, surprised. "No. Pierre."

"Last name?"

"He never said and I never asked." She swallowed. "Pierre said I had talent. Said if I gave him an exclusive he'd kick-start my acting career."

"You believed this Pierre would make you a star?" I tried to keep the incredulity from my voice.

"Cormier insisted Pierre was a high-powered agent. What did I know? He spoke the lingo. Claimed to know all the right people. I trusted him."

Behind us, Johanne clattered china.

"Go on," Ryan said.

"After a few weeks, Pierre said I had to move out

of my house. One night I told my parents I was going to study with friends. I went to a bar instead. When I left, Pierre picked me up and we drove to this big old house in the boonies. The place was a little run down, but better than what I was used to in Rosemère. A couple other girls were living there so it seemed OK. Pierre helped me cut and dye my hair. Said it made me look older. Image, you know."

I kept my hands and eyes very still.

"Took me six, maybe seven months to realize I'd been duped. When I tried to quit, the dickhead threatened me. Said if I talked to anyone or attempted to leave he'd see that I was seriously hurt and my face disfigured."

"How'd you finally break away?"

"Pierre's films all had goofy themes. *Nasty Nunnery. Sorority Sluthouse. Wiki Up.* He thought having a narrative gave his stuff class. That's what he called it, a narrative. His flicks were shit.

"We were in Moncton making a piece of crap called *Inside Acadians*. This other girl and I started hanging out in a bar on Highway 106 after the shoots. Le Chat Rouge. Mr. Bastarache was the owner, and he'd chat us up now and then. One night I had a lot to drink, started whining how unhappy I was. Next morning, Pierre tells me I'm off his payroll and working for Bastarache. Surprised the hell out of me."

"You didn't ask why you'd been fired?" Ryan.

"That was Pierre's style. One day a girl was his darling, the next she was gone. I didn't care. I was glad to be out of the porn."

"Did you know the police were searching for you in Montreal?"

"Not at first. By the time I found out, I thought it was too late. Pierre convinced me I'd be fined, then jailed when I couldn't pay. Pretty soon the media moved on to something else. I didn't see any point in putting myself out there."

"Here's the point."

Ryan curled his fingers in my direction. I gave him the envelope. He laid down photographs of Claudine Cloquet and the girl from the Dorval shoreline.

Karine glanced at the faces. "I don't know them."

Phoebe Jane Quincy joined the lineup.

"Dear God, she's only a few years older than my daughter."

Ryan added the facial reconstruction of the girl from the Rivière des Mille Îles.

Karine's hand flew to her mouth. "Oh no. No."

I didn't breathe. Didn't move a muscle.

"It's Claire Brideau."

"You knew her?"

"Claire was one of the kids living in Pierre's house. She was the one I hung with at Le Chat Rouge." Karine's nose had gone red and her chin was trembling. "She was with me that last night before I got sacked."

"Claire knew Bastarache?"

"It was usually Claire that he hit on. For some reason, that night he was talking to me." Her voice faltered. "Is she dead?"

"She was found floating facedown in 1999."

"Suffering Jesus!" Karine's chest heaved as she fought back tears. "Why the funny sketch? Was she messed up?"

I found the question odd. If Ryan shared my reaction, he didn't let on.

"She'd been floating awhile."

Karine's hands fumbled the latch on her purse.

"Where was Claire from?" Ryan asked.

"She never said." Pulling out a tissue, she dabbed her eyes.

"Claire made skin flicks for Pierre?"

Karine nodded, bunching the tissue in a fist below her nose.

"Do you know where Pierre is now?"

"I haven't seen or heard from him since 1999."

"Could you find his house if you had to?"

She shook her head. "It was too long ago. And I never drove. Never paid attention."

Dropping her forehead to the fist, she drew a long, ragged breath. I laid my hand gently on hers. Her shoulders trembled as tears slid down her cheeks.

Ryan caught my eye and tipped his head toward the door. I nodded. We'd gotten all we were going to get for now, and we knew where Karine Pitre could be found.

Ryan got up and crossed to the register.

"I never meant to make trouble." Gulped, as a sob rose up her throat. "I just wanted out. I believed no one would miss me."

"Your parents?" I asked.

358

Raising her head, she dabbed the wadded tissue from eye to eye. "We never got along."

"Perhaps they would like the chance to get along with their grandchildren." I made a move to slide from the booth.

Karine reached out and grabbed my wrist. "My husband doesn't know about the skin flicks."

I looked at her, unable to imagine what her life had been. What it was now.

"Maybe you should tell him," I said quietly.

Light flashed in her eyes. Fear? Defiance. Her grip tightened.

"Do you know who killed Claire?" she asked.

"You think someone killed her?"

Karine nodded, fingers clenched so tightly the tissue was a tiny white ball.

35

"What now?"

We were in Hippo's car, slipstreaming toward Le Passage Noir. It was past midnight; I was running on less than five hours' sleep, but I was pumped.

"I track Claire Brideau," Ryan said. "And a sleaze named Pierre."

"Cormier pimped Sicard to Pierre for his smut films. Pierre turned her over to Bastarache to strip in his bar. That ought to be enough to charge Batarache."

"Sicard wasn't a minor when she worked for Bastarache."

"She went from Cormier to Bastarache via this Pierre. Phoebe Quincy phoned Cormier. He's probably the one who took the Marilyn photo of her. That links Bastarache to Quincy, at least indirectly."

"Guilt by association." Ryan's terse answers were suggesting a marked disinterest in conversation.

Silence filled the small space around us. To occupy my mind I replayed the interview with Bastarache. What was it he'd said that bothered me?

Then it clicked.

"Ryan, do you remember Bastarache's comment when you showed him the picture of the girl on the bench?"

"He said he was barely out of high school when that kid was playing Indian princess."

"What's wrong about that?"

"It shows Bastarache for the coldhearted bastard he is."

"I printed that frame off the video. Today. Modern printer, modern paper. There isn't a single thing in that shot to indicate time frame."

Ryan glanced at me. "So what made Bastarache think the thing was decades old?"

"He knows what's going on. He knows who that girl is."

I noticed Ryan's knuckles tighten on the wheel.

"If charges aren't filed, Bastarache walks tomorrow."

"It takes evidence to file charges."

I slumped into my seat back, frustrated, knowing Ryan was right. The investigation had produced very little linking Bastarache to any of the missing or dead girls. Sure, Kelly Sicard had danced for him. And Claire Brideau had visited his bar years earlier. But a crown prosecutor would demand physical or much stronger circumstantial evidence. Nevertheless, Ryan's seeming depression surprised me.

"You should feel good, Ryan. Sicard's alive and we found her."

"Yeah. She's a peach."

"You plan to call her parents?"

"Not now."

"I have a feeling Kelly will make contact herself."

"Karine."

"Kelly. Kitty. Karine. You think she told us everything she knows?"

Ryan made a noise I couldn't interpret in the dark.

"My take is she opened up when asked, but volunteered little."

Ryan said nothing.

"She made an interesting comment as you were paying the bill."

"Thanks for the cocoa?"

"She thinks Brideau was murdered."

"By?"

"She didn't say."

"My money's on Plucky Pierre."

"He threatened her. But Bastarache used to hit on her."

I looked at Ryan, a silhouette, then a face slowly illuminated by oncoming lights. The face was steel-jawed.

"You've cleared two cases, Ryan. Cases that were stone-pony cold. Anne Girardin and Kelly Sicard. If Sicard is right, the Rivière des Mille Îles body will be ID'd as Claire Brideau. You're making progress."

"One alive, four dead, two still missing. Break out the sparklers."

A truck whooshed by. Trapped in its wash, the Impala rocked, settled.

Turning from Ryan, I pulled out my mobile and checked for messages.

Still nothing from Harry.

Rob Potter had called at 10:42. He'd analyzed the poetry and come to a conclusion. Though curious, I decided it was too late to phone him.

Leaning into the headrest, I closed my eyes. Thoughts ping-ponged in my brain as we barreled through the night.

Why didn't Harry phone? Sudden jolting images. The goon in Cormier's studio. The Death e-mail and the anonymous call. The pair snooping at my condo.

Cheech and Chong. Mulally and Babin.

What if Harry hadn't taken off on her own?

Don't go there, Brennan. Not yet. If Harry doesn't check in by tomorrow, ask Hippo or Ryan to get a bead on Mulally and Babin.

Was Obéline alive and in regular contact with Bastarache? Why? The man had broken her arm and set her on fire. If so, why the faked suicide?

What conclusion had Rob reached? Had all of the poetry been written by the same person? Was the author Évangéline? If so, had Obéline paid to have the collection published by O'Connor House? Why anonymously? Had Bastarache bullied her so relentlessly she'd felt the need for secrecy in all things?

Had Obéline actually witnessed Évangéline's murder? If so, who'd killed her? Bastarache was a young man at the time. Was he involved? How?

What had happened to Évangéline's body? Had she ended up in an unmarked grave like Hippo's girl, the skeleton from Sheldrake Island? Who was Hippo's girl? Would we ever know?

Had Bastarache killed Cormier? Had Pierre? Had one of them killed Claire Brideau? If so, why? Had one of them killed Claudine Cloquet? Phoebe Quincy? The girl who washed up on the Dorval shoreline? The girl found floating in Lac des Deux Montagnes?

Had those girls been murdered? Were Cloquet and Quincy dead? If not, where were they?

Too many ifs and whys.

And where the hell was Harry?

Hippo was smoking a Player's on the sidewalk when we pulled up at Le Passage Noir. Ryan bummed a match and lit up as I relayed our conversation with Kelly Sicard/Karine Pitre.

Hippo listened, chin rising and falling like a bobble-head doll.

"Went another round with the staff," Hippo said when I'd finished. "Cut 'em loose about an hour ago. Told 'em not to be planning any trips."

"Orsainville call?" Ryan asked.

Hippo nodded. "Bastarache's lawyer's been screaming bloody hell. Unless we find something that lets us charge this prick, they kick him at dawn."

Ryan dropped and heel-crushed his cigarette. "Then let's find something." Yanking the door, he strode into the bar.

While Ryan and Hippo plowed through Bastarache's files, I went to the Impala, got my laptop, and booted. The dial-up connection was excruciatingly slow. Launching my browser, I crawled through "porn producers," "porn makers," "porn companies," "sex film industry," etc., etc.

I discovered the Religious Alliance Against Pornography. Read articles about city attorneys and federal prosecutors pursuing court cases. Saw virtual lap dances, overdone orgasms, and boatloads of silicone. Learned the names of producers, performers, Web sites, and production companies.

I found no one calling himself Pierre.

By four-thirty I felt like I needed a shower. And antibiotics.

Closing the PC, I moved to the lounger, thinking I'd rest my eyes for five minutes. Across the room, I could hear Ryan and Hippo banging drawers, shuffling receipts and invoices.

Then I was arguing with Harry. She was insisting I put on moccasins. I was objecting.

"We'll be Pocahontas," she said.

"Dressing up is for kids," I said.

"We have to do it before we get sick."

"No one's getting sick."

"I'll have to leave."

"You can stay as long as you want."

"That's what you always say. But I've got the book."

I noticed Harry was clutching her scrapbook.

"You didn't see the part about Évangéline."

"I did," I said.

As I reached for the book, Harry swiveled. Over her shoulder I could see a child with long blond hair. Harry spoke to the child, but I couldn't make out her words.

Still holding the book, Harry walked toward the child. I tried to follow, but the moccasins kept sliding from my feet, tripping me.

Then I was peering into sunlight through an iron-barred window. All around me was darkness. Harry and the child were staring in at me. Only it wasn't a child. It was an old woman. Her cheeks were sunken, and her hair was a silver-white nimbus surrounding her head.

As I watched, rents appeared in the wrinkled skin around the woman's lips and under her eyes. Her nose opened into a ragged black hole.

A face began to materialize beneath the woman's face. Slowly, it took form. It was my mother's face. Her lips were trembling and tears glistened on her cheeks.

I reached out through the bars. My mother held up a hand. In it was a bunched wad of tissue.

"Come out of the hospital," my mother said.

"I don't know how," I said.

"You have to go to school."

"Bastarache didn't go to school," I said.

My mother tossed the tissue. It hit my shoulder. She threw another. And another.

I opened my eyes. Ryan was tapping my sleeve.

I went vertical so fast the recliner shot into full upright and locked.

366

"Bastarache will be out in an hour," Ryan said. "I'm going to tail him, see where he goes."

I looked at my watch. It was almost seven.

"You could stay here with Hippo. Or I could drop you at a motel, pick you—"

"Not a chance." I got to my feet. "Let's go."

As we drove, I dissected what I could recall of the dream. The content was standard fare, my brain doing a Fellini with recent events. I often wondered what critics might write of my nocturnal meanderings. *Surreal imagery with no clear demarcation between fantasy and reality.*

Tonight's offering was a typical retrospective from my subconscious. Harry and her scrapbook. Kelly Sicard's reference to moccasins. Her wadded tissue. Bastarache. The window bar imagery was undoubtedly thrown in by my id to portray frustration.

But my mother's appearance puzzled me. And why the reference to a hospital? And sickness? And who was the old woman?

I watched other cars pass, wondering how so many could be on the road so early. Were the drivers going to jobs? Delivering kids to early morning swim practice? Returning home after a long night serving burgers and fries?

Ryan pulled into a lot outside the prison's main entrance, parked, and leaned sideways against the door. He clearly wanted quiet, so I dropped back into my thoughts.

Minutes dragged by. Ten. Fifteen.

We'd been there a half hour when a dream-inspired synapse fired.

Mother. Hospital. Illness. Nineteen sixty-five.

The whisper I'd heard upon reading about the Tracadie lazaretto geysered into my forebrain. Connected with other disparate images and recollections.

I sat bolt upright. Sweet mother of God. Could that really be it?

In my gut, I knew I'd stumbled on the answer. Thirty-five years and I finally understood.

Instead of triumph, I felt only sadness.

"I know why Évangéline and Obéline disappeared," I said, excitement laying a buzz on my voice.

"Really?" Ryan sounded exhausted.

"Laurette Landry started bringing her daughters to Pawleys Island when she lost her hospital job and had to work double-time at a cannery and a motel. Évangéline and Obéline were yanked back to Tracadie when Laurette got sick."

"You've always known that."

"The girls started coming to the island in 1966, the first summer after the Tracadie lazaretto closed."

"Could be there was another hospital in Tracadie."

"I don't think so. I'll check old employment records, of course, but I'll bet Laurette Landry worked at the lazaretto."

Ryan glanced sideways at me, quickly back at the prison entrance.

"Évangéline told me her mother was a hospital employee for many years. If Laurette worked at the lazaretto, she'd have been in close contact with lepers. It's a fact she became ill with something that required daily nursing by Évangéline."

"Even if Laurette did contract leprosy, you're talking the sixties. Treatment has been available since the forties."

"Think of the stigma, Ryan. Whole families were shunned. People were forbidden to hire lepers or other members of their families if the person diagnosed was living at home. And it wasn't just personal lives that were ruined. The presence of the lazaretto had a devastating impact on the Tracadie economy. For years, no product would include the town name in its labeling. Public association with Tracadie often meant a business was ruined."

"That was decades ago."

"As Hippo says, the Acadian memory goes long and deep. The Landrys weren't educated people. Maybe they chose to hide her away. Maybe they distrusted government. Like Bastarache."

Ryan made one of his noncommittal sounds.

"Maybe Laurette was frightened of being quarantined in some lazaretto. Maybe she was determined to die at home and begged her family to keep her condition secret."

At that moment Ryan's cell phone sounded.

"Ryan."

My thoughts jumped from Laurette to Hippo's girl. Had the two actually died of the same disease?

"Got him."

Ryan's voice snapped me back to the present. I followed his sight line to the prison entrance.

Bastarache was walking in our direction. Beside him was a dark-haired woman in a dumpy gray suit. The woman carried a briefcase and gestured with one hand as she spoke. I assumed I was looking at local counsel Isabelle Francoeur.

Crossing the lot, Francoeur and Bastarache climbed into a black Mercedes. Still talking, Francoeur shifted into gear and drove off.

Ryan waited until the Mercedes had merged into traffic, then followed.

36

Ryan and I drove in silence. Rush hour was pumping, and I feared that taking my eyes from the Mercedes might allow our quarry to become lost in the sea of bumpers and taillights flowing south toward the city.

Ryan sensed my nervousness.

"Relax," he said. "I won't lose them."

"Maybe we should follow closer."

"They might spot us."

"We're in an unmarked car."

Ryan almost grinned. "This crate screams cop louder than a light and sound show."

"She's heading into town."

"Yes."

"Think she'll take him to Le Passage Noir?"

"I don't know."

"Then don't lose her."

"I won't."

We were on the outskirts of centre-ville when the Mercedes flashed a turn signal.

"She's going right," I said.

Ryan slid into the turning lane several cars back.

Two more signals. Two more turns. I watched, chewing the cuticle of my right thumb.

"Safe driver," I said.

"Makes my job easier."

"Just don't—"

"Lose her. I've thought of that."

The Mercedes made one more turn, then pulled over on Boulevard Lebourgneuf. Ryan continued past and slid to the curb a half block down. I watched in the side mirror while Ryan used the rearview.

Francoeur placed something on the dashboard, then she and Bastarache got out, crossed the sidewalk, and entered a gray stone building.

"Probably going to her office," I said.

"She stuck some sort of parking pass in the windshield," Ryan said. "If this is her office, she must have a regular spot. Why not use it?"

"Maybe it's a brief stop," I said.

Whatever Bastarache and Francoeur were up to, it lasted long enough for me to grow bored with surveillance. I watched office workers hurrying with lidded cups of Starbucks. A mother with a stroller. Two blue-haired punks with arm-tucked skateboards. A spray-painted busker carrying stilts.

The Impala grew hot and stuffy. I rolled down my window. City smells drifted in. Cement. Garbage. Salt and petrol off the river.

I was fighting drowsiness when Ryan cranked the ignition.

I looked toward the building Bastarache and Francoeur had entered. Our boy was coming through the door.

Bastarache pointed a remote at the Mercedes. The car *broop-brooped* and the lights flashed. Yanking the door, he threw himself behind the wheel and lurched into traffic. When the Mercedes passed us, Ryan let several cars go by, then followed.

Bastarache wound through surface streets onto Boulevard Sainte-Anne, seemingly unaware of our presence. His head kept bobbing, and I assumed he was playing with the radio or inserting a CD.

Several miles out of town, Bastarache turned right onto a bridge spanning the St. Lawrence River.

"He's going to Île d'Orléans," Ryan said.

"What's out there?" I asked.

"Farms, a few summer homes and B&Bs, a handful of tiny towns."

Bastarache cut across the island on Route Prévost then turned left onto Chemin Royal, a two-lane blacktop that skimmed the far shore. Out my window, the water glistened blue-gray in the early morning sun.

Traffic was light now, forcing Ryan to widen the gap between us and the Mercedes. Past the hamlet of Saint-Jean, Bastarache hooked a right and disappeared from view.

When Ryan rounded the corner, Bastarache was nowhere to be seen. Instead of commenting, I worked the cuticle. It was now an angry bright red.

As we rolled down the blacktop, my eyes swept the landscape. A vineyard spread from both shoulders. That was it. Vines for acres, heavy and green.

In a quarter mile the road ended at a T intersection. The river lay dead ahead, behind a trio of quintessentially Québécois homes. Gray stone walls, wood-beamed porches, high-pitched roofs, dormer windows up, window boxes down. The Mercedes was parked in a driveway beside the easternmost bungalow.

The river road continued to the left, but died ten yards to the right. Ryan drove to that end, made a one-eighty, and killed the engine.

"Now what?" I was saying that a lot lately.

"Now we watch."

"We're not going in?"

"First we get the lay of the land."

"Did you really say lay of the land?"

"We sit code six on the dirtbag skel." Ryan responded to my ribbing with even more TV cop lingo.

"You're a scream." I refused to ask what a code six was.

Forty minutes later, the door opened and the dirtbag skel hurried down the steps and crossed to the Mercedes. His hair was wet and he'd changed to an apricot shirt.

Glancing neither left nor right, Bastarache blasted backward down the drive, tires grinding up gravel. Ryan and I watched him gun up the blacktop toward Chemin Royal, leaving behind a ripple of dust.

Reaching into the glove compartment, Ryan withdrew a fanny pack. I knew its contents. Cuffs, extra clips, badge, and a Glock 9mm. Ryan used the thing when not wearing a jacket.

Yanking free his shirttails, Ryan strapped the pack on his belly and checked the string that would undo the zipper. Then he cranked the engine and we rolled.

At the bungalow, we got out of the Impala and scanned our surroundings. The only thing moving was a mangy brown spaniel sniffing roadkill twenty yards up the shoulder.

I looked at Ryan. He nodded. We beelined to the front door.

Ryan rang the bell with the index finger of his left hand. His right was subtly crooked, positioned over the Glock tucked in the pack.

Within seconds, a female voice spoke through the door.

"As-tu oublié quelque chose?" Have you forgotten something? Familiar "you."

"Police," Ryan called out.

There was a moment of silence, then, "You must wait until later."

A burst of adrenaline coursed through me. Though muffled, the voice was familiar.

"We want to ask you some questions."

The woman didn't reply.

Ryan hit the bell. Again. Again.

"Go away!"

Ryan opened his mouth to reply. I grabbed his arm. The muscles were taut as tree roots.

"Wait," I whispered.

Ryan's lips clamped shut, but his elbow stayed cocked.

"Obéline?" I said. "*C'est moi, Tempe.* Please let us come in."

The woman said something I couldn't hear. Seconds later, I caught a flicker of movement in my peripheral vision.

I turned. A pulled window shade was fluttering gently. Had it been raised when we approached the house? I couldn't remember.

"Obéline?"

Silence.

"Please, Obéline?"

Locks turned, the door opened, and Obéline's face appeared in the crack. As before, a scarf covered her head.

She surprised me by speaking English. "My husband will return soon. He will be angry if he finds you here."

"We thought you were dead. I was heartbroken. So was Harry."

"Please leave. I'm fine."

"Tell me what happened."

Her lips drew tightly together.

"Who staged a suicide?"

"All I want is to be left alone."

"I'm not going to do that, Obéline."

Her eyes jumped over my shoulder, toward the road leading to Chemin Royal.

"Detective Ryan and I will help you. We won't let him hurt you."

"You don't understand."

"Help me to understand."

Color rose in the unscarred skin, grotesquely marbling the right side of her face.

"I don't need to be rescued."

"I think you do."

"My husband is not a bad man."

"He may have killed people, Obéline. Young girls."

"It's not what you think."

"That's exactly what he said."

"Please go."

"Who broke your arm? Who torched your house?"

Her eyes darkened. "Why this obsession with me? You show up at my home. You reawaken pain best left dormant. Now you want to destroy my marriage. Why can't you just leave me in peace?"

I tried a Ryan quick-switch. "I know about Laurette."

"What?"

"The lazaretto. The leprosy."

Obéline looked as if I'd struck her. "Who told you this?"

"Who killed Évangéline?"

"I don't know." Almost desperate.

"Was it your husband?"

"No!" Her eyes darted like those of a hunted dove.

"He probably killed two little girls."

"Please. Please. Everything you think is wrong."

Relentless, I kept my glare aimed at her. Kept

hammering. "Claudine Cloquet? Phoebe Quincy? Have you heard those names?"

Reaching into my purse, I grabbed the envelope, yanked out the photos of Quincy and Cloquet, and thrust them at her.

"Look," I said. "Look at these faces. Their parents are in pain that never goes dormant."

She turned her head, but I forced the photos through the crack, keeping them in her field of vision.

Her eyes closed, then her shoulders seemed to turtle in on themselves. When she spoke again, her voice carried a tone of defeat.

"Wait." The door closed, a chain rattled, then the door reopened. "Come in."

Ryan and I entered a hallway lined on both sides with pictures of saints. Jude. Rose of Lima. Francis of Assisi. A guy with a staff and a dog.

Obéline led us past a dining room and library to a parlor with a wide-plank floor, heavy oak tables, a scuffed leather sofa, and overstuffed armchairs. One wall was floor-to-ceiling glass. A stone fireplace rose among the windows, partially blocking a spectacular view of the river.

"Please." Obéline gestured at the sofa.

Ryan and I sat.

Obéline remained standing, eyes on us, one gnarled hand to her mouth. I couldn't read her expression. Seconds passed. A solitary drop of sweat slid down her temple. The tactile input seemed to nudge her to action.

"Wait here." Whirling, she strode through the same archway we'd entered.

Ryan and I exchanged glances. I could tell he was wired.

Morning sun beat down on the glass. Though it was barely eleven, the room was cloyingly warm. I felt my shirt start to wilt.

A door opened, then footsteps clicked up the hall. Obéline reappeared leading a girl of about seventeen.

The pair crossed the room and stood before us.

I felt something balloon in my chest.

The girl stood less than five feet tall. She had pale skin, blue eyes, and thick black hair bobbed at her jawline. It was her smile that snagged and held my gaze. A smile flawed by a single imperfection.

Beside me, I felt Ryan go rigid.

The day had taken a radical turn.

37

I was still holding the photo of Claudine Cloquet. Ryan's MP number two. The twelve-year-old who had disappeared in 2002 while riding her bicycle in Saint-Lazare-Sud.

I looked from the girl to the image. Winter white skin. Black hair. Blue eyes. Narrow, pointed chin.

A row of white teeth marred by one rotated canine.

"This is Cecile," Obéline said, placing a hand on the girl's shoulder. "Cecile, say hello to our guests."

Ryan and I rose.

Cecile regarded me with open curiosity. "Are those earrings *authentiques*?"

"Real glass," I said, smiling.

"They're very sparkly. Sparkly-o."

"Would you like them?"

"No way!"

I removed the earrings and handed them to her.

She turned them in her palm, as awed as if they were the crown jewels.

"Cecile has been living with us for almost three years." Obéline's eyes were steady on mine.

"*Je fais la lessive,*" Cecile said. "*Et le ménage.*"

"You do laundry and cleaning. That must be a tremendous help."

She nodded too vigorously. "And I'm really good with plants. Good. Good-o."

"Are you?" I asked.

Cecile beamed a blinding smile. "My Christmas cactus got a thousand blooms." Her hands carved a large circle in the air.

"That's amazing," I said.

"*Oui.*" She giggled a little girl giggle. "Obéline's got none. Can I really keep the earrings?"

"Of course," I said.

"Please excuse us now," Obéline said.

Cecile shrugged one shoulder. "OK. I'm watching *The Simpsons,* but it keeps going fuzzy. Can you fix it?" She turned to me. "Homer is so funny." She gave the "so" several "o"s. "*Drôle. Drôle-o.*"

Obéline held up a finger to say her absence would be brief. Then she and Cecile hurried from the room.

"Claudine Cloquet," I said, keeping my voice low and steady. Ryan only nodded. His attention was focused on punching his cell.

"How the hell do you suppo—"

Ryan raised a silencing hand.

"Ryan here." He spoke into the phone.

"Bastarache has Cloquet at a residence on Île d'Orléans." There was a brief pause. "The kid's fine for now. But Bastarache is on the move."

Ryan provided a color, model, year, and plate number for the Mercedes. Then he gave the address and location of Obéline's house. His jaw muscles bunched as he listened to the party on the other end. "Let me know when he's netted. If he shows here, his ass is mine."

Ryan clicked off and began pacing the room.

"You think he'll come back?" I asked.

"She's expecting—"

Ryan froze. Our eyes met as, simultaneously, we became aware of a low droning, more a vibration of air than a sound. The droning built. Became the hum of a motor.

Ryan darted down the hall and into the dining room. I followed. Together, we stood to one side and peeked out a window.

A mirage car was cresting the blacktop running from Chemin Royal.

"Is it him?" I asked, whispering pointlessly.

Ryan pulled the fanny pack's zip string. Together we watched the hazy shape congeal into a black Mercedes.

Sudden realization.

"We parked at the curb," I hissed.

"Tabarnac!"

Ten football fields out, the Mercedes stopped, then abruptly reversed in a ragged U-turn.

Ryan sprinted into the hall, through the door, and down the drive. In seconds the Impala shot forward, back tires grinding up ground. I watched until it disappeared over the horizon.

"What is happening? Where has he gone?"

I swallowed and turned. Obéline was in the doorway.

"That girl's name isn't Cecile," I said. "It's Claudine. Claudine Cloquet."

She stared at me, fingers twisting her scarf as they had at the Tracadie gazebo.

"Your husband stole Claudine from her family. Probably forced her to get naked for his sordid little films. She was twelve, Obéline. Twelve years old."

"That's not how it was."

"I'm tired of hearing that," I snapped.

"Cecile is happy with us."

"Her name is Claudine."

"She's safe here."

"She was safe with her family."

"No. She wasn't."

"How could you know that?"

"Her father was a monster."

"Your husband is a monster."

"Please." Her voice was trembling. "Come in and sit down."

"So you can tell me that things aren't what they appear?" I was angry now, no longer trying to be nice.

"Claudine's father sold her into child pornography for five thousand dollars."

That brought me up short.

"To whom?"

"An evil man."

"What's his name?"

"I don't know." Her eyes dropped, came back. I suspected she was lying.

"When did this take place?"

"Five years ago."

The year Claudine went missing from Saint-Lazare-Sud. Five years after Kelly Sicard. Five years before Phoebe Jane Quincy.

Kelly Sicard. A sudden thought.

"Was this man's name Pierre?"

"I never knew."

I turned and looked out the window. The road was empty. The spaniel was now peeing on a post by the T intersection.

Time dragged by. Behind me, I heard Obéline take a chair at the table. The muffled voices of Homer and Marge Simpson floated from a TV somewhere deep in the house.

Finally, I turned back to her.

"How was your husband acquainted with this man who 'bought' Claudine?" I finger-hooked quotation marks around the word.

"He worked for David's father. A long time ago. Before we married."

"So strip joints weren't enough. Your husband partnered up with this sleaze to make kiddie porn."

"No." Vehement. "David hates this man. Occasionally they"—she broke off, cautious about word choice—"need each other."

"So Mr. Evil just handed Claudine over to your husband. What? She get too old for his market?"

Again, Obéline's eyes dived, recovered. "David gave him money."

"Of course. David Bastarache, rescuer of maidens."

I wasn't buying this, but Kelly Sicard's story of liberation from Pierre nagged at me.

I looked at my watch. Ryan had been gone almost twenty minutes.

"Where does this man operate?"

"I don't know."

At that moment my cell chirped. It was Ryan. Bastarache had managed to get onto the twenty and was heading west. Ryan was following, discreetly, hoping Bastarache would further incriminate himself. He'd be a while.

Great. I was carless in Quaintsville for God knew how long.

Feeling trapped, I jammed my phone into my purse. Before the flap settled, it rang again. The area code was unexpected. New York. Then I remembered. Rob Potter.

Eyes steady on Obéline, I flicked on.

"Hey, Rob."

"Do you love rock and roll!"

"Sorry I couldn't return your call last night." I was far too tired and cranky to be witty.

"No problem. You got a few minutes? I have some thoughts you might find interesting."

"Hang on."

Pressing the phone to my chest, I spoke to Obéline. "I need to take this alone."

"Where has that detective gone?"

"To arrest your husband."

She cringed as though I'd threatened to strike her.

"And you're stuck with me."

She rose.

"Don't go hitting your speed dial," I added. "Warning David could end up making you a widow."

Rigor stiff, she walked from the room.

I dug a pen and notepad from my purse. Then I hooked on my earpiece, laid the cell on the table, and resumed my conversation with Rob, glad for a diversion to pass the time.

"Shoot," I said.

"Long or short version?"

"Tell me enough to make me understand."

"Got the poetry there in front of you?"

"No."

Hearing the clatter of cookware, I assumed Obéline had gone to a kitchen not far from where I sat.

"No big deal. I'll review it. Now K is code for poems written by your gal pal back in the sixties, and Q refers to those contained in the *Bones to Ashes* collection."

"Known versus questioned," I guessed.

"Yes. Fortunately for the analysis, as I'll explain, both the K and Q poetry is written in English. Since your friend was a native French speaker."

I didn't interrupt.

"An interesting thing is that, even when people try to disguise their language, or mimic someone else's, a forensic linguist can often see below the surface to areas not under control of the speaker. For example, most people in the United States say they stand 'in line' at the post office. In New York, people say they stand 'on line.' American speakers, either from New York or elsewhere, don't seem to be aware of this. It's very distinctive, but beneath the level of most people's consciousness."

"So someone mimicking a New Yorker would have to know that. Or a New Yorker disguising his speech would have to be aware of that."

"Exactly. But typically folks are oblivious to these quirks. Grammatical differences can be even more subtle, to say nothing of pronunciation."

"Rob, we're dealing with written poetry."

"Written poetry draws on all levels of language. Differences in pronunciation might affect the rhyme scheme."

"Good point."

"Going back to words, and awareness, ever hear of the devil strip ransom note?"

"No."

"It was a case brought to my mentor, Roger Shuy. He looked at the thing, predicted the kidnapper was a well-educated man from Akron. Needless to say, the cops were skeptical. Write this down. It's short, and it'll help you understand what I did with your poems."

I scribbled what Rob dictated.

"Do you ever want to see your precious little girl again? Put $10,000 cash in a diaper bag. Put it in

the green trash kan on the devil strip at corner 18th and Carlson. Don't bring anybody along. No kops! Come alone! I'll be watching you all the time. Anyone with you, deal is off and dautter is dead!"

"One of the first things linguists look for is the underlying language. Is the person a native English speaker? If not, there may be mistaken cognates, words that look like they should mean the same in both languages but don't. Like 'gift' in German means 'poison' in English."

"*Embarazada* in Spanish." I'd made that mistake once in Puerto Rico. Instead of saying I was embarrassed, I'd said I was pregnant.

"Good one. Systematic misspellings can also show a foreign native language. Notice that in the note the writer misspelled 'kan' and 'kops' for 'can' and 'cops.' But not 'kash' for 'cash,' or 'korner' for 'corner.' So it probably wasn't that the writer was educated in a language where the *k* sound was always spelled *k* and never *c*. And over all, the note's pretty fluent."

"So the writer's an English speaker, not pregnant, who can't spell 'trash can.' How did Shuy know he was educated?"

"Keep looking at the spellings. He can't spell 'daughter' either, right?"

"Right. But he can spell 'precious.' And 'diaper.' And his punctuation is correct, not like someone's who can't spell 'cops.'"

"I knew you'd get this immediately. In essence, it's the same thing you do in your job. Look for

388

patterns that fit and don't fit. So if the perp can spell, why doesn't he?"

"To throw the cops off. Maybe in his community he's known as well educated. So instead of hiding his education, his attempt at concealing it sends up a flare. But what about Akron? Why not Cleveland? Or Cincinnati?"

"Read the note again. What words stand out?"

"'Devil strip.'"

"What's your word for the grass strip between the sidewalk and the road?"

I thought about it. "No idea."

"Most people haven't a word for it. Or if they do, it's a local one. County strip. Median strip."

"Devil strip," I guessed.

"But only in Akron. Not even in Toledo or Columbus. But no one's aware. Who ever talks about devil strips? You still with me?"

"Yes."

"So language varies by educational level and geographical region. You can also throw in age, gender, social group, and just about every other demographic feature imaginable."

"Language demonstrates what group you belong to."

"You've got it. So the first thing I tried with your poems was linguistic demographic profiling. What does the language tell about the writer? Then I used microanalytic techniques to discern in each set of poems an individualized language pattern, what we call an idiolect. Based on all this, I was able to do the authorship analysis you requested, and answer the question: Did the same person write both sets of poetry?"

"Did she?"

"Let me go on. This analysis was especially interesting, since the *K* poems were composed by a French native speaker writing in English. As any foreign language teacher knows, you try to speak a second language using the linguistic system you already know, your native tongue. Until you get good, your native language bleeds through into your acquired one."

I thought of my own use of French. "That's why we have accents. And funny sentence structure. And word choice."

"Exactly. For your analysis, as I worked through all the poems, when I spotted interesting passages, I put them up for split-screen comparison. On one side, I placed the poems as they are. On the other side, I altered the poems to reflect what a French speaker may have been trying to communicate in English, but failing because she was incorrectly translating from French, her first language, and using false cognates. If the overall coherence of the poem improved due to my changes, I took that as evidence the writer was perhaps Francophone. Do you want me to take you through some examples?"

"Bottom line."

"It's pretty obvious that both the *K* and *Q* poems were written by a native French speaker with limited formal schooling in English."

I felt a hum of excitement.

"Next, I looked for idiosyncratic rhetorical

390

devices common to both the *K* and the *Q* poetry, and any statistically significant skewing of vocabulary or grammar. You with me?"

"So far."

"Listen to these lines from a *K* poem:

"Late in the morning I'm walking in sunshine, awake and aware like
I have not been before. A warm glow envelops me and tells all around,
'Now I am love!' I can laugh at the univers for he is all mine."

The words rising from my past caused a constriction in my chest. I let Rob go on.

"Now listen to these lines from a *Q* poem:

"Lost in the univers, hiding in shadow, the woman, once young, looks
Into the mirror and watches young bones returning to dust.

"In both the *K* and the *Q*, the author meters in dactylic hexameter."

"The same device Longfellow used for 'Evangeline.' My friend loved that poem."

"Dactylic hexameter is common in epic poetry. So in itself the similar metering is not particularly meaningful. But of great interest is that throughout these two *K* and *Q* samples, similar *mistakes* appear consistently. And throughout both, the word 'universe' lacks the final *e*."

"*Univers.* The French spelling."

"*Oui.* Now let's go back to geography. Your friend was Acadian from New Brunswick. She spent time in the South Carolina Lowcountry. Listen to the title poem from the *Q* book, *Bones to Ashes.*"

"What am I listening for?"

"Regional dialect. This *Q* poem contains the motherlode."

Rob read slowly.

"Laughing, three maidens walk carelessly, making their way to the river.
Hiding behind a great hemlock, one smiles as others pass unknowing
Then with a jump and a cry and a laugh and a hug the girls put their
Surprise behind them. The party moves on through the forest primeval
In a bright summer they think lasts forever. But not the one ailing.
She travels alone and glides through the shadows; others can not see her.
Her hair the amber of late autumn oak leaves, eyes the pale purple of dayclean.
Mouth a red cherry. Cheeks ruby roses. Young bones going to ashes."

"Same metering," I said.

"What about vocabulary? You've spent time in New Brunswick and South Carolina?"

"The phrase 'forest primeval' is straight out of Longfellow."

"And refers to Acadia. At least in 'Evangeline.' What else?"

I looked at my jottings. "'Dayclean' is a Gullah term for dawn. And in the South, 'ailing' is colloquial for being ill."

"Exactly. So these two together point to South Carolina."

A poet with ties to Acadia and South Carolina. A poet influenced by Longfellow's "Evangeline." A Francophone writing in English. Talk about a linguistic fingerprint.

Sweet Jesus. Harry was right. *Bones to Ashes* was written by Évangéline.

A flash fire of anger seared through my brain. Another lie. Or at best an evasion. I couldn't wait to confront Obéline.

Rob spoke again.

His words sent ice roaring through my veins.

38

"Wait." I spoke when my lips could again form words. "Back up."

"OK. I said that a speaker's mother tongue often comes to the fore when he or she is under stress. Then you're more likely to use false cognates because emotion is boiling through your native language. It may happen in these lines because of the terrible feelings of viewers, because of the unimaginable yet real images on TV of burning victims leaping to their deaths."

"Read the lines again." It wasn't possible. Rob couldn't have said what I thought I'd heard.

Rob repeated what he'd read.

"I see the terror that comes from hate
Two towers fall while men debate
Oh where is God? Even brave people, chair,
*   blessed by fire,*
Jet to death!"

My heart was banging so hard I feared the sound would carry across the line. Rob continued talking, oblivious to the emotions raging inside me.

"'Chair, blessed by fire' isn't very coherent in English, but the medium is poetry, and in poetry the flow of information and the frames of reference elicited are expected to be murky and different than in everyday speech. Except in these lines it *is* almost everyday speech, at least in French. *Chair* is flesh. And *se jeter,* here the verb 'jet,' roughly means 'to throw yourself.' And *blesser* means 'to injure.' In French this verse means 'Oh where is God? Even brave people, flesh wounded by fire, throw themselves to their deaths!'"

"You're certain it's a reference to nine-eleven and the World Trade Center?" Impossibly calm.

"Has to be."

"And you have no doubt the poems in *Bones to Ashes* were written by my friend Évangéline."

"None. Can I finish explaining how I arrived at that conclusion?"

"I have to go now, Rob."

"There's more."

"I'll call you."

"You OK?"

I clicked off. I knew it was rude and ungrateful. Knew I would later send flowers or cognac. At that moment I didn't want more talk.

The poems were all by Évangéline, and some were recent.

Down the hall, a door opened. The argument between Homer and Marge grew louder.

At least one poem was written after September 2001.

The argument concerned a trip to Vermont. Homer wanted to drive. Marge preferred flying.

I sat motionless, paralyzed by the implications of Rob's findings.

Évangéline was alive in 2001. She had not been murdered decades ago.

Bart and Lisa joined the debate, advocating a motor-home holiday.

Obéline had lied about Évangéline dying in 1972. Why?

Was she truly mistaken? Of course not, she had the poems. She must have known approximately when they were written.

A murmured giggle augered into my musings. I looked up. The room was empty, but a shadow crossed the floor at the doorway.

"Cecile?" I called out softly.

"Can you tell where I am?"

"I think"—I paused, as if unsure—"you're in the closet."

"Nope." She hopped into the doorway.

"Where is Obéline?"

"Cooking something."

"You're bilingual, aren't you, sweetie?"

She looked confused.

"You speak both French and English."

"What does that mean?"

I took another tack.

"Can we chat, just you and me?"

"Oui." She joined me at the table.

"You like word games, don't you?"

She nodded.

"How does it work?"

"Say a word that describes things and I'll make it round."

"*Gros,*" I said, air-puffing my cheeks.

She screwed up her face. "You can't do that one."

"Why not?"

"Just can't."

"Explain it to me."

"Words make pictures inside my head." She stopped, frustrated with her inability to clarify. Or with my inability to understand.

"Go on," I encouraged.

"Some words look flat, and some words look crookedy." Scrunching her eyes, she demonstrated "flat" and "crookedy" with her hands. "Flat words you can make round by adding *o* at the end. I like those. You can't do that with crookedy words."

Clear as a peat bog.

I thought about my initial exchange with Claudine. The girl spoke a jumbled Franglais, seemingly unaware of the boundaries between French and English. I wondered what conceptual framework divided flat from crookedy words. "Sparkly" and *drôle* were obviously flat. *Gros* was crookedy.

"Fat." I tried my initial word in English.

The green eyes sparkled. "Fat-o."

"Happy."

She shook her head.

"Fort."

"Nooo. That one's crookedy, too."

"Fierce," I said, baring my teeth and curling my fingers in a mock monster threat.

"Fierce-o." Giggling, she mimicked my fierceness. Whatever semantic ordering her mind had created would remain forever a mystery to me. After a few more exchanges, I changed topics.

"Are you happy here, Cecile?"

"I guess." She tucked her hair behind her ears. Smiled. "But I like the other place, too. It has big birds on poles."

The house in Tracadie. She'd probably been there when Harry and I dropped in.

"Can you remember where you were before you lived with Obéline?"

The smile collapsed.

"Does thinking about that place make you sad?"

"I don't think about it."

"Can you describe it?"

She shook her head.

"Was someone mean to you?"

Claudine's sneaker made tiny squeaks as her knee jittered up and down.

"Was it a man?" Softly.

"He made me take off my clothes. And." The jittering intensified. "Do things. He was bad. Bad."

"Do you remember the man's name?"

"*Mal-o.* He was bad. It wasn't my fault."

"Of course it wasn't."

"But he gave me something cool. I kept it. Want to see?"

398

"Perhaps later—"

Ignoring my reply, Claudine shot from the room. In seconds she was back carrying a woven leather circle decorated with feathers and beads.

"It's magic. If you hang it over your bed you're sure to have good dreams. And—"

"Why are you harassing Cecile?"

Claudine and I both turned at the sound of Obéline's voice.

"We're having a chat," Claudine said.

"There are apples on the counter." Obéline never shifted her scowl from my face. "If you peel them we can make a pie."

"OK."

Twirling her dream catcher, Claudine stepped past Obéline and disappeared. In moments, the sound of singing drifted down the hall. *"Fendez le bois, chauffez le four. Dormez la belle, il n'est point jour."*

I translated the child's tune in my head. Chop the wood, heat the oven. Sleep, pretty one, it's not daytime yet.

"How dare you," Obéline hissed.

"No, Obéline. How dare *you*?"

"She has the mind of an eight-year-old child."

"Fine. Let's talk about children." My tone was polar. "Let's talk about your sister."

All color drained from her face.

"Where is she?"

"I've told you."

"You've told me lies!"

Slamming both palms on the table, I leapt to my

feet. My chair capsized and hit the floor like the crack of a gun.

"Évangéline wasn't murdered," I said, tone as hard as my expression. "At least she didn't die at sixteen."

"That's nonsense." Obéline's voice wavered like an audiotape that's been overplayed.

"Harry found *Bones to Ashes*, Obéline. I know Évangéline wrote those poems. Some of them as recently as 2001."

Her eyes darted past me to the window.

"I know about O'Connor House. I'm tracking the purchase order. I'll bet Virginie LeBlanc will turn out to be you or Évangéline."

"You stole from me." She spoke without bringing her eyes back to mine.

"I hate to break it to you, but what you and your husband have done is infinitely worse than pinching a book."

"You misjudge us, and make hurtful accusations that are untrue."

"What happened to Évangéline?"

"This is none of your business."

"Was that the reason? Business? What the hell, the kid works for Daddy. It's not in the job description, but I'll strip her, tie her with ropes, and take a few shots. She's young and poor, needs the work. She won't rat me out."

"That's not how it was."

I slapped the table so hard Obéline flinched. "Then tell me. How was it?"

She spun to face me.

"It was my father-in-law's business manager."

Tears wet the gnarled flesh. "He forced Évangéline to do it."

"Mr. Evil No Name." I wasn't buying it. If there was such a person, Obéline had to know who he was.

"David fired him the day of his father's death. I only found out about the pictures later."

"What happened to Évangéline?" I'd keep hammering the question as long as I had to.

She stared at me, lips trembling.

"What happened to Évangéline?"

"Why can't you leave well enough alone?"

"Well enough? Who's well enough? Évangéline?"

"Please."

"What happened to Évangéline?"

A sob rose from her throat.

"Did your husband kill her?"

"Don't be crazy. Why do you say this?"

"One of his henchmen?"

"David would never let anyone hurt her! He loves her!"

Obéline's hand flew to her mouth. Her eyes widened in horror.

As before, I felt a coldness spread through me.

"She's alive," I said quietly.

"No." Desperate. "David loves her memory. Her poetry. My sister was a beautiful person."

"Where is she?"

"*Bourreau!* Leave her alone."

"I'm the bully?"

"You will only cause her pain. You will only hurt her."

"Is she with this man?"

I remembered Obéline's words from earlier. How had she put it? David and this man needed each other.

"She won't want to see you."

"He's hiding her, isn't he?"

"Pour l'amour du bon Dieu!"

"What? Did hubby swap your sister for Claudine? Needed a newer model?"

Obéline's face tightened into a mask of fury. When she answered her voice had gone harder than mine.

"J'vas t'arracher le gorgoton!" I'll pull out your windpipe!

We locked glares, but I looked away first. Was I feeling a touch of uncertainty? A motor sound drifted in from outside. Grew louder. Stopped. Shortly, the front door opened. Closed. Footsteps ticked up the hall, then Ryan strode into the dining room.

"Ready to roll?"

"Definitely."

If my vehemence surprised Ryan, he didn't let on.

"What about Claudine?" I asked, scooping my notes and phone into my purse.

"Social Services is right behind me."

"Bastarache?"

"Handed him off to the Trois-Rivières SQ. They'll stay on him. Looks like he's heading to Montreal."

"Hippo?"

"Flying to Tracadie later today. Plans to squeeze

Mulally and Babin, check out some things that turned up in Bastarache's files."

I turned to Obéline.

"Last chance."

She offered nothing.

I put all the menace I could into my parting words.

"Mark this, Obéline. I won't stop until I find your sister. And I'll do everything I can to see that your husband is prosecuted for kidnapping, child exploitation, child endangerment, and anything else we can think to pin to his sorry ass."

Obéline spoke softly and with an air of sadness.

"I know you want to do good, Tempe, but you will cause harm instead. You will harm the people you are trying to protect and those who have helped them. Poor Cecile finds happiness here. Social Services will be a nightmare for her. And if you find Évangéline, it will cause her pain. May God bless you and forgive you."

The quiet force of Obéline's words pushed away my anger. I was pleading now.

"Please, Obéline, please tell me what I must know to bring the man who hurt Évangéline and Cecile to justice. Please do this."

"I can say no more," Obéline murmured, not raising her gaze to mine.

39

As we sped across Île d'Orléans I recounted my conversations with Claudine and Obéline.

"Double-barreled ambush." Ryan sounded impressed. "Your husband's a smut bandit. Your sister did bondage."

"Obéline claims David is innocent of all the things of which I suspect him, and, in fact, helped some of the girls. Remember our conversation with Kelly Sicard."

"Where does she lay the blame?"

"On a former employee of her father-in-law."

"Who?"

"She didn't know, or wouldn't reveal his name. Says David fired him in 1980. The fact is that someone murdered several girls and the only link we have is Bastarache. I can't ignore that."

Ryan veered onto an entrance ramp. There was a short descent, a deceleration, then the Impala lunged forward and we were on the twenty. I fell silent, allowing Ryan to focus on driving.

As we ate up asphalt, my thoughts meandered through the events of the past twenty-four hours. David Bastarache. Kelly Sicard. Claudine Cloquet. The sodden and bloated body that was Claire Brideau.

Harry. It was now Wednesday. I hadn't seen her since Sunday night. Hadn't heard from her since she called my mobile on Monday morning.

One image fragment bumper-rode the tail of another. Évangéline in ropes. A girl on a bench. Claudine, a walking tragedy. The mixed-race teenager dragged from Lac des Deux Montagnes.

Might Évangéline still be working in the porn industry? Might that be the secret Obéline was hiding?

Sound bytes replayed over and over. Sicard discussing the anonymous Pierre: *I wore moccasins while a guy in a loincloth fucked me.* Bastarache's troubling comment: *I was barely out of high school when this kid was playing Indian princess.*

I felt another shoulder-tap from my id.

Bastarache knew the bench-girl video had some years on it. The filming had been done in his house. The guy had to be dirty. Or did he? How old had he been then? What was his role in the Bastarache family business?

The tapping continued, insistent.

The human brain is, well, mind-blowing. Chemicals. Electricity. Fluid. Cytoplasm. Wire it up right and the thing works. No one really knows how.

But the brain's parts can be like governmental agencies, closing ranks to hoard their special knowledge. Cerebrum. Cerebellum. Frontal lobe. Motor cortex. Sometimes it takes a catalyst to get them to share.

My neurons had ingested, but not fully digested, a larder full of data in the last few days. Suddenly, something shifted. My lower brain contacted my upper. Why? Claudine Cloquet's dream catcher.

"What if Obéline is telling the truth?" I asked, sitting up straight. "What if our perv *is* the guy who worked for Bastarache's father?"

"Right."

"When Harry and I were in Tracadie, Obéline mentioned a former employee of her father-in-law. Said her husband fired him and the parting wasn't amicable."

Ryan didn't comment.

"This former employee designed the sweat house that was later converted to a gazebo. He was nuts into Native art. Carved benches. Totem poles." I paused for effect. "Kelly Sicard said Pierre forced her to wear moccasins. What was Bastarache's remark when you showed him the print of the girl on the bench?"

"The kid was playing Indian princess." Ryan was with me.

"There was nothing in that picture to suggest a Native American theme. And the videos Sicard listed. Think about the titles."

"*Wamp Um. Wiki Up.* Sonovabitch."

"Claudine had a dream catcher. Said she got it

from the man she lived with before Obéline. What if Cormier's 'agent' friend, Pierre, is the same guy Bastarache fired? The same guy who had Claudine?"

Ryan's knuckles tightened on the wheel. "So how does Bastarache fit in?"

"I'm not sure." I started tossing things out without really thinking. "Bastarache is a kid. He sees skin flicks being made in his home. He resents it, vows to pull the plug the minute the old man kicks."

Ryan rolled that around in his mind.

"What did Claudine call this creep?"

"She didn't know his name. Or wouldn't say it." I told him about the word-rounding game. "Claudine perceives adjectives as either flat or crooked. Flat ones she adds an *o* to, crooked ones she doesn't. It's not logical, just some aspect of her unique cognitive mapping. She just said the guy was bad. *Mal-o.*"

Ryan's eyes pinched in thought. Then he added another contender to my list of what-if's.

"What if *mal* is a crooked adjective? One that can't be rounded."

"So you can't add an *o*."

"Exactly."

I saw where Ryan was going. "What if it's a name? Malo." Neurons fired. "Pierre Malo."

Ryan was already reaching for his cell. I listened as he asked someone to run a check.

We were moving west with a sea of cars. I watched their tailpipes. Sunlight on their trunks and roofs. Chewed a cuticle.

We were an hour out of Quebec City when Ryan's mobile warbled.

"Ryan."

Pause.

"Où?" Where?

Pause.

"Shit!"

There was a final, shorter pause, then Ryan snapped the lid and tossed the phone to the dash.

"What?" I asked.

"They lost Bastarache."

"How?"

"Bastard pulled into a rest stop. Entered a restaurant. Never exited."

"He abandoned the Mercedes?"

Ryan nodded. "He was either picked up or hitched a ride."

I repeated Ryan's sentiment. "Shit."

Minutes later it was my phone.

I'd had virtually no sleep in the last forty-eight hours. I was running on doses of a cat nap and pure adrenaline. What happened next was my fault.

Checking the caller ID, I felt a rush of relief. Followed by annoyance.

Driven by the latter, I clicked on but said nothing.

"You there, big sister?"

"Yes." Frosty.

"You're peeved." Harry, the master of understatement. "Now, I know what you're going to say."

"Where the hell have you been?"

"Yessiree. That's it. I can explain."

"You needn't bother."

"I wanted to surprise you."

How often had I heard those words?

Ryan's cell warbled again. I heard him answer.

"Who's that?" Harry asked.

"What is it you want?"

"Before you go round the bend getting all pissy, let me tell you what I learned."

"How about telling me where you've been?"

"Toronto. Talked with Flan O'Connor. Scored some interesting info."

"Got something to write with?" Ryan asked, still holding the phone to his ear.

"Hold on," I said to Harry.

"Where are you?" she asked as I laid the phone on the dash.

I dug paper and pen from my purse.

"Thirteen Rustique."

I jotted the address Ryan was repeating.

As I finished, Harry's voice buzzed from my cell. I ignored her.

"Pierrefonds to Cherrier. Left about a mile after Montée de l'Église." Ryan looked a question at me. I read the directions aloud.

"Below the golf courses and nature preserve. Got it." Ryan clicked off.

"Pierre Malo lives outside Montreal?" I asked, scribbling the last bit of information.

Ryan nodded.

"Holy hell, Ryan. That's probably the house Kelly Sicard described."

"Good possibility."

"And remember how vehement Bastarache was when he told us to look in our own backyard?"

"I took it as his way of saying fuck off."

"Obéline said Malo and her husband had some sort of working arrangement. Said they needed each other. Think Bastarache could be going to hook up with Malo?"

"He was pointed toward Montreal."

I reread the directions.

"What nature preserve?"

"Bois-de-L'Île-Bizard."

I felt the wings of my throat constrict.

"The boat ramp!"

"What?" Ryan switched lanes to pass a Mini Cooper.

"Suskind's diatome analysis tied the Lac des Deux Montagnes body to the Bois-de-L'Île-Bizard boat ramp."

"You're sure?"

"Yes!"

"That ramp's practically in Malo's backyard." Ryan's jaw muscles bunched, relaxed.

A terrible thought. "If Malo somehow got Phoebe Quincy through Cormier, the same way he got Kelly Sicard, he could be holding her at that house."

A sharp whistle came from my cell.

I'd forgotten Harry was still on the line.

"Yo!"

I picked up my phone. "I've got to go."

"You really figured out who snatched that little girl?" Harry sounded as excited as I felt.

410

"I can't talk to you now."

"Look, I know you're mad. I was thoughtless. Let me do something to make amends."

"I'm going to hang up now."

"I want to help. Please. Wait. I know. I can go there and keep an eye on the place—"

"No!" It came out more of a shriek than I'd planned. Or not.

"I won't *do* anything."

"Absolutely not."

Ryan was throwing me questioning glances.

"I'm not stupid, Tempe. I won't go ringing this guy Malo's bell. I'll just keep him in my sights until you and Monsieur Marvelous land."

"Harry, listen to me." I forced calm into my voice. "Do not go anywhere near that house. This guy is deadly. He is no one to play around with."

"I'll make you proud, big sister."

I was listening to dead air.

"Holy mother of God!" I hit *Redial*.

"What?" Ryan asked.

"Harry's going to stake out Malo's place."

"Stop her."

Harry's phone rang and rang, then went to voice mail.

"She's not picking up. God, Ryan. If we're right about Malo, the guy's a monster. He'll kill Harry without breaking a sweat."

"Call her again."

I did. Voice mail.

"She'll never find Malo's place," Ryan said.

"She has GPS on her phone."

411

Ryan's eyes met mine.

"Reach in back and hand me that LED."

Unclasping my belt, I swiveled and lifted a portable strobe from the floor.

"Clip it onto your sun visor."

I secured the light with its Velcro straps.

"Plug the cord into the lighter."

I did.

Ryan flipped the high beams to alternating flash.

"Lower the visor and flick that switch."

I did. The LED started pulsating red.

Ryan hit the siren and mashed pedal to metal.

40

A siren and strobe will get you where you're going. Pronto.

Two hours after leaving Île d'Orléans, Ryan and I were closing in on Montreal. The return journey had definitely kept my attention. I rode with palms flat to the dash and side window, lurching and bouncing as Ryan accelerated and braked.

L'Île-Bizard lies northwest of Montreal, at the western tip of the town of Laval. Crossing onto the island, Ryan cut to the forty, diagonaled southwest through the city, then shot north on Boulevard Saint-Jean.

Off Pierrefonds, we winged right and rocketed across the *pont* Jacques-Bizard. At midbridge, Ryan killed the lights and siren.

Most of L'Île-Bizard is taken up by golf courses and the nature preserve, but a few neighborhoods straggle the periphery, some old, some new and so far upmarket the prices would never be broadcast.

Malo's street was just past a small tangle on the island's southern edge.

Ryan slowed as we passed Rustique, but didn't turn. Thirty feet down, he made a U-ey, doubled back, and crept by for a second look.

The street appeared to be strictly residential. Large old homes. Large old trees. I saw no one moving among them.

Again reversing direction on Cherrier, Ryan slid to the curb, positioning the Impala for optimal surveillance. *His* optimal surveillance. I had to crane around him to see.

Rustique was one block long, with what looked like a small park at the far end. Six houses on the left. Six on the right. Set far back on deep, narrow lots, the frame structures all looked tired, in need of paint and probably plumbing and wiring.

A number of residents had taken a shot at lawn care and gardening. Some were enjoying more success than others. Outside one faded Victorian was a carved wooden plaque saying 4 Chez Lizot.

"It's like Bastarache's setup in Tracadie," I said.

"How so?"

"Dead-end street. Back to the river."

Ryan didn't reply. He'd pulled binoculars from the glove compartment and was scanning up one side and down the other, assessing.

I looked past him again. Three cars were snugged to the curb, one near Cherrier, one at midblock, one farther down by the park.

The Lizot's sign suggested even numbers were on the right. I counted from the corner.

"Number thirteen has to be that double lot last on the left." I couldn't actually see much. Malo's property was surrounded by six-foot chain linking overgrown with vines. Through gaps in the foliage I could make out pine, cedar hedges, and one enormous dead elm.

"Love what he's done with the landscaping." My anxiety was fueling imbecilic jokes.

Ryan didn't laugh. He was punching buttons on his phone.

"Can you read Malo's sign?" I asked.

"Prenez garde au chien."

Beware of the dog. No joke there.

"I need you to run three DBQs, type one." Ryan was asking for a trace on auto licenses, speaking, I assumed, with the desk officer at SQ headquarters. He waited, then read the plate number off a beat-to-hell Mercury Grand Marquis parked just down from Cherrier.

"Murchison, Dewey. *Trois Rustique. Oui.*"

I eyeballed the brick-and-frame bungalow five up from Malo's. It was obvious Old Dewey wasn't sitting on a fat portfolio.

"Nine. Four. Seven. Alpha. Charlie. Zulu." Ryan had moved on to the Porsche 911 halfway down the block.

After the heart-thumping drive, the warmth and stillness in the Impala were dulling. I listened to Ryan's end of the conversation, suddenly aware of a stunning exhaustion.

"Vincent, Antoine." Ryan repeated the name. "Any Vincents living on Rustique?" Ryan waited. "OK."

My arms and legs were starting to feel like pig iron.

"Hang on." Grabbing the binoculars, Ryan read off the license of the late-model Honda Accord at the far end of the block. After a pause he asked, "Which rental company?"

My exhaustion was gone like the flash of a shutter. Eyes squinting, I focused on the Accord.

"Got a number?" The voice speaking to Ryan said something. "Sure you're not too busy?" Beat. "Appreciate it."

Ryan closed but didn't toss his cell.

"It's Harry." My voice was amped. "I know it is."

"Let's not jump to conclusions."

"Right."

I threw myself into the seat back and folded my arms. Unfolded them and started gnawing the cuticle.

"The Merc and the Porsche belong to locals," Ryan said, never taking his eyes from number thirteen.

I didn't bother to comment.

Seconds dragged by. Minutes. Eons.

The Impala seemed suddenly oppressive. I lowered my window. Sickly warm air floated in, bringing the smell of mud and mown grass. The cawing of gulls.

I jumped when Ryan's cell warbled in his hand.

Ryan listened. Thanked the caller. Disconnected.

"Harry rented the Accord on Monday morning."

My eyes flew down the block. The car was empty. The park was empty.

"I'll call her." I reached for my purse.

Ryan shot a restraining hand to my arm. "No."

"Why not?"

Ryan just looked at me. Like mine, his eyes were full of fatigue.

My mind did a frightening connect. If Harry was on Malo's property or in his house, a ringing phone might compromise her safety.

"Jesus, Ryan, you really think she's gone inside?" Been taken inside? I couldn't say it.

"I don't know."

I knew.

"We need to get her out."

"Not yet."

"What?" Sharp. "We just sit here?"

"For a while, yes. If *I* go in, *I* will do so with backup. Note the pointed use of the first-person singular."

The sun was low, bouncing off windows and car hoods, bronzing the river, the park, and the street. Sliding on shades, Ryan draped both arms on the wheel and resumed staring down Rustique.

Planetary movement ground to a stop. Occasionally Ryan glanced at his watch. I checked mine. Each time less than a minute had passed.

I switched from working the cuticle to picking at threads in the armrest. Switched back. Despite the heat my fingers felt icy.

417

We'd been watching ten minutes when a Camaro came hard up Cherrier and turned onto Rustique, running so fast its tires squealed softly. The driver was a murky silhouette behind tinted glass.

A silhouette I recognized.

"It's Bastarache!"

We watched Bastarache angle to the curb outside number thirteen, jump out, and throw open the Camaro's trunk. Extracting a bolt cutter, he strode to the fence, positioned the blades, and snapped the handles. After boot-kicking the gate, he disappeared from sight.

The first shots sounded like firecrackers, the pops coming so fast they seemed connected. In the park, a cyclone of gulls rose and swooped over the river.

"Shit!"

Ryan activated and keyed the radio. A dispatcher came on. Identifying himself, Ryan gave our location and requested backup.

"Listen to me, Tempe." Ryan was unholstering the Glock as he spoke. "I am deadly serious. You are to get on the floor and stay put."

Silently, I slid from the seat, keeping my eyes above the dash for a view of the street.

"Do not leave this car."

Using the houses for cover, Ryan worked his way down Rustique, Glock pointed downward at his side. Back to the chain linking, he crept to Malo's gate, peered in, then vanished.

I crouched on the floor of the Impala, terrified,

palms slick with sweat. It seemed hours. In actuality, it was less than five minutes.

I was trying to stretch my cramped legs, when my cell phone chirped. I groped it from my purse.

"Where are you?" Harry was using her whisper-shout voice.

"Where are *you*?"

"I'm in a park near Malo's house. Feeding the seagulls."

"Jesus Christ, Harry. What were you thinking?" My comment failed to reflect the relief I was feeling.

"I may have heard shots."

"Listen to me." I employed the same tone Ryan had just used with me. "I'm at the corner of Cherrier and Rustique. Ryan has gone onto Malo's property. Backup is en route. I want you to get as far from that house as possible without leaving the park. Can you do that?"

"I see a monument to some dead guy. I can hunker behind that."

"Do it."

By hoisting my butt up onto the seat, I was able to see a pink-clad figure scuttle from left to right at the river's edge.

I was returning to my crouch when two muffled shots rang out.

My heart stopped.

I listened.

Impossible stillness.

Dear God, was Ryan in trouble? Harry? Where was backup?

Maybe it was fear for my sister. Or Ryan. What I did next was mad. I did it anyway.

Firing from the Impala, I sprinted across Cherrier and diagonaled the first lawn on the left side of Rustique. Keeping to house shadows, I ran to number thirteen, back-skimmed the fence, and paused, straining to detect any sound of movement.

Screaming gulls. The hammering of my own heart.

Barely breathing, I peered through Malo's gate.

A gravel drive led to a dark brick house with garish pink mortar. To its right stood a similarly constructed three-car garage. To its left stretched a lawn latticed by shadows of the dead elm.

I went stiff, fighting the adrenaline that was stirring me to action. A form was seated at the base of the tree. Had I been spotted?

Five seconds dragged by. Ten.

The form didn't move.

After waiting a full minute, I rechecked my surroundings, then crept down the drive. Each crunch of gravel sounded like an explosion. Still the form remained lifeless, a life-sized rag doll rippled by spider-thread shadows.

Closer to the tree, I could tell that the form was a man. I'd never seen him before. A long, dark tentacle scrawled the front of his shirt. The man's eyes were closed but he appeared to be breathing.

Half crouching I scuttled across the lawn.

And stopped cold.

Two dogs strained on chains attached to bolts set in concrete. Each was huge, with a sleek brown and black coat, small ears, and a short tail that suggested Doberman. Each growled viciously.

I raised a cautioning hand. The dogs grew frenzied, snarling and slathering, eyes savage in their desire to attack.

In the distance I heard the faint wail of sirens.

I backstepped cautiously. The dogs continued lunging and snapping, each body thrust threatening to wrench the bolts free from their moorings.

On rubber legs I scrambled back to the front of the house. To the right of the door I could see a partially open window. Crawling through a square-cut cedar hedge, I stretched on tiptoes and peered in. Though a chair back obstructed my view of the room, I could clearly see three men.

One word hammered home.

Endgame.

Ryan was holding a Winchester twelve-gauge while pointing his Glock at Bastarache. Bastarache had a Sig Sauer 9mm pointed at a man I assumed to be Malo.

Malo's back was to the window. Like Bastarache, he was big and heavily muscled.

The sirens were growing louder. I guessed backup units were now crossing the bridge.

"You miserable sonovabitch," Bastarache was yelling at Malo. "I knew your demented perversions would screw us all sooner or later."

"You're what, Dudley Fucking Do-Right? You went in with eyes wide, Davey-boy."

"Not kids. I never agreed to kids."

"They want to be stars. I give them their dream."

"You promised me you cut that shit out. I believed you. Now I learn you been lying all along." Sweat dampened Bastarache's hair. His shirt was plastered to his chest.

"Easy." Ryan tried to defuse Bastarache's anger.

Bastarache jerked the Sig Sauer toward Ryan. "From the questions this guy's asking, I'm guessing you killed some kids."

"That's ridiculous." Malo gave a nervous laugh.

"Look at me, ass wipe." Bastarache leveled the Sig Sauer on Malo's face. "You've brought a murder investigation down on me. I've had cops up my ass for days."

Raising both palms, Malo reoriented toward Bastarache.

My mouth went dry with shock.

Though older, artificially tanned, and more fit, Malo bore a striking resemblance to Bastarache. A resemblance that could only be explained by genes.

Bastarache continued his harangue.

"You killed those girls. Admit you did it."

"That's—"

"No! More! Lies!" Bastarache's face was raspberry.

"They were sluts. I caught one stealing from me. The other was a junkie." Malo swallowed. "You're my brother, Davey. Take this guy out." Malo made a nervous gesture toward Ryan. "Take him out and we're home free. We find another place—"

"You draw attention to me. To my business. To people I care about. You've lost every bit of your brain. Cops been tailing me since Quebec.

Something happens to this one and they'll know who to look for."

"She's fine."

"Your deviant shit threatens everything. You polluted my father's house. That's why I dropkicked you the first chance I had."

Bastarache was moving the gun with sharp, jerky motions. "You're just like your whore mother."

"Lay your gun on the floor, Dave." Ryan, the negotiator. "You don't want to hurt anyone."

Bastarache ignored him.

"You care about nothing but money and your own sick pecker. But now you threaten *my* house. People *I* care about. Because of you they're gonna find her and lock her away."

"You're a head case," Malo scoffed. "You live in the dark ages."

"Head case?" The gun was trembling in his hand. "I'll show you a head case. Your head all over that wall."

A woman spoke from just below the window. Her voice sounded wheezy and winded.

"If you hurt him, it harms us."

I strained to see the woman, but the chair back blocked her from view.

The sirens were now screaming down Rustique. Tires screeched, doors opened, feet pounded, radios sputtered. A man's voice called out, another answered.

Bastarache's eyes darted to the woman. In that instant, Ryan tossed the Winchester behind him and sprang.

The shotgun skidded across the floor and ricocheted off a baseboard. Malo spun and bolted from the room.

I turned and yelled, "Coming out the front!"

Three cops raced up the driveway. One shouted, "*Arrêtez-vous!* Freeze!"

Malo cut toward the garage. The cops overtook him, slammed his body to the brick, and cuffed his wrists.

Bounding into the house, I hooked a right through a set of double doors into the parlor. A cop followed close on my heels. I heard Ryan tell him to radio for an ambulance.

Bastarache was down on splayed knees, hands cuffed behind him. The woman crouched by his side. Her arm circled her waist. One hand lay on his shoulder. A hand that possessed only three knobby fingers.

"I'm such a fuckup," Bastarache mumbled. "Such a fuckup."

"Shhh," the woman said. "I know you love me."

A shaft of fast-dropping sun flamed the dark curls framing the woman's head. Slowly, she raised her chin.

Agonizing realization curdled my innards.

The woman's cheeks and forehead were lumpy and hard. Her upper lip stretched to a nose that was asymmetrically concave.

"Évangéline," I said, overwhelmed with emotion.

The woman looked my way. Something flashed in her eyes.

"I've seen the Queen of England," she rasped, chest heaving, tears snaking serpentine trails through her flesh.

41

A week passed. Seven days of recovery, celebration, parting, revelation, confession, and denial.

I slept for twelve hours following the incident at Malo's house, awoke rejuvenated and harboring no grudge against my sister. Harry had survived her escapade in the park. One Jimmy Choo leopard thong sandal had not. Gull guano.

Harry explained that she'd driven to see Flan O'Connor in Toronto. She wanted to surprise me with a scoop on Obéline and the poetry. Her big discovery was that O'Connor House had only operated from 1998 until 2003. Ironically, the information turned out to be merely cumulative to what we already knew about time frames.

Harry flew home to file for divorce and sell her house in River Oaks. Having enjoyed downtown living, she'd decided to search for a condo that would allow her to live car-free. I suspected her plan was unworkable in a town like Houston. I kept it to myself.

The feast of Saint John the Baptist, la fête nationale du Québec, came and went. City crews swept up, the fleur-de-lis flags came down, and Montreal's citizenry turned its attention to the annual rites of jazz.

Through conversations with Ryan and Hippo, I learned many things.

The man slumped by the tree was a Malo thug named Serge Sardou. When Sardou challenged Bastarache's charge up the driveway, Bastarache shot him. The wound caused a lot of bleeding but only minor muscle damage. Sardou started bartering as soon as the anesthesia wore off.

Turned out Mulally and Babin had been smitten with the Escalade, not with Harry and me. It was Sardou who'd threatened me by e-mail and phone. And, my personal favorite, thrown me down the stairs. Malo had asked him to recover the contact sheet of Évangéline, and to back me off. Sardou decided to double-task at Cormier's studio.

Bastarache and Malo both went directly from Rustique to jail. Bastarache claimed self-defense, saying Sardou had threatened him with the Winchester. A lawyer had him out on bail the next day.

Based on statements from Sardou and Kelly Sicard, Malo was charged with three counts of homicide and a zillion counts of offenses involving kids. Unlike Bastarache, Plucky Pierre was going nowhere soon.

Wednesday, June 27, I was in my lab at Wilfrid-Derome. Five boxes lined the side counter, remains packaged for release to next of kin.

Reading my handwritten labels, I felt a bittersweet sense of accomplishment. Geneviève Doucet. Anne Girardin. Claire Brideau. Maude Waters. LSJML-57748.

Cause of death would never be determined for Geneviève Doucet. No matter. Poor Théodore was beyond understanding. Or blaming. Maître Asselin would be collecting her great-niece's bones.

There would be no justice for little Anne Girardin, Ryan's MP number three. Daddy had died of a self-inflicted bullet to the brain. But Adelaide had been located and could now bury her daughter.

From age seventeen to nineteen, Claire Brideau had starred in dozens of Peter Bad Productions. Pierre Malo. Peter Bad. Pure poetry.

We'd guessed right about Cormier. The photographer had funneled girls to Malo in exchange for a few bucks and a steady supply of pedophile smut. Kelly Sicard had been one. Claire Brideau had been another. There would be no more. Fearing Cormier might roll to save himself, Malo had killed him.

According to Sardou, in 1999, Malo strangled Brideau in a rage for lifting money from a nightstand in the house on Rustique. Ordered to dispose of the body, he'd offloaded Brideau from a buddy's boat into the Rivière des Mille Îles. She became Ryan's DOA number one.

Ryan's DOA number three, the Lac des Deux Montagnes floater, was identified as sixteen-year-old Maude Waters. The previous year, Maude had left her home on the Kahnawake Mohawk Reserve hoping to make her way to Hollywood and a star on the Walk of Fame. Instead, she ended up with Malo doing porn.

Malo was claiming Maude OD'd while living in his house. Sardou's version had Malo strangling Maude because she'd threatened to leave. As with Brideau eight years earlier, Sardou was ordered to dump the corpse. Feeling invincible, the loyal employee simply drove a few blocks and tossed Maude from the Bois-de-L'Île-Bizard boat ramp.

LSJML-57748. Hippo's girl. For now, the Sheldrake Island skeleton would lie under an anonymous iron cross in the lepers' cemetery in Tracadie. But I was working with an Acadian historian. With luck, and hard work, we hoped to learn who she was. The lab in Virginia had sequenced DNA from her bones. Perhaps someday we might even find a relative.

The lab door opened, breaking my reverie. Hippo entered, carrying coffee and a bag of St. Viateur Bagels. As we spread cream cheese with little plastic knives, I considered what I'd learned of the saga of Évangéline.

I'd been right. Laurette Landry had worked at the lazaretto, and had lost her job upon its closing in '65. Years later, she developed leprosy. So great was the family's distrust of government, Laurette was hidden away with Grand-père Landry. At fourteen, Évangéline became the family's primary breadwinner and nurse.

While Laurette was alive, Évangéline lived at home and worked days for David's father, Hilaire Bastarache. Upon her mother's death, she assumed the position of resident housekeeper.

At that time Pierre Malo, Hilaire's illegitimate son, was also living in the Bastarache house. Malo pressed Évangéline into posing for him, threatening her with loss of her job. David Bastarache had fallen in love with Évangéline. Appalled by his half-brother's activities, he vowed to sack and boot Malo as soon as control fell to him, as Hilaire had told him it would.

Though I'd gained some insight into Bastarache's character, the man still mystified me.

"Explain it to me, Hippo. How could such thinking exist today?"

Hippo chewed as he gave my question thought.

"Every Acadian kid grows up on tales of ancestors being hunted down and deported. Le Grand Dérangement still haunts us as a people. And it's not just ancient history. Acadians see their culture as constantly threatened by a hostile, Anglo-dominated world."

I let him go on.

"How do you keep alive your customs and language while your kids are watching *Seinfeld* and listening to the Stones? While their city cousins can barely *parler* a few words of French?"

I took the questions as rhetorical, and didn't answer.

"We Acadians have learned to hold on to our identity no matter what life throws at us. How? Partly through sheer obstinacy. Partly by making everything larger than life. Our music. Our food. Our festivals. Even our fears."

"But it's not the 1800s," I said. "Or even the 1960s. How can Bastarache distrust hospitals and government that much?"

"Bastarache is Acadian by nature. He also operates businesses that run close to the line. On top of all that, he's got personal baggage. Vile father. Deviate brother. Mother shot. Homeschooled." Hippo shrugged. "The guy seems to genuinely love your pal. Didn't want her harmed. Did what he thought was best to protect her."

Malo had been right about one thing. Obéline and Bastarache were living in the dark ages with regard to their attitude toward Évangéline's disease. Like the nursing nuns of a century before, Obéline had sacrificed for leprosy, committing to a loveless marriage in order to care for her sister. Bastarache had been complicit in hiding Évangéline away.

"Obéline lied about seeing Évangéline murdered," I said. "To throw me off. She also let everyone believe Bastarache was responsible for the broken arm and the fire."

"He wasn't?" Hippo was thumbnailing something from a molar.

I shook my head. "Because of the leprosy, Évangéline had little feeling in her hands and feet. Obéline cracked her ulna attempting to stop Évangéline from falling downstairs. It was also

Évangéline who accidentally set the house on fire.

"She also lied about the poetry book. Obéline had it published as a birthday gift for Évangéline. Anonymously, since no one was to know her sister was alive."

Having achieved success with the molar, Hippo was cream-cheesing a second bagel. I continued talking.

"The great tragedy is that Évangéline could have led a relatively normal life. Multidrug therapies are readily available and patients usually show improvement in two to three months. Fewer than one tenth of one percent of those treated fail to be cured."

"There still much leprosy around?"

I'd done some research on that.

"The global registered prevalence of leprosy at the beginning of 2006 was almost two hundred and twenty thousand cases. And it's not just Africa and Southeast Asia. Thirty-two thousand of those cases are right here in the Americas. Over six thousand in the United States. Two hundred to two hundred and fifty new cases are diagnosed each year."

"I'll be damned."

"Bastarache and Obéline did for Évangéline exactly what had been done for her mother, never realizing the enormity of the mistake."

"One thing I don't get. Bastarache hated Malo. Why stash her with him?"

"Évangéline had only been at Malo's house a short time. When Harry and I dropped in on

Obéline, Bastarache freaked. Figured if we found the house in Tracadie there was a possibility we could also find the one on Île d'Orléans. When Ryan and I actually did show up there, he panicked and raced back to move her again."

My eyes drifted to the row of neatly labeled boxes. Geneviève Doucet, left to mummify in her bed by poor deranged Théodore. Anne Girardin, killed by her father.

I thought of others. Ryan's MP number two, Claudine Cloquet, sold to Malo by her father. Évangéline, locked away by her would-be husband and her sister, though undoubtedly with her own consent.

"You know, Hippo, the bogeyman's not always hanging out in the school yard or at the bus depot. He can be the guy in your parlor hogging the remote."

Hippo stared at me as though I'd spoken Swahili.

"Someone right there in your own family. That's often where the threat is."

"Yeah," Hippo said softly.

My eyes settled on the name now attached to the girl from Lac des Deux Montagnes. Maude Waters. Maude had also had movie star dreams. Was dead at sixteen.

My thoughts veered to Malo. He'd claimed no knowledge of Phoebe Quincy. Again, his employee had told a different tale. Sardou stated that he'd seen Phoebe at the house on Rustique. But only briefly.

Phoebe remained missing.

Ryan's DOA number two, the girl from the Dorval shoreline, remained unidentified.

Symbolic, I thought, of the many children who are murdered each year, or those who simply vanish, never to be found.

"Back to the streets," Hippo said, pushing to his feet.

I rose, too. "You did a crack job on these cases, Hippo."

"Got two more to close."

"Do you think Phoebe Quincy has been piped into some underground pornography pipeline?"

"I prefer to think she's alive, but, one way or another, I won't quit looking until I know. Every day I'll come to work and every day I'll keep searching for these kids."

I managed a smile. "I bet you will, Hippo. I bet you will."

Hippo's eyes bore into mine. "Sooner or later I will have answers."

Friday morning, I boarded a flight to Moncton, rented a car, and drove to Tracadie. This time Bastarache answered the door.

"How is she?" I asked.

Bastarche did a "so-so" waggle of one hand.

"Is she taking her meds?"

"Obéline's giving her no choice."

Bastarache led me to the room at the back of the house, excused himself, and withdrew. I thought about him as he walked away. Strip clubs, cat houses, and adultery, but the guy drew the line at child pornography. And loved Évangéline. Go figure human nature.

Évangéline sat in an armchair gazing out at the water.

Crossing to her, I wrapped my arms around her shoulders and drew her close. She resisted at first, then relaxed against me.

I held my old friend as tight as I dared for as long as I dared. Then I released her and looked into her eyes.

"Évangéline, I—"

"Do not speak, Tempe. There is no need. We have met. We have touched. You have read my poems. It is enough. Don't despair for me. We are all creatures of God, and I am at peace. You have given me a great gift, my dear, dear friend. You have reopened my childhood. Sit with me awhile and then return to your life. I will keep you always in my heart."

Smiling, I drew graham crackers, peanut butter, and a plastic knife from my purse and laid them on the table. Added two Cokes in six-ounce glass bottles. Then I drew a chair close.

"You can't really visit Green Gables," I said.

Acknowledgments

As usual, this novel was a team effort. Let me introduce the team.

I owe massive thanks to Andrea and Cléola Léger, without whom this story might never have been written. Andrea and Cléola introduced me to the warm, generous, and effervescent world of the Acadian people. *Merci. Merci. Mille mercis.*

I am enormously indebted to all those who welcomed me during my stay in New Brunswick. This list includes, but is hardly limited to, Claude Williams, MLA, Maurice Cormier, Jean-Paul and Dorice Bourque, Estelle Boudreau, Maria Doiron, Laurie Gallant, Aldie and Doris LeBlanc, Paula LeBlanc, Bernadette Léger, Gerard Léger, Normand and Pauline Léger, Darrell and Lynn Marchand, Fernand and Lisa Gaudet, Constable Kevin Demeau (RCMP), George and Jeannie Gaggio, and Joan MacKenzie of Beaverbrook House. Special thanks go to those in Tracadie, especially Claude Landry, MLA, Père Zoël Saulnier, and Raynald Basque and the staff at Cojak Productions. Soeur Dorina Frigault and Soeur Zelica Daigle, RHSJ (Les Hospitalières de Saint-Joseph), generously opened their archives and provided a tour of the museum and cemetery at the former site of the lazaretto.

Robert A. Leonard, PhD, professor of linguistics and director of the Forensic Linguistics Project, Hofstra University, interrupted his busy schedule to provide guidance on forensic linguistics. (You were really a founding member of Sha Na Na? Yes, Kathy. No way. Yes, Kathy. Awesome!)

Ron Harrison, Service de police de la Ville de Montréal, provided information on guns, sirens, and a variety of cop stuff.

Normand Proulx, *Directeur général,* Sûreté du Québec, and *l'inspecteur-chef* Gilles Martin, *adjoint au Directeur général, adjoint à la Grande fonction des enquêtes criminelles,* Sûreté du Québec, provided statistics on homicides and information on cold case investigations in Quebec.

Mike Warns, design engineer, ISR, Inc., fielded endless questions and coached me on techie stuff. A true Renaissance man, Mike is also largely responsible for the poetry.

Dr. William C. Rodriguez, Office of the Armed Forces Medical Examiner, and Dr. Peter Dean, HM Coroner for Greater Suffolk and South East Essex, helped with details of skeletal and soft tissue pathology.

Paul Reichs provided valuable input on the manuscript.

Nan Graham and my Scribner family made the book a lot better than it might otherwise have been. Ditto for Susan Sandon and everyone at Random House UK.

Jennifer Rudolph-Walsh supplied countless intangibles and the usual unflagging support.

A useful resource was *Children of Lazarus: the story of the lazaretto at Tracadie* by M. J. Losier and C. Pinet, Les Éditions Faye, 1999.

Read on for an exclusive extract from the
new Temperance Brennan thriller

Flash and Bones

Coming in September 2011 from
William Heinemann

1

Looking back, I think of it as Raceweek in the Rain. Thunderboomers almost every day. Sure, it was spring. But these storms were over the top.

In the end, Summer saved my life.

I know. Sounds bizarre.

This is what happened.

Bloated, dark clouds hung low to the ground, but so far no rain.

Lucky break. I'd spent the morning digging up a corpse.

Sound macabre? Just part of the job. I'm a forensic anthropologist. I recover and analyze the dead that present in less than pristine condition – the burned, mummified, mutilated, dismembered, decomposed, and skeletal.

OK. Today's target wasn't actually a corpse. I'd been searching for overlooked body parts.

Short version. Last fall a housewife vanished from her rural Cabarrus County home. A week ago, while I was away on a working vacation in Hawaii, a trucker admitted to strangling the woman and burying her body in a sandpit. Impatient, the local cops had sallied forth with shovels and buckets. The bones were delivered to the Mecklenburg County Medical Examiner's office in a Skippy peanut butter carton.

Yesterday, my aloha tan still glowing, I'd begun my analysis. A skeletal inventory revealed that the hyoid, the mandible, and all of the upper incisors and canines were missing.

No teeth, no dental ID. No hyoid, no evidence of strangulation. Dr. Tim Larabee, the Mecklenburg County Medical Examiner, asked me to have a second go at the sandpit.

Correcting screw-ups usually makes me cranky. Today, I was feeling upbeat.

I'd quickly found the missing bits and dispatched them to the MCME facility in Charlotte. I was en route to a shower, a late lunch, and time with my cat.

It was one fifty p.m. My sweat-soaked T was pasted to my back. My hair was yanked into a ratty knot. Sand lined my scalp and undies. Nevertheless, I was humming. Al Yankovitch, 'White and Nerdy'. What can I say? I'd watched a YouTube video and the tune lodged in my head.

Wind buffeted my Mazda as I merged onto southbound I-85. Slightly uneasy, I glanced at the sky, then thumbed on NPR.

Terry Gross was finishing an interview with Kay Ryan, the US poet laureate. Both were indifferent to the conditions outside my car.

Fair enough. Philadelphia is five hundred miles north of Dixie.

Terry launched into a teaser about an upcoming guest. I never caught the name.

Beep! Beep! Beep!

'The National Weather service has issued a severe weather warning for parts of the North Carolina piedmont, including Mecklenburg, Cabarrus, Anson, Stanly, and Union Counties. Severe thunderstorms are expected to move through the area within the next hour. Rainfall of one to three inches is anticipated, creating the potential for flash flooding. Atmospheric conditions are favorable for the development of tornadoes. Stay tuned to this station for further updates'

Beep! Beep! Beep!

I tightened my grip on the wheel and goosed my speed to seventy-five. Risky in a sixty-five mph zone, but I wanted to reach home before the deluge.

Moments later Terry was interrupted again, this time by a muted *whoop-whoop*.

My eyes flicked to the radio.

Whoop!

Feeling stupid I checked the rear view mirror.

A police cruiser was riding my bumper.

Annoyed, I pulled to the shoulder and lowered my window. When the cop approached, I held out my license.

'Dr. Temperance Brennan?'

'Looking somewhat worse for wear.' I beamed what I hoped was a winning smile.

Johnny Law did not beam back. 'That won't be necessary,' indicating my license.

Puzzled, I looked up at the guy. He was mid-twenties, slim, with an infant mustache that appeared to be going nowhere. A plaque on his chest said R. Warner.

'The Concord Police Department received a request from the Mecklenburg County medical examiner to intercept and divert you.'

'Larabee sent the cops to find me?'

'Yes, Ma'am. When I arrived at the recovery site, you'd left.'

'Why didn't he call me directly?'

'Apparently he couldn't get through.'

Of course not. While digging, I'd locked my iPhone in the car to protect it from sand.

'My phone is in the glove compartment.' No need to alarm Officer Warner. 'I'm going to take it out.'

'Yes, Ma'am.'

The numbers on the little screen indicated three missed calls from Larabee. Three messages. I listened to the first.

'Long story, which I'll share when you're back. The Concord PD received a report of a body at the Morehead Road landfill. Chapel Hill wants us to handle it. I'm elbow deep in an autopsy. Since you're in the area, I hoped you could swing by to check it out. Joe Hawkins is diverting that way with the van, just in case they've actually got something for us.'

The second message was the same as the first. Ditto the third, but more terse. It ended with the inducement: You're a champ, Tempe.

A landfill in a storm? The champ was suddenly not so chipper.

'Ma'am, we should hurry. The rain won't hold off much longer.'

'Lead on.' I could not have said this with less enthusiasm.

Warner returned to his cruiser, whoop-whooped, then pulled into traffic. Inwardly cursing Larabee, Warner, and the landfill, I palm-slapped the gearshift and followed.

Traffic on I-85 was unusually heavy for mid-afternoon. As we approached Concord, I could see that the Bruton Smith Boulevard exit ramp was a parking lot.

And realized what a nightmare this little detour of Larabee's would be.

The Morehead Road landfill is back fence neighbor to the Charlotte Motor Speedway, a major stop on the NASCAR circuit. Races would be held there this weekend and next. Tomorrow's qualifying would determine which lucky drivers would make the cut for Saturday's All Star Shootout.

Two hundred thousand avid fans would pour into Charlotte for Race Week. Looking at the sea of SUVs, campers, pick-ups, and sedans I guessed that many had already hit town.

Warner rode the shoulder. I followed, ignoring the hostile glares of those cemented in the logjam.

Lights flashing, we snaked through the bedlam on Bruton Smith Boulevard, past the dragway, the dirt track, and a zillion fast food joints. On the sidelines, the tattooed and tank-topped carried babies, six-packs, coolers, and radios. Vendors sold souvenirs from folding tables beneath improvised tents.

Warner looped the surrealistic geometry of the speedway itself, made several turns, then rolled to a stop outside a small structure whose siding might once have been blue. Beyond the building loomed a series of mounds resembling a Martian mountain range.

A man emerged and issued Warner a yellow hardhat and neon orange vest. As they talked the man pointed at a gravel road rising sharply uphill.

Warner waited while I received my safety gear, then we proceeded up the slope. Trucks rumbled in both directions, engines churning hard going in, humming going out.

When the road leveled I could see three men standing by an enormous dumpster. Two wore coveralls. The third wore black pants and a long-sleeved black shirt over a white T. Joe Hawkins, long-time death investigator for the MCME. All three featured gear identical to that lying on my passenger seat.

Warner nosed up to the dumpster and parked. I pulled in beside him.

The men watched as I got out and donned my hardhat and vest. Fetching. A perfect complement to my current state of hygiene.

'We gotta quit meeting like this.' Joe and I had parted at the sandpit barely an hour earlier.

The older man stuck out a hand. 'Weaver Molene.' Molene was flushed and sweating, and filled his coveralls way beyond their intended capacity.

'Temperance Brennan.'

I'd have skipped the handshake, given the black moons under Molene's nails, but didn't want to be rude.

'You the coroner?' he asked.

'I work for the medical examiner,' I said.

Molene introduced the younger man as Barcelona Jackson. Jackson was very thin and very black. And very, very nervous.

'Jackson and I work for BFI, the company that manages the landfill.'

'Impressive pile of trash,' I said.

'Site's got a capacity of over two and a half million cubic meters.' Molene ran a dingy hanky across his face. 'Friggin' weird Jackson stumbled onto the one square foot holding a stiff. Or maybe not. Probably dozens out there.'

Jackson had mostly kept his eyes down. At Molene's words, he raised then quickly dropped them back to his boots.

'Tell me what you found, sir.'

Though I spoke to Jackson, Molene answered.

'Probably best we show you. And quick.' He pocket-jammed the hanky. 'This storm's coming fast.'

Molene set off at a pace I would have thought impossible for a man of his bulk. Jackson scampered after. I fell into line, paying attention as best I could to the uneven footing. Warner and Hawkins brought up the rear.

I've excavated in landfills, am familiar with the aroma of *eau de dump*, a delicate blend of methane and carbon dioxide, with traces of ammonia, hydrogen sulfide, nitrogen, hydrogen chloride, and carbon monoxide added for spice. I braced for the stench. Didn't happen.

Good odor management, guys. Or maybe it was Mother Nature. Wind swirled dirt into little cyclones and tumbled cellophane wrappers, plastic bags, and torn paper across the landscape.

Our course took us the length of the active landfill, down a slope, then around a series of what appeared to be closed areas. Instead of raw earth, the tops of the older mounds were covered with grass.

As we walked, the rumble of trucks receded and the whine of fine-tuned engines grew louder. Based on the changing acoustics I figured the speedway lay over a rise to our right.

After ten minutes, Molene stopped at the base of a truncated hillock. Though tentative grass greened the top, the side facing us was scarred and pitted, like a desert butte gouged by eons of wind.

Molene said something I didn't catch. I was focused on the exposed stratigraphy.

Unlike the sandstone or shale making up metamorphic

9

rock, the mound's layers were composed of flattened Pontiacs and Posturpedics, of squashed Pepsis, Pop-Tarts, Pringles, and Pampers.

Molene pointed to a crater in a brown-green layer eight feet above our heads, then to an object lying about two yards off the base of the mound. His explanation was lost to a clap of thunder.

Didn't matter. It was obvious Jackson's 'stiff' had dropped from the mound, probably dislodged by the previous day's storm.

I crossed to the thing and squatted. Molene, Warner, and Hawkins clustered around me but remained standing. Jackson kept his distance.

The object was a drum, approximately twenty inches in diameter and thirty inches high. Its cover lay off to one side.

'Looks like a metal container of some kind,' I said without looking up. 'It's too rusted to make out a logo or label.'

'Flip it.' Molene shouted. 'Jackson and I turned the thing bottom-up to protect the stuff inside.'

I tried. It weighed a ton.

Hawkins squatted and, together, we muscled the drum upright. Its interior was filled with a solid black mass.

I leaned close. Something pale was suspended in the dark fill, but the pre-storm gloom obscured all detail.

I was reaching for my MagLite when lightning sparked.

A human hand flashed white in the electric brilliance.

Dissolved to black.

Virals

Kathy Reichs

Tory Brennan is as fascinated by bones and dead bodies as her famous aunt, acclaimed forensic anthropologist, Tempe Brennan. However living on a secluded island off Charleston in South Carolina there is not much opportunity to put her knowledge to the test. Until she and her group of technophile friends stumble across a shallow grave containing the remains of a girl who has been missing for over thirty years.

With the cold-case murder suddenly hot, Tory realises that they are involved in something fatally dangerous. And when they rescue a sick dog from a laboratory on the same island, it becomes evident that somehow the two events are linked.

On the run from forces they don't understand, they have only each other to fall back on. Until they succumb to a mysterious infection that heightens their senses and hones their instincts to impossible levels. Their illness seems to have changed their very biology – and it's clear that the island is home to something well beyond their comprehension. It's a secret that has driven men to kill once. And will drive them to kill again . . .

WILLIAM HEINEMANN: LONDON

Spider Bones

Kathy Reichs

Dr Temperance Brennan spends her working life amongst the decomposed, the mutilated, and the skeletal. So the two-days-dead body she is called to examine holds little to surprise her. Until she discovers that the man is John Lowery, an ex-soldier who was apparently killed in Vietnam in 1968. So who is buried in Lowery's grave?

The case takes Tempe to an organisation dedicated to bringing home the bodies of unidentified soldiers where she must examine the remains of anyone who may have had a connection to the drowned man. It's a harrowing task, but it pays off when she finds Lowery's dog tags amongst the bones of a long-dead soldier.

As Tempe unravels the tangled threads of the soldiers' lives and deaths, she realises there are some who would rather the past stayed buried. And when she proves difficult to frighten, they turn their attention to the one person she would give her life to protect . . .

arrow books

206 Bones

Kathy Reichs

**'You have an enemy, Dr Brennan. It is in your interest
to learn who placed the call . . .'**

A routine case turns sinister when Dr Temperance Brennan is
accused of mishandling the autopsy of a missing heiress. Someone
has made an incriminating accusation that she missed or concealed crucial evidence. Before Tempe can get to the one man
with information, he turns up dead.

The heiress isn't the only elderly female to have appeared on
Tempe's gurney recently. Back in Montreal, three more women
have died, their bodies brutally discarded. Tempe is convinced
there's a link between their deaths and that of the heiress.
But what – or who – connects them?

Tempe struggles with the clues, but nothing adds up. Has she
made grave errors or is some unknown foe sabotaging her? It soon
becomes frighteningly clear. It's not simply Tempe's career at risk.
Her life is at stake too.

arrow books

Devil Bones

Kathy Reichs

An underground chamber is exposed in a seedy, dilapidated house with sagging trim and peeling paint . . .

In the dark cellar, a ritualistic display is revealed. A human skull rests on a cauldron, surrounded by slain chickens and bizarre figurines. Beads and antlers dangle overhead.

Called to the scene is forensic anthropologist Dr Temperance Brennan. Bony architecture suggests that the skull is that of a young, black female. But how did she die? And when? Then, just as Tempe is working to determine the post-mortem interval, another body is discovered: a headless corpse carved with Satanic symbols.

As citizen vigilantes, blaming Devil-worshippers, begin a witch-hunt, intent on revenge, Tempe struggles to keep her emotions in check. But the truth she eventually uncovers proves more shocking than even she could have imagined . . .

arrow books